The SEED of CORRUPTION

A NOVEL

A.I. Fabler

W&L
Wild & Lawless

Also by the author:
'AGENDA 2060: The Future as It Happens'
Published 2021
www.agenda2060.com

ISBN 978-0-473-62326-5 (Epub)
ISBN 978-0-473-62327-2 (Kindle)
ISBN 978-0-473-62328-9 (PDF)
ISBN 978-0-473-62329-6 (Apple Books)

W&L
Wild & Lawless

PO BOX 34595, BIRKENHEAD, 0746, NEW ZEALAND
Creative Management and Licensing
E: wildandlawless@aifabler.com

This version designed and edited by:
David Prendergast, Book Designer; Robin Fuller, Copy Editor.
Typeset using 12pt Garamond

For Sean deRedcliffe

None goes his way alone.

*M. de Serisy pointed out that the major interests
of the country sometimes required secret illegalities,
crime beginning only when State means
were applied to private interests.*

—Honoré de Balzac, *A Harlot High and Low*

PREFACE

In June 2004, I travelled to Vietnam, alone. It was a trip that my son, Hugo, and I had planned to make together, but he died at the age of thirty-five from a grand mal seizure in his sleep. So, I went while his memory was still strong, taking the route and the transport modes we had decided upon together. I rode by motorbike, bus, and train from the sodden canals of the Mekong Delta to the freezing hillside tracks of the Northern Highlands, writing down what I encountered each day, wondering how he would have interpreted it all.

While I was there, bird flu was shutting down the markets and daily life, first in Vietnam, then throughout Southeast Asia. That wasn't the story I was following, though it became the backdrop to my own. My story was of a semi-reclusive wildlife painter, tracking down the source of a counterfeit copy of one of his paintings in Vietnam, while wrestling with a growing awareness of the personal corruption that lies at the heart of his own artistic and financial success. On this journey of exploration of his own moral ambiguities, he also has to deal with the corruption he discovers in the international aid agencies operating on the ground. This is territory famously explored by Joseph Conrad in *Heart of Darkness*.

I was following a narrative line developed from a series of events I had witnessed over a number of years, which found unusual endorsement (and amplification) on the ground as I travelled in Vietnam. Like a river, the journey carried me forward into territory I hadn't expected to visit, until soon, thanks to the bird flu epidemic, I was stumbling into a high-stakes international conspiracy far beyond the capacity of my lead character to withstand. As such, whole passages are basically written just as they actually happened. Others were inspired by what I saw and heard along the way, or in some cases, what I subsequently learned. I filled entire notebooks, which required no redactions after the event. They sit in my desk drawer today, telling it just as it happened. As far as truth goes, this is as close to it as fiction can get. But the story itself remains fiction.

On 22 January 2020, *The New York Times* ran the headline 'As New Virus Spreads from China, Scientists See Grim Reminders'. The virus was initially named SARS-CoV-2 after being identified as genetically related to the coronavirus responsible for the SARS outbreak of 2003. For over a year, mainstream media, leading scientists, and health bureaucrats worldwide maintained the line that any suggestions that the virus had originated in China's Wuhan laboratory were 'conspiracy theories'. Social media sites deplatformed users who dared to even raise such suspicions. During that time, a publisher who had been sitting on my manuscript of *The Seed* came back to me to advise that there was a need to maintain a united front in the face of the COVID-19 pandemic and avoid anything that encouraged 'conspiracy theories'.

To label a belief as a 'conspiracy theory' is to imply that it's false. More than that, it implies that people who accept that belief, or even those who want to investigate whether it's true, are irrational. The term is used to stigmatise and marginalise people whose beliefs conflict with the officially sanctioned or orthodox beliefs of the time (whether rightly or wrongly).[*]

So, why did that publisher take fright at the possibility of a 'conspiracy theory' label?

The answer, perhaps, lies in the parallels that emerged between the bird flu version of SARS and COVID-19. *The Seed of Corruption* takes place during the former. It was not common knowledge then that both China and the United States were experimenting with the manipulation of SARS viruses in contravention of international protocols, *just underreported.*

In contrast, it was no secret that the United States Secretary of Defence, Donald Rumsfeld, was a major shareholder in the company that developed the drug Tamiflu in response to the bird flu pandemic hysteria promoted at the time, or that the US military under his command stockpiled this drug and persuaded up to sixty allied nations to do the same, at huge cost, despite Tamiflu having little or no preventative or curative effects. It was no secret—*just underreported.*

For some time, *The Seed of Corruption* was an unfinished story ... prophetically, as it turned out.

At the end of the day, writers, being human, have to allow themselves enough faith in humanity to be able to get up the next morning. Faced with mankind's iniquity, they're tempted to pull the last punch rather than land it. That's what I did when I stopped writing *The Seed of Corruption* in 2019. And look what happened next: COVID-19, a virus concocted from a witch's brew of lies, corruption, incompetence, and greed, spread disease and insanity across the world with a speed and ease that no creative writer would have dared to imagine possible. How will that story end? With the truth *underreported* would be my guess.

This story is far from over. In mankind's competition between good and evil, I don't yet have the courage to declare a winner.

—A.I. Fabler, 2022

* Refer to 'Conspiracy Theories: The Philosophical Debate', ed. David Coady 2019, pub. Taylor & Francis

ONE

In the deserted foyer of the Grande Rivière Hotel on the western bank of the Hau River was a well-thumbed copy of a French magazine, *Geographique*, devoted to the life-forms that inhabited the region of the Mekong Delta. Anton Faraday, having just returned from an excursion on the river and wondering what to do next with his day, found himself reading about an enigmatic creature known as the freshwater snakehead fish. The story immediately grabbed his attention, for something he had seen just that morning drove him to find out more.

Describing the land-walking snakehead fish as 'something from a bad horror movie', Interior Secretary Jean Yealands said this week that she wants the US to ban it. Growing to three feet or more in length, it can slither across land, staying out of water for up to three days, eating any small animal in its path, including humans. A native of Asia, its only predators are crocodiles, alligators, and larger versions of itself.

The description was enough to stop him in his tracks. It fit perfectly with depictions of the first creatures on earth to emerge from the water, yet according to the theory of evolution, the freshwater snakehead fish should have spent the last four hundred million years evolving into something else. It hadn't; it was still just a fish.

Faraday was a painter of wildlife. Evolutionary biology was very much his thing, so it wasn't surprising that chance encounters with creatures like this could lead his thoughts down byways seldom travelled by the average person.

He took the magazine and wandered out onto the hotel veranda terrace, thinking, among other things, that there were little chinks in the armour of evolutionary theory, like this example, which suggested that the next few million years might be difficult ones for supporters of Charles Darwin, unless they believed that the evolutionary tide had turned and life was heading back under water. There were many intelligent people who believed that the beginning of the end was already underway, that the Earth had already started the process of turning into a burned-out cinder, and that eventually the oceans would vaporize and the planet would be engulfed by the sun. Higher life would be extinguished in much the same way it had come into being: little by little, and eventually, all land-based creatures would be driven into the sea by the scorching heat, until even the oceans became too hot for complex life. In the end, the last life-form would look very much like the first one: a single-celled bacterium that farted.

For reasons that were not then clear, the image of the snakehead fish was destined to imprint itself like a watermark on his feelings about life from that day forward, even though his journey in Vietnam had barely begun and he hadn't even caught a glimpse of the iniquity that lay in wait for him, let alone danced with it and felt its warm breath on his cheek. All that was yet to come. Perhaps some places held an ineradicable scent of pain, a history that forewarned of the future, and the fish was just a harbinger of what was yet to befall him.

It was mid-June, a steam bath devoid of oxygen, and he'd been out on a barge on the Mekong River since six thirty that morning, the only passenger on a vessel built for two hundred.

The Mekong River had begun its life as a slow drip high in the mountains of Tibet, where the sun was barely warm enough to thaw the permafrost even in the summer months, and eventually it formed a trickle that ran south through China, Laos, Cambodia, and Vietnam, gathering up other trickles as it went, until—forty-five hundred kilometres later—it was discharging thirty-eight thousand cubic metres per second into the South

China Sea. Most of that water came from the monsoon rains that fell from May to October, and by Faraday's calculation, a large proportion of those cubic metres must have fallen that day—mostly on him. Which was why no one went to the Mekong Delta in the wet season. Which was, presumably, why he'd had the boat to himself.

He'd ridden down from Ho Chi Minh City the day before in a taxi whose accelerator and horn seemed to be stuck and whose brakes didn't work. The people were rather proud of the new road they'd built out of old Saigon into the Mekong Delta, but when he arrived at the Grande Rivière Hotel, Cantho, his gratitude that he was still alive was palpable, because for millions of Vietnamese, a new road was a conveniently dry, flat place for setting up shop and lighting the brazier, rather than a place for cars.

Cantho was the transportation centre of the Mekong Delta, a spaghetti noodle junction of waterways that had no signposts or speed limits and teemed with traffic twenty-four hours a day. Because the delta regularly flooded, the houses along the riverbanks were built on high bamboo stilts, and the biggest structure in town was a giant illuminated billboard mounted on a multistorey bamboo scaffolding advertising Tiger beer.

From what he could see, most people lived on boats. They ate, slept, fornicated, and gave birth on them, emerging out of the labyrinths of canals and muddy creeks at the crack of dawn to trade produce with each other in the floating markets. The river was their highway, their lavatory bowl, and their food basket. When the sun was shining—which it had for only the briefest moment that morning—the water was the colour of mushroom soup; the rest of the time, it looked like grey porridge. Into this porridge, the people cast nets, pulling aboard a dubious harvest of empty bottles and plastic bags, which they sifted through lazily and without anticipation before throwing them back in the water again. Occasionally, they landed a small, startled fish that flopped about in the bottom of the boat, gasping for air.

He'd been told by the hotel concierge in Saigon that one went to Cantho to see these things: the floating markets, the men casting nets. That's why he was there, taking a break from the quest that had brought him so urgently to Vietnam, pretending to be a tourist. He hadn't planned the excursion on the boat. It was offered to him free of charge by the hotel, where he was paying eighty dollars a night as the only guest in a state of unexpected luxury.

When the rain had momentarily lifted, he'd asked his guide, Canh, if they could get off and walk so he could take some photographs. Canh had boasted that he taught English at university, but he seemed to struggle with understanding any questions, so the conversation quickly ground to a halt.

Without speaking, they walked for an hour along the muddy tracks beside the canals, avoiding puddles and bowing their heads politely to anyone they encountered. The houses were small two-room affairs nestled beneath tangled canopies of breadfruit and durian trees. The doors were open, the rooms within dark and quiet. As if sensing their presence, people came to the doorways, smiling, and followed them with their eyes, the smiles fading slowly from their faces like memories as the two passed. There were no sounds; the air was too heavy. Water filled Faraday's hair, clothes, and shoes, running down his forehead and the small of his back.

Yet the lens of his camera kept leading him on, to the open doors of the houses, or towards the women washing clothes and dishes in the canals. The canals were deep, with steep banks that the women were forced to clamber down with the help of bamboo poles in order to squat in the mud at the water's edge. Flood levels were marked on the canal walls by scum lines of rubbish, and the water in which the women did their washing looked like it had been used for boiling old newspapers until it achieved the consistency of cellulose.

Faraday was used to photographing wildlife, not people, and he didn't know the protocol here. Could he presume the right to peer so intimately at these Vietnamese women like this, zooming in on their bare knees and feet, capturing their slender fingers sluicing scraps of food from the bottoms of their cooking bowls?

Abruptly he found himself stopping beside a canal and focusing on one scene in particular. The water flowed slowly past a young woman's feet, dampening the buttocks on which she squatted, soaking the bottom of her fuchsia dress, the skirt of which she had tossed over her shoulder to protect it. She seemed to wash to a rhythm that he was unable to hear. Her long-haired head followed the flow of the water until, like a twig caught in the eddies of a stream, it was released from the water's flow and flicked back to begin again. In her case, the water was not for cleansing; it was an emollient, calming and softening her. There were no utensils in her hand, and although her eyes were not closed, for some reason he presumed she couldn't see.

He pressed the shutter button and lowered his camera. The scene was so foreign to him in every respect that in that moment, he realized he knew nothing. He only knew that he would never know enough. His life's journey had not begun when he was born; it would not begin until he consciously started it. And what if that moment never came? What then...?

The girl suddenly stood up and pointed at the water. Bubbles were rising there—not the tiny, isolated farts of single-cell amoebas that disturb the surface of all wetlands, but large, oxygen-charged bubbles of determined life. They fractured the surface, eager to escape, and the water erupted like overheated molten chocolate.

She was pointing in delight, for him and all to see.

The surface of the water stretched and gave way, revealing a human face. The eyes opened, then the mouth. The girl laughed, a high-pitched screaming from the throat, as if she had seen or sensed the spirit creature of the deep.

Canh shouted excitedly, 'The snakehead fish! The snakehead fish!' and danced on his toes as if stamping on cockroaches.

The face retreated beneath the water, and Faraday stepped back quickly from the edge of the bank, clutching his camera for support. In that moment, he truly believed that it was the creature Canh identified as a snakehead fish that he'd seen, and the glimpse of a human face rendered it demonic. He felt as though all the remaining air had disappeared from his lungs, and his ears were suddenly flooded with sound. What he heard may in truth have been rolling thunder, or it may have just been his imagination conjuring up the phantom that haunts the fields of death, yet somehow he was sure that what he heard and saw so clearly in that instant had happened there many times before. In fact, what was happening in that moment was that Faraday was sensing the haunted spirit of Vietnam for the first time. It was a feeling he would encounter again before his journey ended, and it was not just a product of his imagination, but a palpable presence.

Of course, the spot where he was standing was not singularly different than any other spot in Vietnam. In this place, bombers had once sprayed defoliants, mercilessly wiping out all plant life. Then in the autumn, the bombers returned with napalm, so that everything above ground, alive or dead, was burned. The heat would have been so intense that all the oxygen was consumed, and anything living below ground or seeking refuge in the water inhaled only fire when it resurfaced.

He'd seen the photos in the War Crimes Museum in Saigon (which the United States had insisted be renamed the War Remnants Museum, or else it would block the country's aid program). In an attempt to avoid the cyclo driver who he knew was waiting outside the museum to bully him into an unwanted tour of the city, he had gone through the displays twice, taking his time, not realizing what was happening to him. Not realizing that he was being irradiated by those images. Not realizing anything … only asking himself, where the fucking hell had he been all his life, not knowing about this?

As he walked away along the canal bank to return to the boat, he looked back. The girl and the man who had finally emerged from the water were laughing for the heavens to see, tears as clear as crystal rain falling from their faces into the thick grey slime that engulfed their feet. No, not a snakehead fish at all; just the spirit of one.

Was it here that Faraday's journey had begun?

TWO

'How was your morning?' the American girl asked, coming out onto the veranda terrace for lunch at the same time as Faraday.

'Great! I've been on the river.'

'Was that you? I heard they sent out the *Lady Hau* with just one passenger. You must feel honoured! I saw them lugging back all the food.'

'I'd have been just as happy in a sampan. They didn't need to lay it on.'

'Hey, mister, that would have been lateral thinking, and maybe loss of face, too. The Vietnamese are not good at either. And what do you think of the rain?'

'I like it. It's very atmospheric.'

'Clears the air, that's for sure. It'll be cooler now. So, why are you here?'

'To find out how they cook the fish,' he lied.

'Oh! They used to do cooking classes when the last chef was here. He was French. The new chef is Vietnamese. He doesn't speak English.'

'And why are *you* here?'

'I'm employed by the hotel to teach English to the staff. It's a real problem. I actually have a room full of them waiting for me right now, so I'm going to grab a sandwich and run. They're really happy to have a guest out of season though, so I'm sure you won't want for anything. It's just you and me.'

Somehow, at her suggestion, they agreed to have dinner together that evening.

* * * *

This must be where it began, then.

Her name was Caroline Brinkley, and she came from New Jersey.

'My name's Caroline Brinkley. And yours?'

'Anton. Anton Faraday.'

'You a Brit? You sound like a Brit.'

'No, Rhodesian. But I live in London.'

'Rhodesian? That's Zimbabwe, right? That nice Mister Mugabe! I guess London is the best place to be.'

Caroline was tall, with dark hair that was coiled up out of sight, and she was dressed in white cotton long sleeves and a skirt, which made it difficult to see whether she was skinny or just thin, and created the look of one prepared for an assault by mosquitoes. She taught English, she said, because it was an easy thing to do, though it was boring, and the money was no good. She spoke French and Vietnamese, hence her value to the hotel. All this he learned in the first minute.

'I'm kinda filling in with this hotel job,' she explained. 'I freelance for a Southeast Asian news bureau—mostly travel articles and follow-up pieces for local stories. That's what I am at heart: a journalist. But freelancing is an erratic source of income at best. It's too slow to rely on all the time. You can't be choosy if you want to make a living in Vietnam, so after I leave here, I'm off to do a stint with a kind of NGO.'

'A kind of what…?'

'NGO: non-governmental organization. It's a catch-all for do-good groups. Asia is full of them.'

'Yes, of course. And how did this come about?'

'Well, it's a long story…'

It was, indeed, a long and winding story, which she launched into without hesitation as he downed the large pitcher of Tiger draft beer he'd ordered before it could turn lukewarm, relieved that he didn't have to bear the burden of making conversation. While he watched and listened to her as she swept through the large empty dining room and out onto the covered veranda, talking animatedly to the waitresses and filling the place with noise (so it was easy to forget momentarily that they were the only people there, and that the candles on all the other tables, laid out so neatly with starched white tablecloths and sparkling silver cutlery, did not need to be lit), her confidence struck him in stark contrast to the shyness of the young Vietnamese staff. Yes, she was American, and there was a certain cultural imperialism—or at least a lack of awareness—that went with that, but this seemed more like a genuine enthusiasm for people. As that was not something he felt obliged to share, he steeled himself against it.

She was pretty—he'd noticed that when they met earlier in the day, and he put it down to her youth—yet he had the feeling she tried not to be. Behind her tortoiseshell glasses, and the absence of any apparent grooming, was a young woman whom he assumed (correctly, as it turned out) to be in her early thirties—maybe ten years or so his junior—with a confidence that was not the least bit self-effacing. Her attitude made it clear that they were two strangers in a distant land who, finding themselves alone at dinner time, were merely taking comfort in a common language. He had no idea at that stage that what she was going to tell him would lead them both, by degrees, to the edge of perdition ... but that was way off in the future.

She recommended the basa fish fried in lemongrass and onion. It arrived quickly, still sizzling and smelling of other herbs that he couldn't identify, as fresh as the scent of rain in the air and as volatile as the invisible electrons that rushed about the verdant gardens like Ariel in *The Tempest*, gathering up static to deliver to the clouds, readying them for the thunderstorm that would soon become a counterpoint to their conversation.

'My brother is *Vietnamese*,' she began playfully, widening her eyes for effect. 'Well, looking at me, it's pretty obvious he's not a blood brother. My parents adopted him as an orphan, the sole survivor from his family of boat people who tried to escape in the eighties.'

She peered at him quizzically, expecting a response. He didn't have one.

'Anyway,' she continued blithely, 'from the age of three, I've had a Vietnamese brother. That usually surprises people. My mom and dad are just ordinary Irish Americans from New Jersey, but they have this thing about taking people in. Growing up, I always seemed to be trying to explain it to people. My *Vietnamese* brother! That word is so highly charged, what with the war and everything, that no one in America knows what to do with it. It's like a hand grenade when you throw it into conversation back home, even today. When you've grown up with it, like I have, you really get to see it.'

He nodded sympathetically, though he was far from convinced that sympathy was what she sought. 'So, this is what prompted you to come to Vietnam?' he asked, more interested in the flavours that underlay the fish.

'Sure. Though Tuan—that's his name—pretended to hate Vietnam with a vengeance, he always wanted to return, so when I started travelling, I arranged to meet up with him in Hanoi. I knew a little bit of the language from what he'd taught me growing up, but not enough to clearly understand or to get a job, so when I arrived, I was pretty much in his hands.'

'He was returning to discover his roots,' Faraday suggested vaguely.

She took off her glasses, folded them neatly, and placed them to one side, then picked up the tea candle from the table and held it just inches in front of her face, peering so intently into the dancing flame that she appeared faintly cross-eyed. 'Just when you think you know, you find out you don't know, and never will,' she said quietly. 'That's one thing I've learned in Vietnam for sure.'

She looked up, and she wasn't cross-eyed at all. Her eyes were green and streaked with candlelight, and there was an edge to her voice—more Irish than American, he suspected, which made him regret the unthinking ease with which he'd taken her up on her suggestion to join her.

'Was there a problem?' he asked. The rapidity with which she'd slid into her story convinced him that she needed someone to tell it to.

'A problem? How can I explain it? I'd been his sister for twenty something years, right? He was raised in New Jersey, went to college in Brooklyn, and ate turkey for Thanksgiving, just like everybody else. Then in Hanoi, he turned into a gook. That's a term of hostility and contempt, in case you didn't know, which is what he suddenly displayed towards me. Not that we spoke much—not for the first week anyway, as he was working all the time. I'd arrived believing I was coming to meet up with my brother, and I found this total stranger instead.'

'In what way?'

'Like, just cold and angry. I can't explain it. Anyway, eventually he announced that he was going to take me to the house of some uncle, whom I'd never heard mentioned before, and who lived outside the city on the road to Bac Ninh. He was very up and down, very agitated, and by the time we got there, his behaviour was quite bizarre, like he was on speed or something. Well, I soon realized that my brother and this uncle had an ongoing disagreement, and from the tone of their voices behind closed doors, I could pick up that it wasn't going well. On top of that, he hardly even introduced me, so there I was with all these strangers looking at me, thinking, 'Who is she? What is she to him? Girlfriend? Wife? Does she have a name...?' It was a very weird moment.'

From her clipped tone, he gathered that it was not a moment for which she'd had much tolerance.

'I can imagine,' he said, trying to sound sympathetic. 'Did you find out why he behaved like that?'

She smiled, but only with her mouth. 'He's Vietnamese.'

She drank some water, looked out into the dark night, looked back at him, and shrugged. That seemed to be the end of it. Faraday concentrated on his fish and struggled to think of something to say. The way she'd launched straight into her story, sweeping the conventions of small talk aside, had put him off balance, and her intensity made him slightly uncomfortable.

'I'm afraid I've only been here a few days,' he admitted eventually, 'and I have no experience of the Vietnamese at all. You'll have to explain.'

If he sounded a bit like a prig, it was probably because he was torn between the appeal of sharing a meal with company, and the unappealing prospect of being potentially misunderstood. There was no denying that she was attractive, and two strangers meeting in a remote hotel in a foreign land was a cliché that hung above his head as obvious and threatening as the storm clouds that rumbled ever closer. Still, it had been her suggestion.

'I'm sorry,' she said, presuming he'd lost interest. 'I don't know why I'm telling you this.'

'You're telling me because you need to talk about it,' he suggested, 'in order to make sense of it.'

'That's right!' she agreed. 'When your own counsel fails you, take the counsel of a stranger. Isn't that how it goes? Do I sound like I need counselling? Anyway, you're going to have to hear me out, because you're stuck with me now; there's no one else in the hotel to talk to. You're trapped.'

Finding delight in this obvious truth, she shook her head like a black ibis emerging from a lagoon, and her hair, dark as the night, suddenly fell loose from her crown in an unexpected release. He sat up sharply, animal instincts telling him that the barometer had shifted, and the storm that had been circling them was now fixed in its direction.

'You see, that's what they're like,' she whispered, leaning forward, but speaking so softly that he had to lean forward, too. 'If they need to express something that's too awkward to say, they just don't say it. Believe me, you will never know in this country what's *not* being said. My guess is that the problem between my brother and his uncle had everything to do with the rift between those that stayed and those that left. I call it "Vietnam's incurable sickness". There are whole generations who will have to die before they can let it go. Anyway, next thing I know, he disappears back to Hanoi in a huff.'

'Who? Your brother?'

'My brother. He leaves the goddamned house and never comes back. So, there I am, left on my own with this uncle and his family, trying to figure out who I am, an American girl with no name who's been dropped on them without any warning by a nephew who's behaving like a little shit.'

'Sounds like a great welcome to Vietnam! What was their reaction?'

'I guess you could say they were somewhat bemused. It was obvious I had nowhere else to go at that moment, so they were very kind to me. Hospitality is seen as a duty here. I stayed the night, and somehow one night turned into a few days. I managed to explain my relationship with Tuan, and his uncle and I quickly became friends, though the subject of my brother's angry departure was pointedly never mentioned again, and I sensed that I would never be told why. You've got to understand, life is not easy for people in Vietnam, and not only because of the war. There are invisible threads that keep them bound, like Gulliver, unable to move. They're cultural bindings that we in the West can't even see, let alone understand—the ties of family and ancestry, which they call *nghia*, and of filial and patriarchal obligation, called *on* … and most of all, of *face*.'

'If by *face*, you mean 'pride,' then we all have *face*, to a degree,' he suggested. 'It's not unique to Asia.'

'Not so strong that we'd rather die than lose it.'

'I guess not. But after just three days in this country, it's a little early for me to be an expert.'

At that moment, Prospero whispered in Ariel's ear, and the wind began to whip the tails of their tablecloth and rattle the fronds of the queen palms. Boys in crisp cotton uniforms ran out of the shadows, zigzagging across the terrace beside the swimming pool, snatching up cushions and towels from the lounges where they'd been set out for the imaginary guests at the first sign of sunlight that afternoon. An umbrella toppled over, taking a table with it.

'I suppose I should have told them I wouldn't be swimming,' Faraday said apologetically.

'Wouldn't have made any difference. They'd still have put the towels out.'

'Inflexibility, or *face?*'

'Both.'

He began to like her laugh, even though she still disturbed him. It was warm and inclusive, wanting to be friendly, but there was an edge to it that suggested she had her own firm views of life, and a seriousness that forced him to listen. The story was still far from its end.

The uncle, it emerged, had a problem that had been burdening him for a long time, and he had conceived the idea that Caroline might be able to help him with it.

'He asked me to go with him up into the highlands of Lao Cai, near the Chinese border, to a small village, which I gathered was where his wife had been born. And on the way, he explained that he had a cousin there who was not happy, trapped by both *nghia* and *face*, who had struggled since the end of the war to support an extended family, and for whatever reason, they felt an obligation to help him in some way. It all had to do with what had happened during the war, and he wondered if I could maybe write a story about it.'

She was frowning now, intent on getting the recounting exact, which confirmed Faraday's belief that the story needed to be told, if only so that she could get it right in her own mind. His face must have shown puzzlement at this point, for she broke off and looked around the room, as if for an explanation, which brought the young waitresses in their elegant white *ao dais* fluttering to their table for fear that something was wrong. Faraday took the opportunity to order another beer, and a dry napkin to replace the one he'd saturated with sweat from his hands and forehead, which, presumably due solely to the humidity, wouldn't stop running.

'Didn't you think that was strange,' he asked, 'you being American…?'

She hesitated a moment, then smiled ruefully. '… and Americans being responsible for the war, you mean?'

'The war was hardly America's finest hour,' he mumbled apologetically.

'No, you're right. Hey, I make no excuses, but you'd be amazed how forgiving the Vietnamese can be. We weren't the first to stage a major bloodletting on their soil, you know. If you read their history, you can't help but conclude that there's a kind of madness that possesses people when they come here. As soon as their will is opposed, they engage in an orgy of killing. And the reason the Vietnamese are so accepting may well be that they secretly hold themselves responsible. It's like battered wife syndrome: 'If he keeps beating me to pulp, I must somehow deserve it.' You have to wonder how many deaths they would have to suffer before they really got angry.'

She shrugged. Lean limbs, he thought, olive skin, and not an ounce of body fat. So confident, and so unlike him. And she knew that he didn't have a clue about Vietnam, that he couldn't write five hundred words about it that would add to anyone's understanding of it.

'So, what do *you* do?' she asked suddenly.

'I'm a painter of wildlife.'

* * * *

At the very edge of human vision, high above the arid savannah, the martial eagle soars for hours, riding the thermal updrafts, stiff-winged and barely moving, watching for signs of life and death below, with eyes aligned in parallel that see perfectly that which other creatures lack the facility to focus upon. And when it falls in a long, flat glide, dropping a thousand metres out of the bright sky, latching fast and silent onto its victim's neck, the kill is like a sudden flash of blinding light. But when it glances up and looks around, it is bemused by the proximity of things, its far-sighted vision now unsuited to close examination of the corpse trapped in its talons. That is the look he captured in his long-focus lens. He painted the eyes in solid ivory black washed with a thin film of raw umber. The reflected light from the bleached sky was a fleck of titanium white hatched with aurora yellow. After the kill, there was always a strange moment of peace, a calm he had never understood, but which seemed to frequently follow danger.

19

* * * *

'Oh!'

The white in Caroline's eyes was the reflection of the tealight on the table between them, and her focus was far away, beyond her question, as if she had only asked in order to be given time to think. But he felt a sense of calm in that moment, as if her beauty left him no choice but to volunteer for danger. It may have been a momentary lapse into fatalism, or a surrender to the overwhelming unfamiliarity of the surroundings, but in hindsight, he believed he was beginning to will it to happen—even though, at that stage, the events about to unfold were still beyond the limits of his vision.

'It's possible that the Vietnamese don't resent death the way we do,' she said, as if it had suddenly just occurred to her. Her eyes started to come back into focus.

'What makes you say that?'

'Because they make their lives such unnecessary torture. My God! Is it possible we *all* do that? Do painters of wildlife do that? Is mankind so fucked that none of us know how to keep it simple anymore? … Okay, don't answer that. You don't know me. It's not a fair question.'

No, he didn't know her. And in any case, the question was too big to attempt an answer on their first meeting. But give it a week or so, and they would both be attempting to answer even bigger questions—questions that no one should be asked to answer—but they didn't know this at the time. In the context of their first meeting, he treated it as a throwaway line.

'So, you went with this uncle to visit his cousin,' he prompted. 'What was the story he had in mind?'

'He wanted me to hear first-hand about how people who had aligned with the wrong side during the war had been persecuted, almost to the point of extinction. It was to be his way of acknowledging that he understood how they had suffered, though I couldn't quite see how it would repair whatever had gone wrong within their family. Actually, I doubt that Uncle ever believed it would. The point you have to understand is that this is Vietnam. Expressing sympathy can threaten the other person's pride—their *face*—and knowing that, maybe he thought the gesture would be elevated and made more noble by my participation. Does that sound like crap? It *is* crap. Believe me, we Westerners will never understand these people.'

'Okay,' he interrupted, a little disappointed by the sudden collapse of her story, 'let's not be defeated by this. I refuse to accept that the Vietnamese—or anyone else, for that matter—can never be understood. Let's accept that *face* would not allow this man to accept sympathy, for whatever reason. Maybe it's a male thing. Maybe your uncle raised the stakes by having the story told in front of a woman—an American woman, no less. Perhaps you need to be a man to understand. Maybe it's got nothing to do with being Vietnamese at all.'

She laughed, but more out of politeness this time. Apparently he was off the mark, and apparently it wasn't the end of the story.

'Look, it can be very frustrating, no matter how well you think you know them, because they really are their own enemies at times. But I'm getting to the explanation of how I became involved in the NGO. Are you interested or not?'

'Of course,' he acknowledged. 'Actually, I'd forgotten that was where we were meant to be heading.'

'Okay, then. The story was not a new one, because it's played out all over the country since the fall of Saigon in 1975. But it was particularly cruel as applied to some of the hill tribes, like the Nung, who'd helped the enemy by acting as mountain guides, and the younger generation is still suffering the effects more than forty years later. And this was an old man in his late sixties telling the story.'

'Hardly 'old'!'

'Old for Vietnam—a lot older than you or me. Anyway, I listened to his story, and then I wrote a piece that got picked up by *The New York Times,* and sometime later, I got this letter from the Vanderbilt Foundation, asking if I could help them contact the tribe and arrange an introduction. It was signed by a Violet Dunleavy, who, as it turns out, was born Violet Vanderbilt.'

'As in …?'

'As in *the* Vanderbilts? I had no idea at that stage. It's not a common name, as you may know. Depending on your viewpoint, they could be considered American royalty. Not that I'm a believer in royalty, you understand; I leave that to you Brits. Anyway, I decided to search online, and I quickly found Violet Dunleavy, "of the Vanderbilt family", and what kind of work the foundation does.'

At this point, the advance guard for the approaching rainstorm arrived, widely spaced, but with heavy splashes that hit the ground like seagull droppings. The waitresses fluttered about like birds too nervous to land, wondering in which language they should warn of the coming disaster, but Faraday sensed that Caroline was finally reaching her denouement.

'Go on,' he encouraged her. 'I want to know how this ends.'

'Well, it turns out that it's a charitable foundation that's active in South America and other Third World countries, providing wells for clean water and all that stuff.'

'So, you figured they wanted to do the same thing in Vietnam?'

'You got it. I sent a reply, asking what they had in mind. Then some weeks later, when I was back in New York, I got a phone call from Violet's secretary saying that Violet had been in the Philippines and Africa, and now she was about to go down to Ethiopia, and her schedule was very full, but she'd like to schedule a time to meet and talk. Which we did. She listened to the story of my visit to the village and how we'd gone there essentially to help, then she said, "Alright, so what are we going to do?" Well, she's very high-powered and used to making the decisions. "So why's she asking me?" I thought. What did I know? I wasn't even sure what she meant. "Well, if we're going to be able to improve their situation, you're going to have to help me," she insisted. She practically told me it was my responsibility!'

'So, she put it back on you,' he stated. 'That's the sure sign of a true leader.'

'Tell me about it! She chairs God knows how many boards and foundations. Like, this is one heck of a lady.'

'So, what did you do?'

'Well, the more I thought about it, the more I realized I wanted to return to Vietnam. Something had gotten hold of me, and it kept drawing me back. So, what we agreed was that her foundation would fund a project here, and I'd help get the Nung tribe involved—which would benefit Uncle's cousin—and then I'd get a feel-good story out of it, plus a decent fee from her NGO.'

At that moment, the rain came down onto the roof of the veranda like a dam had burst above them. Faraday reflexively grabbed his camera and concentrated on manually overriding the shutter speed, so he could freeze the curtain of falling water against the brightly lit backdrop of the empty foyer beyond. The curse of digital cameras was the laziness they induced.

'What sort of project?' he shouted over his shoulder.

'Digging freshwater wells in the tribal villages in his region.'

'How will that help your uncle's cousin?'

'He acts as the liaison and organizer for the tribe, and in return, we fund a poultry farm for them.'

'Will it work?'

'Yes.'

'What about his *face*?'

'It's not charity. It's a payment for his services that benefits the whole tribe, as well as his own family.'

'Congratulations!'

'Thank you. If nothing else, I should be able to file a great story.'

THREE

The rain didn't stop as expected, but continued its relentless hammering on the roof and grounds that cancelled out all attempts at further conversation. They agreed to call it quits and maybe meet again in the morning over breakfast or for lunch, as Faraday was due to catch a launch at one thirty to take him upriver to Chau Doc on the Cambodian border.

As he lay on top of the bed with the ceiling fan drying the sweat on his naked skin, he sensed that Vietnam was infecting him in a way he had never experienced before. Like the rain and humidity, it saturated the senses and monopolized the mind. It was elusive yet intimate, teasing yet evasive, begging for its secrets to be discovered while hiding them from discovery. The enigmatic face of Asia is often presumed to mask profundity, yet in his experiences to date, it only masked a single-minded pursuit of money. What made Vietnam feel so different, then? Why did it arouse this perception of hidden drama, this presentiment of impending ill fortune that had dogged him from the time he'd landed at the Ho Chi Minh airport?

He thought about the river, how powerfully it flowed, so dense and impenetrable, hiding its contents, a source of life that somehow reeked of death, as if the blood of centuries had seeped out of the hills and surrounding marshes, feeding its insatiable appetite. He thought about the crocodiles and alligators that infested the mouth of the river, and he wondered why they wouldn't come up into the creeks and canals of Cantho, where the women washed their cooking pots while their men lay obliviously submerged.

And yes, he thought about the darkness that lay in the depth of Celtic women's eyes, born long ago from the horrors of Spanish galleons foundering on the wild coast of Kerry, from famines and bombings and wailing songs of grief, a darkness that never completely disappeared, even in New Jersey, in the land of the free, always carrying an edge of danger and unpredictability.

It had been a simple mission that brought him here, but already its purpose was becoming obscured, and it seemed that a new purpose was being born, though its nature and shape were still a long way from being revealed to him.

There was no sign of Caroline at breakfast the following morning, so he ate alone, feeling listless from the lack of sleep and disappointed by the absence of her company. The rain had lifted for the moment, and he had time to kill until after lunch, when his boat was due. So, he walked in the gardens for an hour or so, then returned to the lobby to read the only paper in English, *The Phnom Penh Gazette*.

Come mid-morning, the hotel's conference room doors were thrown open, and the hotel staff streamed out, including Caroline. She was now dressed in the hotel uniform—a Vietnamese-style silk pyjama suit—and wore flat-heeled leather sandals that clapped briskly on the polished stone floors as she strode towards him, breaking into a broad smile and removing the tortoiseshell glasses that seemed designed to give her an air of authority. The edge of darkness from the night before had been banished from her eyes by daylight.

'Anton, you're still here!' She beamed.

'Killing time till my boat arrives.'

'Great! I'll kill it with you. I'm off duty now, and I wanted to ask what brought you to Vietnam, because I told you my story, and I got the feeling last night that you're not just a tourist. Are you going to tell me?'

She had a terrific smile and eyes that drilled into him. He had no choice. 'Well, that, too, is a long story…'

* * * *

Maybe this was where the journey began.

In the first week of June, he'd been due to give an address on the importance of stylistic tagging to first-year students in the painting department of his old alma mater, the Royal College of Art in Kensington. The invitation to speak was intended as a compliment, but he'd started to regret accepting it. The fact that he was free to choose the topic hadn't helped at all, for with every passing hour, he'd become more and more convinced that his thesis— that every painting should carry the artist's personal marker somewhere within it—not only revealed the degree to which art was corrupted by commerce, but unsubtly confirmed the degree of his own corruption.

In previous years, he'd have welcomed the chance to open students' eyes to the commercial realities they would face in the real world. He'd have been happy as Larry to expound at length on what he cynically referred to as 'the gallery trade,' and to hell with the risk of damaging their tender artistic sensibilities. At the ripe old age of forty-five, however, he had to admit that Anthony John Faraday—Anton to his friends, such as they were, and AJ to the art-buying public—was having a mid-career crisis, characterized by a growing decline in motivation and confidence. But whereas most such crises arise out of an accumulation of disappointments and underachievement, his, believe it or not, had its roots in success. He'd become trapped in a genre that richly rewarded him (the painting of wildlife), and as a result, he felt incapable of escaping it. Indispensable to this success were the stylistic markers, clear as the thumbprint on a John Dory, which identified a work as unmistakably his. But now that he'd chosen to mount an argument in favour of such devices, he had to wonder whether his own markers had become the very trap that imprisoned him.

He'd gotten up early on the appointed day to try and resolve this dilemma in his mind, practicing his speech while fiddling about with an unfinished canvas. The tone of the speech, even in the confines of his own head, concerned him, laced as it was with hints of disenchantment. It was not a tone he was eager to reveal to students half his age, arrogant little arseholes that they were, brimming with the confidence and blissful ignorance of youth. Yet despite the early start and his determination to keep it positive, it had been an unproductive morning, so when he heard the doorbell ring at an unusual hour for visitors, he willingly put down his paintbrush and hurried down the short flight of stairs from his studio with the eagerness of someone willing to switch his attention to a much more compelling event.

He wasn't disappointed.

It was another indifferent London day outside, grey and airless, clogged with the smell of half-burned diesel fuel. The painful howl of an exhausted bus grinding its way up Kensington Church Street swept in through the door as he removed the security chain to open it, and he must have screwed up his face in distaste, for in front of him, backing away defensively at the sudden appearance of this unwelcoming countenance, was a rather nondescript bloke in a black raincoat whose face looked vaguely familiar.

'It's a bad time to call unannounced,' the nondescript bloke apologized, 'but the early bird, so they say…' His head nodded up and down like that of a pigeon looking for a seed of encouragement. Under one arm, he carried a large, flat package wrapped in brown paper. 'This can only be done in person, and I took the chance that I'd find you in, as we're only around the corner, so to speak. Jonathon Appleby from Christie's, South Kensington.'

'Jonathon…?'

'Appleby! Hopefully I'll only need to disturb you for a moment, but I felt I had no choice but to come right to the source. We've been asked to sell one of your paintings, you see, and I suddenly had an awful feeling that it wasn't quite right.'

'In what way?' Faraday demanded suspiciously.

'That's what I hoped you could explain. It's just a feeling, but I'd rather be safe than sorry, and I thought you'd be the first to agree with that. It's not often that your work comes through our salesroom, and it wouldn't do anyone any good if, God forbid, we were found to have sold a fake.'

The package was awkward to handle, so he rested it on one toe while waiting for Faraday to reply. There wasn't a great difference in their ages, but the man from Christie's had that air of mannered deference, common to auction room and funeral parlour staff, which managed to induce a passive acquiescence in others.

'No, I suppose not,' Faraday conceded meekly.

Thus granted the seed of encouragement he sought, Appleby hopped forward, took Faraday's hand, and shook it rather limply, then stepped politely into the hallway, bringing with him a faint vapor trail of recently chewed peppermints. 'Do tell me if it's not a convenient time,' he offered. 'I know how you artists hate being interrupted at a critical moment.'

'No, no, it's fine. I was about to make some coffee anyway. So, what's the subject?'

'A panda bear.'

Faraday spun around and stared in disbelief. 'Give it to me.'

Pulling away the paper wrapping, he propped it up on the kitchen table, his mind spinning.

'I've been through all the catalogues of your exhibitions over the years,' Appleby professed, 'but I couldn't recall this painting. So, I looked on your limited editions site, and there's no mention of a panda there, so naturally I became suspicious.'

'That's right; it's never been reproduced.'

The coffee was forgotten as he stared, flabbergasted. Of all the paintings he had ever done, this was the one that he had never expected to see again. In some people's eyes, it was the one he never should have painted.

'Did you know that these things can eat over a hundred pounds of bamboo shoots a day?' he said, marking time. 'They're forever hungry. Don't be fooled by the black-eyed Susan looks and the cuddly shape; they'll happily scratch your eyes out. Nu Nu here was a gift to the nation from the Chinese government back in the eighties. Pandas were used as surrogate emissaries of peace, despite their vicious temperaments. Nixon got one. Pompidou got one. I guess it proves that looks really are everything. Zoos love them. I photographed her in 1994, just before she was sent to Mexico.'

'So, it *is* one of yours!' He popped a peppermint into his mouth and crunched it with delight. 'Thank heavens for that.'

'Oh, yes, I remember it well,' Faraday said, stepping forward for a closer look, but already aware that Appleby's relief was going to be short-lived.

* * * *

How the water of one's life flows, he thought: small, unnoticed raindrops that grow into trickles; trickles that grow into streams; streams that become roaring torrents; torrents that sweep you away.

'There was a time when pandas were big news,' he explained to Caroline, recalling that moment as they sat in the foyer of the Grande Rivière Hotel. 'They got more magazine coverage than Prince William and Kate get now, and the whole damned nation took their failed mating attempts very personally indeed. It might have been a bit before your time, but when it was announced that Nu Nu was being sent to mate in warmer climes, an epidemic of anthropomorphic grief swept across Britain. Crowds of people lined up for hours to peer wonderingly into those dark eyes and wish that they, too, were pandas. Of course, any behavioural scientist with a background in biology can tell you that the pupil of the human eye dilates with sexual arousal, and the enlargement provides an unconscious signal to the mate, which acts as a further attractant. This in part explains the sex appeal of unusually dark-eyed people, such as Catherine Zeta Jones and Johnny Depp. It also explains the marked appeal of the panda.'

'The things you learn!' She laughed. 'I'd always presumed our pupils expand during sex because the lights are low. Have you made a study of this?'

'Don't confuse me.' He blushed. 'I'm just telling you about the panda. This is a painting I had not expected to ever see again, though in hindsight, I now realize it played a significant part in shaping my career. For reasons that I'll explain, the panda is off limits to wildlife painters, but at that time, I was still a student, and I'd been at the London Zoo with my camera and decided to get some shots of her before she left. The queues were enormous, and I never got closer than ten rows back from the perimeter of the enclosure, waiting for heads to move out of the way so I could get a brief glimpse of black-and-white fur. More out of exasperation than hope, I aimed my lens, zoomed in, and waited for the obstructing heads to part and provide me with a fleeting view. It was like shooting through a keyhole. Framed by a circle of anonymous heads and necks, poor old Nu Nu looked baffled, alone, and imprisoned in the bright afternoon sunlight. The focal depth blurred the backs of the spectators, rendering them into amorphous shapes, which is how I ended up painting it.'

'Sounds interesting. Go on.'

* * * *

'I remember this painting well,' he told Appleby. 'It was my crowd-pleaser piece for the graduation show at the RCA a year later. I owe a lot to that painting.'

The stylistic tags were already there, which surprised him. He thought they'd evolved consciously over time, but it appeared from the evidence of Nu Nu that they'd been dictated by the limitations of the photographic image.

'It's not the sort of subject matter you'd expect to see in the harsh

30

environment of today's RCA,' he joked, delaying the moment. 'Animals and babies are too deeply contaminated with sentimentality for today's contemporary artist. Babies are for burning! Animals are only permitted to populate nightmares!'

'That would explain why I hadn't seen it,' Appleby enthused, 'and presumably, that would also explain why it isn't in your catalogue of prints. An early student work, now verified by the artist himself—the perfect provenance! Buyers always love that.' His head started ducking up and down like a bird again as the prospect of a good price and a healthy sales commission promised to be the worm that made his early start to the day worthwhile.

'Yes, that's certainly how I painted her,' Faraday murmured, peering more closely at the unframed canvas on the table. 'Only this one wasn't painted by me.'

It was one of those moments when the source of the vague anxieties and dissatisfactions that had been plaguing him was suddenly illuminated, allowing him to see it clearly for the first time. He wasn't thinking about the consequences of being faced with a fake. He was thinking about the consequences set in motion by the original, the cheesy bloody panda, and how they had affected his life.

He'd known the rules when he painted it. The consensus of opinion at the RCA had long been that paintings of animals were not serious art (which made it all the more surprising that years later, they'd asked him— a wildlife painter—to be a guest lecturer). He must have been aware, even in his student days, that he'd been pushing his luck using such a subject for his graduation piece. But seeing it again made him wonder whether the animal subject matter wasn't incidental to the manner in which it was painted. He could just as easily have taken the same stylistic approach to another subject, surely, and that must have been what the selection panel thought as well.

One's destiny is determined by such apparently random choices.

Something had made him put the panda into that graduation show.

Could it have been a simple misjudgement on his part? Today's students were busy addressing issues of identity and coercive violence, referencing their deconstructionist checklists for any hidden taboos that might inadvertently pop up to shame them. They'd die a million deaths rather than be caught painting a panda. Perhaps he was just lucky enough to have been there in the period that spawned neo-expressionism, a period characterized by feeling-laden brushwork and primal imagery. Neo-expressionism had its checklists, too, of course. Allegory and metaphor were in there somewhere. This wasn't just a painting of a cuddly bear; this was a blatant cry for freedom, a plaint against bondage and the cult of beauty.

Referencing the failure of pandas to successfully mate in captivity, he'd added an explanatory inscription to the painting. Seeing it again, he now read it softly under his breath:

Peel back the mask of my allure,
and you will find that the mourning of my life
has killed the seed within.

It was a cheap trick, that reference to the bear's infertility. But as tricks went, it was a successful one, for Ralph Lutyen—*the* Ralph Lutyen of Lutyen's Gallery, no less—had given him his card and a piece of advice that would never have occurred to him otherwise.

'There's money in animals,' Lutyen said. 'Forget about people. People don't sell.'

Now, as the worm was unceremoniously pulled from his early bird mouth, Jonathon Appleby spluttered in disbelief. 'But you said you recognized it.'

'I do. It's a very good copy.'

'Are you absolutely certain?'

'Absolutely. There are aspects of the brushwork that give it away. I use soft filberts for impasto, for instance, instead of bristle flats as used here—and the scumbling uses a heavier hand than I'd like. In any case, the canvas is wrong. At the RCA, we made our own stretchers, and this one definitely isn't mine.'

'I couldn't put my finger on what it was that disturbed me,' Appleby hastened to explain, 'but I did sense that something wasn't quite right.'

'Quite a bit, actually. The spelling in the inscription is a giveaway, too. It should be "mourning" as in grieving, not "morning" as in daytime. Whoever copied it didn't understand the meaning.'

'Thank heavens I came to see you before it was put up for sale!' Appleby mumbled. 'What a disaster that would have been.'

His disappointment at losing a sale was tempered by relief, but of course that wasn't the end of the matter, as they both knew. There was the potentially embarrassing task of Christie's having to inform the vendor—embarrassing because there was always a lingering suspicion on such occasions that the vendor, despite the requisite expressions of shock and horror, knew damned well it was a fake. In that case, Christie's would remain unfailingly polite, offer their sincere regrets, and quietly mark his card for future reference. But even so, that was not a very satisfying result for the artist.

'I suppose I should feel violated,' Faraday said. 'Is it an insult or a compliment to be copied in this way? Christ, I don't know. However, with this particular painting, there's another issue. You see, the original has never been in the public domain. The last I heard, it was locked away in a private collection in Switzerland, and as far as I know, that's where it remains.'

* * * *

'Let's sit under the umbrella tree,' Caroline suggested. 'I need some air after being locked up in that damned conference room all morning. Maybe they'll bring us some mint tea. Then I want to know what happened next. I mean,

33

who would be so crazy as to knock off one of your paintings if you're so well known and live just around the corner from the auction house? That doesn't sound very smart to me.'

They sat on a wrought iron bench that had been wiped dry by one of the uniformed pool boys, who was then instructed to summon a waitress so they could order Caroline's tea. The underemployment of the hotel staff appeared to make her feel guilty, and she seemed intent on putting as many of them to work as possible.

Despite the frequent torrents of rain, the flamboyant trees and the bougainvillea had managed to hold onto their flowers, and the lawns were the colour of crisp green apples.

'According to Appleby, the vendor bought the painting from a gallery in Vietnam,' Faraday said. 'That's why I'm here.'

At this, Caroline clapped her hands with delight—which brought more staff running from all directions.

'Great!' she enthused. 'So, you're going to nail the bastards! Or have you already? Who were they, and what did they say? I'll bet they just smiled and pretended they didn't understand. They've probably ordered another ten copies just on the basis of your interest. I love it! Knocking off paintings for tourists is big business in Vietnam. You must have seen all the Gauguins and Van Goghs that line the pavements. Hell, you should feel flattered. So, which gallery did he buy it from?'

'If I knew that,' Faraday replied testily, 'I'd have no need to traipse all over the damned country. Unfortunately, you've asked the wrong bloody question.'

'Oh, sorry; it seemed like the obvious question to me. Couldn't Christie's tell you?' She must have sensed from his tone that she'd hit a raw nerve, for she reached over and laid a hand lightly on his arm.

* * * *

By the time Jonathon Appleby had taken his leave that morning, it was almost ten o'clock. He professed to know nothing about the vendor of the forgery, as he hadn't been on the front desk when it was submitted. But he did assure Faraday that he would leave no stone unturned in pursuing the origin of the painting and, hopefully, its perpetrator.

'I know it will seem odd to you after so clearly establishing that it's a fake,' he said, 'but in circumstances like this, we have no option but to return the counterfeit work to its owner. There's no law against copying, you see. The offence lies in passing it off as the genuine article. So, if the vendor pleads ignorance of its origins, there's nothing we can do about it.'

'That's nonsense,' Faraday protested, as pleasantly as possible. 'It's got my signature on it, so the intent to commit fraud is pretty damned obvious.'

'But the vendor might well claim that he or she is actually the only victim,' Appleby explained. 'That's our difficulty.'

Whatever happened, he agreed that Christie's would not part with the painting until Faraday had been informed of the result of their enquiries, and he promised that he'd phone him with an update. It was only after he'd left that Faraday realized he hadn't asked what it was that caused him to doubt the painting in the first place, for the clues that were obvious to the painter would not have been known to anyone who had not seen the original. This thought stayed with him throughout the day as he went off to lecture the latest generation of art prodigies at the RCA on the need to stamp their work with the indelible thumbprint of their own stylistic markers, but it faded over the ensuing days, and when Appleby eventually phoned to say that the vendor had finally taken the painting back (having been informed in writing that it was not genuine), he forgot to ask him that question.

'It was purchased from a gallery in Vietnam, according to the person who picked it up on the owner's behalf,' Appleby said. 'Unfortunately, I can't be more specific than that, as we didn't speak to the owner in person.

Apparently he lives overseas. I rather doubt that we'll be hearing from him again, though. I mean, Vietnam! Really! It's hardly the place to go shopping for bona fide art, one would think.'

But the question that he forgot to ask was only one of many that kept popping up in the days since.

* * * *

Faraday stood up and walked to the edge of the hotel lawn, which was bordered by a low stone wall. On the other side, the Mekong River oozed past like a giant predator. The water was almost on a level with the lawn, and after the next downpour, it could well become higher. Hardwood boats with sharp prows raced past, manned by scowling men in black who clutched long-handled outboard motors that screamed angrily through the vents in the tin cans replacing their missing mufflers. It seemed like a place where killing would hardly be noticed, where dead bodies could be slipped into the water and instantly disappear as if they had never existed, while downstream, at the river's mouth, the alligators waited.

'I figure there can't be that many galleries in Vietnam selling paintings to Westerners,' he explained. 'Locals aren't likely to be buying them—they seem to be flat out just trying to survive—so I'll follow the tourist route, and see the country while I'm at it. It's a great excuse for a holiday.'

'And you had no luck in Saigon?' Caroline asked, trying to show a little more sympathy now that she knew how seriously he was treating the matter.

'No. I'm pretty sure I've eliminated all the possibilities there. I concluded that the knock-off must have been sold as an original, which rules out the mass-production arcades and suggests I'm looking for a more exclusive gallery, and there aren't too many of them. The arcades deliberately copy recognizable, iconic pieces of impressionism. My painting of the panda has never been reproduced, and by rights, it shouldn't be able to be copied at all. If it was one of my published lithographs, I could understand it. I probably wouldn't be bothered to come all this way to track it down, in fact. But the panda is a completely different story.'

'Is that because it's in a private collection? Did you say in Switzerland?'

'That's right. It was bought by the Paladin Foundation for the Environment.'

'An environmental group? That would explain it, then; it must have been copied from one of their brochures or websites. Isn't the panda their logo or mascot?'

'No, you're thinking of the World Wildlife Fund. The Paladin Foundation is very private. They don't do publicity; they do politics. There are reasons, which I won't go into, that make it pretty certain that that painting has never been reproduced publicly. That's why I'm so keen to track down the source.'

While they were talking, a flat-bottomed river boat with the hotel's name painted on the side had pulled into the jetty at the bottom of the garden, and shortly thereafter, the receptionist was waving to him from the foyer, signalling that it was time to settle up and be on his way. They walked back across the lawn together, and past the swimming pool with its rows of white loungers adorned with towels for imaginary guests. The familiar sound of approaching thunder rolled upstream towards them, and the boat boy was already unfurling clear plastic awnings and lashing down the sides of the boat in preparation for the expected rain.

Faraday's contribution to the hotel's overheads that week was eighty-nine dollars, which included the guided morning boat trip to the floating market, the fried basa fish, and the free copy of *The Phnom Penh Gazette* he'd picked up at the front desk (which was to prove very interesting reading).

'I have a feeling there's more to this story than you've told me,' Caroline insisted as they said goodbye. 'You're on an odyssey, and I really want to hear how it ends. Will you let me know?'

So, there and then, as the rain started falling again in the heart of the Mekong Delta, they exchanged contact details before he made a dash for the boat that was waiting to take him upriver to Chau Doc and the Cambodian border. Looking back at her standing on the lawn in the rain, a stranger he'd only known for a few hours, he had no way of knowing that they were embarking on a journey of discovery together.

She was right; there was more to the story than he'd told her, just as there was more to her story than she'd told him. Sometimes it's easier to creep closer to the truth with total strangers, believing there are no consequences since you will probably never meet again … but first, you have to be willing to admit the truth to yourself.

FOUR

Faraday had intended to restrict his student lecture at the RCA to no more than an hour, but the follow-up questions made him run over. For all their carefully cultivated conceit, students could be intimidated by the obscure cleverness of most art lecturers, so he'd kept it plain and simple. Whatever the level of their artistic ability, he emphasized, there were practical and mundane decisions they would have to make in order to get paid for their work. Talent alone was never enough.

As his talk progressed, he sensed that the audience was drowsily content for him to say whatever he pleased; all that agonizing about his tone had been a total waste of time. In the lecture room of the RCA, he probably looked perfectly at home: a little overweight, in a comfortable sort of way; a little shaggy, his dark hair reaching over the collar of his open-necked shirt; eyes slightly bruised and reluctant to focus after so many years of working on his own—the archetypal artist, in fact. There was no outward sign of the self-doubt that had plagued him in recent months ... not that they would have noticed.

'I expect you want me to explain how to make money,' he began, 'or have you already worked that out? I suppose if Damien Hirst can get a million pounds for a sliced pig in formaldehyde, you could try a set of conjoined embryos in a womb of blood-red polycarbonate. It might not be a painting per se, but neither is Tracey Emin's discarded bed linen, so who's to deny that it's art? It must seem so easy. You can almost sense Charles Saatchi's cheque book eagerly awaiting your creative genius.'

They liked that. It was obviously a prelude to telling them how it worked in reality.

'When I graduated from here, I had no idea about the life I was choosing, and I expect you don't either. I never imagined that twenty years on, I'd have already spent half my life in front of an easel, with the rest of my life—forty more years, in all probability ——stretched out before me offering more of the same. I never imagined the physical reality of working alone every day, the radius of my activity limited by the length of my arm, lungs calloused from the vapours of solvents and thinners, imagination tested by the chore of daily routine.'

They wanted to know the codes of behaviour that governed the artist-agent relationship. How important was it to be represented, and how did you go about it? Luckily, everything came back to the development of a clear and recognizable style, which was his basic thesis. But should this development be conscious, or would it evolve on its own in good time?

He decided to show them examples of his own early work, pieces that came to typify the expressionistic style that distinguished his paintings from the hyper-realism that pervaded wildlife art at the time when he was setting out.

'In hindsight,' he explained as the image of a whirring bird came up on the screen, 'this was a risky departure from the established norm. The convention at the time was that nature was already perfect, and the artist's challenge was to portray that perfection in all its minute detail. Of course, I didn't know any of that at the time, not yet being a wildlife painter.'

Like a cynical revisionist, he went on to pretend that every artist's invisible hand can be revealed through practice.

'Everything you do is conscious,' he lied. 'The brush you choose, the colour you mix, the way you apply it. Eventually, you know every technique and every visual effect that can be achieved. Then you become engaged in a never-ending process of editing. All the conscious choices you make

40

during that process will result in your particular interpretation. When you make the same choices often enough, then you will have developed a recognizable style.'

While spouting this nonsense, he chose to ignore the little matter of Nu Nu, whom he'd chanced to paint just the way he'd photographed her—and the serendipitous meeting with Ralph Lutyen, who chanced to encourage him in concentrating on painting wildlife, which he identified as a potentially lucrative market. But then, he couldn't very well tell these eager young faces that life all came down to chance, could he? How fair would that have been?

* * * *

The first thing he'd done after Appleby left his studio was to call Ralph at the gallery. But Ralph was out—gone to an early lunch without his cell phone—so he left a message with his partner, Robbie, asking him to call as soon as possible. By the time his phone rang, the small group of students gathered around him in the RCA cafeteria was questioning whether or not any opinion should—or could—be formed about an artist without reference to his political stance.

'There's the politics of wildlife,' one girl said accusingly, 'but you make no statement about it. There's the politics of money, and you obviously make heaps of that. Not to mention the politics of *celebrity*...'

There was something very sexy about short-haired women with tattoos who tried to hide their prettiness, he thought—and also something very scary. As the other students all nodded in agreement with her, he quietly excused himself.

'I need to talk to you about something,' he muttered on the phone with Ralph. 'It's got me puzzled, and I think we need to sort it out.'

Even at that early stage, he must have been aware that something was growing out of the seed of this counterfeit painting that would prove to be utterly entangling. They arranged to meet at six thirty that evening at The

41

Honeycomb Café and Restaurant in Bayswater, as anything later required a reservation, which they might not have obtained. Faraday chose to walk, because any distance north or south of Hyde Park at that time of day took longer by bus or taxi than on foot. Besides, he had much to think about.

As usual, Ralph arrived late, ensuring that Faraday was well into a bottle of The Hay Paddock Syrah that he'd promised himself on the walk up the hill. So, it was a smiling and affable face with which he greeted his agent, and which he held as they picked their way through the menu. But his mind was already darkening, and inside him a scowl of discontent was developing, and a fierce determination to find out who was pirating his work. In the mildly paranoiac state that had taken hold of him throughout the day, anyone could be guilty—even Ralph.

'Ralph, I was presented today with a counterfeit version of one of my works, passed off as an original.' He tried to make it sound like a mere comment on the traffic, and at first it was treated as such.

'Ah, my dear boy, that's the inevitable price of success! These days, it's unavoidable. What I really should say is congratulations! It's the ultimate accolade. Think of the company you have joined. I salute you.' He lifted his glass to his mouth and drank without properly savouring it, thinking instead of the angel hair pasta that would soon arrive.

'Problem is, Ralph, the painting in question is one that I'd always believed was no longer available to be copied.'

'You've lost me, dear boy. Your work is so widely published now that it's bound to be copied. It's the price of success,' he repeated innocently. His eyes were all over the room, searching for something more interesting.

The angel hair pasta—which arrived very quickly, as Ralph had requested—slipped down his throat, bringing spasms of warmth and joy to his whole body, and he held his napkin to his mouth, lest the joy should pop out for all to see. When the moment had passed, Ralph could trust himself to speak. 'But what do you mean, "it's no longer available to be copied"?'

'I'm talking about the painting of the panda bear, which Kenneth

Johnston bought for the Paladin Foundation on the pretence that it would save us from being sued by the World Wildlife Fund. It was agreed that it would never see the light of day. Remember?'

'Refresh my memory. But please, don't try and spoil my appetite.'

* * * *

Alright: that was easy enough.

Lutyen's Gallery in Mayfair, five thirty on a winter's afternoon. All the talk was of the inevitable collapse of Charles and Di's marriage, but Faraday had other things on his mind as he surveyed the room. They were waiting—a crowd of bright-eyed gallery groupies, a handful of over-anxious artists, and an odd assortment of businessmen, all wearing their silly cocktail party faces—for the arrival of The Duke.

Occupying a prominent position on a large wooden easel (which a Florentine antique dealer had sworn was once used by Fra Angelico himself) was Faraday's painting of *The Indochine Tiger*. This was an animal that he'd found tied to a steel peg in the back garden of a Meo village hut on the road to Doi Inthanon, where he'd stopped for a bowl of green frog curry and rice on his first trip to Thailand. It was a very fit-looking tiger, fed each day on restaurant scraps, yet despite its bulging neck and muscular shoulders, it had somehow lost the strength to compete with the puny rope that held it in place. That's the way Faraday had painted it ... but looking at it now, so prominently displayed for all to see, he had begun to have concerns as to whether the treatment worked. He had three other pieces in the exhibition, but this was the one that bothered him.

The Fra Angelico easel stood beside a lectern against a wall bearing the legend L.U.T.Y.E.N.S in large gold-leaf letters that shone ostentatiously under the spotlights, carefully positioned to ensure they could be clearly read in any press photograph (but would be difficult for a subeditor to crop out without also cutting into The Duke's head). By the door, a long table welcomed guests with champagne glasses and press releases. The importance of the occasion was signified by a massive table display of white lilies—difficult to obtain at that time of the year, and impossible to ignore.

Ralph expertly worked the room, gracing each group with a full display of his gleaming teeth and immaculately coifed grey hair. As usual, he was a little too smooth for politics, a little too cultured for business, and a little too impressive to be running an art gallery. In those days, he was at his peak, the room fully under his control.

'Anton, I want you to meet Kenneth Johnston. He wants to talk to you about one of your paintings.'

'You don't like the tiger?' Faraday asked nervously.

'I think it's exceptionally well executed, and I like the rhino, too. I don't care for the panda, though—particularly the bars.' He was quite small but didn't realize it, a sandy-haired forty-something with a Scottish accent and enough confidence to fail to directly meet Faraday's eyes, as if knowing that he would interest him anyway.

He was right. 'The bars are what keep her in,' Faraday replied amiably. 'They may look like cuddly animals, but there's nothing pleasant about them at all. They have a particularly nasty temperament, probably due to the fact that they're perpetually hungry.'

He might have added that the bars were the whole point of the bloody painting: sad little eyes, steel fucking bars.

'Oh, it's not *me* that takes issue with it, you understand; it's our colleagues at the World Wildlife Fund,' Johnston explained easily. 'They're very concerned over any representation of the panda, and I suspect they would not be well pleased with the way you've portrayed it. We're talking an image thing here. Consider the millions of stuffed panda bears that accompany little children to bed at night, and the cuddly creatures that adorn their collection buckets and posters. They feel a sense of proprietorial right, you see, having funded the Save the Panda campaign in China … not to mention the copyright ramifications.'

Faraday was incredulous. 'The what?'

'The portrait of the panda is the subject of a worldwide copyright, which the World Wildlife Fund has spent millions registering. Prior consent is required for its use. It's a royalties issue.'

Before Faraday could splutter his indignation, Ralph cut in. 'Mr Johnston has pointed out that The Duke is the president of the WWF, and we run the risk of provoking a reaction from him. So, I'm going to quietly remove it from display.'

* * * *

'Yes, yes,' Ralph acknowledged, 'I remember now. Johnston then offered to buy it on behalf of the Paladin Foundation, and we all agreed it would never be reproduced. The beginning of a very lucrative relationship, if I may say so.'

'We both agree on that, Ralph.'

'Those paintings he went on to commission from you, and the special edition portfolios they used for fundraising purposes, really set the benchmark price for your works. You have a lot to thank Mr Kenneth Johnston for, God rest his soul. It was a very fortuitous meeting.'

'For all of us, apparently, though I still have trouble getting my head around how it all worked financially. I left that to the two of you. You're the money man; I'm just the bloody artist.'

'And we're both good at what we do, Anton.' Ralph pointed the corner of his raised napkin at him in emphasis, just in case he'd missed his meaning.

'So, why do I still have this feeling,' Faraday asked quietly, 'that there was something shonky about it all, Ralph ... something you've never properly explained?'

Even though he made a point of peering intently into the depths of the Syrah, he sensed that Ralph's eyes were off in flight, searching the room, seeking the cause of his confusion. Ralph was more than twenty years older than his protégé, and despite the food, he'd kept himself in good condition. But it had been a long while since Faraday had examined him without the blur of over-familiarity. His eyelashes had gone white, weakening the intensity of his eyes, and his skin now had the mottled red shine of an un-summered older man. God, he was well into his sixties already! They'd known each other for over twenty years.

'I don't understand,' Ralph said finally. Then, feeling some need to be adamant, he repeated himself: 'I don't understand what you just said.'

Faraday lifted his eyes from the wine to Ralph's shirt, careful to disguise his inner intensity. 'Well, in hindsight, you'd have to say that the prices negotiated were suspiciously high for an unknown artist. How the hell did that work?'

At that moment, large red capsicums, stuffed with a pilaf of herbed rice and veal and pork forcemeat, landed on Ralph's placemat, the steaming hot vapours rising visibly towards his nostrils, such that he momentarily lost his focus. 'Sage,' he murmured. 'I smell sage and thyme, and thankfully, a hint of shallots rather than garlic. I am becoming so resistant to garlic! Don't you agree?'

By comparison, Faraday's simple pasta and salad reeked of self-denial. He wished he'd ordered the capsicums instead, but it was too late.

'Tell me again how it worked,' he prompted, 'because we both know that I was an unknown artist with no previous sales history. How the hell did you justify the prices?'

Baked capsicum holds its heat long after it reaches the table, and Ralph was forced to restrain himself. 'Well, that was the whole point, my dear boy.' He reluctantly laid down his knife and fork while waiting for the dish to cool. 'You were presented as the new-found prodigy, the very latest thing. So, had there been a history of previous sales, it would have been impossible to command the prices we obtained. That's what was so clever. There were twelve sponsors who seed-funded the Paladin Foundation.

Johnston invited each of them to pay for the acquisition of one of your "brilliant" paintings to go into a permanent collection. It didn't really matter what each of the sponsors paid, because they were already committed to paying the Foundation's costs one way or the other anyway—but for you, it was an incredible stroke of luck. The difference between what you received and what the sponsors paid was the proceeds of Johnston's fundraising. And then, of course, there was the further fundraising through the sale of the limited-edition prints once the collection was complete. If you don't mind my saying so, you were a very lucky young man.'

As he watched the first forkful of crimson capsicum prepare to enter Ralph's mouth, Faraday felt a familiar wave of dissatisfaction sweep over him. Perhaps this was why he took no pleasure in his success. All along, he must have suspected what Ralph was now telling him: he'd just been fucking lucky.

His meagre plate of linguine suddenly went cold.

'In the right place at the right time—is that how you'd put it?' he demanded, pushing the plate away from him. 'Just a lucky accident that had nothing at all to do with talent?'

'Don't be so sensitive, Anton; it isn't like you. Yes, of course it took talent. Your style is unique and inseparable from the content. But we can't deny the element of good fortune that surrounded the commissioning of those paintings by Kenneth Johnston, or the impact on your career, now can we? It takes an awful lot of luck to succeed in your game. We've got art schools in every borough and county of Britain, turning out thousands of graduates every year, and every one of them suffers from the delusion that they'll make a living from it. I mean to say, how many empty living room walls do they think there really are? No, no, dear boy, let's not delude ourselves: Johnston gave you your chance, and you took it with both hands. That's your talent, you see; you know when you're onto a good thing. You're not infatuated with your own genius, thank God.'

Faraday refrained from ordering another bottle of The Hay Paddock

Syrah and passed on Ralph's offer to share a dessert. No, he was not a genius. He just painted pictures of animals—a safe, dull, and unimaginative pastime which, thanks to Kenneth Johnston, enabled him to earn a lot of money.

'Getting back to the subject of the panda,' he persisted, 'is there any way of finding out whether it's still in the Paladin Foundation's collection, and whether or not they've ever had it reproduced? Is there someone who would know that?'

'I can ask, I suppose.' Ralph looked less than certain. 'Since the Mont Blanc Tunnel fire, and Johnston's disappearance from the scene, I've had no further contact with them. They're a bit of a mystery, actually. I've never quite worked out what it is they do. But I'll try, dear boy; anything for you. Just give me a little time.'

Faraday walked home feeling flat and listless, convinced that what he needed was a vacation. Oh, yes, the Mont Blanc Tunnel fire that Ralph had mentioned—he had successfully forgotten that one. With so many victims reduced to mere bone and ash, that disaster had become a convenient graveyard for people from neighbouring countries who chose to drop off the map at that time. But who had started the rumour that Johnston was one of those who had gone missing, and what was its purpose? For as he was soon to learn, there had been no truth in it.

FIVE

Business class was full on the flight from Bangkok to Ho Chi Minh City, and Faraday found himself sitting across the aisle from an Indian man who seemed oblivious to the in-flight rules forbidding the use of cell phones. First class, on the other hand, had been only sparsely populated as he walked through: two Thai businessmen in dark blue suits, and a middle-aged European whose thinning sandy hair was all that was visible of him as he lay back under a blanket, already fully reclined without bothering to wait for take-off. It was clear the man didn't plan to stir for the entire flight, and as Faraday passed on through to find his own seat, he thought that was not such a bad idea.

When they landed an hour and a half later, he had just reached the point where several unsuccessful attempts to nod off had left him feeling heavy and more tired than when he started. He was in no hurry to get to his feet as the stewardess pulled back the curtain separating first class from business, leaving the aisle space and the overhead compartments to the chatterbox Indian man and his cell phone. Only when economy class passengers started pushing through from the rear did he reluctantly rise and file after the man, who was held up by a stewardess trying to retrieve a bag from one of the first class overhead compartments. Smiling an apology, she then turned and ran for the exit door, calling out a passenger's name.

By the time Faraday had negotiated the stairs down onto the tarmac, the first class passengers were already entering the terminal, walking fast. Clearly they knew something he didn't, so he elected to hurry, too. The terminal was vast but empty, coming as a shock after the chaos of Bangkok and London. Only one immigration booth was even manned, and it was showing every sign of quickly becoming a choking point. Vietnam was a communist country; officialdom ruled. The two Thai businessmen from first class were being interrogated like spies—but in the distance, already through immigration and walking briskly, briefcase in hand, was a sandy-haired but slightly balding figure in a rumpled, light tan tropical suit who must have been the sleeping man from when he boarded the plane, and who now, at a distance, looked vaguely familiar. Whoever he was, he must have travelled this way before, as he clearly knew the system. Faraday watched in envy as the man was waved through customs and out the door before the Thai businessmen had even gotten their passports stamped.

Behind him, the queue began to stretch across the terminal floor and out the door, and by the time he reached the cavernous new baggage hall, his suitcase had been around the carousel enough times to become giddy, and the man with the briefcase had long since scuttled off into the dark night—unaware, as was Faraday at that moment, of their relationship to each other. It was only when he was finally in a cab, directing the driver to the Rex Hotel, that he recalled the name the stewardess had called out as she retrieved the bag from the overhead compartment: 'Mr Johnston,' a short, sandy-haired, slightly balding man who had looked vaguely familiar at a distance, but whom he had no reason to believe might be known to him at the time.

* * * *

Conquering the city that is home to your arch-enemies, then immediately naming it after yourself is a great way of rubbing people's noses in it. For Ho Chi Minh and his comrades, Saigon had been not just the home of

America's lackeys, but a cesspit of shame and dishonour, a slime bath in which the nation's traitors swam. And for all the ruthless cleansing undertaken by the victorious North Vietnamese Army, a very faint stench remained.

The Rex Hotel, which Faraday had booked while still in London, had been built by an acolyte of the royal family in the days when the French governed while the locals served, and the fledgling bird of nationalism, in the form of the Revolutionary Youth League, was still growing its feathers. The governing presumption among many at the time was that all things French were inherently superior, and the Rex had the look of a building striving to foot it with the grandeur and elegance of Paris, but falling just short. To Faraday's eye, the grandeur was heavy-handed and ill-informed, though its shortcomings were likely overlooked in the days when the ballroom was overflowing with Catherine Deneuve lookalikes and their arrogant colonial husbands in blue-and-gold-braided uniforms.

Faraday paid the cabbie, acknowledging his advice that he'd probably chosen the wrong hotel and would have been better off in a cheaper part of town, then climbed the steps in search of a welcoming bed. The cavernous foyer and ballroom were both empty, and the announcement of his name at the front desk was met with a smile of embarrassment before being passed along the line of idle staff for someone else to deal with, until finally, on the fourth try, he was admitted and given a key so he could find his own room. The languorous inactivity within the hotel suggested that communist Vietnam was still learning commerce from a ministry handbook, yet there was a strong whiff of self-doubt among the staff, as if the colonial power had only just left without explaining to anybody how to run things. If the new power was communism, it was strangely self-effacing.

The following morning, his request at the front desk for guidance in locating art galleries garnered only two recommendation: the Fine Art Museum and the Ben Thanh Market. Eager to get started—and feeling strangely excited by the prospect of confronting a counterfeiter—Faraday set out with energy and focus that he felt had been missing from his life in recent times. He was traveling with purpose now, curious yet apprehensive. What if he were to discover there was no skill required in flawlessly imitating his work? What if the copyist had no regard for his art at all? More than just a forensic investigation, this was potentially his own unmasking that he was engaged in. Perhaps it was that very prospect that energized him: the opportunity to learn the truth about himself.

The pavement at the hotel entrance was wide and empty, the manicured gardens opposite were clipped and tidy, and across the square, the grand facade of the freshly painted Hotel de Ville shimmered in the morning sunlight, just as it would have in provincial France. A neat little row of bright red taxis was lined up like Tonka toys, and the smiles of the uniformed bell boys as they opened the doors for him were wide and friendly as he stepped outside.

According to the street map, the Ben Thanh Market was only a few hundred metres away, so he walked to the corner and stopped to get his bearings. God, it was hot... And there was a noise like swarming locusts, for the road was filled with a thousand motorbikes, none of them with mufflers or any appreciable sense of left and right. Crossing to the other side was unthinkable, so Faraday turned right, clinging to the relative safety of the sidewalk.

Throughout Asia, the allure of the indoor market was the insight it provided into the agglomeration of crap that now littered the world: knock-off Louis Vuitton satchels that wouldn't withstand a week of travel, peaked caps embroidered with the logos of New York universities, and fake Nike trainers that cut the foot off at the ankle within ten minutes of putting them on. And of course, there was food: whole meals for the price of a sachet of ketchup in the real world, cooked in aluminium pots that stood on braziers in the narrow, crowded aisles that swam with garbage and humanity, served in dishes washed in buckets of cold water drawn from the nearest river—water that would serve as the base for tomorrow's noodle soup.

The Ben Thanh Market was no different. The soup was called *pho*, and it was so cheap that in England or the United States, there was no longer coinage small enough to pay for it. What made it so palatable were the many days devoted to boiling the chicken bones and meat scraps, and the subtle hit provided by the last-minute addition of fresh chili, lemongrass, and fish sauce. While slurping *pho*, squeezed into a space half his size and perched on a stool just large enough for one buttock, Faraday managed to regain a modicum of courage to face the mayhem of the streets again, and then— upon being shooed along to make room for more customers—he fought his way through the labyrinth of aisles in search of one of the back entrances.

Like Les Halles, on which the area was modelled, the streets surrounding the market were filled with retail shops and restaurants. It didn't take him long to locate the art gallery mentioned by the hotel staff, though it turned out to be less of a gallery and more of an arcade, a long, high passageway linking two streets. The walls were lined with row upon row of large, brightly coloured canvasses, some already mounted on stretchers, others pegged to wires and hanging loose.

Seated on white plastic chairs before rickety wooden easels were four young men, busily working up copies of Henri de Toulouse-Lautrec, Franz Marc, Edgar Degas, and Piet Mondrian. With paintbrushes in one hand and photo clipboards in the other, they wore the dull, expressionless faces of factory workers. The copies they were making were not exact, but good enough to be recognizable. Freed from the need to be original and allowing themselves some latitude with colour, they worked confidently and at great speed, dutifully ignoring all passers-by, including Faraday. Clearly, they were pieceworkers, and this was a sweatshop.

The manager of the shop was a young woman wearing a white blouse and a bright white smile. 'You like art?' she asked.

'I do. Do you have any paintings of animals?'

'Animals? Wait, please.'

She ran over to a table and returned with a large, well-worn copy of *The Great Art Galleries of the World*. 'You find for me?' She smiled.

Faraday made a pretence of looking, but all he could find was Franz Marc's *The Large Blue Horses*.

'How about wildlife?' he suggested. 'Lions, tigers, panda bears…?'

'You have picture?' she suggested brightly. 'We copy for you.'

'Thank you,' he said stupidly.

They smiled at each other, nodded, bowed, looked at the paintings on the wall, smiled some more, bowed again, and then, realizing they had nothing more to say, Faraday left. Well, he thought, trying to be philosophical about it, that experience had certainly put any pretensions about the importance of art firmly in their place.

Three doors down was a shop selling counterfeit CDs and DVDs. Just like the art gallery, they only bothered to copy what was popular: iconic music and movies, focusing on those that were instantly recognizable. Figuring that he needed a quick fix on the history of Vietnam, he splashed out three dollars and bought copies of the movies *Indochine, The Quiet American,* and *Apocalypse Now*—the French and British perspectives, followed by the American.

Waiting for him on the street as he emerged was a one-armed cyclo driver who was determined to claim him as his personal property. 'I take you to museum now?' he asked cheerfully.

For a moment, he considered diving back into the market again to escape this unwanted attention. But something told him that would just start a battle of wills that he was bound to lose. Going with the flow might be a less stressful approach to the challenges that Vietnam seemed to offer.

'Alright!' he agreed. 'One US dollar per hour, and you take me first to the Fine Art Museum and wait.' The Lonely Planet guide had prepared him well, and his trousers pocket was filled with a handy stash of one-dollar notes, one of which he held up for the driver to see.

'Then I take you to Pham Ngu Lao for shopping. I know very good shops. You like massage?'

The Fine Arts Museum proved to be a temple of art nouveau décor housing an eclectic collection of paintings that ranged from heroic realism and aggressive abstraction to European kitsch and sacred Cham. It seemed that the pillage and rape of their country by successive waves of invaders had not dulled the Vietnamese will to paint at any time in the previous century. Exploding bombs and tortured prisoners were rendered with the same vigour and intensity as purple irises, and the contemporary art on sale to the public demonstrated a common ability on the part of the artists to capture the essence of any style with great proficiency. It was clear that the Vietnamese had an unusual talent for painting. But neither here nor at the Vinh Loi Gallery, which was his next stop, or at the upmarket lobby shops of the five-star hotels near the river was there any evidence of artistic interest in wildlife, or a willingness to suggest an artist who might accept a commission to copy a work that was not in the public domain.

After four hours, he returned to the hotel, desperate for air conditioning, and asked for a DVD player to be sent up to his room so he could watch *The Quiet American* while his body temperature recovered from the boiling point. After the movie ended, he fell asleep briefly, wondering what it was that prevented the Vietnamese from wanting to kill all Westerners on sight.

The American War had been over for more than forty years, but Saigon was one of those places, like Berlin, that seemed made for war. There was war of a kind on the streets twenty-four hours a day, and some spots in town gave the impression that they wouldn't come alive again until there was another one. Their history hung about them like a shadow of shame. The Rooftop Bar at the Rex Hotel was such a place. Though Michael Caine had stayed at the Continental while filming *The Quiet American*, by all accounts, it was the Rex where the real-life Colonel Lansdale and his fellow CIA conspirators drank while dreaming up their wild games of intrigue and betrayal. They had no business even being in the country, of course, and ultimately they achieved nothing but pain and devastation, but that hadn't stopped them from acting with total self-righteous conviction. They plotted the destruction of people with the same detachment as they plotted the destruction of the jungle, over ice-cold Budweisers and bourbon and Cokes.

Faraday headed for the bar immediately upon awakening, desperate to replace the fluids that anxiety and humidity had drained out of him during the day. With the movie still on his mind, that shadow of shame seemed to blanket the room. Perhaps the rattan furniture was newer than he would have expected, and the potted plants were a little stiff and ugly, rather than the seductively exotic tropical ones he'd imagined. The band was playing 'Volare' which predated the French War—let alone the American one— and in keeping with all government tourist hotels, there was a make-work scheme in place that required no less than three people to eventually bring him his beer—not the Budweiser that Colonel Lansdale would have been drinking, but Tiger, the local brew. The beer was cold enough to freeze his third eye, and there were searchlights playing in the night sky, as if no one had heard that the air raids had stopped forty years ago.

After his failed endeavours on the street that day, he was feeling a bit chastened. The skill of the copyists had shaken him. They were remarkably young, and they worked very quickly, capturing the essence of the works they were copying without difficulty. Yet he'd been taught that the ability to sit and observe, finding in the surface of things a composition and structure not readily apparent to a non-painter's eye, was a quality that came only with time and practice. It was a lot easier to observe objects and landscapes than it was to observe people, yet the copyists had no difficulty with any of it. And the ease with which they switched styles made a mockery of intellectual interpretations of the artistic process. The Vietnamese copyists knew all the tricks, and it was obvious that a facility with technique could seduce most people into believing in the quality of the artist. Why not, then, just be a copyist?

By his third drink, the righteous indignation that had spurred him to come to Vietnam had already abated, leaving him teetering in that narrow space between self-pity and self-disgust. Holding onto artistic pretensions seemed so trivial in a country that had suffered so much trauma. Were not painters merely Neros fiddling amidst the flames, musicians playing outside the oven doors of death camps, making a pretence of civilization?

Who gave a damn, anyway? They were only bloody pictures. *Go ahead and copy them*, he thought. It wouldn't harm the world in the slightest way.

SIX

He woke with a thick head. Where was he? Oh, yes: returned from a futile and depressing tour of the galleries of Saigon. Back in his room at the Rex Hotel, having tipped the bar staff with a restraint that he hoped proved his relative sobriety, he'd approached the rest of the evening with the passivity of a man resigned to his own weaknesses. He'd watched another movie, fallen asleep, and hoped to be revisited with a sense of purpose upon awakening in the morning. It was a mood that perfectly matched that of the principal protagonist in *Apocalypse Now*, a mood in which the struggle to control life by understanding it slipped away silently, like a corpse into water. Sleep became that water.

When he woke with a start, heart pounding, he believed at first that it was a jungle ambush in which he, along with Martin Sheen, was being attacked. In fact, it was only his cell phone ringing; the movie had finished.

'Anton, dear boy! What time is it: early or late?'

Ralph Lutyen: moist of lip, mellifluous of tone, his voice always carrying the undertone of an unasked question in addition to the one being asked.

'Late.'

'I thought so; you never answer your phone during the day. Have you caught any geese yet…?'

'Geese…?'

'… on your wild goose chase.'

'Ah. Very good, Ralph, very good. No, no geese, and no pandas either. What about you?'

'Well, dear boy, I did as you asked and spoke to the good people at the Paladin Foundation in Geneva, and you'll be pleased to hear that your beloved Nu Nu is hanging on their boardroom wall and hasn't budged since he arrived there. I am assured of that absolutely.'

'It's a she. What about reproductions?'

'Anton, please! What about "Congratulations, Ralph"? I went to great trouble tracking down this information for you. Besides, you're forgetting the reason why they bought this painting in the first place. Don't you remember the conversation?'

'Remind me.'

'It was two fingers up to the World Wildlife Fund. Mr Van Heeren made some very strong statements about it at the time, as I remember. Surely you haven't forgotten? Kenneth Johnston introduced you.'

'No, I haven't forgotten. Who did you speak to?'

'Van Heeren's secretary. The phone number for the Foundation is an 0800 charity number. They couldn't help me, so I phoned Anglo Swiss BioLab, Van Heeren's pharmaceutical company. Sure enough, she was able to give me the assurances you wanted. Quite the detective, don't you think? I'm not just a pretty face, you know.'

'Did you ask her about Kenneth Johnston?'

'Why on earth would I do that? He's long gone. I told you, he was rumoured to have died in the Mont Blanc Tunnel fire.'

'So you did.'

* * * *

'Let me introduce you to the artist, then. This is Anton Faraday, sir, and you have bought his painting of the panda—which, for the sake of good relations with our wildlife colleagues, has been removed before The Duke arrives. Mr Faraday, this is the chairman of the Paladin Foundation, Mr Van Heeren.'

Johnston clicked his heels on completion of this introduction, and Faraday wondered idly if he had a military background. Ralph rubbed his hands together and pursed his lips with pleasure.

Van Heeren, on the other hand, was about as animated as a rock. 'You have chosen to paint the panda as a prisoner behind bars,' he said, 'just as the World Wildlife Fund is a prisoner of outdated ideas.'

His voice had a familiar ring to it. German? No … South African. That was why it was familiar: it was the voice of Faraday's youth, as well as the voice of Rhodesia.

Van Heeren didn't offer his hand. 'The panda will not be saved by breeding in captivity,' he continued. 'It will only be safe when human beings are eliminated from its environment. Humanity, Mr Faraday, has become a plague in some respects. The human species has become so numerous that it threatens the very survival of the planet. I would never argue this point of view in public, of course, or let the World Wildlife Fund know that I think they have chosen the wrong animal as a symbol for their cause. Coincidentally, you have captured my point perfectly in your painting, whether consciously or unconsciously, and that is why I decided to buy it and keep it for our viewing only: as a reminder.'

No response was expected, which was fortunate, because none came to mind. Johnston and Ralph both smiled and nodded as if in the presence of a sage, while Faraday mumbled politely.

'How did you like my painting of the rhino?' he asked.

'I like the rhino even better than the panda,' Van Heeren replied. 'You are lucky that it did not kill you. That is the most dangerous animal in all of Africa. But I see you survived.'

The cue for light laughter was duly noted by all who were listening.

'But, Mr Faraday,' he said, his voice now deeper and accompanied by an admonitory finger, 'the survival of that rhino is less certain, I think.'

Now he did offer his hand in greeting, and in the same movement, swept Faraday to one side. 'Good, good, *ja...*' His head nodded rapidly. 'We will buy the rhino, too.'

He spun around to challenge all three of them, arms akimbo, fists on his hips. 'What do you have to say to that?'

In that instant, Faraday had been overwhelmed with guilt and couldn't think properly. It was the irrational thought that this powerful, all-knowing man was about to unmask him. It was what he had said about the survival of 'that rhino', as if he knew something that Anton had never dreamed anyone could possibly know. Guilt and the fear of being suddenly exposed caused him to panic. Put simply, in this moment of triumph, he was convinced he was about to be undone, his secret revealed.

'I'm sorry,' he blurted out, 'but the rhino is no longer for sale.'

Quite rightly, Ralph and his clients looked at him as if he had lost his mind.

'I forgot to tell Ralph that I wished to withdraw it,' he added lamely.

In truth, the story he'd told people about his experience of hunting the rhino with his camera in order to paint it wasn't the full story. In the full story, the rhino had been shot dead at his feet by poachers who hacked off its head for the prize of its horn—and who only refrained from killing him, too, because they had once worked on his father's farm, and they had led him to where the rhino was grazing. Why had they taken him there? Because he asked them to. Because he gave them money. Because all that mattered to him was his painting, and all that mattered to them was survival in a land that was being torched by the crazed inhumanity of Robert Mugabe.

'Don't be silly, Anton,' Ralph interrupted him impatiently. 'You know the rules; unless it has a red sticker on it at opening time, it is available for sale. If Mr Van Heeren wishes to purchase it, I will be delighted to sell it to him.'

So, the Paladin Foundation got its painting, Faraday got his fee, the farm workers got their illegal bounty—and the black rhino got shot.

There never was any likelihood that the story of the killing by the poachers would reach the outside world, of course—not unless Faraday was the one who told it. But guilt distorts one's reasoning, and he continued to be wary in Van Heeren's company as a photographer ushered them to stand alongside the painting, so that Lutyen's Gallery should receive maximum coverage in the art world's media pages.

* * * *

All of that had immediately sprung to mind when Ralph Lutyen called him in his room at the Rex Hotel and told him that he'd spoken to Van Heeren's personal secretary at Anglo Swiss BioLab, and she had assured him that the painting of the panda had never left the wall since the day it was purchased, and it most certainly would never, under any circumstances, have been allowed to be reproduced, for the same reason that it had been purchased in the first place.

'So, it seems your forgery remains a mystery,' Ralph concluded. 'With Kenneth Johnston out of the picture—if you'll excuse the pun—I'm afraid there is nothing more I can do to help.'

Which is where Faraday would have left it, too, if Ralph hadn't then added, half to himself, 'Of course, with young Kenneth, you really never knew...'

SEVEN

By his second day in Saigon, the streets no longer held any fears for him. He'd learned their rules and thus freed himself of guidebook hang-ups about how to strike a bargain and avoid getting conned. The touts were all still there, pulling at his elbow and jostling for attention as he emerged from the hotel, but now they quickly fell away, recognizing from the look in his eye that he would be more work than he was worth.

After his call from Ralph the night before, he'd finished watching *Apocalypse Now* in his room, sliding into its mesmerizing depiction of barbarism as if watching a psychedelic slide show on the necrosis of the soul. Anesthetized by the pitiless malignancy of war, the Americans seemed driven to commit more and more atrocities in order to keep themselves alive until, in the end, their brains were addled by evil.

Lying on a bed in a hotel in Vietnam was definitely the right place to watch that film, he thought, although from the vantage point of peace, it was impossible to fully understand war, and the best he could do was try and understand where the war had left the Vietnamese people. Compelled then by a sense of duty, he sought out the broken-toothed cyclo driver who'd been hounding him the previous day and told him to take him to the War Crimes Museum.

'Thirty thousand dong.' The driver grinned.

'No, I'll give you fifteen.'

'No, no, no-o-o … too little … too little!'

'Okay.' Faraday started to walk away.

'Alright, alright! Fifteen thousand.'

After just one day, Faraday already understood a few things about Vietnam.

The War Crimes Museum was a rather down-at-heel collection of concrete sheds surrounding a yard littered with scrap metal in the form of rusty old tanks, broken helicopters, and ancient field guns. It was clearly not a place they'd poured money into; perhaps that helped maintain the purity of its message. The weaponry looked like it had been welded together in someone's backyard, but inside the buildings, the reality emerged from a devastating collection of photographs with understated captions. Like a witness at a school massacre, Faraday wandered from room to room, numbed but entranced, knowing he would never comprehend the fear and frustration that had driven the Americans to lash out at everything that moved in this damned country, everything that refused to lie down and be beaten, every man, woman, and child whom they came to believe in the end had to be burned, bombed, tortured, and killed.

* * * *

These were the images that filled his mind as he peered through the boat's clear plastic awnings into the driving rain as they sped upriver from Cantho to Chau Doc, following his farewell with Caroline Brinkley days later. His eyes became Martin Sheen's eyes, every passing boat potentially filled with insurgents, every paddy field a hiding place for Viet Cong submerged just beneath the water, breathing through straws. All he could think was how scared those Yankee kids must have been.

The small provincial town of Chau Doc had two claims to fame. It was the last stop on the river before entering Cambodia, and it was the centre of an unusual and highly productive method of fish farming. Nevertheless, it was hard to see why the French owners of the Victoria Hotel chain had decided to build on the riverbank there, for the town was a decaying slum, and the decay was so corrosive that it had already invaded the unapt monolith they'd constructed, causing the grout lines of the swimming pool tiles to ooze a calcareous slime and the balconied facade to be streaked with tear stains of concrete cancer.

There was a push to promote the river as a high-speed highway to Phnom Penh, avoiding the tortuous roads. Maybe that's why they'd built a hotel there. But any investment in an area that had been washed for centuries with tidal waves of invasion and retreat remained an act of faith, and any population that included Khmers and Chams—two mortal enemies living in close proximity—only added to the mystery of mankind's continued survival.

Arriving wet and unimpressed, Faraday was relieved to find signs of other guests and a hand-addressed envelope of welcome awaiting his arrival. The heat was less oppressive here than in Saigon, but he was already beginning to flag as they escorted him to his room overlooking the river. Once alone, he unceremoniously spread himself out like a starfish on the crisp white bedcover beneath a gently revolving fan and fell gratefully into a deep, unaided sleep, only to be woken sometime later by the television turning on, presumably thanks to a time switch. The American president—or his body double—was making drowning noises about the Middle East on BBC World News, and behind him was a waxwork model of the grinning British prime minister, nodding like a toy dog with a spring-loaded neck.

The light was fading quickly outside, and he opened the balcony shutters to survey the river as the setting sun laid a pale carmine wash over the landscape, the water oozing like molten plastic on its slow journey towards the South China Sea. Beneath the balcony, two sampans had rafted up, tying their bows to the hotel railings, and their occupants were preparing to settle down for the night, dousing their charcoal cooking burners and spreading a frayed plastic sheet between the gunwales under which they planned to

65

sleep. The light waning suddenly at the end of the day played tricks on his eyes, but in the distance, he thought he could see a small corrugated iron city floating in the middle of the river, houses surrounded by water as if washed away by floods, their chimneys filling the pink and grey sky with clouds of white smoke. It was too late to set up his camera, so he closed the balcony doors and went back inside to kill the television just as the phone rang.

'You survived the journey, then?'

It took a moment for him to recognize her voice, though there was something instantly familiar about the tone, amused and mocking.

'Was there some doubt that I would?'

'I didn't want to tell you when you left, but people have been known to die of boredom on that trip.'

'Then they can't have seen *Apocalypse Now*. I had my heart in my mouth every time we passed another sampan.'

'That's the artist in you—too vivid of an imagination. Vietnam's the safest country in the world now. You should try New Jersey.'

'No, I shouldn't; life's short enough as it is. Are you ringing to say they made a mistake with my bill this morning?'

'I'm ringing to check whether Michel, the executive chef, has contacted you yet. I told him you were coming, and that you might be interested in a cooking course, knowing how you like food and all. He said he'd look after you.'

'How very nice! There's a letter here which I haven't opened. Let me look…'

Sure enough, the hand-addressed envelope he'd picked up at reception contained an invitation to make himself known to Michel Lahoud at dinner that night.

' "My good friend Caroline tell me you are interesting in the cuisine Vietnamese",' he read, mimicking an accent. ' "I will be happy to show." It's signed, "Michel". What's this "good friend" stuff?'

'He's a kind of boyfriend … once.'

'A French "kind of boyfriend" who cooks…'

'You'll like him. I told him to look after you.'

'That's very nice of you. How do I pay you back?'

'Phone me when you get to Hanoi. I'm going up there at the end of the week, wearing my NGO hat, to check out the poultry farm. You've got my mobile number. Maybe we can have a meal together. I could help you track down that painting you're after. Hanoi's the place if you're looking for galleries.'

'I'm starting to get the feeling that I'm on a wild goose chase there. As far as everyone is concerned, the original has never been shown or reprinted, so it's a mystery. Still, I'm here now, and I'm certainly going to keep looking. A meal together in Hanoi sounds like a great idea. I'll call you when I arrive.'

After she hung up, he poured himself a drink from the mini bar and headed for the shower. He'd intended on turning in early and not bothering with dinner, but now for some reason, he was no longer tired. Yes, cooking was his thing, but he wondered how she'd picked up on that.

Michel was not difficult to find. He was in his mid-to-late thirties, with the Foreign Legion haircut that suits premature balding, a nick out of his left ear, and a fingernail missing from one hand. A packet of cigarettes bulged in his breast pocket beneath his chef's jacket, and he fingered it while he spoke, as if trying to decide whether he should just undo the jacket buttons and give into his craving.

'You want to learn Vietnamese cooking?' he asked effusively, not bothering with an extended greeting. 'I tell you all you need to know. Come with me to the kitchen. We will have something special.'

He seemed delighted to have someone to entertain. Though English was his second language, he was clearly relishing the chance to use it.

'The secret is the *nuoc mam*, you know—the fish sauce. And cook very quick. No baking, only grill or fry. And *bouillant*, of course. This is the same for *Thailande* and *Cambodge*, I think. Very quick, very fresh, because there is no refrigeration and no oven. Chili, lemongrass, *des herbes*. Hot, sweet, sour, all mixed together. This is all you need to know. What you like for *diner*?'

He spoke rapidly, clanging empty pots together for emphasis and diving into his jacket pocket for the French cigarettes that were clamouring for his attention. The Vietnamese staff in the kitchen continued working quietly, paying no attention.

'I hadn't really thought...' Faraday contemplated the question. 'Chili crab with lemongrass?'

'I have a better idea. You like good food, I can see that.' He inhaled deeply. 'I have something special. We'll have a little feast, okay? Lobster! You will be my guest, and we'll pretend we are in France. Fresh lobster *au beurre blanc*. Tomorrow you can eat all the Vietnamese you want.'

Faraday accepted the invitation with enthusiasm and sat on a stainless-steel bench while Michel went to work. Their talk was small and light at first: the hotel, the weather, the non-existence of roads, and the ridiculously low prices. There were no other customers in the dining room, and the kitchen staff went outside, apparently to smoke as well. Accustomed to European prices, Faraday hated to think how much it had cost to put fresh lobster in the hotel fridge, but it was not an issue that appeared to bother Michel. Everything was cheap here, he said, and for him, everything was free. He worked quickly, treating the preparation of food as a form of martial arts that required an economy of movement with a hint of low-level violence. Judging by his rather damaged appearance, Faraday got the feeling that he wouldn't be averse to displaying those same qualities in a dark alley.

Between them, however, there lay an unanswered question that needed to be gotten out of the way.

'How long have you known Caroline?' Faraday asked eventually.

'Not long. I meet her in Cantho at the hotel. She tell me about her brother. She tell you, too?'

'She told me that's what brought her here, to Vietnam.'

'Listen…' Taking a bottle of Chablis from the fridge, Michel poured them both a glass. '… this thing with her brother. He is not really her brother. He is Vietnamese; she is American. A cat is not a dog, and a dog is not a cat. Do you understand what I mean? Women want all the world to be 'appy and everyone to be nice. Then, they think, there will be no more problems. Ha!' He snorted derisively. 'People blame France and the Americans for killing Vietnamese. What happens to reality? The French and the Americans tried to stop the Vietnamese from killing each other. That was their mistake. The North wants to kill the South. The Khmers want to kill the Chams. Everyone has tried to kill the Montagnards at some time or other. You will see. The problem now is the boat people, like Caroline's brother.'

'How so?'

'They are fucked in the head. How do you say…? What they want is revenge. I tell this to Caroline. Because they escape to the West, they think they are more brave and more smart. For them, the people who stay behind are to blame for everything. They are inferior. Yes, this is true; this is how they think. They think the people who stay are lazy and corrupt because they are communists, or they are lazy and cowards because they allowed themselves to be humiliated and punished in re-education camps. So they deserve nothing. They are traitors. They have destroyed the country. This is how the boat people think.'

'Is this how Caroline's brother thinks?'

He shrugged. 'Of course.'

'And what do the locals think of the boat people?'

'They think the same: they think they are lazy and corrupt and cowards, too. It is nature.'

'It seems that she had a row with her brother, and there was an argument with an uncle. So, what would the brother make of this NGO she's working for that's helping his uncle's friend get started with a poultry farm?'

'Boat people don't believe in charity. Charity is for the weak.'

'And you told this to Caroline?'

'Of course.'

He grinned and sat back expansively on the stainless-steel bench, the wine cradled in his hand. 'Tell me,' Michel said, changing the subject, 'what better can a man have than fresh lobster and lemon butter, with a glass of Chablis and a friend to share it with? Is this not good? Now, what is the best meal you have ever had? And let me guess: it was in France.'

The best, or the most memorable? Yes, it had probably been in France— just across the border from Geneva, in fact. But why had that meal instantly sprung to mind?

'It began with the specialty of the house,' Faraday recalled, trying to remember the exact time and place, 'which was larks' tongue pâté, reflecting the name of the restaurant, which I believe was the *Alouette*.' For some reason, the detail was imprinted in his memory with such clarity that it was almost like a video recording. Had he recounted this story before…? 'The pâté was served in a bird-sized oval dish, and the lid was made from an embalmed lark, complete with feathers. That took a bit of getting used to, but the pâté had a smooth, rich consistency, enhanced with goose liver and truffles, wrapped in bacon, and sealed with aspic. Set in the aspic was a mosaic of larks' tongues. From memory, I think there were thirty of them.'

'*Magnifique!* I envy you. And the wine?'

'Le Montrachet.'

'*D'accord!* And after the pâté…?'

'We went for the quail. Madame recommended it—and to accompany the quail, a bottle of Chateauneuf-du-Pape, which managed to disappear without our noticing.'

As he explained all this, Michel took another Chablis from the fridge.

'That wine was replaced in time with a Romanée-Conti,' Faraday continued. 'Hardly a backward step, I thought, though I have to admit to feeling a little shell-shocked by the cost of it all.'

'Clearly you were with *gourmands*. That is the most essential ingredient for a great meal.'

'No, I wouldn't describe them as that, not really.'

'And the quail? How is it?'

'I couldn't work out how the hell they'd managed to make such a little bird so plump and moist. And the golden colour—what the hell was that?'

'Meadow saffron.'

'Right! Well, my mind wanders after the quail. I remember it was served with a *compote des cerises* and a basket of fine potato ribbons, deep fried and woven into the shape of a nest. An appropriate resting place for a dead quail, I suppose.'

'Anton,' Michel exclaimed, raising his glass, 'you are a man of my own heart! We like the same food, and we like the same women. Let us drink to French cuisine, and to Caroline.'

'To Caroline…?'

'She must have known we have the same taste in food as we have in women, no?'

The Gallic wink that accompanied this question suggested that Michel had established with unabashed clarity just what sort of boyfriend he presumed Faraday was, and feeling certain that he had found a soulmate who would be willing to kick on and drink the night away, he suggested summoning two Vietnamese girls from the staff quarters to join them. This assumption about his relationship with Caroline, however, combined with his own recall of the events surrounding that meal in the restaurant outside Geneva, killed any enthusiasm Faraday may have held for partying on in the kitchen. After they'd finished eating, he decided to pack it in, making an excuse about the need to rise early.

A recurrent anger that he believed he'd successfully buried over the intervening years since that night proved to be still lurking just beneath the surface of his emotions, and telling the story about that dinner had brought it suddenly back to life. He resented Michel for his crudity, and he resented Caroline for her poor taste, but most of all, he resented his own inability to let go of his anger at what was past.

EIGHT

The proper place to start, he realized later that night, was in Geneva, not London or Vietnam. He'd chosen to push Geneva as far back into the underground cave of his subconscious as it would go, bricking it up against chance discovery and planting an impenetrable thicket of thorns in front of its entrance to mask its whereabouts. Geneva was so long ago and ill-remembered, he liked to pretend that it was possible to forget what had happened there. But his recall of the meal at the *Alouette* restaurant, as he'd told it to Michel, proved that he hadn't forgotten at all; he had merely shifted his point of view so that he was looking at the details of the events that didn't matter, rather than those that did.

Following Van Heeren's purchase of the panda and the black rhino, Kenneth Johnston had conceived the idea of commissioning twelve paintings of animals that were threatened with extinction. The black rhino would be one of them. The panda was disqualified by virtue of its association with the World Wildlife Fund. The concept had involved many phone calls from Johnston, and long hours of negotiation by Ralph on Faraday's behalf. With his career as a bankable artist very much at the unattested stage, Faraday had neither the ability nor the confidence to conceive of the prices that Ralph, as his agent, was willing to demand, so he stayed out of it as long as possible. But once the bones of the deal had been solidified, it came time to put the flesh on it.

'We're calling it the Harbinger Collection,' Johnston told him over the phone, 'because the extinction of these animals would be the harbinger of doom for all wildlife. I want you to bring your partner, if you have one, and come to Geneva at the end of the month so we can have a little ceremony, and then I want to talk to you about some ideas I have for a special print run. Can we set a date now and stick to it? I have important people I need to take into account.'

Though he wasn't completely comfortable with the idea of committing the next two years to a single project, the money Ralph had negotiated for him was more than he would have anticipated from ten years' work under normal circumstances, so it was inevitable that he would agree. A deadline was set to fly to Geneva as arranged at the end of June, accompanied by his then girlfriend, Helene, as they planned to go on down to Amalfi for the summer.

Of all the thorns he had planted in the impenetrable thicket masking the entrance to his subconscious, Helene was still the sharpest, no matter how heavy the gloves he wore. If he could have removed her from his memory of those events, he might have been more comfortable, and certainly more objective, in recalling them. Yet it was precisely Helene's presence that should have been the clearest clue as to the nature of Kenneth Johnston. If Helene hadn't been there—if they had broken up before he went to Geneva, rather than after—would he have formed a clearer picture of the man with whom he was dealing?

But something had happened during his conversation with Michel that had pried open that entrance to his subconscious he had been so carefully guarding.

As Johnston had explained it over the phone, the ecological challenges facing the world were unlikely to be solved by children shaking collection buckets in shopping malls on Saturday mornings. Global problems would only be resolved by those who effectively controlled the globe: the financiers and industrialists who were the principal initiators and beneficiaries of globalization. The Paladin Foundation for the Environment had been founded by twelve such individuals (with its name taken from the twelve heroic knights of the court of Charlemagne, no less), each of whom had nominated ten other Names who, by dint of money or political influence, could support the Foundation's aims.

'As networks go, Anton, this is the ultimate. Forget Harvard and Yale, Skull and Bones, Scroll and Key, and Wolf's Head; they're just varsity frats. But don't ask me to name Names, because that would be more than my life is worth. These are people who can quietly pick up the phone and make things happen. They have the power and the influence, and the reason this works is because it is totally private. All you see is the name on the letterhead.'

Therefore, it was no surprise, after Johnston picked them up from their hotel to take them to his headquarters, to find they were located on the top floor of the International Bank for Global Settlements, a discreet elevator ride up from the bank lobby, conducted by a uniformed lift attendant who delivered them into a marble and cherrywood world of panelled hallways and closed office doors. A receptionist ushered them into a meeting room and offered them coffee, but the available magazines and newspapers spoke to a world interested in money rather than animals, and there was no signage.

Johnston disappeared for ten minutes, returning with an air of jaunty satisfaction to whisper in Faraday's ear that Charles would be with them in a minute—a message that was accompanied by a conspiratorial tapping of the nose and a wink to Helene, but whose meaning was lost on Faraday. They then followed him down the corridor to another panelled room, this one large enough to house an enormous round table inlaid with a stylized brass representation of the world. Leather chairs ringed the table, and the walls were bare except for just one painting: Faraday's black rhino.

'Soon there will be twelve paintings on the wall,' Johnston announced, 'one for each Paladin. The one drawback to my plan is that it may take too long for Anton to complete them. But the wait will be worth it,' he added, squeezing Helene's arm reassuringly.

There was just a hint of criticism in his voice, letting Faraday know that he'd be most unhappy if they were to be kept waiting unreasonably.

At that moment, Faraday was ashamed to admit to himself that he felt remarkably smug. The room was windowless, the walls divided into twelve equal timber-veneer panels framed with decorative mouldings, just waiting, according to Johnston, for his paintings. It was as if the surroundings, so redolent of wealth and security, would subtly shift the status of the animals from endangered to protected. In this perfectly square room with this perfectly round table with its inlaid image of a world that seemed so perfectly designed, God's creatures would be safe—and he, Anthony John Faraday, would have helped to make them so.

Ostensibly, the purpose of their visit was to sign the contract 'as a matter of record' and agree on the list of endangered animals to be painted. With a view to personalizing the occasion for publicity purposes, a photographer was already at work with a lighting assistant, setting up for a shot to be taken in front of the black rhino. Johnston and Helene retired to the leather chairs circling the round table while Faraday stalked the room in nervous excitement.

Just as the photographer finished trialling his camera exposures, the door was thrown open, and Charlemagne himself entered.

'Charles! Mr Van Heeren!' Johnston exclaimed, leaping to his feet.

Van Heeren's presence immediately filled the room.

'Mr Faraday, you have agreed to do our paintings, I hear.'

Faraday sensed as soon as Van Heeren entered the room that this man was every bit as dangerous as any animal he would ever face. But he chose to ignore it; that was the effect that people in power had on others. Besides, Faraday had already been corrupted by the money on offer. The empty panels around that table of influence were his alone to fill, and his commitment to filling them would allow many doubts and compromises to slip by before he would willingly surrender that right.

'This concept,' Van Heeren said, 'it is clever, *ja?* The artist creates his painting of the living animal, but no one can recreate the living animal once it is extinct. So, how will we feel if the day comes when we have only the memory, dried oil on stretched canvas, the images as meaningless to us then as images of the brontosaurus are to us now? Will we be content?'

He paused. 'I think not,' he whispered.

Oh, he was good, finger tapping out each syllable like a musical counterpoint on the side of his chin as his voice rose and fell sonorously.

'You see, we are sharing a dream. It is the same dream God had. Some say we have no right to aspire to God's dreams; they should be beyond us. I say that it is our duty to aspire to them. If we are unable to conserve and protect the habitat in which we live, then we have no right to be masters of it. The earth is our home, and we share it with the animals. They are our living barometer. If we let them perish, then we, too, are at risk.

'Your paintings will stand as a reminder that each of us is committed to our role. As yet, we cannot create life, other than our own, but the first step in the mastery of our planet is preventing the destruction of life. Wildlife and habitat are in our hands, and it is humanity that threatens their survival.'

Viewed years later, the photograph taken of the artist and the chairman of the Foundation standing before the portrait of the charging black rhino didn't quite capture the expression Faraday had tried to convey at the time. Neither concerned Greenie nor talented artist, he looked instead like a very young man somewhat out of his depth.

That evening, Johnston invited Faraday and Helene to dinner.

'We'll drive out to Saint-Julien, just across the border. There's a great little restaurant there called the *Alouette*—that's "lark" to you. Two Michelin stars, and they take Amex. I've booked a table for eight thirty.'

'Are you sure?'

'What do you mean, 'am I sure'? You have to go all the way to Lyon to find another two-star Michelin! This place has got eight crossed corkscrews and the *Palme d'Or d'Escoffier*; of course I'm sure! Besides, we need to discuss some copyright issues. I want to persuade you to let us print reproductions, and you know what they say: the way to a man's heart is through his stomach.'

Ralph had already prepped Faraday on the subject of reproductions, so he was ready for the conversation, though it took a while coming, as the food commanded centre stage.

Recalling the details of that dinner later in his bed at the hotel in Chau Doc made him realize how many clues he had missed along the way. Across the Swiss border lay the headquarters of two of the major world organizations devoted to saving wildlife. Across the table sat one of their senior executives … and they began by eating larks' tongues. At the time, he thought it was very funny. There was no moral; there was nothing to understand.

Now he wondered whether he hadn't been deliberately avoiding the clues. After all, wasn't life easier when one chose not to examine things too closely?

As the bottle of Romanée-Conti arrived, Johnston had explained his proposal.

'It may surprise you to know, Helene, that Anton is not the only artist at this table. I, too, am an artist; mine is the art of raising money.'

'Very good,' Helene replied approvingly. She liked him. Apparently, she could see exactly what he was.

'You see, people are happy to part with money, provided there is some pleasure in it, some reward or recognition. The anonymous donor who gives secretly, never allowing his name to be revealed, is, in my experience, only giving out of guilt, or under duress. It contradicts human nature. No one hesitates to drop a coin into the box each year for the War Widows Fund, never asking what happens to the money, or whether there are even any war widows still living. Why? Because they get to wear a red poppy for everyone to see. They are thanked; their generosity is recognized. Whether it's one pound or twenty thousand pounds, the principle remains the same. For the twelve Paladins of our Foundation, the twelve paintings they will see at our headquarters will be the red poppies that commemorate their generosity and give them a warm glow of self-satisfaction each time they gather round the table to discuss the salvation of the world. Do you understand where I'm coming from, Helene?'

'*Oui*, I do.'

'And when you have an organization that relies on the anonymity of its benefactors in order to be effective, the symbolic equivalent of the red poppy becomes extremely important. But having met the needs of the twelve Paladins, I now face another challenge: how to acknowledge the hundred and twenty influential Names who are the secret foot soldiers of the Paladin Foundation?'

He paused dramatically, looking first at Helene and then at Faraday, before draining his glass, not expecting an answer. 'So, this is my proposition…'

The proposal was quite simple. The eleven new paintings they were going to acquire, along with the black rhino, would be reproduced in a limited edition of lithographs, beautifully packaged in bound folio sets, signed by the artist, and personally inscribed with the signature and crest of Charles Van Heeren, chairman of the International Bank for Global Settlements and president of Anglo Swiss BioLab, one of Europe's richest men.

'For the one hundred and twenty Names, this will represent a gift of inestimable value, tastefully recognizing the financial contribution they are being asked to make to the Foundation. For Anton, need I say, this will be an enormous coup. Just imagine having your work occupying pride of place on the coffee tables of the world's richest and most powerful men and women, your photograph and biography there for all to see. It has to be the ultimate accolade. But for this to happen, we have to overcome one little obstacle.'

'You don't own the copyright,' Faraday stated flatly.

The Johnston smile could easily be taken for a grimace, were it not for the sharp bark of amusement that accompanied it, which seemed open to many interpretations.

'Which is what we are here to discuss,' he replied amiably, reaching across and patting Helene on the hand, as if the two of them were somehow in this thing together. 'But I'm sure you knew that.'

The confident and predatory way in which Johnston spoke in front of Helene should have warned Faraday that he was in the company of a man who would take liberties, he realized now. His social ease and glib fluency suggested he'd never found others taking offence to be an obstacle to his own smooth progress, but at the time, Faraday had found this amusing— attractive, even. After all, these qualities had allowed for the gestation of an idea that would fuel Faraday's success as an artist to a level beyond his wildest dreams. Why on earth would he have questioned them?

Then Ralph, thinking out loud, had muttered over the phone from London, 'Of course, with young Kenneth, you never really knew...'

So now, he'd be damned if he could sleep for thinking about it.

NINE

Unable to sleep, Faraday lay on the bed and immersed himself in *The Phnom Penh Gazette* that he'd picked up from the reception desk at the Grande Rivière Hotel in Cantho. Nearly four decades had passed since the Khmer Rouge had marched their fellow citizens out of Phnom Penh into the fields and killed them—killing so many that no one could count them, cutting them down like sugar cane, obediently hacking them to death until their arms ached. Almost forty years, yet the unreality of it all continued to infect Cambodian life, and *The Phnom Penh Gazette* was riddled with it.

The front page featured a photo of Khieu Samphan, Pol Pot's faithful lieutenant and head of state, alongside the main story that "Khmer Rouge guilt not clear". Was he being tried at last, Faraday wondered? No; they were quoting a letter he'd written some years prior, complaining about a mildly critical review they'd published of the book he'd written justifying his role in the slaughter of three million people. There was no chance, however, of his being tried for the atrocities he'd committed, because the United Nations, at the insistence of the United States, would only be willing to prosecute a case for genocide, not for crimes against humanity. *The crime of genocide is narrowly defined, and specific intent to destroy a group is the most difficult to prove, particularly without a confession,* the Gazette reported. Apparently, it wasn't clear that the Khmer Rouge intended on killing *all* Cambodians, though they might have been planning to kill *all* Buddhist monks.

This didn't do anything for Faraday's mood. Sighing, he turned the page... NGOs, it seemed, had been trying unsuccessfully to get the United Nations to act since the early 1980s. And right alongside that story was another:

Convoy to save children:

A convoy of buses will leave Phnom Penh today to begin The Salvation Convoy, a weeklong journey through Cambodia to raise awareness of and gather information about child exploitation. Nearly a hundred participants from more than thirty NGOs will visit the provinces to raise awareness with officials, local project workers, and children, according to organizers from the NGO coalition COSECAM.

Now, as he turned the pages further, NGOs started to leap out of the text at him like his own initials. Acronyms lined up by the score to promote their just causes: anti-paedophilia, anti-human-trafficking, human rights, AIDS awareness, workers' rights, women's rights, water purity, and wildlife conservation. The place was overrun with them, arguing their cases on the basis of increasingly apocalyptic statistics, competing with each other—if he could read between the lines—for the highest moral ground. There were so many of them that the English language *Phnom Penh Gazette* read like their in-house journal. This was a totally new phenomenon for Faraday; he doubted that anyone he knew would have been aware of it either. What degree of naivety or arrogance motivated these people, he wondered, and why were they so prevalent in Southeast Asia?

Throwing the paper away, he turned to the mini bar instead. One cognac and a Drambuie later, and he was finally asleep.

That night, he dreamed he was under water, but for some reason, he was still able to breathe. Orange flames danced on the surface of the water, and a familiar face swam in and out of view, peering down at him and speaking slowly, ponderously, in a sad and wistful tone, strained and remote, as if at the end of a long, hollow pipe. What it had to say seemed to take all night, and Faraday tossed and turned trying to make sense of it.

'The genius,' the voice kept saying, 'the genius to do that ... and the will.'

It would be weeks later before he would remember where he'd heard those words before, and by then, the feeling of drowning would no longer be confined to his dreams.

At 5:00 a.m., he got up with the sun and went out onto the balcony. It was already hot, around thirty degrees, and the two families who had rafted up in their sampans beneath his window the night before had now finished breakfast and were packing up their charcoal burners and preparing to head out midstream to join the floating melee of boats assembling downriver for the morning market. The houses he'd seen in the distance in the fast-fading light of dusk were now clearly visible as floating corrugated iron sheds, like Midwestern hay barns swept together by the torrents of water flooding out of Cambodia.

He was not alone at breakfast. Three German men held an earnest and prolonged conversation with the hotel manager, who was also German. A middle-aged French couple spoke in hushed tones and avoided his morning greeting, and a pretty young woman in hotel uniform ate fresh fruit with great delicacy, using a knife and fork, with all the lightness of touch of an eye surgeon, never taking her eye off the kitchen door. Relying on a hastily formed prejudice, and without any proof, Faraday concluded that her interest was directed towards the arrival of the executive chef. However, when the door swung open and the waitress arrived with Faraday's herb omelette and black coffee, she was followed by a young man in a crisp white shirt, navy-blue trousers, and polished black shoes who introduced himself as Trih.

'Good morning, Mr Faraday. My name is Trih. You sleep well?'

The pretty young woman stopped eating her fruit and laid down her utensils, watching Trih's every move.

'I am your guide this morning,' he continued confidently, spreading his upturned hands as if offering the entire world and bowing in a manner that seemed designed to mock servitude, albeit good-naturedly. 'When you are ready, of course.'

'I didn't realize I'd booked a guide.'

82

'Oh, yes, it's part of the package. I am the best! I guide you for two hours, and then you are an expert on Chau Doc. Please, finish your breakfast and meet me at reception in one hour—unless you already have plans...?'

'No, no...'

Unlike Canh from Cantho, Trih spoke a sort of English that would make Faraday increasingly curious as the morning went on. He was clearly very bright, and contrary to most Vietnamese, not at all diffident. After finishing breakfast and retrieving his camera from the safety deposit box in his room, Faraday went downstairs to find him waiting on the pier in front of the hotel, where they'd landed on arrival the day before. He was itching to get started.

'Let's skip the floating market,' Faraday suggested. 'I've already seen how you trade fruit and vegetables in Cantho. Show me some other interesting stuff.'

'Okay, we go to Cham village, and you can see the people who make silk for no money—and then I show you the fish farm, where people make good money.'

He gave the boatman a crisp instruction, and they headed across the river at full speed to the other side, nosing into a side creek and clambering out onto some slippery stone steps that had Faraday sliding on the slime, unable to trust his footing. Trih waited impatiently for him at the top, then set off briskly down the path at the top of the embankment towards the Cham village.

'Anything you want to photo, just do it. Anything you want to know, just ask.'

Through the doors of the village houses, they could see women swathed in silk working at their looms, and their verandas were swathed in silk also: cerulean blues, fuchsia pinks, violet, and tangerine. The footpaths were the rich acorn brown of the delta silt made slippery by overnight rain, and in the dense green undergrowth, lizards scurried rapidly for cover as they passed. There were no men, only women—and the women looked away shyly and moved back inside their doorways whenever they saw the raised camera.

'Where are the men?' Faraday asked.

'At prayers. They are Muslim. The women work; the men pray.'

'Can I see?'

A young girl began to follow them at a distance, stopping when they stopped, shadowing their progression along the tree-lined path that seemed to be the only road through the sparse village, hesitant but attentive, like an unclaimed puppy, all dark eyes beneath lowered lashes, feet light and ready for flight, yet not attempting to hide her presence.

'Does she want something?' Faraday asked after a while.

'Yes.' Trih studiously ignored her and kept walking while Faraday paused to take her photo, expecting her to giggle and run away. But she held her ground impassively, then continued to follow them past the white-walled mosque and schoolyard and the curious stares of the village women in their doorways, stubbornly persisting as if invisibly tethered to Trih's indifference.

They paused at the mosque door and looked in cautiously.

'Where are the older men?' Faraday asked. They were all young—Trih's age or less.

He shrugged. 'Dead. The Khmer Rouge came here.'

He was keen to keep walking, but he had nothing further to offer on the subject, preferring to question Faraday instead: where did he come from, what was his work, and did he like the hotel? He appeared to have no interest in the people of the village or their history.

'Your English is very good,' Faraday told him. 'Do you think one day you'll become the hotel manager?'

Trih laughed. 'No, I want to make money. Come.'

He led at a fast clip out of the village, away from the river and into the paddy fields that stretched northeast across the flat plains towards Phu Tan and the southern Cambodian border. The green, quilted landscape was devoid of trees or houses, a vast canvas of post-painterly abstraction composed of billions upon billions of rice seed heads, sewn together with

84

the silt-grey thread of hand-dug flood channels.

'This land is for rice,' Trih explained over his shoulder. 'Rice takes one hundred days from planting to harvest. Before now, they used to plant also with potatoes and other things. We call it a 'rotation.' Now they plant only rice, three times a year. This is better; it makes more money. But not all the land is good for growing. I will buy that land and make it pretty. I plant trees and make everything nice, and then I wait. Price goes up, I sell.' A matter-of-fact shrug of his slight shoulders suggested that this was no pipe dream, but more of a foregone conclusion.

'You're going to be a property developer!' Faraday challenged him.

' "Developer", yes!' He clearly liked the sound of the word, giving no indication that it had bad connotations in a communist state.

'And are you allowed to buy this land?' Faraday asked curiously. 'Do you need government permission to divide it up?'

'Of course.'

'That isn't a problem?'

'No problem, no. You just need to ask the right person. You need to pay money to the right person.'

'And you know that person?'

'Because of my family.'

Faraday thought about that for a while as they gazed out over the vast patchwork of misty, irrigated countryside that had been plucked and planted by thousands of peasant hands, like a gigantic act of agrarian pointillism repeated over and over for centuries. What the young man had said, and the way he'd said it, sounded all too familiar—but not in this place, of all places.

'Where will you get the money to buy the land?' Faraday asked at last.

'I will borrow it, of course.'

'And why will they lend it to you?'

'Because of my family.' He smiled. It was simple. 'You want to see the fish farm now?'

They turned east, following a path along the top of a causeway that looked like an informal rampart encircling the village. The air was so heavy with moisture that the sunlight had become diluted and the colours saturated, fully absorbed. There were no boundary lines amidst the limitless expanse of rice paddies (other than the irrigation channels), no houses and no trees, no dogs, bicycles, or birdsong. The girl had long since stopped and gone back the way they'd come.

'Which is the land you'll purchase?'

'There.' He pointed. Ahead of them, between the causeway and the low-lying paddy fields, was an area of higher ground that seemed at a distance to be an outcropping of limestone or white clay, and beyond it, the causeway turned back towards the village and the tributary of the river where they had come ashore. Rich soil, saturated with water and supporting thousands of acres of fast-growing vegetation, has no discernible smell, yet gradually Faraday became aware of a dank odour, penetrating and astringent, more animal than vegetable, and heavy like the moist, lethargic air.

As they drew closer, the clay-coloured ground began to move, like a mound of meat smothered in white maggots, and the smell grew fouler— not the smell of death, but the malodorous stench of over-abundant life, fetid and rank—and the maggots revealed themselves to be white ducks squatting in a field of mud. The density of the ducks was so great that they were forced to lay their beaks on each other's backs with no room between them, and they emitted a faint and constant fluttering sound, as if asleep and dreaming. All that held them in place was a straggly netting fence propped up with bamboo stakes, following the contour of the mound and the boundary of the causeway.

'Poultry farm,' Trih said dismissively. 'Poultry can live anywhere.'

Next to the field of ducks was the field from which they had recently come: a dense, dark expanse of green and black slime that smelled of ammonia. Standing barefoot and ankle-deep in the slime, a solitary woman was slowly shovelling it into wicker baskets. Full baskets of slime were lined up neatly beside the causeway, awaiting collection, and as they passed, she looked up at them with a faint smile of satisfaction—for a job well done, or for a job worth doing, or just for having a job, maybe.

Faraday held a handkerchief to his nose and mouth and tried not to breathe.

* * * *

Trih was equally keen on putting the smell of duck excrement behind them and returning to the boat waiting at the landing steps. He was a man in a hurry, warning Faraday that he'd said his services as a guide only lasted for two hours, and he meant it. There wasn't going to be any lingering. Soon they slid back down the landing steps to the boat and headed out into the main stream towards the floating city of corrugated iron sheds, the traffic on the waterway now requiring them to stay alert.

'Fish farms,' Trih said, gesturing ahead. He didn't waste words.

The iron sheds that looked like hay barns were moored in the fast-flowing waters of the main stream. They were built on floating platforms constructed from bamboo poles lashed to oil drums, and steel nets were visible, suspended just beneath the platforms as holding pens for the fish.

'Each farm costs twenty to thirty thousand dollars to build!' Trih shouted as they roared amongst them. 'The cage hold one hundred and twenty thousand fish. When they grow to one kilo each, they sell them. They do this twice a year.'

'Good money?'

'Good money! You make thirty thousand dollars a year US.'

He pointed the boatman towards the nearest one, and they clambered aboard without asking, Trih running about while treating it as his own, taking great delight in scooping up handfuls of dry fish food from a sack and throwing it into an open hatch in the deck, where a feeding frenzy of fish immediately churned the water into a boiling lather. The shed appeared to be someone's home; the man and woman who occupied it stood back shyly in the shadows.

'Thirty thousand dollars is a lot of money for Vietnam,' Faraday commented. 'But these people don't look that rich.'

Trih laughed. 'Of course not.'

'So, other people own them?'

'Some people own many.'

'And you need special permission?'

'Of course.'

Faraday was catching on fast.

'Here.' Trih held out a bowl filled with fish food. 'You feed them. It makes you feel very powerful.'

The food smelled vaguely familiar. 'What is it?'

'It is broken rice and duck shit. Very good; makes them grow fast.'

Duck shit...? The woman with the wicker baskets? Faraday walked to the edge of the trapdoor and looked in. The water was dark and still. Then he cast a handful of the dry food, and before it even reached the surface, there was a flash of silver light, like lightning arcing out of the depths and leaping towards his outstretched hand. Gasping, he stumbled backwards, spilling some of the food from the bowl onto the deck. Fish flew forth from the water, landing at his feet, flapping like angry piranhas—like the snakehead fish of his imagination—and Trih laughed hysterically, excited by his fear.

'They eat you! They eat you!' he cried delightedly. 'You make good fish food! They eat anything. See? Okay? Easy to make money when you know.'

* * * *

That morning stayed in Faraday's mind as he travelled on to Hue the next day. There had been something familiar about Trih's untroubled arrogance. He was good-looking, intelligent, and fortunate enough to be well connected in a country where the winners had not hesitated to show the losers where they belonged. But his insouciance went beyond either the confidence of youth or the reliance on party connections. Whatever it was, it was innate.

Faraday's allotted two hours had passed, but Trih determined that he needed to go upstream to the Cambodian border, which he was assured he would find interesting. Chau Doc was on the Bassac River, which ultimately met up with the Mekong, but there were so many tributaries and canals interlacing the delta that it was easier just to think of it as one. In the end, all water flowed to the sea, and they headed against the flow before turning into the Vinh Te Canal, where they cut the engine while Trih explained that this waterway was man-made, following the border out to the coast at Ha Tien.

'Eighty thousand men,' he said, waving an arm, 'dead.'

'Eighty thousand men died building it?'

'Yes. Die.' He seemed somewhat disinterested in the figure, just as he had been in the absence of older men in the Cham village. 'You see the boy over there on the channel marker?'

Faraday could see a young child clinging to a buoy in the middle of the stream. 'Yes. What's he doing there?'

'See the orange flag?'

'I see an orange plastic bag.'

'That is the signal.'

'For what?'

'To tell the smugglers that the police are not here.'

'… Do the police not realize that?'

'Oh, yes, they do. It also means for them to stay away.'

'Why?'

'They have been paid already.'

He pointed down the canal, where an endless passage of two-man canoes were crossing at high speed from one side to the other, one man paddling, the other doubled over with a television strapped to his back.

'At the border, TV costs thirty dollars,' Trih mused wistfully. 'In Saigon, it sell for three hundred dollars. Good money.'

He was clearly keen on Faraday seeing this, so he obliged by taking photographs—something he'd failed to do at the poultry farm. Though Faraday didn't pick up on it at the time, he thought later that Trih had taken him to see the smuggling because he wanted him to see his country in the best light: entrepreneurial, innovative, making money. He was proud of that, and he assumed all Westerners would admire it as well.

On the way back to the hotel, Trih led them into the covered market, searching for a specific vendor. 'You like Mont Blanc pens?' he asked. 'Very cheap. Counterfeit. No one can tell.'

'How much?'

'You give me twenty dollars, I buy four.'

He bought five and put one in his pocket.

Back at the hotel, Trih politely pointed out that they had gone over the two-hour time allowance, and thus Faraday should pay an extra ten dollars directly to him, because he was now working on his own time. They smiled, shook hands, and parted. Without realizing it, the young man had demonstrated something about the nature of corruption that Faraday had previously chosen to overlook: that in some cultures, it was seen as opportunity and just reward.

TEN

The route Faraday was following around Vietnam was a well-trodden one. His stop in Chau Doc had been the exception, brought on by his desire to immerse himself in the environment that so tellingly underscored the emotional impact of *Apocalypse Now*. But he had determined at the outset that wherever the travel brochures sent the Western traveller, that was where he would find the art galleries he was seeking, so after returning to Ho Chi Minh City, the next stop was Hue.

Being close to the midpoint of such a long, skinny country that stretched the entire length of the Indochinese Peninsula, it was easy to see why the city had been chosen as the seat of power by the pre-Western rulers of the Nguyen dynasty. Dynastic rule was all about power, and power was all about control. From this midpoint, Nguyen Anh and his successors had been able to exercise control over both the north and the south. If you didn't have control and wanted to seize it, this was where you came—as the French had in 1885, and the Viet Cong in 1968, each taking care to liquidate with ruthless efficiency any representative of the power they were displacing, whether architectural or human.

Despite the carnage and destruction wrought during the 1968 Tet Offensive, there was still ample physical evidence of the Nguyen belief that order could be imposed upon nature and the landscape just as easily as upon people. The streets were wide and lined with trees, the ramparts and moats of the Citadel as imperious as those of Versailles. Grand architecture, like power, relied on grand conceit. Over a period of two weeks, when General Westmoreland had tried to take back the city from the communists, US bombs had razed the area inside the Citadel, killing ten thousand people. But despite the bombs, the stone ramparts remained, waiting in mute splendour for the next power elite to claim them—which, recognizing their pull on tourists, the government of the socialist republic had belatedly done.

Faraday had booked a hotel in the Old Quarter, consciously trying to move himself away from the seductive comforts of the luxury hotel chains, somewhere closer to where he felt Vietnam saw itself residing. Despite his relative financial comfort, a liberal art school streak still resided in him that made him averse to treading the same ground as the moneyed classes. This reverse snobbery had him plumping for a room rate of twenty-five dollars a night that included 'breakfast, bath, and window'. The window looked out onto a courtyard where *xe om* motorbike taxis came and went all night, and the need to keep the curtains drawn was so inarguable that the management had nailed the hems to the sill. Outside, it was thirty-six degrees centigrade, and inside, it took the air conditioning fan two hours to reduce it to a bearable thirty. If he left the room for any reason, removing the keys from the power switch at the door, the air conditioning would go off, and the temperature would immediately creep back up. It didn't take long before this became his primary preoccupation.

As he lay on the bed in Hue, waiting for the room to cool down and the sun to set, so he could venture out for dinner without melting, he had a sudden urge to call Ralph. It was now mid-morning in London, and he knew Ralph would be drinking coffee, waiting for his stomach to start rumbling so he could go to lunch.

'Dear boy, are we still sleuthing in Vietnam,' Ralph asked facetiously, 'or are we now back in civilization?'

'Very much in Vietnam.'

'Well, I admire your tenacity, though personally I think what you're doing is like looking for a pin in a paddy field. Not even the full might of Microsoft or Hollywood lawyers could stop those people from copying things. Quite frankly, you're wasting your time.'

'Quite likely, Ralph. But you know what they say: the journey is more important than the destination, et cetera. New surroundings always get you thinking, and I've been thinking that maybe all is not what it seems sometimes. So, I have a couple of questions for you.'

'Make them easy,' Ralph sighed.

'You organized the printing of the Paladin Portfolios. How many were printed?'

'You know the answer to this: one for each of their one hundred and twenty Names, no more. That was the agreement.'

'And that's how many were printed: exactly a hundred and twenty?'

He could sense Ralph sitting up straighter in his button-backed leather chair. 'That's what we ordered, yes.'

'And that's what you printed—exactly.'

'What has this got to do with the fake panda? The panda wasn't even part of the portfolio.' He sounded annoyed by the question.

'It wouldn't have been less than a hundred and twenty, obviously,' Faraday persisted, 'but might it have been more?'

'More? I don't know what you mean.' His vowels had retreated to the back of his throat. 'Where is this leading?'

'I seem to remember some discussion about overruns…'

'Ah, overruns!' His vowels relaxed again. 'Yes, there are always overruns on print orders; it's insurance against rejects. The cost in printing is the set-up, so it costs nothing at all to make an extra print or so. Five percent is the usual figure. As you know, with all your work, we are very strict in insisting that the overruns are destroyed once we are satisfied with the quality of the agreed-upon number. Moores and Stiles are required to issue an auditor's certificate verifying that fact. It is an essential part of the process protecting copyright. The whole point of the Paladin job was that the only copies in existence would be those that were hand delivered by Security Express to Johnston's list of Names, and that the printing plates would then be destroyed. You remember how strict we were.'

'Yes, I remember you saying the same thing when I was autographing the frontispiece sheets. But I seem to remember that there were a few more than a hundred and twenty, and I just wondered what happened to them. At the time, I was rather naive about the process and didn't take much notice.'

'Odd that you should be asking such a question now. What prompted it?'

Ralph seemed strangely subdued … or was that just Faraday's imagination?

'Not so odd, really. You hinted yourself that Johnston was a little fast and loose in some respects, and it occurred to me that the value he had placed on each portfolio could have made a few spare copies worth quite a bit of money. Just a thought.'

What was truly odd was that he hadn't asked at the time. As well as being young and naive, he had also been in a mild state of shock at such unexpected early financial success. One morning in Trih's company had finally begun to awaken him to the ways of the world. But Ralph was right: it had no bearing on the source of the counterfeit panda, because that image had never been part of the portfolio. What was different now, perhaps, was that the counterfeit painting had made him aware of the general potential for opportunistic fraud, and now all the other transactions he had taken at face value were beginning to nag at him also—and there was nothing in Ralph's explanation to stop that nagging from becoming more persistent.

* * * *

There was a deaf man who ran a restaurant on the north bank of the Perfume River in Hue. Because the food was very cheap and had long been featured in the Lonely Planet guidebook, lots of tourists went there, particularly Australians. A narrow set of concrete steps led from the small open kitchen up to a very rudimentary dining room and balcony that had probably not changed since the Tet Offensive, save for the graffiti covering the walls. As it turned out, the deaf man encouraged the graffiti by handing out red marker pens. The deaf man's daughters took the orders and cleared the tables, disappearing at intervals to breastfeed their infants in an adjoining back room, while the deaf man's wife crouched on the kitchen floor over a single gas ring and a small charcoal burner.

The deaf man smiled continuously as he moved about the crowded dining room, no doubt believing that the walls of his establishment were being adorned with snippets of cosmopolitan wisdom, like a compendium of the world's great cultures. On the wall next to Faraday's table was one such scrawled message: *Rosalie Taylor gave me head on the bus to Danang, May 20, 2001.*

Politely declining the marker pen, he avoided the poultry dishes and ordered the fresh seafood hotpot.

Though there were already forty diners in the restaurant, the fish stew came quickly. Chasing it down with a Tiger beer, he wiped his hands on the chilled wet napkin that one of the daughters managed to produce at exactly the right moment, then made his way down the narrow stairs to settle the minuscule bill. The deaf man was waiting for him, red marker pen in hand; he wasn't going to let Faraday pay until he wrote something on his wall. So, he dutifully drew a crab, an octopus, and a fish and enclosed them in a hotpot, just like the one the man's wife had cooked for him.

'God bless you,' the deaf man said with a slight bow.

Maybe he did understand the graffiti after all.

The *xe om* motorcycle drivers were queuing up on the pavement outside, but Faraday still had some thinking to do, so he opted to cross the river and walk until he found a bar with air conditioning, taking note of the lobby galleries of the two smart hotels on the river as he passed, which he would visit the following morning. The thinking to be done involved the potential for personal profit that a few extra unrecorded print portfolios could have provided for Johnston in his fundraising position at Paladin. Faraday hadn't wanted to acknowledge it, but there had always been a whiff of extravagance to Johnston's dealings: the cavalier approach to pricing the original paintings (Ralph had explained, unconvincingly, that they needed to be expensive, or they would not have carried the necessary cachet); the sum that Johnston had given away so lightly in order to secure the copyright; the lavish celebratory dinner, charged to American Express.

He'd chosen not to take notice of all that, let alone do the sums. But with so much money passing through Johnston's hands, the potential for some of it to stick without being noticed must have been evident to a man like him. Or was that just how people behaved when they were spending other people's money? But it was all long ago now; he'd had no contact with Johnston for years, and Nu Nu the panda remained firmly fixed to the wall of Charles Van Heeren's Geneva office. So, who had commissioned the copy of that painting, and why?

The following day, he made the obligatory visits to the Imperial Enclosure in the Old Citadel and the Tomb of Tu Duc at Luu Khiem Lake, checked out the art shops and the main hotels without success, and then, continuing his ruse of 'doing it tough', he purchased a ticket for the bus to Hoi An. Compared to the cost of a private car, this saved him all of twelve dollars, but it added immeasurably to his sense of self-esteem—until he began to realize that backpackers used the dollars they saved as a trade-off for time and dignity lost. As he was driven around Hue in a small van for an hour while they picked up people from café bus stops, it quickly became clear that elements of futility were required for the backpacker process to work. Once the small van was filled to bursting, they were all emptied out onto the pavement and left to wait until a bigger bus arrived to collect them.

It turned out that the pavement where they were emptied out was the very place where they had started—and when the bigger bus arrived, it was already three quarters full, so the passengers had to be off-loaded with their luggage before they could all be loaded on again.

In the course of this madness, Faraday got to talking to the small middle-aged man with a bright smile who was sitting beside him. Things could be a lot worse, the man assured Faraday. While travelling in Laos, he said, the next bus out of Vientiane, immediately behind his own, had been shelled by rebels, and everyone aboard had died. Then, getting off in Cambodia one night, he had a pistol held to his head by the police, who promptly relieved him of his passport and wallet … although in Vietnam, he assured Faraday, this was most unlikely to happen, as the government had officially removed all the guns.

His name was Duc, and he was returning to his home in Sinho, which was in Northwest Vietnam. But first he needed to go to Hoi An to talk to some people who wanted him to act as a guide in the mountains to the north of his tribal area, which he knew well. That was why he was on the bus, he said: to meet these people, who would pay well for his services, and his village needed the money.

Between Hue and Hoi An was a steep hill that required considerable effort for buses to climb on a hot day, laden with tourists and their backpacks. At the top of the hill, the buses stopped to catch their breath, allowing the touts to waylay their passengers with cold drinks and souvenirs. Behind them was a view of Danang, a blighted strip of coast where the American Army had parked its armaments and ice cream machines until driven out during the war, leaving behind bomb craters, brothels, and Nissan huts. Honouring the tone thus set, the inheritors of this hard-won victory had turned Danang into a monument to all that was ugly in Western culture. Breeze-block motels lined the white foreshore, and cheap strip malls backed by acres of unpainted fibro workshops now claimed the land that had once claimed so many lives.

'Next stop is Marble Mountain,' Duc announced knowingly, studying his map.

For Faraday's part, he was content to occupy himself with his endlessly fascinating edition of *The Phnom Penh Gazette*. Why this single issue of a low-circulation journal that he'd plucked by chance from the front desk of an empty hotel in the Mekong Delta should have taken on a talismanic quality was not yet clear to him, but each time he dipped into it, he sensed the existence of an encoded subtext that, if only he could decipher it, would illuminate the increasingly dark path on which he felt himself traveling. The world of his imagination, relying as it did on the limited nutrients provided by the British press and the cosy complacencies of his London contemporaries, had made no allowance for the existence of this abused continent. What the hell was going on here? Caroline had been right: 'You'll never know what's *not* being said,' she had warned. But what she hadn't warned him about was that much of what *was* being said made no sense at all, which was why he was forced to read many of the passages in *The Phnom Penh Gazette* more than once.

Snorting in disbelief, he found himself discussing one such passage with the man beside him. 'You've just been in Cambodia,' he said. 'Perhaps you can help explain this to me. Apparently, there is outrage in Phnom Penh over the claims of an American researcher that barely two thousand victims of human trafficking had been located in Cambodia's population of, quote, "18,256 prostitutes", unquote. The local NGOs are upset because they claim there are actually eighty thousand to a hundred thousand prostitutes in Cambodia, and this researcher's figures could affect their funding.'

He turned to Duc to check that the man understood what he was saying to him. He knew it was an unfair question to put to a stranger like this, but he couldn't help himself.

'How on earth do they count them, I want to know?' he went on. 'Do they knock on every village door, asking how many prostitutes there are? Is it now possible that there are more people looking for women and children to rescue than there are victims? But here's the quote I need you to explain to me: " 'It is only in the mind that the problem has changed,' commented a spokesman for the Coalition to Address Sexual Exploitation of Children in Cambodia; 'nothing has changed on the ground.' " Does that mean what I think it means?'

'That depend on what you think it mean,' Duc answered politely.

'I think it means that facts are not important.'

'Then that is what it mean.'

Faraday refolded the paper carefully and replaced it in his camera satchel, suspecting that the NGO mindset could easily prove to be an obstacle to his feeling comfortable in Caroline's company, should they arrange to meet in Hanoi as suggested—something that he realized he was now looking forward to.

At the bottom of the hill, the bus stopped again in a small town, and they were emptied out into a car park beside a large white-stone quarry. Every shop in town, bar one, was dedicated to the sale of marble statuary: lions rampant, dolphins standing on their tails, Venus, Cupid, and Archangel Gabriel—one-ton souvenirs that would require a crane and a forklift to get them home. Faraday and Duc took a table in the one shop that didn't sell statuary and ordered mint tea.

'How did you get your wallet and passport back?' Faraday asked, picking up on their earlier conversation.

Sitting opposite him, rather than side by side as they had been on the bus, Faraday was now more curious about his companion, and that curiosity could be attributed as much to Duc's appearance as to the dramas he had endured on his travels. He was dark-skinned, with a flatter, broader face than the average Vietnamese man, and his hair was longer, but what set him apart was his clothing, best described as 'safari chic'. Short and stocky, he bore a paunch that stretched his white tee shirt beneath a fly-fishing waistcoat with multiple zippered pockets that he fingered constantly, as if trying to remember what each one contained. His trousers were generously zippered, too, providing homes for various traveling paraphernalia and permitting the leggings to be removed, turning them into shorts. His shoes were the latest Nike trainers.

'I follow the policemen who have taken it,' he replied matter-of-factly. His English was good.

'Except for the evidence that you are sitting opposite me, apparently unharmed, I'd have to say that sounds like a fairly risky thing to do. What happened?' Faraday asked sceptically.

'I tell them I want them back.'

Duc held his teacup in two hands, blowing gently across the surface of the liquid without drinking. There was no evidence that he was making a wry joke. His lips were compressed solely for the purpose of blowing, and his eyes remained focused on the hot drink, calculating the moment when its temperature would be right for consumption. Before that moment came, he put his cup down and reached between his legs for the backpack he'd held on his knee throughout their journey. Allowing for the possibility that he had misinterpreted the nature of the event described, that it was not a mugging at all, Faraday refrained from further questions while Duc struggled with the drawstring that sealed the top of his tightly packed bag, eventually producing a tight wad of clothing that appeared to be underwear. He laid the wad on the table and carefully unwrapped it, revealing a small pistol.

'Cambodia and Laos very dangerous,' Duc said sternly, as if Faraday had somehow been making light of it. 'No one pay police. No one care if they die.'

He returned the underwear and gun to his backpack, and they drank their tea in silence until the bus was ready to depart again, his words hanging uncomfortably in the air like an uninvited confidence. Back on the bus, Faraday tried his hardest to look like a man who hadn't just seen a gun, and Duc radiated the nonchalance of a man who didn't carry one—but that may just have been Faraday's imagination.

Nevertheless, he couldn't help but wonder what the hell he had meant.

'No one care if they die'? Did he mean no one cared if the *policemen* died? Or was he just saying that life was cheap? Had he used the gun, or had he just threatened them with it? And why the fuck did he show it like that? Why would he do that?

* * * *

In Hoi An, it was the heat that found him out, soft and fat like a well-fed pig. Sweat oozed from his skin, filling every fibre of his clothing, dropping as heavy and clear as glycerine from his forehead and nose as he skulked in the shadows, hiding like a fugitive from the sun, hulking his suitcase through the narrow, car-free streets in search of his hotel, the Vinh Hung One.

'You'll love Hoi An,' Caroline had breezily promised him over dinner in Cantho. 'It's everybody's favourite. But it's small, so you'll need to book.' Thank God she'd warned him, he was thinking, but she hadn't mentioned the heat, or the special pungency of sweat driven by anxiety. As if that anxiety was not already high enough after seeing a gun produced from Duc's rolled-up underwear, it was raised even further by the warnings of the tout who had joined the bus at Marble Mountain to hawk available beds at a hotel on the outskirts of town.

'All Hoi An fully booked!' he'd shouted shrilly. 'Last chance for bed, or the bus take you back to Danang!'

Most of the passengers looked alarmed and put up their hands for the out-of-town option he was offering, while Duc snorted disdainfully, and Faraday hastily re-read the printout of the internet booking he'd made through the Grande Rivière Hotel in Cantho to be sure he could trust it. In a safe and sane world, he probably could. In the world he was now encountering, he was far from sure.

'Good luck with your job,' he said, shaking Duc's hand. 'After your experience, I think I'll be avoiding Cambodia.'

The bus had terminated at the tour booking office on Tran Hung Dao, leaving him with four blocks to walk to the hotel. There were no taxis because vehicles were banned from the Old Town, and amazingly, no cyclos or *xe oms* either. The streetscape was a fusion of the Cote d'Azur and Chinatown, but at siesta time. He had no choice but to walk.

Despite his belief that he was traveling light, the contents of his leather 'weekender' bag quickly turned to lead in the heat. His feet swelled and his shoes shrunk until every footstep made him wince, and by the time he finally reached the front door of the Vinh Hung One, his brain was shutting down from exhaustion.

The hotel had been created out of an eighteenth-century Chinese merchant's house, painted black throughout with a red tiled floor and black lacquered furniture. Peering into the gloom, he was immediately convinced that he had made a mistake and would soon be heading back to Danang; it didn't look like a hotel at all. But then he was greeted by a female voice.

'Ah, Mr Anthony! We wait you.'

The sound was like spoons playing on crystal glass, a sing-song voice tripping on the verge of laughter. From the dark recesses of the house, a young woman encased in a gold embroidered *ao dai* ran forward with her hand outstretched. 'You have good journey?'

'My name is Faraday,' he responded dully. 'I have a booking.' The copy of the email correspondence clutched in his damp hand had turned to pulp.

'Yes, yes, Mr Anthony. We have special room for you. I send you email.'

'And my name is Faraday,' he repeated, just for clarity. The last thing he wanted was to be kicked out of his precious room later because the real Mr Anthony had arrived.

The sound of spoons on crystal glass echoed again through the lobby. 'Yes, Mr Anthony.' She beamed. 'And first name Faraday—but I do not know you, so is not polite.'

He laughed, and she laughed. It was clearly going to be easier if he accepted a temporary name change.

'And we have email come for you, Mr Anthony. I put it in your room.'

ELEVEN

How did the cooking class go with Michel? the email read. *Did you learn anything? I'm in Hanoi Tuesday. Violet is arriving from Africa. Give me a call if you want. C.*

The hotel room was painted throughout in black gloss enamel: black floor, black ceiling, black walls, black shutters closed against the heat of the day. The four-poster bed, slept on by Michael Caine himself during the making of *The Quiet American* (the catalyst for his choice of lodgings), groaned beneath his weight. How had she suddenly become 'C' after just one meeting and a phone call? Was she the same Irish-American girl who had spilled out the history of her extended family to a complete stranger one night in the middle of a thunderstorm and dressed as if she'd embarked on an ethereal dream, or was she the cool and collected journalist in the elegant silk uniform who could confidently coach staff in three languages as to the expectations of the Western way? And which of those was the woman that Michel assumed Faraday knew the way he apparently knew her?

On searching the email for clues, he realized she'd found his booking confirmation from the Vinh Hung One on her hotel's email files and merely sent back a reply marked for his attention. But she seemed to be saying that it was now his turn to call her, as if she'd started a conversation and now he was obliged to continue it. In two short lines, she'd managed to convey that he had an obligation to report on his meeting with her French boyfriend, and an obligation to rendezvous with her in Hanoi. On top of that, Violet Dunleavy coming into her life now meant that she had come into Faraday's life as well. How had this happened when he couldn't even remember Caroline clearly enough to draw her likeness?

Then he did something that, for him, was completely out of keeping: he retrieved her number on his cell phone and called her for no apparent reason.

'Are you keeping tabs on me?' he asked, without even thinking to make an introduction. 'Because I feel like I'm being spied on.'

'You made it to Hoi An, then? I just wanted to be sure you were still in one piece. After a night with Michel, that isn't a given. How was it?'

'I learned a lot—maybe more than I wanted to. I was surprised by your choice of boyfriend, if you really want to know.'

This was not what he'd intended to say, and he immediately wished he hadn't said it.

'He's full of shit, and he's not a boyfriend ... but he *is* a good cook. Knowing how you like food, I thought you might find him interesting. He speaks well of you, too.'

'What did he say?'

'He said you're an uptight Brit. You refused to have fun.'

'He wanted to go drinking and talk about women. That isn't my style.'

'He was right, then: you *are* an uptight Brit.'

She was laughing at him, which he didn't like, and she seemed to have missed the point that he was defending her reputation. Maybe she didn't care about her reputation.

'Does this Vanderbilt-Dunleavy woman know the reality of duck farming in Vietnam?' he asked, deliberately changing the subject, and angry at being laughed at. 'Have you told her what it entails? Because in Chau Doc, I saw it close up, and I can tell you that it isn't pretty. In fact, it's pretty disgusting. If she thinks she's going to be flying in for a photo opportunity as the Great Western Benefactor giving a leg-up to poor Asian peasants, she'd better be ready for the smell, aside from everything else. And with so many of you

104

NGOs running around Asia, telling the locals how to live, you can bet your bottom dollar there's someone promoting the cause of animal rights. Wait until *they* latch onto how poultry is farmed. Isn't there some other way of helping your uncle's cousin than funding a poultry farm?'

He didn't know why he was suddenly going down this track. It was hardly likely to endear him to her, coming at her with a barrage of criticisms on the basis of a chance encounter with the realities of duck farming Chau Doc-style.

'I don't know what you saw,' she answered coolly. 'The Vietnamese have been farming poultry for hundreds of years. I think you can presume they know what they're doing.'

'Keeping them in pens with no room to move? Ducks with no wings, drowning in mud and excrement? That's what I saw. Waterfowl need clean water and space. They need to forage and fly. I'm no expert, but there's something not right with it, that's all. You might as well know.'

He wished he hadn't even started. Perhaps he'd felt a need to give the call a purpose other than just his desire to talk to her, but now it was developing a life of its own.

'What you probably saw were Pekins,' she said. 'Domestic ducks don't have proper wings. They're not made to fly, they're made for herding, selected for generations for their ability to find food in harvested rice fields, swamps, and waterways. At night, they pen them in, and the following day, they move them on. There's no cruelty involved. Believe me, I've read up on it. Is that why you rang? Do you have a special thing for waterfowl?'

Her slightly mocking tone was hard to read. This was the second time they'd spoken in three days, but neither of them was acknowledging any significance in that. She'd called him first with the introduction in Chau Doc, which was very considerate of her, but it had no other significance. He'd called her next because he was concerned that her charity work might backfire on her, and that was being considerate, too … at least, that was the line he was maintaining.

'Perhaps you're right,' he admitted. 'I do have a soft spot for waterfowl. I'm even a paid-up member of the Wildfowl & Wetlands Trust, so seeing ducks like that gave me a bit of a shock.'

'Well, I'm sorry you disapprove, but a flock of ducks in Vietnam can support a number of families, Anton. They're not going to raise them in any way that would compromise their health or growth rate. It may not look pretty, but you can bet it's well thought out.'

She was right. All of this was crap, he suddenly realized.

'Maybe I'm too sensitive about animals,' he admitted. 'I have a guilty conscience, you see.'

'Because you make money from painting them?'

'Something like that.'

'Well, farming ducks isn't going to make anyone rich in Vietnam, but it will provide them with a living, and no one needs to feel guilty about that. Besides, what Violet is providing is help in establishing clean water. The poultry part of it is Uncle's initiative.'

They agreed to change the subject and spoke instead about his encounters along the way. She liked his recounting of the inscription he'd seen on the wall of the deaf man's restaurant. He liked that she was comfortable with his sense of humour and not averse to a bit of vulgarity. The events of the days since they met had left him with the feeling that a thought had skipped him by without his properly noticing it, something relevant that he would only recognize if he went back over the days and concentrated harder on giving the thought definition. But the more they talked, the more he realized that conversation was the thing that was missing from his life, and that thoughts that remained unspoken were unlikely to reveal deeper meaning.

'Did he really say that—that I was an uptight Brit?' he interjected once they were relaxed again. 'The fucking French are an arrogant bunch. Did he tell you he tried to fix me up with a Vietnamese girl?'

'You don't say! Don't you like girls? Or are you married? I never thought to ask. When you meet men who're traveling, they never admit to being married.'

'No, I'm not married. Come to think of it, I'm hurt that you never thought to ask.'

Her laugh suggested she knew him better than he knew himself. But what he couldn't fathom was how and why they had insinuated themselves into each other's lives so easily.

* * * *

'An uptight Brit who refused to have fun.' It could just as easily have been Helene that said that, he thought, though maybe in slightly different words. He had succeeded in not thinking too much about Helene for a number of years, but suddenly, here in Vietnam of all places, she'd resurfaced—and the connection was Kenneth Johnston.

In addition to not thinking about Helene, he'd also managed to not think about the Paladin Foundation. Since Johnston had disappeared from view, Paladin had ceased to play any part in his life. He'd hidden away in his studio behind a self-imposed workload, blotting out the memory and the implications of that night at the *Alouette* until, unexpectedly, on the road in Vietnam, the memories had come pouring back in—and with them, a hurt he had tried to deny.

* * * *

They'd moved on to the dark chocolate wafers wrapped in edible gold leaf before the subject of the copyright agreement had been raised, at the risk of spoiling the meal.

'Ralph Lutyen is adamant that we never surrender the copyright on paintings,' Faraday finally had the courage to explain, 'for what I believe are very valid reasons. To see them reproduced everywhere on calendars and placemats would kill their value stone dead. I have to accept Ralph's advice.'

'I agree, Anton, I agree,' Johnston replied. 'That's why my proposal would be limited solely to the hundred and twenty copies distributed to the anonymous Names. There would be no question of them being seen everywhere. Quite the opposite! These are extraordinarily private and discreet people of considerable standing. Only a few trusted people even know who they are. It is precisely this exclusivity on which we rely. That's what Ralph and I agreed on.'

'He agreed?'

'Ralph would arrange the printing, you see. It would have to be of the very highest quality, and he's the expert. His auditors would supervise all aspects of security and distribution. The printing plates would be destroyed, so there would be no opportunity for abuse of copyright, ever. The originals would be secure in the boardroom of the Paladin Foundation. As for the rights to reproduce these works, Ralph thought that twenty thousand pounds would be a suitable fee. That's twenty thousand pounds on top of what we've already paid for the originals. What do you think?'

Before he could answer, Helene had intervened. 'And how much you get for your Foundation … from each of … *les Nommes*?' she asked, looking at Johnston in a way that Faraday would eventually come to realize she had never looked at him, and Johnston's answering smile had been filled with both admiration and pleasure.

'Twenty thousand pounds, if you must know. But you have to remember, it's all for charity.'

'Charity or no, I think Anton must get fifteen percent, *non*? It is normal.'

Each held their gaze steady, like gamblers at the table, locked in an intimate challenge of wills. It wasn't her money, and it wasn't his either. But when he agreed to it, it must have been a signal that he was willing to pay for whatever it was she was asking of him, which turned out to not be money at all.

Faraday, of course, was so busy running a calculator in his head that he missed what was really happening. It was only months later, after he and Helene had parted, that she admitted that, at some time during the meal, Johnston had somehow managed to proposition her, suggesting that she meet him for a weekend at the Ritz in Paris. But that was no reason to be angry with either of them. It was just something that he'd recently had cause to recall.

* * * *

After promising Caroline again that he would meet her in Hanoi, he hung up and took a much-needed shower. He hadn't mentioned Helene to her, of course, but for some reason, her challenge about whether he was married or not (or whether he liked women or not) had left him wanting to explain that he was not incapable of a relationship—and he had to admit that urge was quite meaningful in itself. The prospect of meeting her again in Hanoi lifted his spirits, and he lingered in the shower, calling up the image of her that had imprinted itself most clearly on his memory: the moment when she had shaken her head, like a black ibis emerging from a lagoon, and her hair, dark as the night, had suddenly fallen loose from her crown in an unexpected release, just before the wind had whipped their tablecloth as if Prospero had whispered in Ariel's ear, and they had been driven inside.

Afterward, feeling a lot better with a clean, dry shirt and socks and the realization that the cold, reviving shower would always be there to return to, he set out slowly in search of art galleries, pretending that the evening was cooler. Perhaps it was the encounter with the gun on the bus, or maybe it was the undercurrent of his conversation with Caroline, but he felt slightly on edge, unsettled, like a soldier forced to wait too long for the order to invade, needing a release through action.

The cobbled lanes of Hoi An took less than an hour to walk. It was an hour of increasing unreality as the feeling grew that the town was a dreamscape, a Beijing-style Disneyland version of how the Cote d'Azur might look through Asian eyes. As day turned to night, seemingly in an instant, the cafés and tourist shops switched on their yellow lights and paper lanterns, and the guests of the fully booked hotels woke from their siestas, rubbed their eyes, and took their jaded appetites and wallets in search of stimulation.

Quaintness and charm adhered to the town like a coat of paint, and the locals wore permanently pleasant if vacant expressions, as if they had recently bought into an absurd cult. Apparently that cult was devoted to shopping as a way of life, and the absurdity of it was that these people had only recently been communists, fighting for their lives against the imperialist enemies who were now their customers. Faraday still didn't trust it, this apparent ability to bury the hatchet. It was simply unnatural. No German would ever be safe in the back streets of Birmingham or Liverpool, just as no Englishman could expect safe passage in Hamburg or Dresden—not while there was still an Englishman or German alive who remembered the Second World War and could still draw breath. Enmity never died. So, where had these people buried their hatchet, he wanted to know, and what would cause them to rush to retrieve it?

There were two art shops selling 'original' paintings. Modigliani was big, as was Gauguin. Braque and Picasso were available for those with a taste for the less obvious, but there was no sign at all of A J Faraday's world of art in either style or content, nor any willingness on the part of the shopkeepers, when pressed, to try and find it. While not advancing the purpose of his journey, this was reassuring in its own way, for had his style and content been as recognizable and easy to copy as that of Modigliani and Gauguin, he had no doubt that it would have proven impossible to stop them from doing so.

The girl at reception in the gold silk *ao dai* had told him to eat at Restaurant 888 and provided him with a map which, because the town was small, had very few streets on it. Thus Restaurant 888 was easy to find, and he entered its courtyard looking overweight, sweaty, white, and obviously out of place. There were no other customers, and he accepted a welcome in English and a seat outdoors before devouring an ice-cold Tiger beer like his life depended on it. Then he was mysteriously left alone, without a menu or offer of further service, for ten minutes, an inattention that was untypical of Vietnam, and which eventually prompted him to go indoors in search of the waiter who had greeted him.

Inside the restaurant, the tables were laid, but the chairs were empty, as if there had been a sudden evacuation. There was no sign of either customers or staff. The walls were decorated with posters featuring colour photographs of rainforests and calls to action from the World Wide Fund for Nature. In the bottom corner of each poster was the ubiquitous stylized logo of the giant panda with the acronym WWF. Through a closed door came sounds of laughter and animated discussion, and Faraday pushed it open to reveal a crowded kitchen with twenty or so Westerners gathered around the cooking area, and two Vietnamese chefs who were cutting and slicing while commentating in broken English. His interest in joining the cooking class was immediately aroused, but sadly, as the young waiter who'd first greeted him quickly explained after rushing forward in embarrassment for having forgotten him, he had arrived too late; the class was just ending, and he would need to book for the following evening. He was, however, invited to join those who had just completed the class in consuming the product of their studies: prawn and duck with green mango salad, grilled aubergine with crab, and tamarind snake-headed mullet soup.

'Knowing how you like your food,' Caroline had said when speaking of Michel, 'I thought you might find him interesting.'

What had she observed in him, over the one meal they'd shared together? He pondered this later that night as he lay awake in bed. He'd ordered the basa fish fried in lemongrass and onion together with other herbs that he hadn't been able to identify. It had been served sizzling hot on a wooden platter, and he'd bent over it inhaling the aromas. Then, looking up into her dark eyes, he had smiled in obvious relish—a relish she hadn't missed, it seemed, and which must have encouraged her to trust him in some way, for she had then gone on to tell him about her personal life as if they were intimates. How could he have revealed so much to her in that one moment over food, such that she had felt moved to involve him in her life? Perhaps she'd recognised that his obvious relish was less for the basa fish than it was for the allure of her dark eyes and teasing smile.

TWELVE

The encounter with Trih had inadvertently narrowed his food choices. The pungent aroma of the Pekins swarming in the mud of the paddy fields, as well as the feeding frenzy that the dried duck shit had inspired in the caged basa fish, stayed with him. But these weren't the only intimate experiences of poultry he was destined to encounter on this trip, and the next one was to prove equally interesting.

At 4:00 p.m. the next day, lying on his bed in his black-lacquered room at the Vinh Hung One hotel, naked except for his underpants, having retreated from the thirty-eight-degree-Celsius inferno of the streets outside to listen to the labouring sounds of the overloaded air conditioning fan, he was roused by the unexpected jangle of an old-fashioned telephone.

'Could you meet me please, Mr Anthony, sir, in the lobby?'

'Who are you?'

'I will wait. Thank you.'

There it was again: that back-to-front name thing. Oh well, at least he'd rested long enough to stop sweating. He hoped it wasn't about the bicycle that he'd rented earlier for fifty cents a day and left leaning against the hotel's front steps until he was ready to return it in the evening. The car-free area of the town was so small that he'd seen everything three times in the first hour and decided to park it up. If they wanted it back, he was quite agreeable, but if it had been stolen, he might have a problem. He pulled on some clothes, grabbed his room key, and made his way downstairs.

The young man in the white shirt and black pants waiting at reception looked vaguely familiar—and distinctly nervous.

'I am sorry, sir,' he said, 'but your cooking class cannot be provided.'

Of course, that was why he recognized him: he was the young waiter from Restaurant 888.

'We wish to apologize very much for your inconvenience and invite you attend a birthday party.'

'A birthday party? Whose birthday?'

'Mr Jason, sir. He is the owner of our restaurant, and also of the Red Windmill. The Red Windmill is where you book the cooking class we must cancel.'

'I thought I booked at Restaurant 888.'

'No, sir, that cooking class not possible. You book at the Red Windmill.'

Leaning on the reception desk, her chin cupped in one hand, the girl in the gold embroidered *ao dai* watched this exchange with interest and delight. It was Faraday's turn to ask the next question, but he elected to pass.

'Mr Jason ask that you please forgive,' the young man continued, 'and please accept invitation to his party.'

'Where is the party to be held, and who is Mr Jason?'

'At the Red Windmill. I am to take you.'

Faraday looked at the receptionist for guidance. Was this how things were done in Vietnam? She nodded.

'Mr Jason own The Explorer restaurant,' she said, smiling enthusiastically, 'and the Rainforest Café also. You go, Mr Anthony?'

What the hell, he thought. He had nothing else planned, and he had to admit to a certain curiosity as to what sort of person would own four establishments in one town in a country that preached collectivism and was rumoured to still be operating forced-labour 're-education' camps.

'Tell Mr Jason I'll be happy to accept.'

The arrangement was that at 6:00 p.m., he was to go to Restaurant 888, and from there the young waiter would escort him to the party, which was across the river on the southern outskirts of town. In the meantime, Faraday would return his bicycle, have another cold shower, put on a new ten-dollar, made-to-measure cotton shirt that he'd ordered from a nearby shop that morning, pop some business cards and dollar notes in his breast pocket, down a whisky from the mini bar, brush his teeth, and set off, not knowing what to expect other than the unexpected.

What was completely unexpected was to find another cooking class just getting underway as he arrived at Restaurant 888.

'Welcome, welcome!' a large, ebullient Vietnamese man was shouting to new arrivals as they filed in. 'Welcome to all cooks!' His well-fed confidence and air of proprietorship led Faraday to assume that this must be Mr Jason.

'Oh, no,' the young waiter corrected him, 'he the manager. His name is Hi.'

'But isn't this the cooking class I booked?'

'No, sir, this class is full. Your class at the Red Windmill.'

'I see. And what is your name?'

'My name Hi also.'

'Family name?'

'First name. Mr Jason ask me to show you his photo gallery, then we go to the Red Windmill.'

Through a side door opening from the restaurant and fronting onto a back alley was another room set up as a gallery, devoted solely to large colour photographs of wild animals, around a dozen in all, frameless and mounted behind glass. They were amateur but effective, not of *National Geographic* quality, but reliant on natural light rather than Photoshop manipulation, not unlike the photos that Faraday himself might take in the wild. The animals appeared to all be native to Southeast Asia, if not to Vietnam. He recognized the long horns and white facial markings of the saola, otherwise known as the Asian unicorn, which he'd been led to believe could no longer be found in the wild, and there were gibbons and reptiles that he couldn't name. The Asian elephant and Indochinese tiger, though, were part of his own repertoire.

'Is this Mr Jason's hobby,' he asked Hi, 'or has someone else taken these photos?'

'Mr Jason give money to save animals. He want you to see.'

Well, if nothing else, the World Wide Fund for Nature posters in the outer room now had an explanation, but greater clarity was unlikely to be forthcoming, so long as Hi's understanding of his questions remained so proximate. After giving a decent and polite period of attention to the photographs, Faraday led them back through the restaurant, where the mostly American and British tourists were now excitedly filing into the kitchen in pursuit of Mr Hi, the manager, who was loudly chanting the ingredients of *nuoc mam cham* like a religious mantra. Though Faraday knew he should obviously be asking why he had not been offered a place in this cooking class rather than an invitation to the birthday party of a complete stranger, he also knew that it was unlikely to evince an answer that would satisfy, so he left it unasked. Does life only progress if there is complete understanding, or is it the misunderstandings that pry open the cracks and let the light in?

As they prepared to climb onto Hi's motorcycle for the ride out to the Red Windmill, Hi asked if he could have one of Faraday's business cards. Faraday had known for years that to travel in the East without a business card was to travel naked, so he had come prepared, though his was the card of a man who clearly didn't do business at all. A. J. (ANTON) FARADAY, it baldly proclaimed, along with a website, an email address, and a cell phone number—no physical address, and no explanation. He couldn't even bring himself to add the word PAINTER.

'For Mr Jason,' Hi added.

'Of course,' Faraday replied.

'Mr Jason say you are a very important man.'

Hi ran back into the kitchen and returned with a sack, which he asked

Faraday to hold while he kick-started the motorbike. Then he waited for Faraday to climb onto the pillion and find somewhere to tuck his legs before engaging the gear and heading off down the cobbled street towards the river bridge.

'Who told him that I was important?' Faraday shouted.

'The manager at the Vinh Hung Hotel,' Hi shouted back.

When the sun goes down in the tropics, the sky turns black. The white headlight of the small, noisy motorbike twisted and turned in front of them as they negotiated the wooden bridge out of town and turned down the rough riverbank road towards the party, Faraday's arms wrapped around the slim torso of the serious young man who was delivering him to his master. The air buffeting their faces and clothing was still hot, but the speed of the bicycle made it seem drier, and in the dark, they were greeted by smells that would have gone unnoticed in the bright glare of daylight: jasmine, frangipani, sewage, and the faintly honeyed aroma of the young man's warm skin through the polyester fibre of his white shirt.

In the days that followed, Faraday would revisit the events of the party at the Red Windmill many times in search of clues as to their meaning, but that night, he was clueless.

The sack that Hi had asked him to hold was reasonably heavy—about ten kilos, he guessed—and he had no idea what it contained until, shortly into their journey, he felt it moving in his lap and realized that it contained something living. It was a somewhat unnerving feeling, having an unknown animal moving about in his lap while he was precariously holding on with one hand to ensure he wouldn't fall off a motorbike that was traveling at a fair clip down a dark and bumpy road, and his shouted enquiry about what the hell was in the sack was either drowned out by the racket or was not understood by the young man driving. When they finally made it to their destination, he was relieved to discover that the sack simply contained four live chickens destined for the restaurant kitchen.

At the time, he gave them no second thought.

117

The windmill for which the place was named was lit up with light bulbs like a gaudy Parisian nightclub, while in contrast, the restaurant beside it was an elegant symmetrical structure with a floating tile roof supported by ebonized columns, with large, red lacquered doors opening on a dimly lit interior of white tablecloths and stained bamboo furniture: an upmarket Westernized take on an imperial banquet room. The party, however, was not in the restaurant; it was on the lawn that sloped down to the towpath bordering the river, and of all things on a hot and sticky tropical night, it was centred around a roaring log fire set in what appeared to be a concrete replica of a sampan.

Jason Turnbull had separated himself from the group gathered by the fire as soon as he heard the motorbike approaching, and he emerged from the darkness as Faraday dismounted, an aura of bright light bulbs from the windmill outlining his silhouette, so that Faraday had trouble making out his appearance. The voice was an instant giveaway as to his Australian nationality, but there was no immediate clue as to his age. He was slim, languid, and casually dressed in the long sleeves and loose, long trousers favoured by people who have experience in living in the tropics.

'You must be the famous painter of wildlife,' he said, not offering his hand. 'I'm Jason Turnbull. We heard about you. Glad you could come. There's a bar, a barbecue, and a bunch of expats all talking bullshit. Hi will take you back once you get sick of it. What did you think of my gallery?'

He didn't wait for an answer, but turned as if someone invisible had tapped him on the shoulder and began wandering slowly back in the direction of the bonfire. Hi took the sack from Faraday and tipped its contents onto the ground: four uncomplaining chickens, just as he had seen them many times in the markets, with their feet tied and their wings clipped. While Hi stuffed them back in the bag and headed off into the restaurant, Faraday followed his host towards the fire. There was music playing, and someone without much of a voice or even a memory for the words was exhorting his companions over the microphone, without any apparent luck, to *'dance, dance, dance to the ten guitars'*. It was a predominantly male gathering, with one notable exception, who detached herself from the group to advance on Faraday in response to the host's whispered instructions, stopping in his path and pressing her palms together with her fingertips touching her forehead before bending very slowly forward in a graceful bow. Her dress was traditional, a white silk *ao dai*, but slit on one side from her ankle to her hip in a most non-traditional display of alluring leg that revealed itself as she walked. She didn't speak, but gestured with her hands for him to follow her to a table laden with food and drinks, where she mimed for him to help himself before bowing again and slipping away into the darkness.

'There's two reasons, right there,' a voice beside him said. 'When they look like that and have the good sense not to speak, why the hell would you ever want to go back to a white woman?'

The man was in his middle fifties, overweight and untidy. The accent was somewhere north of London and south of Manchester. His drink of choice was Heineken, which he replenished from a large tin bathtub filled with bottles and ice, tossing his empty into a plastic bin.

'How long you been here, or are you just visiting?' he asked once he'd taken a long, satisfying swig. His eyes were quick and intelligent, darting about like that of a rodent searching for an escape route while simultaneously searching for food. He had the jaunty confidence of a man who cared little about how he looked, and even less about anything else.

'No more than a week,' Faraday replied. 'And you?'

'Make that twenty. Years, not weeks. I passed the point of leaving a long time ago. Living in someone else's country relieves you of the need to care. Whatever you don't like doesn't bother you; it's someone else's problem.'

'And what don't you like about Vietnam?'

'All the foreigners.'

Faraday decided he liked him. His name was Dave, and as close as he could tell, he was a journalist—or if not a journalist, a publisher in the throes of launching an English-language paper 'for the NGO market'.

'Like *The Phnom Penh Gazette*,' commented Faraday knowingly.

'No,' Dave replied, 'more like *Time Out*. Where to eat, where to drink, who's fucking who: only the things that matter. Everyone here thinks that what they're doing is so important that it's going to change the world, but what they don't realize is that most people in the world are only interested in getting enough to eat and drink and having an orgasm, a decent shit, and a peaceful night's sleep. So, what do you do, and where do you do it?'

'I'm a painter from London.'

'Houses, or pictures?'

'Animals. Wildlife.'

'That's why you're here, then.'

'What do you mean?'

'That's why you're invited. Jason's a big cheese in conservation. Animals are his currency. It's rumoured that the money he makes from his restaurants is fed to the rangers in the national parks, who filter it down to the poachers to bribe them to catch endangered species live. Who would know? And the Jamaican-American guy he's talking to works for some outfit called the Paladin Foundation. He counts wild elephants. Check out his gold watch! There's money in wildlife. But then, you should know…'

Faraday didn't react. Without articulating the thought, he knew there was something not quite right about this seemingly innocent reference to Paladin. But he was scrambling to assimilate all the other things that seemed wildly improbable about the night, as if he were mildly hallucinating, and he couldn't immediately think of a question to pose to Dave that might convey his doubts about what he'd just been told.

Meanwhile, finding in Faraday a fresh new audience for his well-rehearsed cynical views of the world, and quietly admiring the size of the chardonnay that he observed him pouring for himself, Dave took the newly arrived wildlife painter in tow to stir things up among the expats gathered around the barbecue. Communities who saw each other frequently, as these people clearly did, liked nothing better than newly arrived outsiders to whet their appetites for conversation, providing as they did an opportunity to repeat histories that had otherwise become boring, or perhaps to reshape them for the benefit of someone who was in no position to criticize their veracity. Dave's introduction reflected all of this.

'Listen up, *Nams*, we have a visitor from the Old World, all the way from London! So, sharpen your minds and mind your language, because you are now in the presence of a chardonnay drinker.'

'What news do you bring from GHQ?' asked a tall, muscled man with the cropped hair and tattooed forearms of an axe champion. The half-hearted smile accompanying the weak joke suggested that anything said or done could go either way, pleasant or threatening, and it would make little difference to him.

'Chardonnay is back with a vengeance,' Faraday replied pleasantly, raising his glass. 'That's the good news. Everything else in Britain is much the same.'

Where had he seen this man before? Africa, probably. Mercenary. Ex-SAS. He was a type, very useful to have around when trouble was brewing—depending on who was paying him.

'The country's lost its guts,' the man confirmed, as if that were inarguable, 'and now they're drinking chardonnay. No wonder it's fucked.'

'Well,' Faraday conceded, 'I'm guilty of that, as you can see. But I'm just an effete, poufy artist from London—hardly representative of the great nation as a whole. The great nation continues to get wasted on lager, if you find that more reassuring.'

Dave laughed and clapped Faraday on the back. 'John here is scouting Vietnam for a suitable place to open a bar. He could take you on as his drinks adviser. What are you going to call the place, John?'

'Pommy John's. What else would I call it?'

There were five of them in this group around the fire, including the host, Jason Turnbull, as well as a good-looking black man in blood-red, sleeveless trekking jacket and white trousers who stuck out his hand and introduced himself as Sam. His accent was conspicuously Jamaican-American, and his teeth were conspicuously white, but the most conspicuous feature of all was the gold watch on his left wrist. Perhaps it was the events subsequent to this meeting that would elevate Faraday's awareness of the watch, but even in the moment of introduction, it seemed like a planted clue—except at that stage, he was not aware of what he was searching for or why. In the context of what was to happen on this journey, it would become a silent footfall.

Faraday shook the extended hand and smiled amiably.

'You're in the wildlife business, Dave tells me. As is Jason, I believe. I saw the photographs back at the gallery. If those are the animals threatened with extinction in Vietnam, it looks like you've got your work cut out for you.'

'We do our best,' Jason replied. 'Don't we, Sam?'

'Some programs work, and some are a lost cause. But like Jason says, we do our best.'

'The biggest threat to wildlife in this country,' Dave interjected, 'is the swarm of foreigners trying to save them. We used to have fanatical Christian missionaries exploring far-flung climes in search of lost souls. Now we have the new fanatics: the eco-warriors, Gaia's foot soldiers, haunting every rainforest and wetland in search of creatures to be saved, and pointing their fingers at the material man like he was some sort of plague. I think I preferred it when it was just Christ being shoved down our throats. I prefer my religions just plain stupid; at least you can laugh at them.'

'Who the fuck's Gaia?' Pommy John asked.

'The Greek god of the Earth,' Jason replied matter-of-factly. 'A conceptual theory given the status of a deity. You are Gaia, John, and so am I; so is everything we do.'

He didn't appear the slightest bit disturbed by Dave's portrayal of him, and neither did Sam. And while Faraday recognized the stereotype that Dave had in mind, having encountered it with ever-increasing frequency throughout his career (most noticeably among the tedious young students he lectured at college), there was nothing in the speech or demeanour of these two 'eco-warriors' that suggested missionary zeal, or rejection of 'the material man'. To the contrary, they seemed extremely comfortable with materialism.

'Hi tells me you have four restaurants in Hoi An,' Faraday remarked to Jason. 'That must keep you busy. Presumably the wildlife thing is an interest on the side.'

'I'm in property, not restaurants,' Jason replied vaguely, giving the impression of being only partly in the conversation, as if trying to listen to music at the same time—music that no one else could hear. Then, without warning or excusing himself, he wandered off distractedly into the darkness beyond the firelight, just as Faraday was about to ask him how he'd obtained the photographs in the gallery, particularly the one of the Asian unicorn, or saola. It was the subject of a painting that he'd long had in mind, if only he could get close to one.

'Turnbull has a way with the local government that none of us understand,' John said with undisguised sarcasm. 'I've been looking for a place to open a bar for four months, and I can't even get one to lease, but he keeps acquiring property that he doesn't even want. Fuck if I know where he gets his money from, or who he's paying. He refuses to say.'

'Maybe it's not money he pays with,' Sam answered quietly. 'Maybe it's favours.'

'Same thing,' Dave snapped. 'Don't be cute with us, Sam. We know you can't operate without a bagman behind you. Anyway, I'm here to drink the host dry. Who wants another?'

Dave and Pommy John wandered off to the bar for replenishments, and Sam chuckled as if the conversation so far was a repeat of every conversation, though Faraday's assumption that this group knew each other well enough to meet regularly was based solely on the tone of the banter. But that tone may have been common to all expatriates who found themselves living in Vietnam.

'Tell me about your work with elephants,' Faraday asked. 'Dave said something about you counting them. Presumably that means a census?'

'That's exactly what it means, man. We are counting the elephants in the wild. There used to be thousands, and now there are maybe only a hundred—probably less, no one knows. We have a program to track their migration with satellites, because it's important to know where they go, and why, if we're going to increase their numbers.'

'I saw some elephants in Thailand, being used for logging in the forests. Are these the same type?'

'Yes, but elephants are tribal. Herds live in their own areas and follow their own trails. Cambodian and Laotian elephants might meet and mate on the borders, depending on whether males are present in the group. See, only the males have tusks, and most mature male elephants have been slaughtered by poachers, so now there are mostly females surviving, and they get pushed further and further into remote habitats by the encroachment of people. We didn't know how to follow them, but now we got tiny transmitters to send out their location.'

'How do you implant the transmitter?'

Sam paused and peered at Faraday suspiciously. 'You got a special interest in these things, or what?' he demanded.

Faraday shrugged. 'I guess I do,' he conceded. 'Everyone loves elephants.'

'Oh, yeah, ain't that for real!' He smiled, then raised an arm and squinted straight along it, as if aiming a rifle. 'We tranquilize them with an airgun. First, we gotta get close enough, you know. That ain't easy. We work with the hill tribes where possible; they know how to find them. It's rumoured that the biggest concentration of wild elephants is now in Myanmar— Burma! Eighty percent of that country is forest, so it's perfect cover for them. But of course, no one has been able to get in there. We now have three tracked herds in the Central Highlands of Vietnam, and we're about to start tracking on the Chinese border in the Northwest. Man, that is steep country! Without a guide, we got no chance.'

124

'I met a man on the bus from Hue who's a mountain guide from that region. His name is Duc. Said he was coming to meet someone about a job. Was that you?'

' "Duke"? As in Ellington?'

'I don't know. I presumed it was his first name. He spoke good English.'

'If he's a guide from Bac Ha, could well be. What did he say?'

'Nothing, just that he's a mountain guide.'

'We're always looking for those.'

'And who's "we"? Dave said you work for the Paladin Foundation. I didn't know Paladin did that type of thing.'

'You know them?' Sam looked surprised.

'If it's the same outfit: the Paladin Foundation for the Environment?'

'That's the one.'

'Well, just by chance, I do know them. I did a series of paintings for their headquarters in Switzerland. It was quite a few years ago now, but I was always under the impression that they weren't involved in fieldwork. It sounds as though something has changed.'

Sam sipped his drink and didn't reply, but Faraday felt that the easy conversation was no longer easy.

'Listen,' he continued, 'I don't suppose you've ever met a guy named Kenneth Johnston, have you?'

At that moment, the most dreadful noise burst through the loud speakers that had earlier relayed someone's poor karaoke rendition of 'Ten Guitars'. It hit like the grating screech of a cockatoo combined with a fingernail scraping across a blackboard. Faraday flinched in pain and reflexively spun around in search of its origins. Dave and John were doubled up, too, and Dave pointed in mock horror beyond the bar where they were standing towards a small wooden platform on which had been mounted a stand-up microphone, amplifier, and speakers in front of a large flat-screen TV. At the microphone stood the delicate figure of the beautiful girl in the white silk *ao dai*, attempting to sing what might have been a

Vietnamese version of 'Happy Birthday', but in a key that was beyond musical transcription.

'Holy hell, what sort of noise is that?' Faraday exclaimed, but when he turned back to the companion to whom he was complaining, he found that Sam had disappeared into the darkness.

THIRTEEN

'If you are possessed by an idea,' Thomas Mann wrote, 'you find it expressed everywhere'. Because a part of Faraday's life had died when Helene stopped returning to his Kensington home at the end of her long-haul flights, and he couldn't find an explanation for it, he became convinced that disappointment of some sort was always lurking and likely to strike at any time. After eight years of cohabitation, the lack of warning or any explanation from Helene felt closely akin to a death. When the heart aches, perhaps it longs for a funeral. But instead of facing up to his own hurt, he found himself conjuring up predictions of hurt by others, something he chose to blame on his African childhood. Perhaps 'predictions' was overstating it; they weren't even premonitions, just feelings linked irrationally to anything that could present itself as a portent. And the gold wristwatch was one such omen.

When Dave and John's conversation had moved on to local gossip, Faraday took the chance to move away. Beyond the circle of light cast by the bonfire, the lawn leading down from the restaurant to the river was pitch dark, and he strolled across it among the groups of party-goers at a sufficient distance so that he was not obliged to engage with them, but ready to do so if he should spot the two people he'd met earlier. The significance of Sam's abrupt disappearance needed to be tested, and there were question marks hanging over Jason Turnbull and his reason for inviting Faraday to the party. There was no sign of either of them, however, leading Faraday onward to climb the steps of the restaurant itself.

As he paused in the doorway, there was something in the hollow echo of his voice as he called out 'hello' in the empty room, something about the anonymous figures gathered together in groups in the darkness of the lawn, and something about the eerie disappearance of his hosts into that darkness that imparted the qualities of an evil eye to the cockatrice carved in the lintel above his head. Despite the heat, Faraday shivered. For all that it felt melodramatic, he was struck by the sense that a spirit had been let loose that night, ill-willed, demonic, a denizen of darker lights. He was certain that what was disturbing him was the enigmatic telling of a number of deliberate lies, and if the feeling of evil was to be banished from Jason Turnbull's garden, those lies needed to be identified and then confronted.

Returning to the table by the bonfire, he poured himself another glass of wine, helped himself to a prawn dumpling, and waited to insert himself back into Dave and John's conversation, which had regressed into a discussion about the annoying tendency of the local girls to fake an orgasm.

'Any idea what happened to our host?' Faraday interrupted. 'I need to be getting away to Hanoi in the morning, and his boy is supposed to be giving me a ride back.'

'He'll be smoothing out his path with the local hierarchy,' John replied disdainfully. 'It's payday.'

' "Payday"?'

'Whenever there's a party at the Windmill, it means that the paymaster has just called with his magic briefcase,' Dave explained cheerfully. 'It takes money to play these games.'

'What games?'

Dave threw back his head and laughed. 'NGO games! They're the only game in town. Haven't you noticed?'

Faraday shrugged, not really feeling any the wiser. 'I'm just passing through,' he mumbled.

At that moment, he heard a motorbike starting, and he looked over to where Hi had dropped him off to see the dim figure of the young man now signalling for Faraday to join him. He said a perfunctory goodbye, asking that they extend his thanks and apologies to the host, then made his way across the lawn to ride back through the hot, dark countryside and bang on the locked doors of his hotel.

* * * *

'How old are you, Hi?'

'Twenty years.'

'Do you think you'll own a restaurant one day?'

'No, sir, I have no money. Everything must go to family.'

'Why?'

'It is my duty to support my mother and my brother.'

'What about your father?'

'They took away his land, and then they took him away also, so I must take his place.'

'When did this happen?'

'Since I am nine.'

'Keep the six-dollar deposit for the cooking class,' Faraday said, 'and keep this ten dollars as well.'

It didn't pay to be on the losing side in Vietnam, he thought, but maybe the concepts of *nghia* and *on* that Caroline had explained to him when discussing filial obligations would have been some consolation to the boy. By all accounts, there were millions of young people in Vietnam who had suffered the accident of having parents on the wrong side in the war, and yet, on the surface, Vietnamese society seemed so benign.

* * * *

The following morning, he hired a limousine to take him to Danang International Airport for his flight to Hanoi, the primary purpose now being his anticipated meeting with Caroline, pushing the search for the source of the counterfeit painting temporarily into the background. He never had figured out why the management of the Vinh Hung One hotel had told Jason Turnbull that he was 'very important'. They had a copy of his passport, as well as access to his room, and he had no doubt that the instinct to enquire about strangers was still strong in a communist country. A quick Google search would have identified him as a painter of wildlife. Turnbull had an interest in the same subject, and as the owner of four restaurants in a small town, perhaps he was someone who was kept informed about people passing through. But when they'd met, he'd shown no particular interest in Faraday or his work, so why had he bothered to invite him?

Maybe they'd just confused him with the real Mr Anthony. Maybe in Vietnam, Mr Anthony was a name with connotations that only people who were not what they seemed could understand. Or maybe it was the work of the impatient muse who seemed to be gathering up clues and dumping them at his feet, crying out, 'There you are! Now for God's sake, get on with it!' This same muse had apparently driven him so purposefully to Vietnam on short notice without a clear agenda, and even at that stage, she seemed determined that he should find evidence of the presence of Kenneth Johnston.

But a Google search would also have linked him to Paladin, an organization that didn't have field agents or public programs, supposedly pursuing its ecological objectives through the influence of a well-connected financial and political network. So, what the hell was it doing tracking elephants, and who was the so-called 'bagman' supplying the money?

FOURTEEN

Even while competing with the shrill noise of Hanoi Airport's concourse, Caroline's voice over the phone managed to convey strain and anxiety.

'Oh! Hi! I was expecting someone else, but it's *you*. Good! Things have been so hectic! We said we were going to meet up, right? I've forgotten, did we say when? Look, there's been a major disaster. Some sort of disease has broken out in the Highlands, and the government is slaughtering all the poultry there. Obviously, the duck farm idea is off the agenda. Violet Dunleavy arrives in the morning, and we were due to go up to Sapa together and visit the village, but I don't know what's going to happen now. Everything's up in the air. Where are you?'

'I've just arrived at Hanoi Airport, and I'm about to get a taxi and look for a hotel.'

'Come and stay at the hotel I've booked for Violet. It's small but it's clean, the rooms have their own shower and air conditioning, and it's in a great part of town. I'm sure they'd have a room for you. Do you want me to ask?'

Yes, he thought that sounded like a good idea, he replied, realizing as he did so that he was deliberately making his response sound offhand, which was revealing in itself. By the time she rang back and confirmed the hotel's availability and address, however, he was able to act more natural.

'I'm sorry about your developments,' he sympathized. 'Maybe it just

131

means a delay. I can't imagine the Vietnamese eliminating poultry from their diet for too long. Once the outbreak is contained, they'll be able to start again, surely.'

Her voice brightened. 'I like your attitude,' she said breezily. 'When you get here, we'll go out for dinner. I'm starving!'

The hotel was in the Old Quarter, where the streets were narrow and in places impassable. The taxi he caught from the airport had absolutely no regard for people or motorcycles, beeping its horn every second of the way, which did nothing for Faraday's nerves. And the street where he was dropped off was not the street where the hotel was located, because that street—as best he could understand—had a one-way entrance that would have involved another long and painful journey.

'One hundred meters!' the driver shouted, pointing to the opposite side of the road before driving off.

The noise of the traffic was relentless and impatient, the overwhelming clamour of a thousand motorcycle horns. Yet above that noise, shriller and more insistent, was a mounting chorus of urgent, high-pitched cries.

'Sir! *Sir! SIR!*'

The cries grew ever louder and more alarming in their desperation, directed at Faraday. They came from youths on motor scooters, driving towards him down the footpath. They came from men on huge tin tricycles, trying to mount the curb to reach him. And they came from a man with one eye who suddenly got hold of his shirt sleeve and seemed willing to stand on Faraday's feet to stop him from moving.

Saigon had already prepared him for this; it was in the guidebooks, and forewarned was forearmed. Shaking himself free, he picked up his pace.

'No!' he shouted to all of them. 'No, thank you, I want to walk. Okay? I walk!'

The din grew louder. A man with no legs tried to join in, shuffling backwards while dragging a begging bowl with one hand and screaming something that sounded like *'Mummee!'* in a frightening falsetto. Faraday's

132

own legs grew longer as he strode determinedly to the nearest corner. In those same guidebooks, he'd read that the remarkable thing about crossing the street in Vietnam was how infrequently people were killed, all things considered. That was something he tried not to think about as he stood on the corner, working up the courage to cross. Looking straight ahead like a blind man, he dived in, his camera satchel and travel bag clutched so tightly to his side that they were bruising his flesh.

By the time he reached the other side, rivulets of sweat were running down his temples. This was not the condition in which he wished to meet Caroline, so he slowed down and sought out a shop with air conditioning that could lower his temperature, spotting a flower shop with sliding glass doors and the welcoming sign of heavy condensation on the inside of the windows. Pink, blue, and white hydrangeas, pyramids of scarlet, orange, and yellow roses, sunflowers, and carnations greeted him, and the air was heavy with the scent of gardenias. Feeling a little light-headed (from the relief of crossing the street safely, perhaps), he found himself susceptible to the idea of purchasing a small bouquet. Perhaps it was just because he had taken the liberty of using someone's shop solely for the purpose of cooling himself down. It was the least he could do; besides, they would brighten up his hotel room.

After selecting a bunch of pink and white carnations, he wandered towards the back of the shop, where he could hear voices. Rounding a heavily laden kumquat tree, he came upon two women talking animatedly at a long wooden counter. The woman on the serving side of the counter was dressed traditionally, laughing so deeply at the story being told by the woman on the customer side that her eyes were closed, and it took her a moment to notice Faraday's presence and acknowledge him.

'*Xin chào?*'

'Just these carnations, please.'

The woman with her back to him turned around, smiling. 'Are those for me?'

'Caroline! I was just on my way to the hotel.'

'This *is* the hotel. Isn't it great? I wish every hotel lobby could be so pretty! And you didn't answer: are those flowers for me, or someone else?'

'For you, of course. But unfortunately they're no longer a surprise.'

'Oh, yes they are!'

She stepped forward and kissed him on both cheeks.

* * * *

Just as she'd promised, the room had its own shower and air conditioning, and the scent of the flower shop wafted up the stairs behind him. Caroline's and Violet's rooms were on the first level, and he was two floors above them, with windows looking out across tiled roofs reminiscent of the 5th and 6th arrondissements of Paris.

His enthusiasm for the evening ahead had fallen with every step that he'd taken climbing up to his room. Her lightness had not lifted his mood; it had merely emphasized his own heaviness. Who and what was she? He only knew what could be easily seen: the hair, the hands, the eyes and mouth. But of the person, he knew nothing. It was absurd to think that on the basis of one unplanned lunch together and two or three casual phone calls, he should now be checking into the same hotel as her just seven days later. Even though the suggestion had been hers, he should have insisted on making his own plans. The last thing he wanted was for her to think he was pursuing her. Perhaps, he thought, it would be better if he cried off dinner and went and explored the galleries on his own. But he'd already agreed to it, so he felt he had no choice.

* * * *

The restaurant was in the front courtyard of a house in the Old Quarter, two streets away from their hotel. She knew the area well, she said, having

134

lived there when she first arrived from New York. It was always busy, always presenting new things to charm her: smells, colours, flavours, and sounds that were quintessentially Vietnamese, which was to say, experiences richly layered with a thousand years of history and culture, some French, some Chinese. She walked the street confidently, well at home, unaware of Faraday's mixed feelings, which he had no option but to very quickly put aside. Curiously, not one single cyclo driver or beggar came near them as they walked.

'I told you I was starving!' she proclaimed, leading the way and taking control. He didn't mind that aspect of her in the slightest—and neither did the restaurant staff. She'd been there before.

'We want that table by the little fountain. The water absorbs the humidity and calms the senses. When were you born? I'm a Pisces—a water sign. Be warned, we water signs are intuitive and intense! We run deep, like a river. What are you?'

'No idea. Taurus, I believe, whatever that is.'

'You're an earth sign! Of course you are. Taurus never quits. Solid as a rock, but ruled by Venus, and loves his food and wine, so you're going to love this place. Let me order.'

Which she did.

'Taurus likes to be spoiled, and Pisces is controlling; it's a perfect match. This way, I get to order the fresh seafood hotpot, which is to die for and needs two ravenous people to do it justice. You *are* ravenous, aren't you?'

'Hell, yeah!'

But Taurus, the fixed earth sign, he seemed to recall, loves to wait; it never rushes in.

'So, tell me about this flu outbreak. How bad is it?' he asked.

'As bad as it gets. Triple bad! A calamity—and just as we are about to get started. The worst part is that I haven't been able to warn Violet; she's somewhere in the air. I feel like I'm dragging her all the way to Vietnam for nothing.'

It seemed that influenza outbreaks were not new to the Highlands, but there were vaccination programs and regular monitoring of markets, which were supposed to keep it under control.

'According to Uncle, the authorities get heavy and order flocks to be culled, in order to shake up the local farmers and teach them a lesson about vaccinating their birds. It's just our luck that this has happened in Lao Cai, just as he was arranging to purchase a flock for his cousin's village. Now everything is on hold.'

'Well, like I said, I can't imagine Vietnam without poultry, so it will only be temporary. It will happen in time.'

She laughed. 'Thank God for Taurus! "Be patient and hang in there, Caroline. A little less of the emotion, please." '

She was laughing at herself, not at him.

'And there's no reason why it should hold up your well-digging program, is there?' he persisted.

Without replying, she reached into her shoulder bag and took out a pair of reading glasses, slipped them on, and leaned forward, peering at him closely, studying his face. Apparently satisfied, she removed the glasses and sat back smiling, just as the seafood hotpot arrived in a ceramic urn that was placed on a gel flame burner between them.

'Whole crab, baby octopus, clams, and white fish fillets,' she recited, 'with vermicelli and egg noodles, poached in a fish sauce broth enlivened with shrimp paste, chilies, chives, and watercress. Have you ever smelled anything like that in your life?'

'You sound like you've spent too much time with that bloody French boyfriend of yours. That's how he speaks.'

'He's not my boyfriend—and I don't much like him either, as it happens. But Vietnamese food brings out this thing in me. Now, I've just had a thought: how about coming up to Sapa with Violet and me on the weekend? You can be our Taurus rock sign...'

'Earth sign.'

'... Taurus earth sign, that helps us keep our feet on solid ground. Though I'm a modern girl and wouldn't like you to think I'm admitting to any weakness, it could be kind of useful having a man around.'

' "Useful"?'

'Well, you know what I mean. Besides, Sapa's got galleries for the well-heeled. You might find what you're looking for.'

FIFTEEN

The reason he came to Hanoi, of course, was to trace the source of the counterfeit painting. If it was not to be found in Ho Chi Minh City/Saigon, or along the Hoi An-Hue tourist trail, then inevitably, it must have been purchased in Hanoi. That was pretty much what Caroline confirmed after dinner as they returned to the hotel and climbed the stairs to their respective rooms. And if he struck out in Hanoi, then Sapa would be his only remaining chance.

'You'll find some pretty swanky galleries on Pho Trang Tien, at the southern end of Hoan Kiem Lake, towards the Hanoi Opera House. That's where I'd start. It's a bit of a walk, but not too far, and there's plenty to see on the way. I'd come with you, but I'm picking Violet up from the airport, and then I've arranged a car to take us to Bac Ninh to meet with Uncle. I don't know what will happen from there, but I guess things will be clearer by tomorrow night. Hey, I really enjoyed our talk! Thank you for telling me about yourself. And think seriously about coming up to Sapa with us, won't you? Maybe we can catch up sometime tomorrow night.'

What talk was that, he wondered as he returned to his room—or more specifically, which part of their talk had she enjoyed? Had he really told her about himself? He'd talked about painting and the type of lifestyle that involved, but he wasn't aware of telling her about *himself*—certainly not to the degree that she'd told him about *herself*. When people said how much they'd enjoyed talking, they usually meant how much they'd enjoyed talking about themselves. He certainly hoped he hadn't been guilty of that.

He'd mentioned his shock—outrage, even—at discovering how entrenched the self-appointed charity organizations were in this part of Asia. They were everywhere, un-mandated except by their assumed moral right.

'I guess my simple view of the world is that it operates on two levels: the political and the economic,' he'd told her. 'But what I've come to realize is that there's a whole new other environment that floats amorphously above, between, and around these levels, somehow free and detached from normal rules. What's the appropriate term? Pan-national? Supra-national? Who do they answer to? Maybe I've been locked away in my own little private world for too long. Don't take this as a personal criticism of what you are doing, of course; I think it's very worthy…'

'… "Worthy"…?'

'Worthwhile! Worthwhile and practical! What's top of the list in survival needs? It's clean drinking water; there's no argument. But unless I'm mistaken, this Violet woman is not running a stateless global organization staffed with money launderers and soldiers of fortune who pass brazenly through sovereign borders, flashing the equivalent of a Mickey Mouse badge as their sole form of identity, chanting, "Save the animals from extinction!" or "Save the children from paedophiles!" or "Save unemployed girls in poor, rural villages from being offered money by fat German men in return for playing with their willies!" '

'Anton!'

'Do you think I'm exaggerating? Believe me, this NGO thing is the main game in Asia. But back in the world I come from, no one is talking about it. I feel like I've been living in a cave. That's what it's like, being an artist. As Ralph Waldo Emerson said, "To wade in marshes and sea-margins is the destiny of certain birds, and they are so accurately made for this, that they are imprisoned in those places." Trapped at my easel all day, I no longer feed my mind with new information or experiences. Maybe somewhere along the way, I've ceased to listen. News and current events have become a seamless babble, instantly forgotten. It's quite clear to me that I have no idea what's going on outside the sanctuary of my home and studio.'

Caroline leaned across the table and patted his hand consolingly, putting on a mother's voice filled with soothing sympathy. 'There, there, Anton; everything will be alright. The world can be such a confusing place at times, but Mummy will look after you.'

He remembered thinking, as she slowly withdrew her hand, that her touch felt nothing but completely natural. Why should that be?

'Alright.' He shrugged. 'I'm out of touch. I need to get out more. So, here I am: I'm *out*! Now what would you like to know?'

'Tell me about your work. What's the subject of your latest painting?'

'The weaver bird. It's unfinished.'

The last occasion on which he'd worked on it had been the morning that Christie's came calling. As usual, he'd been up early, painting in his studio at first light. On his easel, a South African weaver bird had been hovering before its nest for a number of weeks now. The male of the species, it was caught in the act of using saliva to cement the fine foliage it had collected in order to make its distinctive round nest, which hung precariously from the branch of a thorn tree and was designed to attract a mate. If the male bird didn't get it right, he wouldn't be mating that year, for the female weaver bird was pretty fussy and would give it a thorough inspection before agreeing to move in, hence the frantic air to his gyrations.

'I'd started the painting in April, when the sun above London was weaker and my colours deliberately brighter. Gradually, the days lengthened, and my palate had become more subdued. I was used to this, of course, having worked in the light of my second-floor studio window for so many years. Really, I was only fiddling with the thing, fluffing about, not quite ready to finish it. There was the inconsistency in the palette I'd used, which only I was able to see, but more than that, I didn't feel fully comfortable with my handling of it. Starting out, I had written in the margin:

The sun vaults over shortening shadows, and the veldt bristles with corn. Flat green strips of cabbage palm are weaved and spittled, Stripped and torn as the weaver builds his nest.

'That's one of my signature elements, you see: giving it a pseudo-poetic twist to imply that it's more than just another bloody animal painting. I'm stuck with it now; if it doesn't contain some piece of doggerel, people don't believe it's a Faraday painting. Anyway, since writing that, I had then learned that, once mated, the male leaves the nest and goes off to build another. The whole process takes place again and again, on and on, right through spring and summer, until the weaver is worn ragged and his last nest is finally rejected—whereupon he dies. That's what I should have written about.'

'You're kidding! How tragic!'

'I kid you not. So much for polygamy, I say! Somehow, I doubted my ability to capture the irony of the situation in one frozen fragment of time, hence my half-hearted daubing. Luckily, I was saved by the doorbell and the man from Christie's. Which, as you know, is the reason I'm here now, and why the weaver bird sits unfinished on my easel in London.'

Tapping his chopsticks on the side of his soup bowl, he looked about for the glass of wine they'd forgotten to order.

'Nature really can be cruel,' she said with mock seriousness.

'It's simply a metaphor for how women treat men.'

'Ah, so you're a chauvinist!' she announced triumphantly.

Perhaps that was what she'd meant when she thanked him later for telling her about himself.

So now, here he was the following morning, outside the Foreign Language Bookshop on Trang Tien, for the first time with a feeling of certainty that he was about to unravel the mystery of how a copy of a painting that was hanging in the Geneva office of the chairman of Anglo Swiss BioLab had come to be offered for sale in London. It might not be the first gallery that bore fruit, or even the second or third, but the sense of inevitability was so strong that he took it for granted that the course he'd followed to get here was somehow predetermined, as if a trail had deliberately been laid out for him to follow.

In fact, it was the fourth gallery, a white-walled space with a sleek entrance that could just as easily have been found in Manhattan or Mayfair, were it not for the strange juxtaposition of styles on display. It was the familiarity of those styles, rather than any recognition of the subject matter of the paintings, that alerted him. If that wasn't an Andrew Wyeth, he thought, it was near-as-dammit, and very well executed—and Hockney may not have painted that particular California swimming pool, but if he had done, that's exactly how he would have done it. Unlike in Manhattan or Mayfair, however, there were no accompanying descriptions or prices, and the paintings appeared for the most part unsigned.

A decent period passed in which he was undisturbed by gallery staff, allowing him to fully inspect the thirty or so paintings on display. While eclectic in style and derivation, they were each, in their own way, commercially appealing: appealing subjects of an appealing size, competently rendered and reassuringly familiar. His own work, he instantly realized, would not have looked out of place there. Perhaps that was what suddenly gave him confidence, for the first time since he'd arrived in Vietnam, that it was not such a wild goose chase after all.

If the period permitted him to inspect the works undisturbed showed an understanding of art gallery protocol on the part of the owner, so did Faraday's unmistakable clearing of the throat once he was ready to be served. A door opened, and a woman in a black skirt and white blouse entered silently. She was Eurasian, a little too tall to be Vietnamese, forty or forty-five-ish, with a European hairstyle and a cool but pleasant smile. He had no doubt that her English would be perfect before she even opened her mouth.

'Is that an Andrew Wyeth?' Faraday asked. 'There's no information.'

'It looks like a Wyeth,' she answered, walking towards it as if the suggestion were a novel one.

'Only it isn't signed,' Faraday pointed out. 'No signature at all.'

She paused to consider that observation, then appeared to have a thought. 'Would you like it to be signed?'

He wasn't quite sure how to answer that, so he took another tack. 'Is it original?'

'Oh, yes, all of our works come with a certificate of origin from the artist.'

'But the artist is not Andrew Wyeth.'

She walked over to the painting and touched the edge of it lightly to confirm that they were speaking of the same thing.

'This painting is the work of a well-known Vietnamese artist who specializes in Realism. If you would like to meet with him, the gallery can arrange that. The price of this painting is six thousand dollars US. We have other examples of his work we can show you as well.'

'Thank you.'

'And you can discuss the question of a signature with him directly.'

He hesitated. What sort of question was going to lead him to the information he sought: a direct question, or an oblique one? He suspected it would not be a string of questions focused on the authenticity—or otherwise—of unsigned works.

'I'm particularly interested in paintings of animals,' he volunteered. 'Wild animals such as tigers, rhinos, and elephants—even panda bears. Do you have anything like that?'

'We have no such works in our current show, as you can see, but we do have artists on our books that may be capable of producing what you have in mind. Are you only interested in original paintings? Because we have a fine selection of limited-edition lithographs as well, including a small number by a well-known *Tieng Anh* artist. Is that something that might be of interest to you?'

'*Tieng Anh* is what…?'

'I am sorry; that is "English".'

'Oh! Yes, I'd be interested in having a look at those. Would that be an easy thing to do?'

'Of course; it would be my pleasure. Please come to our stock room, Mr...?'

'Anthony. Mr Anthony, from London.'

* * * *

Coming out of the gallery twenty minutes later, he'd turned away from the lake in the direction of the opera house, which he'd seen signposted, and which Madame Roulet confirmed was visible at the end of the street. MADAME ROULET, DIRECTRICE: that was the name on the card she gave him, and her manner and style were unmistakably French, whether natural or adopted.

His intention was to show her that he was out strolling, rather than allow the impression that he'd come to the gallery on a mission. It hadn't been necessary for him to ask direct questions, for he had already learned more than he could have anticipated, and he felt certain there was even more to come. So, he let her watch him stroll in the direction of the opera house, as any tourist from London naturally would, and he liked to think that the look in her eyes reflected her belief that he was a genuine prospective buyer. 'A bientôt!' they'd both said.

'Yes, indeed.'

London was seven hours behind Hanoi. He would have to wait five hours before he could catch Ralph at work, and the waiting would prove difficult. What was he to do? Walk the streets in this heat? Return to the hotel? That option did at least boast the attraction of air conditioning, and he started to do just that. But within two blocks, he realized that his little room up three flights of stairs was not where he wanted to spend half a day twisting and turning unanswered questions over in his mind.

If he had missed it before, it was now overwhelmingly clear that he was in the French District, and soon he found himself standing outside the Metropole Hotel, realizing that a long lunch in a comfortable, air-conditioned restaurant was a more preferable way of killing time than sweating on the pavements of Hanoi. The hotel concierge offered him a choice: French, Italian, or Vietnamese. He chose French, of course, and didn't regret it. Meals were markers; this one would mark the first meaningful comfort stop on his journey of discovery. For the first time since he'd set out impetuously in search of an answer to an undefined but unrelenting question, he could reflect on evidence that was sufficiently clear and mundane enough that he could stop doubting his suspicions. Now, at last, he had some facts.

* * * *

'Ah, Ralph! How is the weather in London? I felt I had to phone you. I've just enjoyed the most magnificent lunch at Le Beaulieu Restaurant in the grandest *fin de siècle* hotel you have ever seen: fresh langoustines in a light salmon roe broth, accompanied by a fennel and dill salad and a glass of your very favourite Muscadet. In Hanoi, would you believe? And if that wasn't impressive enough, a duck *à l'orange* that I'd swear had been poached in those blood oranges you can only buy in Seville. Amazing, quite amazing!'

'Dear boy, are you seriously calling me at nine a.m. to try and make me believe you've had some sort of culinary epiphany—or have you just had too much to drink?'

'Not too much, Ralph; just enough. It was you who taught me to always drink better than I could afford, remember? That way, we never drink too much. No, Ralph, I'm ringing to tell you that it is absolutely true what they say: the world is a very small place. A butterfly flaps its wings in the Amazon jungle, and a jet plane disappears from the face of the earth over the Indian Ocean. A naïve young painter and his trusted mentor sell a limited number of signed and numbered lithographs to a plausible rogue in Geneva under the watchful eye of a trusted firm of auditors, and the capsule of trust that holds that transaction together leaks unexpectedly in a distant land many years later … a land in which the naïve young painter—no longer young—happens to be wandering.'

'Anton! What on earth are you talking about?'

'I have just found a collection of the Paladin lithographs for sale at a local gallery. Three thousand US dollars per sheet, seven out of the twelve subjects remaining from a set numbered one hundred and twenty out of one hundred and twenty. Imagine my surprise.'

'I imagine it is just as great as mine, dear boy! How on earth did they get hold of them?'

'They are being sold on behalf of "a collector". Apparently, the artist is very well known, and this series is extremely rare, never having been offered for sale publicly before. His name is A J Faraday. Sound familiar? They offered to look him up on the internet for me, but luckily I was able to dissuade them from doing so, as of course, the first thing they would have noticed was that the photograph of the artist bore a striking resemblance to me. I say "they", but I actually mean "she": Madame Roulet, *la directrice* of said gallery—very cool, very French, and very flexible on matters of authenticity and provenance, is my belief. You'd be impressed by her.'

'Anton, could you please not play games with me! Did you tell them you were the artist?'

'Good God, no! I'm just a tourist with time and money to spare.'

'Did they give any hint as to who the person is that's selling them?'

'None at all. But when I asked what the price would be for an original version, rather than a print, she said she would have to enquire of the artist. It seems that the word "original" has a different meaning here. What she meant was that she would have to ask how much it would cost for one of the prints to be copied as an "original" painting. So naturally, I asked her to do that.'

'And…?'

'She said that might take a day or two. I'll be going back. But here's the thing, Ralph: these lithographs are the genuine article; they're not from a new set of plates. And that can only mean one of two things: either they are the overruns that you and I discussed the other day, or one of the Names has chosen to sell them. The benefit of a long lunch taken alone is that it gives you time to think. If these are overruns, then the source can only be Lutyen's Gallery, or...'

'Don't even think it!' Ralph shouted. 'That is the most insulting suggestion I have ever heard! Anton, I am furious that you would even allow such a possibility. What sort of person do you think I am that I would stoop to selling a few pitiful prints to a fucking gallery in Vietnam, of all places? Apologize now, or I am going to put down the phone!'

Well, Faraday thought, that had certainly touched a nerve. Ralph did indignation better than anyone he knew. '... Or—as I was about to say, Ralph, if you'll let me finish—*or* the source could be the erstwhile Mr Kenneth Johnston, whose whereabouts are something of a mystery, but whose ethics, by your own admission, would have equipped him perfectly for a little dealing on the side, and whom I think, if you put your mind to it, you could imagine might have found himself with an overrun or two— unbeknownst to you, of course, but not inconceivable.'

'We don't even know that Johnston is still alive!' Ralph protested.

'Oh, he's alive, alright. I'm sure of it. My Bushman's instinct tells me that I have stepped on his footprints, and he's somewhere nearby. I can't tell you how I know; you'll have to take my word for it.'

'Well, if Johnston did manage to divert some overruns for private gain, it is extremely disappointing—although, as you say, he was a little loose in his dealings. That said, I wouldn't want you to be too hasty in reaching a conclusion. You said that the prints were numbered one hundred and twenty out of one hundred and twenty. That's how many sets were produced.'

'Exactly, Ralph! So, the question is whether this is the genuine one-hundred-and-twentieth set, or whether it has just been given that number by someone who knew how many sets were ordered in the first place.'

'There's no way of knowing.'

'That's not necessarily true.'

A thought had occurred to Faraday once before, when he was speaking to Ralph after arriving in Hoi An. It had been on the tip of his tongue to ask about it, but he'd let it slip because, at the time, it had little relevance to his main concern: the search for the origin of the counterfeit panda. It came up when Ralph was explaining the auditor's role in the printing and distribution of the Paladin lithographic portfolios. The only copies in existence, he had explained, would be those that were hand delivered by Security Express to Johnston's list of Names, and the printing plates were then destroyed. Someone else in addition to Johnston, he now realized, must have had that distribution list.

'I appreciate that it was a few years ago now, Ralph, but I want you to explain to me how the distribution of those printed portfolios worked. There was Johnston, who provided the list of Names and their addresses; there were the auditors, who oversaw the printing and supplied the certificate authenticating the destruction of the plates; and there was Security Express, who then carried out the registered deliveries. At least, I presume they were registered; I can't imagine items of that value being sent any other way. My question is this: what happened to the distribution list? Who was responsible for filling out those one hundred and twenty individual consignment notes? I simply cannot imagine our friend Kenneth rolling up his sleeves to do such a job, so who was it? Was it the auditors? A customer relations manager at Security Express? Or someone else entrusted with the job, who may also have had a list of the folio numbers assigned to each recipient, and who had a role in overseeing the whole process, someone like…'

'… Like…?'

'Well … like you, Ralph.'

148

SIXTEEN

Ralph Lutyen.

The Jewish son of a picture restorer father from Highgate and a hosiery buyer mother at Selfridges, Ralph had West End tastes and ambitions almost from birth—ambitions he had been determined to indulge, no matter what the cost. From their one or two brief meetings at gallery functions in the early days, Faraday deduced that it was his mother who had been the greater influence, proudly displaying that maternal willingness some women have with their only son to spoil him and overestimate his abilities for all to see. Ralph could do no wrong in her eyes, and that made Ralph positively shimmer. Whenever she died, the light from that shimmer was sure to dim somewhat. Ralph's father, on the other hand, could probably have been credited with having quietly instilled in him an insider's awareness of the techniques, pitfalls, and rewards of the art trade, and whether subliminally or by direct instruction, he had made an excellent job of it.

Establishing a gallery in the West End was not for the faint-hearted; even Faraday, who had no exposure to business, understood that. The remorseless demands of the inexorably rising Mayfair rents, the staff salaries, the lavish catalogues and equally lavish advertising, the entertaining, and the burgundy Rolls Royce with the LUTYEN vanity plate parked at the front door created an equally remorseless need to keep generating money. Did the circumstances create the type, or did the type create the circumstances? Whichever it was, one thing was clear: Ralph had a pecuniary fixation. That was what defined him—that, and his homosexuality. While the latter had never presented as a problem in their relationship, it had made Faraday aware that Ralph's interest in mentoring him in the early days may have been prompted as much by his being a strapping young man as his being a relatively talented painter. There was, however, an undertone of fondness in their relationship that wasn't solely due to the passing of time.

These thoughts—feelings, really—occupied Faraday as he sat at a pavement table outside the Metropole Hotel at dusk following his long lunch. He'd not finished the duck *à l'orange*, but had gone on to order a *mousse aux chocolat*, which definitely proved a step too far, and the glass of Muscadet that he'd admitted to Ralph had rather too easily turned into a full bottle. All of this necessitated a gentle stroll around the hotel gardens and pool before he spotted the very Parisian kerbside tables of *La Terrasse*, which lured him into sitting down again and engaging in a little people-watching while sipping on a stomach-settling Pernod Ricard. Sometimes it took a drink or two to liberate the imagination, and imagination was required to unravel the information he'd gained at the gallery.

He accepted Ralph's right to be indignant at the suggestion that he might have stooped to selling 'a few pitiful prints to a fucking gallery in Vietnam, of all places.' After all, if he'd wanted to engage in that sort of thing, Lutyen's Gallery in London had a far better list of private collectors at its disposal than 'a fucking gallery in Vietnam'. So why were they being offered for sale here in Hanoi, of all places? It had to be that the vendor considered Vietnam sufficiently isolated from the international art world and was not keen to offer them in a mainstream centre where they would attract attention. The number and quality of galleries that he had seen on Trang Tien that morning, let alone the prices, were convincing evidence that New World and Asian money was circulating there. But perhaps the vendor's choice of a Hanoi gallery to dispose of the collection of lithographs was driven by something far more prosaic. Perhaps it was convenient for the vendor as a frequent visitor to Hanoi—or even as a resident. That definitely ruled out Ralph. But it didn't rule out the possibility that the source of portfolio number one hundred and twenty was one of the Names.

It was amazing how Pernod cleared the mind and stimulated the imagination. He decided to order another one and call Ralph again.

* * * *

It was a funny thing, the mind. It put things away untouched until it was ready to deal with them—things that could seem so obvious when the time finally came. Why was that? Ralph had sworn that the only people who would have a copy of the distribution list for the hundred and twenty portfolios, apart from Johnston, were the auditors, though he didn't fancy the chances of them still having it after so long. In fact, he wasn't sure that they hadn't been told to destroy it once their audit was complete. Johnston, it seemed, was very ticklish about the identity of the Paladin Foundation benefactors, and the possibility of their privacy being disturbed. Nevertheless, Ralph would make the enquiry of Moores and Styles, he said, if that was what Anton desired.

'Only, no promises, dear boy.'

The first Pernod had cleared a space in Faraday's mind and planted the belief that Ralph would have somehow found a way to obtain a copy of that list, if for no other reason than it represented a database of extraordinarily rich and powerful people. After all, Ralph's success was based on the quality of his client (and potential client) mailing lists. The thought of him passing up that opportunity was as unlikely as expecting a hungry dog to pass up a meaty bone.

It was the second Pernod, however, that really illuminated his thinking. Ralph had a pecuniary fixation; any consideration of the man had to acknowledge that first and foremost. But so did Kenneth Johnston. Put the two of them together, and they would have a natural affinity.

It was with this thought in mind that he called Ralph for a second time, hoping he hadn't left the office for an early lunch.

'Anton?'

'As I finished each of the twelve paintings in the Harbinger Collection, you received payment for them, right?'

'Of course.'

'So, who did you invoice: Johnston, the Paladin Foundation, or the individual benefactor?'

'I don't recall, exactly. It was a long time ago, Anton.'

'Well, it's quite simple, Ralph: did Johnston say who to make the invoice out to, or did he take it in his own name?"'

'Johnston never paid for anything himself; he was merely the go-between...'

'So, who actually paid for the Harbinger Collection? Who were those invoices made out to: the Foundation, Van Heeren, who...?'

'I have to think... There were two invoices. Johnson always gave a price. Each painting had a sponsor, you see. I was sworn to secrecy; that's the way he liked it. The sponsor saw the first invoice, presumably, but the Foundation only paid our agreed amount on the second invoice, because they were using the paintings as a way of raising funds, of course.'

Faraday's shoulders slumped, and he rubbed his forehead with his free hand. Lunch was finally catching up with him. 'And the amount on that second invoice was what we got. That's right, isn't it, Ralph?' he insisted, keeping his voice deliberately calm.

After all the years of speculation, it was absurd that it had come to this. He felt empty—and Ralph had suddenly gone silent on the other end of the phone.

'How much did Johnston ask you to add to each invoice for *him*?' He was careful to ask this very gently; it was too late to be angry.

'I'm not sure what you're asking.'

'Yes, you are. How much did you add for Johnston?'

'I've never cheated you, Anton. I hope you're not suggesting that.'

'Not for a moment.'

Faraday thought he could hear Ralph's chair creak. In his mind's eye, he could see his pursed lips, the little signs of agitation that he would attempt to convert into injured pride.

'I had rather hoped that my efforts on your behalf over the years would have been appreciated.'

'They have. How much?'

Ralph's voice grew momentarily remote as Faraday sensed him looking around the room for a way to escape. 'In business, you know, it quite often happens...'

'WHAT? Speak up!'

'... It quite often happens that people ask for a different value invoice for some reason or other ... such as insurance. You know, it isn't always easy to get insurance companies to come to the party when a painting has increased in value, so it helps to anticipate that at the time of sale. It may not be quite ethical, but it's just one of those things a dealer has to consider. The artist isn't compromised in any way, I can assure you of that.'

Ralph paused to listen.

'How much?' Faraday repeated softly.

Ralph's chair creaked again, and he sighed. 'You wouldn't expect someone like Johnston to put so much business your way without getting something in return, would you? I didn't like doing it, but those are the ways of the world.'

And, of course, he'd taken commission on the added sum, Faraday thought. No, he could see that Ralph wouldn't have liked doing that. 'Two thousand? Three thousand? Five...?'

'He's a man who likes to dine at Mirabelle's. Don't tell me you never suspected; you can't be that naive.'

No, nobody could be that naive—not if they were honest with themselves.

Now it was Faraday's turn to sigh. 'I would appreciate it, Ralph, if you could look back and see whether any of the invoices had Foundation member names on them. Not now, but in the next day or so, if you wouldn't mind. And I don't care about the amount you loaded on. White the figures out, if you want. It's the names I'd like to see … for purely sentimental reasons, not that it means anything now. Oh, and better still, that distribution list also: who got which copy of the numbered sets. Perhaps you've got the consignment notes somewhere. I want to know where Madame Roulet got those prints.'

It had all seemed so long ago. Maybe that's why he suddenly felt so tired now … or could it have been the alcohol?

SEVENTEEN

While the architecture and pavement café theme of *La Terrasse* seemed faithfully copied from a Parisian style manual, the sidewalk promenade Faraday studied as he finished his second Pernod was quintessentially Vietnamese. Parisians strolled at twilight in order to see and be seen, their self-identity being their purpose in living. The residents of Hanoi, on the other hand, were scurrying to achieve yet another task in an already busy day, their economic imperatives overriding any urge for self-advertisement. It was interesting to observe, but not particularly appealing, and his mind wandered to Caroline and the arrangements they'd made, if any, for meeting up again. They'd both been vague on the subject, Caroline indicating that she'd be tied up with Violet all day and was unsure of her movements, while for his part, he'd made no suggestions one way or the other. Just what was he expecting—or more importantly, what was he hoping for?

Now that he felt sure that Hanoi was going to yield the answers to his questions about the counterfeit painting, he felt awkward about accepting her suggestion to accompany them to Sapa. Checking out its galleries was no longer a valid excuse, and tagging along on a mission in which he was not involved would leave him feeling like an unexplained appendage. The worst part of that scenario was that the only possible explanation for the appendage was that he was pursuing Caroline romantically, which was absurd. He'd met up with her hoping for nothing more than some pleasant company to relieve the self-absorption that was the downside of traveling alone for any length of time. It was nothing more than that, and he was sure it was nothing more than that for her as well. He'd give her a call tomorrow, and maybe they could meet for coffee or something—and if she was busy with other things, that would be fine. No doubt he would be busy, too.

Standing up to look for a waiter to bring him the bill, he suddenly found himself right in the path of Madame Roulet.

'Monsieur Anthony, *bon soir!*'

'Ah, madame! Yes, indeed, *bon soir.* You've finished work for the day?'

'My assistant runs the gallery in the evening so I can eat with my husband.'

'How nice!' He smiled warmly, and she smiled warmly back. Away from the gallery, her demeanour was distinctly less formal, her accent distinctly less French. She was, he now realized, a good-looking woman: Eurasian— or Amerasian, probably, given her age—with the jet-black hair and olive skin of her Sino heritage, and the broader mouth and rounder eyes of her Caucasian bloodline.

'Do you have time to join me briefly for a drink?' he asked impetuously. 'I'd welcome the company, if it's not going to hold you up.'

Looking at her watch, she hesitated for the obligatory moment expected of a respectable woman, then graciously accepted. He was going to have another Pernod, he said, a drink that he only ever drank when in France.

'Which is where I feel I am in this part of Hanoi. I'm sure everyone says the same thing.'

Yes, she agreed, everyone said the same thing. Since the American War, the government had restored the French Quarter, and it was very good for tourism.

To his delight, she elected to join him in having a Pernod also. 'We can pretend we are in the real France.' She smiled.

They talked a bit about tourism and how the country was changing so fast, about the factories being built, and about the money being invested by foreign companies. He gathered these were all things that she welcomed.

'And you, Mr Anthony: what is the business that brings you to Vietnam?'

He couldn't be certain, but he had the distinct impression that while he was ordering the drinks, she had somehow undone one of the buttons on her white blouse; he hadn't noticed her breasts before, but he was now suddenly—and most agreeably—very conscious of them.

'Wildlife.'

'Wildlife?'

'Yes, I'm involved with a conservation group documenting endangered species.' This, he assured himself, was the unchallengeable truth.

'So, this explains your interest in animal paintings?'

He hesitated, running his fingers through his hair in a way that he had been assured in the past was boyish and engaging, then opted to release himself from the constraints of absolute truth.

'Well, actually, my interest in animal paintings is a private one, not directly connected with my work. I started dealing in art in an amateur sort of way as a hobby, and to make a profit on the side. There isn't a great deal of money to be made working for conservation organizations, and buying and selling art is something I can do in my spare time. Which is why I was visiting your gallery today. The interest in animal subjects is a relatively new focus for me. I believe there could well be a growing demand.'

'Where have you seen this demand?'

'Well, to be honest, I haven't seen it to date. People like David Shepherd and A J Faraday sell well, but in London, and also in New York, the Impressionists and Moderns dominate the art market. But having said that, the originals of those lithographs you showed me today would sell extremely well at auction at Christie's or Sotheby's, for instance, being produced by an established artist. Being prints, however, it's too easy to research them on the internet, so there is little opportunity for someone like me to make a substantial gain from them—but original work not previously seen is another matter altogether.'

As she leaned forward to add more iced water to her Pernod, there was no doubt in Faraday's mind that Madame Roulet had deliberately released a button on her blouse and shed her gallery formality; she wanted to do business.

'So, an original version of one of those Faraday prints would be of interest to you, but not the print itself?'

Her question was so matter-of-fact that he hesitated before answering, not sure whether she'd intended the implication that he heard so clearly, or whether in fact there was none. 'As I see it, an actual original by that artist would be beyond my pocket, and so well catalogued that it would be unlikely to be found at a bargain price.'

'But a work that wasn't catalogued...?' She sat back and crossed her legs, watching him with interest as she delicately sipped on her drink through a straw. He hoped he wasn't misreading her, because he sensed he was close to having the answer he was seeking.

'Like the Andrew Wyeth in your gallery, you mean?'

'For many of our clients, that is a very desirable Wyeth. It is an excellent painting, don't you think?'

'Yes, it's very well executed and ... convincing, I thought.'

'In London or New York, such a Wyeth would be neither affordable nor available, but here in Hanoi, it is both of those things. Isn't that what you are looking for when you say you are interested in paintings of animals, Mr Anthony: affordable and available—something you can sell at a profit?'

He had to laugh. He'd seen it in Trih, his young guide in Chau Doc, who was unashamedly planning his career as a property developer around the strength of his connection with government officials who could be bribed, and who had matter-of-factly explained the profit margins of smuggling to Faraday, a complete stranger, as if he were discussing the price of fruit and vegetables, unhampered by false notions of honesty or petty legalities. If this conversation were taking place on Bond Street or Park Avenue, he would say that the woman sitting opposite him was a crook. But somehow,

158

here in Vietnam, he found something refreshingly honest in what she was saying.

'You're quite right, of course,' he agreed. 'Affordable, available, and *convincing* is what I'm looking for. I think you understand my needs completely.' Smiling, he raised his glass to her. 'But where would I find an original Faraday, for instance, that hadn't been catalogued, and how would I provide it with a provenance credible enough to enable me to on-sell it at a profit? That's the challenge.'

'That may not be as difficult as you think.' Her mouth played with the drinking straw as she sucked down the remains of her drink, searching the ice cubes for any last vestige of flavour while holding Faraday with her eyes, making him wait. Then she set her empty glass down with a finality that signalled it was time for her to go.

'If you come to the gallery tomorrow morning at ten o'clock, Mr Anthony, I will introduce you to someone who may be able to answer those questions for you.'

'Really?'

'What you are asking, he has already done. It is up to you.'

'I'll be there at ten, then.'

As he stood up to acknowledge her departure, he could have sworn that she had somehow managed to do up the button on her blouse again without his noticing.

* * * *

By the time he got back to the hotel, Caroline had gone out to dinner with Violet Dunleavy, leaving a note under his door to say she would speak to him in the morning, but was counting on him accompanying them to Sapa the following night. He'd deal with that tomorrow, he thought, by explaining that his personal affairs were coming to a head, and he could no longer afford to leave Hanoi.

He was relieved and glad to be left alone with his thoughts. He was also, he realized, mildly drunk—although the light-headedness may have been partly due to the relief he felt, having finally arrived at the destination that had brought him impetuously on this journey. In the morning, he felt certain, the mystery of the forged painting would at last be solved.

He got up early, had breakfast beside the lake, and arrived at Madame Roulet's gallery at ten o'clock, as arranged. If, as he believed, he was about to meet the forger, he wondered whether he would become angry. To come face to face with someone who had stolen his identity and artistic creation was new territory for him. However, to his surprise and discomfort, as the moment approached, it was not anger he felt, but self-consciousness. Having someone flawlessly follow his every brush stroke was akin to listening to someone impersonating him. Worse still was the realization that in order to construct an accurate copy, the forger was required to deconstruct the original—a process that would inevitably expose its banality. Only another painter could know the truth: that every picture came down to no more than an assembly of pigments. That's why he felt exposed.

But as Ralph had already pointed out, attracting the attention of a forger was really the ultimate form of flattery. Besides, copying in Vietnam was just an admission that the counterfeit artist had no confidence yet in their own style and subject matter, but when it came to technical competence, they appeared to be utterly professional.

He'd travelled a long way to arrive at this moment, and from the description Madame Roulet had given the evening before of an original Faraday, uncatalogued, he was certain that she could only have meant his painting of Nu Nu. If she had been referring to any other painting or print by A J Faraday, it would have been catalogued and identifiable as a copy. The panda was his only subject that had never been reproduced. Though presumably, following the example of the Wyeth, she may have been referring to a Faraday lookalike rather than a direct copy of something he'd already painted.

160

As it turned out, in the event, the man himself turned out to be perfectly likable—as were most Vietnamese, in his experience—and Faraday felt no resentment towards him whatsoever. He was much older than Faraday had expected. All the painters he'd seen in the galleries and arcades to date had been young. It didn't just apply to painters; a generation had been sliced out of the population of Vietnamese males, seemingly removing all those who had been of fighting age in the sixties and seventies. This man, well into his sixties, had somehow managed to avoid the slice. He smiled a lot, but he didn't speak; Madame Roulet did the speaking. Hien was his name, a much-admired painter in his own right, she said. In fact, he was the only person she trusted with truly important assignments, such as the one she had mentioned the previous evening—the one which, by coincidence, featured the famous painter of wildlife whose work he was interested in buying. She couldn't show him the actual painting that Hien had produced, but she could show him a photograph … which she did.

It was not a photograph of the counterfeit painting at all, but a photograph of the original, hanging in the office of Anglo Swiss BioLab in Geneva. He knew that immediately, because the counterfeit copy had a mistake in the spelling; this one was exactly as he'd written it.

'*Voila!*' she proclaimed.

'Ah, a panda!' he announced innocently. 'Very appealing.'

But it begged the obvious question: if this was a photograph of the genuine, uncatalogued original, which she had already hinted Mr Hien had previously copied for someone else, what was she proposing that he commission—surely not another copy?

'Is this the actual painting you are offering for sale?'

She laughed. 'Oh, no. What I am offering you is the opportunity to buy the original copy that has already been created by Mr Hien. You see, our original purchaser is keen to on-sell, and if you are interested, I will get in touch with him. It might take a day or two; he is not expected back in Hanoi until after the weekend.'

'I see.'

Now that he'd seen the photograph of the genuine original, he knew she could only be referring to one person. The painting of Nu Nu had hung for two days in Lutyen's Gallery, and thereafter solely in the chairman's office at Anglo Swiss BioLab in Geneva. As far as Faraday knew, Ralph Lutyen had no plans to come to Hanoi, so that ruled him out—and the chairman of Anglo Swiss was hardly a candidate for lower-level art fraud. That left only one person, who, as Faraday had since recalled, had commissioned a photographer in his presence to take photographs of his paintings in the Geneva office. It was the person he had suspected all along: none other than Kenneth Johnston. Unfortunately, he would have to wait until after the weekend to be able to confront him and confirm it.

'Tell me, madame, is your client also involved in wildlife conservation, like me?'

'No, no,' she replied. 'He works at the Embassy.'

EIGHTEEN

The emotional high that swept him back to his hotel room was fuelled by a sense of triumph and anticipation, but it was the note under his door that tossed his good sense and previous resolution out the window and had him quickly packing his bag and running down the stairs to tell the concierge that he would be gone for two nights. What good was his excitement going to do him if he had to bottle it up all weekend alone—and who else was there to share it with?

The night train to Sapa was a magnet for street hawkers. As fast as they were shooed away by guards, they reappeared like persistent flies from between the carriages, leaping over the iron tracks in front of moving trains with trays of packaged sandwiches, canned soft drinks, and hand wipes, as if the travellers whose custom they sought hadn't been fed in days.

Ask for a soft berth, the note from Caroline had instructed, *and go to counter 3, where they speak English. Try and get on the Victoria Express, train SP3, leaving at 9:50 p.m. Violet and I will be in the dining car. I've booked you a room in Sapa, so don't let me down. I promise you won't be bored.*

Counter 3 had been empty, and at counter 10, they told him that the Victoria Express was full, but he could have a soft berth on another part of the train. He would need to cross the tracks, because the Sapa train left from a different terminal—though 'terminal' was not quite the right word for it, as there were no boarding platforms or signage, and only blind faith and an unofficial porter to guide him over four tracks to a carriage that apparently equated to one of the numbers on his ticket. The soft berth turned out to be a couchette with four bunks, two of which were assigned to a young American couple with earnest frowns and Abercrombie & Kent satchels, and the third was for a besuited Vietnamese man so locked away in his private thoughts that he emitted no energy that required acknowledgement. Not everyone, it seemed, was put off by the news of the influenza outbreak. Faraday's was a top bunk—the last one available on the train, apparently—and he threw his bag onto it and squeezed out a trusting smile for the young couple as he went in search of the dining car.

It would have been fair to say that despite his initial excitement, he was not comfortable acting so impetuously. Faraday was a man who liked things to be planned out, and if that wasn't possible, he liked plenty of time and space around the unplanned events, so he could exercise his options. He hadn't seen or spoken to Caroline since the night he arrived in Hanoi, and he'd been rather thrown by the assumption in her note that his lack of definitive response to her invitation implied acceptance on his part. A lack of definitive response was a necessary feature of Faraday's need to be free to exercise his options. The assumption that this lack of response could be read as acquiescence was not what unsettled him, however; that had more to do with his reservations about leaving Hanoi at a critical moment, with important questions still to be answered.

Now that he was sure that Kenneth Johnston was the source of the photograph of the painting of Nu Nu, as well as the person who had commissioned the copy to be made of it, his mind was not changed by Madame Roulet's claim that he worked at the Embassy—but it had left him with a niggling detail that needed to be cleared up. She may simply have been mistaken about him working there. It was quite common for people to use their country's embassy as an address when coming and going in a city abroad; perhaps it was as simple as that. For a man who was dabbling in counterfeit art dealing, it would have the advantage of allowing him to avoid providing a fixed address. *Kenneth Johnston, c/o the British Embassy, Hanoi*: there, it was the perfect *poste restante*.

But he would have preferred to have time to check that assumption out, and the Embassy closed at 3:00 p.m., before he was able to get there, so now he had to wait until after the weekend to enquire. 'After the weekend' was when Madame Roulet expected her client to be returning to Hanoi. Meanwhile, was he in the mood to tag along on a journey he'd had no part in planning? And if so, as what—a new-found friend, a potential lover, or someone to share the conversational load with Violet Dunleavy? What exactly was his role?

It was in this frame of mind that he eventually found his way to the back of the train and the Victoria Express dining car—where he was to find that he was, in fact, all of those things.

* * * *

Violet Dunleavy was a piece of work: five-feet-nothing of unmoisturized wrinkled skin, topped by a twisted-wire hairdo above a penetrating set of falcon's eyes that could spot prey from ten thousand feet. Faraday knew he had no more than a minute or two in which to decide whether to love her or loathe her. He opted for something in between.

'I hope you know what you're dealing with here, Anton,' she snapped, pointing a piece of bread at Caroline like a witch doctor pointing a bone. 'This girl can cause an awful lot of trouble if she sets her mind to it. One minute, I was happily at work, trying to persuade a Somalian warlord not to dispose of his mutilated victims in our newly dug wells. Next thing, she has me on a plane to Vietnam, on account of an article she wrote about a tribe that got into trouble for helping our marines find their way around the mountains. What if they don't want our damned charity now? I blame Caroline for this. Be warned: this woman is trouble.'

While she didn't laugh herself, she gave them permission to laugh, waving the hand with the bread in it like an orchestra conductor signalling the violas, her eyes darting about at everything within range, never missing a beat. When she dunked the bread in her glass of red wine, then noisily sucked it dry before swallowing the bread whole, that was when Faraday softened to her.

'Well, she talked me into boarding this train with no idea of where we're heading or why,' he replied, 'so I guess you must be right, Violet: she's certainly persuasive.'

And wasn't that the truth, he thought. But here he was—and there was no denying that a point had now passed beyond which he couldn't keep pretending that nothing was happening between them. So, alright, something *was* happening ... but what was it? As she was the one taking the initiative, she must know better than him—but if she did, she wasn't saying. Faraday was a man who needed things to be clear, and until they were, he reserved his position.

'I decided we could do with a man on this trip,' Caroline responded teasingly, 'in case we encounter a problem that needs brute force to resolve it. They have their uses, you know, Violet, and Anton was the only one I could find who spoke English and seemed to be at a loose end. He's a painter, and he needs to get out more. He's spent too much of his life locked away in his studio, he says. The mountain air will do him good; it'll put some colour into his cheeks.'

'Do you mind?' Faraday protested. 'You're talking about me as if I were your child.'

Violet pointed another piece of bread at him. 'To us women, Anton, all men are children, and that's what we love about them—unless they're brutes, in which case we should have nothing to do with them. Even the greatest lover or the most courageous general is still a child to us women. Being all big and manly doesn't fool us a bit; we know you're just too scared to cry. And hopping from one bed to another? What's that but a desperate search for more and more approval from the mothers you men can't ever get enough of? No, give in, my dear, and do as she says. Get some mountain air into your lungs, and take a rest from those paint fumes. Why do you paint animals, anyway?'

'Wildlife! I paint wildlife.'

'… Why?'

Christ, what a question! Because Ralph Lutyen had told him twenty years ago that there might be money in it? And how did she know he painted animals—had Caroline told her?

'Because it makes me money.'

'Ah, money! My husband had lots of money, but he never worked in his whole life. He had my money, you see—and I had my family's money. My husband never left his apartment on Fifth Avenue for all the years we were married. There was nothing he wanted to see or do. My family worked for generations at the business of making more money; that was all they ever did, and still do. For myself, I decided that money has a toxic vapor that can poison you if you don't give it air, so I've spent most of my life doing what my friends call "tossing it to the wind". The polite term for it is "altruism", but that's not a term I particularly like. I think I prefer "tossing it to the wind", because that suggests a certain freedom of spirit, which I believe is essential when you're trying to help people. Altruistic people count out their money and look for a quantity of benefit in return. They complain about the poor biting the hand that feeds them—as if the poor should be better trained and more accepting of their place. But what I've found is that giving needs to be free to sometimes miss the mark. That's something I've been trying to explain to Caroline today, about what she's hoping to do for this village in the Highlands. It is not the end of the world if we fail, or if they decide they don't want it. I think she is having difficulty with that idea. Perhaps you can help me persuade her?'

Those falcon eyes had a mischievous glint in them, a flash of titanium white lighting up the burnt sienna and terre verte green of her irises as she lifted her hefty glass of red wine to her unadorned lips and drank thirstily. She was a piece of work, alright.

'I like the drift of what you're saying,' he replied cautiously, 'but I can also understand if Caroline is reluctant to see someone else's money being wasted. You can choose to waste it, maybe, but she can't. As for this influenza thing, I guess that's just unfortunate timing, but it doesn't stop her feeling bad about it—particularly now that you've come all this way.'

'Thank you, Anton,' Caroline chimed in. She leant across and kissed him on the cheek. 'That's exactly what I was trying to say.'

But as nice as this discourse on the art of giving graciously might have been, a thought was coming to mind that he realized might be profitably aired with this woman—a thought that had occupied him since the days of his first encounter with the Paladin Foundation and its mysterious club of rich benefactors.

'It seems to me, however,' he began, choosing his words carefully, 'that for those of us who do not have an inordinate amount of money, there is an unfortunate aspect of altruism that will always dog it.'

'Which is…?'

'The suspect motive. Why does a man who has devoted his whole life to the pursuit of money and power suddenly decide to become charitable?'

A new piece of bread was dunked in the red wine before being sucked dry. 'Are you asking me why *I* do charity work? Or is it a specific type of person you have in mind when you talk of a man who has devoted his life to the pursuit of money and power?' she demanded.

'I think it's the robber baron type that I have in mind, though I accept that not all rich people get that way by being robber barons. I guess Bill Gates might escape that description, but there are many who don't. What causes them to change their spots?'

'Do you have someone in mind?'

'Yes: Charles Van Heeren, the billionaire president of Anglo Swiss BioLab who founded the Paladin Foundation for the Environment. He was my erstwhile patron, so I have a particular interest in him.'

'I don't know him personally, but you seem to be suggesting that because a man has devoted his life to the pursuit of money and power, he is incapable of sincere charity. Actually, when you think about it, the man who has everything is possibly the only one capable of sincere charity. A person who has little or nothing is more likely to be preoccupied with overcoming that condition and knows that there's a limit to what he can give. The truly rich have moved beyond that. So, I have no trouble accepting that a banker or industrialist or whatever, who's used to exercising enormous power over the lives of others, should reach a point in his life where the only thing which truly dissatisfies him is the state of the planet. What's the point in having achieved so much control over your own destiny if the environment in which you operate is being denuded of flora and fauna, and your place in the sun is obscured by clouds of pollution? Most people feel incapable of effecting change in the world. The problems appear intractable, and they lack the money, the power, or the intellect to influence them. Besides, most people have insufficient self-esteem to ever make a start. Compare that to the rich and powerful. They see problems in simple terms. They disregard any conflicts of interest, being used to making their own interests paramount at all times. They have influence, money, contacts; they're used to making things happen. Am I making a reasonable case, or are you still sceptical?'

Faraday smiled ruefully before answering. 'Certainly, I would agree that they have a very high opinion of themselves and their capabilities. I suspect they believe they're capable of achieving anything. That part makes sense, but...'

Unconsciously, his hands turned over on the place mat in front of him, palms up towards heaven. No, this conversation was only giving him more cause to think—but he wasn't quite sure where the thinking was headed.

NINETEEN

It had been a bad night on the top bunk as the train rattled and swayed up the inclines and around the bends on its slow climb out of Hanoi. He slept fitfully, waking each time the carriages ground together as they slowed down, then drifting off as he buried himself in some imaginary dreamscape of heroic fatigue and epic journeys across endless dystopian landscapes. At 4:00 a.m., the wine he'd consumed at dinner asked to be released, just as one half of the American couple below him decided to join the other half in a single bunk—a move that presaged a period of tossing and creaking sufficient to persuade him to hold on and allow them their moment. At 4:45, he could hold on no more, and he slid out of his bunk and walked the corridor in search of a lavatory. It was a time of night that called for a cigarette, but he didn't smoke; time for a brandy, but he had no hip flask; a time when the present already felt like the past.

When the dawn light broke, turning the black and grey of the passing landscape to indigo and purple before the shafting sun cast a cadmium-green wash over the terraced hillsides, all the bladders on the train became active at once, and his quiet place in the corridor became untenable. Returning to his couchette, he claimed his overnight bag, embarrassed the American couple with a broad wink, and retired to a position well away from the lavatory. The Vietnamese gentleman who had occupied the other top bunk joined him and nodded politely.

'Lao Cai at six fifteen,' he informed him, looking at his watch. 'China border. You go to China?'

'No, I'm going to Sapa. Just for the weekend.'

The man nodded, as if that was the right answer. 'Chinese Army destroy Lao Cai in border war, 1979. Now, town is new.'

'New', as it turned out, meant unplastered concrete walls, unadorned windows, unpainted metal doors, and treeless, unpaved streets. Perhaps they had intentionally made it unattractive, so the Chinese wouldn't be tempted to invade again. Faraday climbed down onto the track and went in search of Caroline and Violet, presuming he would have a role to play in carrying luggage. It was cold, and a yellow mist hung over the town like a urine-soaked blanket. The trackside chaos was not helped by the men in uniform blowing whistles. Everyone was confused, acting like frightened refugees rather than privileged tourists. Faraday, an accustomed loner, enjoyed it—until a large Dutch woman accosted him, very belligerent and very worried.

'How do we get to Sapa?' she shouted.

He shook his head and walked on, weaving through suitcases and waving arms. 'The world will not end, madam,' he muttered to himself. 'You will not still be standing here at nightfall; all will be resolved.' And just to make himself feel better, he tossed a token 'sorry' over his shoulder as he passed.

The Victoria Express carriages were at the far end of the train, where all the faces in the distance appeared to be white—all except one. One face was black. Faraday slowed, then stopped, frowning. It was a familiar, handsome face atop a well-built frame dressed in a crimson sleeveless jacket that made him seem even bigger. Where had he seen that face before? Then he started walking again, more quickly. He'd seen it by the light of a bonfire in a restaurant garden in Hoi An. He could hear the accent, American with a West Indian lilt, and his name was Sam. Could he be mistaken? Was it the colour of the jacket that he'd recognized? He'd only glimpsed him briefly, from eight carriages away. Any tall black man in that jacket would catch his eye at a distance.

Suddenly, he could no longer see him. Faraday broke into a trot, pushing past the passengers gathering beside the train, but when he reached the end of the carriages and pulled up, panting, there was no sign of him. Behind the train on the opposite side of the track were vans and taxis with doors flung open and drivers carrying signboards. An ancient Citroën van with dust-encrusted windows and an antisocial muffler was wheezing and farting its way out of the car park and away from the railroad into the bleak breeze-block streets surrounding them.

'Anton!' Caroline called out from behind him.

'Yes!' Faraday shouted out loud. (Almost in triumph.) 'Yes!' (But not knowing why.)

He was breathing heavily, puffballs of vapor forming in the cold air, but for reasons he didn't understand, also feeling a flush of triumph—God knows on what account. That didn't matter; what mattered was that he felt it.

'At your service!' he announced, spinning around.

'Well, you sound as though you slept well!' She kissed him lightly on the mouth.

'I didn't sleep at all—not a wink. I dreamed of you and Violet lying in luxury, while two American newly-weds quietly copulated on the bunk beneath me. Then, just now, I thought I saw someone I recognized, but perhaps I was mistaken. Now I'm ready for breakfast.'

'Well, at least they did it quietly, the newly-weds. I hope they didn't put you off sex?'

She didn't wait for a reply, and he didn't have one.

'Violet has ordered a taxi van to drive us up the hill to Sapa. It's only thirty-seven kilometres, but it'll take us about an hour, apparently. I promise to buy you breakfast when we get there, if you can wait.'

'No, it didn't put me off. And, yes, I think I can wait.' He grinned.

'For what...?'

'For breakfast.'

* * * *

The next time he saw him was in the market in Sapa. Oh, yes, it was him alright: Sam from Hoi An. Already conspicuous enough by dint of his size and colour, he'd made the mistake of pausing to show interest in some local trinket, and had instantly become a magnet for children and tribal women swathed in indigo and patchwork clothing, begging for the attention of his dollars. He was tall and languid, with an easy, crooked smile and that 'Aw shucks, mon' lingering aura of his Jamaican heritage protecting him from hostility, but really (and Faraday could feel it sure as day across the forty meters that separated them), he was not 'Aw shucks' at all; he was sharp as a penlight on a pitch-black night. What else was he? Why was he here? To track elephants? Any galumphing elephant that traipsed across the paddy fields here, making a mess of the irrigation channels and treading on the newly planted rice, would hardly need tracking by satellite. So, what the hell was he really doing that needed the attention of the vastly rich and influential Paladin Foundation for the Environment? And what had he been doing in the garden of Jason Turnbull's restaurant in Hoi An that made him disappear into the night at the sound of Kenneth Johnston's name?

The Sapa market was spread over three levels of what would have been another ugly car park building in any other urban context. The market vendors, dressed in tribal colours, far outnumbered the shoppers. They were small, swarthy people swathed in indigo pantaloons and shirts, or red skirts and tunics elaborately embroidered, or black smocks hung about with silver medallions, hair braided and turbaned, gossiping quietly, like a crowd of extras waiting to be marshalled for an outdoor operatic production. It was less a market and more a social congregation, except on the produce floor, where slabs of meat lay out on wooden planks, crudely butchered with machetes for inspection by the flies, and open to debate as to size and weight. Of ice or any type of refrigeration, there was no sign. Woven baskets filled to overflowing with persimmons and potatoes, tangerines and pomelos, chilies, peppers, and tomatoes were hefted about the floor by little women barely twice their height and weight, and everywhere, children chased visitors, tugging at their sleeves with cheeky grins and broken English, proffering trinkets and soliciting dollars.

Faraday had come down the hill from the hotel after breakfast, leaving Caroline and Violet to plan their meeting with Uncle's cousin and to find an interpreter and guide to take them to his village. The influenza outbreak had cast a pall over the town, according to the hotel's duty manager, and the situation in the villages was highly volatile.

'The Moi only have themselves to blame,' the manager sneered. 'They know that young birds need to be inoculated, but they don't do it, because they think it reduces fertility—and even then, only when there's an outbreak and it's too late. Then, when the government inspectors come to cull the flocks, they herd their birds higher into the mountains, so they can't be found. The virus will never be eradicated until they police these people properly. Meanwhile, we lose customers because guests are too scared to come here, and no one tells the truth about anything. That's the worst of it: no one tells the truth about anything.'

So, Faraday had left them to solve their dilemma on their own, something that he was certain Violet was more than capable of doing. He could see, now that he was reminded of it, that half the stalls in the meat market were empty, bearing posters with drawings of poultry excised with red crosses, and there was a noticeable presence of officious men in green overalls with identity cards pinned to their chests. But he saw no evidence of anything in the behaviour of the locals suggesting panic or despair. The mood was subdued, certainly, but whether that was unusual, he was unable to judge. It was a small town, and he was quite sure that news from the outlying villages would be known to all.

Meanwhile, his interest lay in the whereabouts of the Jamaican-American, Sam. If he was out and about in Sapa, he was sure he would soon find him, for the whole village could be covered in a twenty-minute stroll. Now, having spotted him in the market, his only decision was how and when to confront him, a decision that also turned on the question of why—and that was a question that he found difficult to answer. If he was to greet him purely on the basis of a chance encounter, then he would have done that as soon as he spotted him. The fact that he hadn't done so told him there were other factors at work, and he opted to observe from a distance until those factors became clearer in his own mind.

After he'd eventually shed the swarm of children through the time-honoured expediency of ignoring them beyond the limits of their attention spans, Sam then wandered into the fruit stalls and selected an apple, which he paid for with elaborate courtesy, then slowly strolled the aisles while eating it. He was distracted, frowning frequently at his watch (the conspicuous gold Rolex that Faraday had found so incongruous in relation to his alleged occupation). It was 11:05 a.m., according to Faraday's own watch. By 11:15, Sam began to show signs of impatience, kicking at rubbish on the ground and tossing his head back in annoyance. Taking a cell phone from his pocket, he glared at the screen, punching idly at buttons but making no attempt to make a call. Then, just as Faraday expected him to give up waiting, he was approached quietly by a short, stocky man whom neither Faraday nor Sam, it seemed, had noticed in the crowd. The two men spoke briefly, then the man—dark-haired and dark-skinned, judging from what could be seen of him from behind—led them out of the market towards the steps down to the road outside.

Faraday had observed all this from a landing on the staircase above the produce market, and he momentarily lost sight of them as they descended the stairs beneath him. After waiting briefly, calculating the time it would take them to reach the street, he then ran quickly down the steps, emerging just in time to see them entering a café forty meters down the road. With no plan, no opening line springing to mind—let alone one that would do justice to the elaborate range of theories that had loitered in his imagination since the connection with Johnston had become a possibility—he wasn't yet ready to confront him. Perhaps he was just procrastinating, but he didn't feel right about following them into the café. So, he chose to wait, entering a shop opposite and pretending to browse through the ethnic merchandise while keeping an eye on the café door.

For fifteen minutes, he feigned an interest in hand-embroidered cushions, place mats, and prayer rugs while enduring an enthusiastic lecture on the Black, White, Red, and Green tribal subgroups of the H'mong people, delivered by the lady shopkeeper in an unblushing flow of fractured French and English, punctuated by much laughter. Like most men who use impersonal courtesy as a shield, Faraday did not find it easy to take up people's time in shops when he had no intention of buying, so at fifteen minutes, he was already at the limit of his pretences when the café door opened opposite, and Sam and his companion emerged.

Unfortunately, this happened at the exact moment that the shopkeeper succeeded in putting into Faraday's hands an embroidered woollen shawl he had spent slightly too much time admiring, and while fishing for money in his jacket pocket, sensing that the pair were about to depart in different directions, he missed the opportunity to casually emerge and feign the vague recognition he had decided to reveal to Sam. Too late, his quarry turned abruptly on his heel and strode off rapidly down the hill, with Faraday's transaction still incomplete. Then the front door of the shop opened, and the other man entered, wearing a multi-pocketed fishing jacket that Faraday would have recognized anywhere.

'Bloody hell!' Faraday exclaimed spontaneously. 'If it isn't my bus companion from Hue! How are you, Duc?'

TWENTY

Nothing magnifies friendship like a chance encounter. Faraday, having hailed Duc as a long-lost friend, received an equally warm greeting in return. It seemed the shared bus ride from Hue to Hoi An had created some kind of fraternity that made for a surprising bond. Perhaps it was a product of the unusual proximity of flesh that occurred in such circumstances. Where else would two male strangers press their thighs together for three hours without either complaint or ulterior motive? Or perhaps it was their unconscious recall of the confidence Duc had shared with him when opening his rucksack to reveal his pistol, and telling the story of his encounter with the Cambodian police.

'Marble Mountain—you!' Duc exclaimed in recognition. His enthusiasm at being unexpectedly reunited was a little less effusive than Faraday's, but no less genuine. They shook hands, nodding and grinning.

'Is this your hometown?' Faraday asked.

'No, Sinho is my people town. You like Sapa?'

'I've only just arrived. Perhaps I could buy you a beer or tea?'

'No beer, no tea. I just finish tea, and it not taste good. We buy some hot *pho*. You will like it.'

So, Faraday followed him out of the shop, clutching the bag with his unintended purchase, and they climbed the stairs back up to the produce market, where Duc found seats for them on two overturned plastic buckets as part of a ring of local customers that had formed around a woman tending a large aluminium cooking pot on a small gas burner. There was no need to order; only one dish was on offer. They were each given a bowl and a spoon. As they ate the hot brew, they reminisced about their bus ride, the size of the tourist statuary at Marble Mountain, and Duc's experience with the Cambodian police—mention of which caused Duc to unconsciously pat the rucksack he had been carrying, which he'd placed between his knees when he sat down, suggesting perhaps that it still contained the pistol that had been central to his tale of escape.

'Did you get the job you were going for in Hoi An?' Faraday asked. 'The mountain guide job you told me about?'

'I get the job, but I no want the job. Today I tell them. *Harrumph!*' Duc banged his spoon on the rim of his soup bowl, and the woman cook looked up with a scowl, firing off a pithy epithet that probably defied translation.

'You told them you didn't want the job? Was that job for the man I saw you with coming out of the café? Did he say he wanted you to help them track wild elephants?'

Duc slurped his soup and looked into the middle distance. 'That what they say: they say they are looking for elephants and saola. But there are no elephants in the mountain, no saola. If they want to find them, they must look in the sky.' This he thought was very funny, and clearly he thought Faraday should find it funny, too. 'Like pigs... Is that what you say?'

'Pigs...? Like pigs in the sky... Like pigs might fly... You mean elephants in the mountains are as likely as pigs flying? Is that it?'

'Just like pigs!'

Faraday laughed with him—or for him—slowly grasping his style. A verb or two missing here, some confusion with tense there, if not sense; it wasn't too difficult.

'So, they want you to work for them, but there are no elephants to find—is that what you're saying? Why do they need you as a guide, then?'

They slurped together in silence for a while. The soup had a richness of flavour that defied logic, because it was as light as a rich man's consommé, yet it took hardly any cooking time to create it. Duc very quickly drained the remnants of his bowl, tipping it directly into his mouth, then wiped his lips on his sleeve with a satisfied murmur.

'We have a saying: "When elephants hide, it is not from the tiger, it is from man." If you look for something that you know is not there, you can look forever,' he said with a shrug.

That didn't make sense, Faraday thought. Sam had told him that he was involved in monitoring declining elephant numbers, so it was not out of the question that he would be interested in the remote forest regions along the China and Laos borders, despite Duc's suggestion that it was a waste of time. It would seem, though, that Duc wasn't buying it.

'So, Paladin has some other purpose in mind,' he suggested.

Duc looked at him sharply. 'You know about them?'

'I know Paladin, yes. I met that man you were with in Hoi An. Is his name Sam? He told me no one can agree on how many elephants are left in the wild. It may be two hundred, or it may be less than fifty. If it's as bad as they say, then it makes sense that they would be hard to find. How easy would it be to find a single elephant in these remote mountains? You can see why they'd need your help.'

Duc shook his head. 'Elephants live together; they are not single man or woman. And they make big mess where they go. That is why they get killed. But they do not like the mountain. Mountain is too hard. Only if they need to hide do they go up … just like us. We go higher and higher— but higher is harder. The French call us Montagnards. It means "mountain people". The Kinh and Hoa call us Moi, which means "savages". Why? Because we are not them. We will never be them. So, we are Moi forever … until we are none.'

'Who are the Kinh and the…?'

'The Viet and the Hoa. The Hoa are Chinese. I am Dao, and many hundreds of years, the Chinese have tried to kill us—and the Vietnamese,

179

too—but we go higher, and our ancestors help us survive. Would my ancestors want me to take strangers to places we know, just because they offer money? That is what the Nung do—and now the Nung are dying.'

He didn't appear to be upset by any of this. On the contrary, it seemed to please him, and he reached across and gave Faraday a comradely pat on the knee. It seemed there was some pride in being the persecuted, as if surviving everyone's best efforts to wipe you out only proved your superiority.

'So, why do you think Paladin wants you to work for them, if there are no elephants?'

'Because they look for something in the mountains that not belong to them, and they afraid they get lost.' He laughed loudly, slapping Faraday on the knee again; this was very funny.

Acknowledging the gesture of kinship, Faraday drained his soup the way Duc had done, accidentally swallowing a whole chili that lay in the bottom of the bowl in the process. An explosion of pain spread through his mouth and throat, and he gasped for air. Seeing his discomfort, the woman with the cooking pot thrust a bottle of water into his hand, and he gulped at it desperately, trying to douse the flame. His eyes streamed, and it was minutes before he recovered sufficiently to find the woman waiting for his empty bowl while holding out her hand for payment.

'How much is that?' Faraday asked breathlessly.

'It is ten thousand dong. I pay,' Duc replied.

'No, no, please, let me. But ten thousand dong is only fifty cents; are you sure that's right?' Fumbling in his pocket, he pulled out a one-dollar note. But before he could pass it over, Duc snatched it from his hand, then held it up while talking rapidly to the woman, remonstrating with her until, reluctantly, she produced a ten-thousand-dong note in exchange.

'Must not spoil our economy,' Duc said seriously, passing the change to him. 'Not for elephants, and not for *pho*.'

They wandered back out of the market, pushing their way through the

180

aggressive clutches of tribal street vendors desperate for their custom, and emerged onto the road outside.

'Are you sure about refusing the job?' Faraday asked. 'I seem to remember you saying that guiding is important for your village. Why turn down the money? See what they want you to do. It can't do any harm.'

He was reluctant to break this link to Sam and the Paladin Foundation without finding out more, but he had the distinct impression that Duc had made up his mind not to be involved. Then he had an idea.

'Look, I'm staying at the Victoria Hotel with some friends who may also need a guide, but not to look for non-existent elephants, just to help them with a local project. Where could I find you if they wanted some assistance?'

Duc put down his rucksack and started patting the pockets of his fly-fishing jacket, pulling open the zips and searching the contents one by one. Out came a small tin of matches, a pocketknife, a length of string, a wallet in a plastic bag, a battered cell phone, and—on the third try—a note pad and pencil, also in a plastic bag. There were still three pockets left unopened.

'I will turn phone on here in Sapa for one day,' he said. 'If your friends need, here is my number.'

* * * *

The climb back up the hill to the hotel was steep, with two long sets of steps that took the wind out of him and had him pausing for breath at each landing. Looking back over the valley to the hills that surrounded the town, he could see that the country beyond the terraced hillsides and cultivated hollows was vast and impenetrable. Shifting mists and shafts of sunlight multiplied into the distance, and the mountaintops were like dark green, brooding watchtowers, haunted by the spirits of the dead who silently watched over the world of the living. There was no way of surviving there, for if there had been, then eighty million Vietnamese and twelve hundred million Chinese, ever hungry for land, would have found a way. Only the Montagnards knew how; that was the source of Duc's pride.

The Victoria Hotel would have been at home in Austria, with its pretty gardens, tiled roof, and balconies looking out at the mountain landscape, which made it an anachronism when set among Sapa's crudely utilitarian socialist buildings. But its familiar Western comforts were a welcome haven for Faraday to return to after his morning in the town. Caroline had left a message for him in his room, saying that she and Violet had gone to meet Uncle's cousin and would see him back at the hotel for dinner, so he opted to catch up on the hours of sleep that he'd missed on the train, then went down to the lounge to order the very English repast of tea and sandwiches.

Despite it being the weekend, the hotel was strangely quiet. There was not only an absence of tourists, but a conspicuous lack of staff also. The mood at the front desk was almost furtive, and there was a hesitancy in the response to his order. As he settled into the deep comforts of his wing-backed armchair and gazed out at the mist-laden alpine scene before him, Faraday wondered if he hadn't now had enough of this country. He'd been on the road for three weeks, constantly moving, constantly in search of clues to the mystery as to who had been copying his work. As much as he liked the people and was intrigued by the enormity of difference in the outlook and culture, the truth was that the continual effort required to extract meaning from a language that contained no element of familiarity to his own, either visually or phonetically, and the perpetual floundering as to the motives and intent of a people who viewed life so differently had tired him out, and the exhilaration he had felt the day before was now replaced by a new sense of unease.

In a day or so, he believed he would have incontrovertible proof of the role of Kenneth Johnston in the duplication of his painting of Nu Nu. But then what? Yes, he'd had to find out just for his peace of mind, but what difference would it ultimately make to him? He'd always known the nature of that man. It would prove no more than a confirmation of his prejudices, another twist of the dagger that bore the fingerprints of a failed relationship, as well as the bloodstains of his guilt over his undeserved success.

The encounter with Duc and his inability to properly explain the presence of Sam, the man from Paladin, here in the mountains was of another dimension altogether. It wasn't merely his confusion over finding Paladin to be an active presence on the ground after years of believing them to be covert—if not secret—wielders of influence in high places, so much as Duc's blunt dismissal of their explanation for being there in the first place, and his seeming disapproval. He could accept that Johnston's (and Ralph's) greed might undermine the legitimacy of his commission to paint the Harbinger Collection, but if the legitimacy of the Paladin Foundation itself was now to be questioned, then he really had arrived at a turning point in his career.

And if Paladin was here in the mountains in the form of Jamaican Sam, did that place Kenneth Johnston here as well?

When the tea tray arrived, the sandwiches were impeccably English. White bread with the crusts removed had been cut into three delicate wedges stuffed with each of three traditional fillings: anchovy paste, tinned salmon with cucumber, and chopped egg with mayonnaise. The tea was Twining's, served in a sterling silver teapot, and the cup and saucer were breakfast-sized Royal Doulton. The sugar cubes were set in a silver sugar canister, and the milk was in a small Royal Doulton jug. How could a Vietnamese kitchen hand have got all this so right?

While such a tea service was, in truth, as foreign to Faraday's everyday life as spring rolls and *pho*, nevertheless, there was a comforting familiarity in it that assured him that he did have a home and a place in life. That home was not necessarily England, with all its faults and disharmonies, but it was, at least, somewhere close to that country. Perhaps it was no bigger than the four walls of his studio and the staircase down to his kitchen. He was a painter; that was what he did. The only world he could control was the world he created on his canvas, nature's world filtered through his imagination in a way that he himself found unremarkable, but which, for some reason he didn't understand, could only be rendered once that filtering was complete. When this week was over, that was the world to which he'd return, though not with the same unanswered questions.

TWENTY-ONE

A sombre mood hung around the dinner table at the Victoria Hotel that evening, and no one was more sombre than Violet Dunleavy. And it was apparent that she didn't get her lined visage by hiding her emotions all her life. If she was angry, she scowled. If she was happy, she smiled. Being now sombre, she furrowed her brow and puckered her lips as if she were manoeuvring an olive pip across the front of her mouth, all the while turning her empty wine glass in her fingers as if inspecting a diamond for its best facet.

'Here's a lesson I want you to learn,' she instructed. 'All the moral certainties of your youth will inevitably be exposed as shallow and sham long before you finally have the luxury of dying. I give you this piece of wisdom without charge, because I know it will do you no good. But it's true for all of us.'

There was no reply from either Faraday or Caroline because they had no idea where she was coming from.

'And here's another lesson for you,' she added, after a pause. 'You can't hide from the consequences of being wrong just because millions of other people were wrong as well. Eventually, you'll be called to account one way or the other. Today, I got called to account.'

Caroline was just as glum, but this admission from Violet had her confused. 'I don't see how any of this could have been forecast by us, let alone prevented,' she protested. 'This epidemic is spreading faster than anyone is admitting, and everyone's blaming everyone else. Vietnam's complexities are completely beyond our understanding at the best of times, let alone when lives are being lost, but what's happened here has nothing to do with us. What we've been trying to do is only good. Why would you have anything to account for?'

Violet stopped twirling her glass and reached for a piece of bread. When she was in a mood to lecture, it seemed, she needed something in her hand to call the audience to attention. 'No, my dear, I have a lot to answer for— and what I heard today was something for which I am just as guilty as any American could possibly be.' She pointed the bread at herself. 'I actively participated in the lies that led to this tragedy, and you should know that.'

'You'll need to explain,' Faraday interjected. 'Obviously something has gone on today, over and above what Caroline has told me, which was that Uncle's cousin didn't keep the appointment, and the village appeared to be mostly deserted, at least by the men, which was explained as being a consequence of the influenza outbreak. How does any of this sheet home to you?'

'I think I know what Violet's saying,' Caroline said quietly. 'It's a bit more complicated than that. The virus outbreak is only part of it. What the interpreter told us explains some things that I didn't understand before, but which now make sense, and if I'd asked the right questions in the first place, Violet probably wouldn't be here; maybe none of us would be here. So, the person to blame is me.'

'Can you be a little clearer?'

Caroline took a deep breath and checked with the older woman before beginning. 'The reason the village has been deserted is not just because of the influenza virus, but because the people of that village are being treated as scapegoats for the epidemic—not just by the government, but by the other hill tribes as well.'

'Hold on!' Faraday held up his hand and looked from one to the other.

186

'I thought the whole point was that this cousin—and his family village, presumably—didn't have a poultry farm, which is exactly what you had come to discuss. So, how could they possibly be responsible for the outbreak?'

'Because they're Nungs,' Violet snapped. 'Nungs from the wrong side.'

'Tell me again, what the hell's a Nung?'

Violet appeared too exasperated to explain, so Caroline answered for her. 'They're an ethnic minority, just like the H'mong or the Daos. Uncle is a Nung, and so is my Vietnamese brother. I told you about the article I wrote, that some of the Nung people here in the Highlands had helped the US Special Forces during the war, fighting against the North Vietnam Army and the Viet Cong. Once the war ended, those who didn't escape were imprisoned and persecuted by the new regime, and their family land was taken from them. Many managed to escape later, or to smuggle their children abroad as refugees or "boat people", and if they were really lucky, they found their way to America. That's how my brother got adopted by my family. But those who stayed had an awful time, and being deprived of land, they were often exposed to starvation. Uncle can't have been one of those on the wrong side, but clearly his cousin was. I wrote about it. For most of the eighties, the Vietnamese government had a policy of forcibly settling up to a quarter million Vietnamese in the mountain regions every year, as a way of squeezing out the minorities. Being at the bottom of the heap, the Nungs from the wrong sub-tribe had no chance. Now that I know this, the tensions between Uncle and his cousin suddenly become clearer— and it explains the argument between my brother and Uncle, too. At least, I think it does, but that's probably not straightforward either. What the Vietnamese who stayed think of the Viet Kieu who left, and vice versa, is not easy to summarize. Anyway, I should have known about all of this before allowing Violet to be talked into coming here to help.'

'Like Trih and Hi,' Faraday mumbled to himself. 'It doesn't pay to have been on the wrong side in Vietnam, that's for sure.'

He could see Caroline's discomfort, but he wasn't sure that she deserved it. She herself had been at pains to warn him when they first met that it was impossible to tell with the Vietnamese what was *not* being said—for reasons of *face* and family and ancestry. She couldn't have guessed at all these things if they'd chosen not to explain them to her. But what was her brother's role in all this? As he had benefited from a US upbringing, wouldn't he have sided with the cousin who had suffered as a consequence of his loyalty to the American forces? So, why did he quarrel so angrily with his uncle for trying to help him?

'There seems to be a lot of unanswered questions here,' he observed. 'I can see why you're so deflated. So, what now?'

Caroline looked to Violet, and Violet frowned even harder. She didn't give the impression of being a person who was unable to make decisions, but just at that moment, she did not appear ready to do so. Her mind was still catching up on unfinished business, and the hand holding the bread bobbed up and down at a steadily increasing pace until eventually it threw the bread down and slapped the table.

'Caroline's not to blame for anything here,' she declared, 'and neither are the Vietnamese. I'm angry at myself.'

The thought working its way through her mind needed time to reach expression. They fiddled with their napkins and waited.

'At the age of fifteen, I was a wartime pen pal,' Violet announced. 'Ain't that sweet?'

They waited.

'I was an idealistic little thing, full of so much passion and pride. Why, I was certain I could change the goddamned world! Well, I certainly helped change *someone's* world. See, the strength of an idea doesn't rely on it being right, only that it's firmly held. Ignorant young people can be far more dangerous than well-informed older people, for the very reason that when you're young, you crave the rapture of evangelism like some people crave sex. When I was fifteen, I didn't want sex; I wanted to believe in Daddy— and the biggest Daddy of all was Lyndon Johnston, our president, our

Super Daddy. And Super Daddy was saving the world from Evil Communists who had brainwashed hordes of yellow Gooks to slaughter our Brave Boys in foreign jungles, which would allow those Evil Communists to leapfrog like dominoes into the unprotected countries of the Free World and eventually enslave us all.

' "Oh, Mr President," we sighed at my waspy school for young ladies from Republican Land, "thank God you are there to protect us with your wisdom and your courage, and thank God for the few heroic yellow Gooks who have chosen to support our Brave Boys in this titanic struggle against the Evil Communists, and thank God for our kind and caring school teachers for letting us write letters to those heroic yellow Gook supporters of America's fight for Freedom, and praise be to God that our letters of support will give them the courage to fight to the death, knowing that in America, there is a young and grateful girl who just wants the chance to live her life free of the fear of being enslaved by the Evil Communists. Oh, and by the way, Mr President, wouldn't it be better if everyone in the world could just be American?"'

Violet turned from one to the other, trying to provoke a response, but both Caroline and Faraday were too stunned to speak.

'That's right, that was me writing that crazed nonsense—sweet little me. Now it's almost inconceivable that a person would support America's actions in the war in Vietnam, right? Who would want to be associated with that kind of person? Not me; not Violet Dunleavy. The only thing I can say in mitigation is that the war dragged on long enough for me to grow up a bit, and for everyone with half a brain to realize what a crock of shit it was. But by then, it was too late. My evil little letters were already out there, doing their stuff—and who'd have thought it would take the slaughter of Vietnam's poultry, fifty years later, for my own chickens to come home to roost?'

She coughed out a dry, cackling laugh that was hers alone to release. The other two remained silent.

'So, now you know, Caroline, why I responded so quickly to this chance to make amends. When I read your article about the fate of the Nungs, I realized that it was a chance for me to revisit my past and cure an infection that had never been properly treated—one that I had convinced myself had never done anyone any harm. Maybe that's what I was hoping to prove: that my youthful ignorance had never done anyone much harm; it was no more than an embarrassment.'

Having gotten that out of her system, Violet decided it was time to have another drink and order dinner. That was the one thing Faraday liked about her; he didn't like drinking alone. She drained her glass of Burgundy and ordered another.

'So, what now?' Faraday asked at length. 'Do you wait for things to calm down, then proceed with the plan of providing village drinking water with their help? Or is the proposal off the table?'

The two women looked at each other and didn't reply. They all decided to have the suckling pig, though Caroline, whose body had no need for such pretensions, asked that they leave off the crackling and the *dauphinoise* potatoes. Anton, the only one of the three who could possibly have benefited from eating a little less, murmured that he couldn't imagine pork without crackling—or potatoes, for that matter.

Having ordered, Caroline returned to the subject reluctantly. 'It's really up to Violet,' she conceded. 'The idea was that Uncle's cousin, Nung Ton Phuc, would help with the village water program. The government prefers the idea of creating bores for the supply of clean water in the mountain villages, because the traditional open wells are unsanitary. But bores need electricity of some sort, even if just a small generator, and that's just not possible in the remote areas. Now that I can sort of understand why the cousin wouldn't take charity from Uncle, I can see why it was necessary for him to pass off the work of setting up the water program as an exchange for the poultry farm for his family village. The problem is—'

'The problem is,' Violet interjected, 'we don't know where the hell he is. He's disappeared up in those goddamned mountains with most of the other men from his village, and who would know where, or what the heck they're doing?'

'Seems that the Nung tribes—this one, at least—are still open to earning money from foreigners who want to be taken into remote areas,' Caroline explained. 'With them being treated as pariahs by the government, as well as by rival tribes, it may be their only option for earning money. The women in the village don't know what they're doing, or won't say, and the interpreter wasn't very helpful. We got the impression we could be waiting around a long time.'

'Meanwhile,' Violet cautioned, lowering her voice, 'there's an elephant in the room that needs mentioning. Look around. There are people dying out there by the score—and that's what we should be talking about. Thank God it's not contagious. Just stay clear of poultry.'

* * * *

When Violet announced that it was time for her to go to bed and send some emails off to her people in Mogadishu, telling them to make sure 'those goddamned warlords' weren't dropping their victims down the water wells any more, Caroline and Faraday decided to take a walk in the hotel gardens overlooking the town of Sapa, so he could tell her about his travels and what he intended to do now that he had tracked down the counterfeit painting. The night was cool, the mist damp, even though it was late June. That, of course, was why people came up to the mountains: to get away from the oppressive heat of Hanoi.

For some reason, they were awkward with each other. Having a third person present had made things easier, and now that it was just the two of them (and despite them having been alone together on the two—was it only two?—occasions they'd met previously), they were suddenly self-conscious.

'I'm sorry about Violet,' she said.

'I like her. She's real.'

'She doesn't hold back. She told our guide today that his job was to ask questions, not to avoid them. She doesn't realize that here it's rude to be inquisitive, and there are some personal matters you never discuss. Sometimes you can sit and drink tea with people for days here before they finally tell you the simplest little thing that has been on their mind. She wants answers. This is Vietnam; they don't give you answers—unless they're obvious answers, in which case, you didn't need to ask in the first place. I've tried to explain this to her.'

'Well, she's an alpha female. If she were an alpha male, you'd expect her to be that way. I like her honesty. Considering her background, she's got a pretty clear-eyed view of the world. The super-rich don't need empathy or understanding to get through life; they'll happily deal with Hitler and Genghis Khan, because they feel equal or superior to them. From what you've told me, she's from that same world and sees it for what it is. Her way of apologizing for the super-rich is to give help to the people at the opposite end of the scale. But she's not afraid to admit her faults. She doesn't see herself as a saint. That story about her wartime letters was pretty revealing.'

Caroline smiled ruefully. 'I had no idea. That floored me. I'd pegged her for a Hanoi Jane—you know, bravely championing the other side against the brutal imperialism of the United States—and all along, she was rooting for Uncle Sam, which is now so politically incorrect that it's almost laughable. Shows how much the world has changed.'

'Not completely. More of your compatriots still stand up than stay seated when the band starts playing and Johnny goes marching off to war again. More of my compatriots, too. What will be interesting is to see whether Uncle's cousin now regrets taking the American side, and how he'd react if he heard Violet's story. Does he know anything about her? Do you think he could have got cold feet?'

Caroline stopped walking and held him back by his arm. 'Do you know, apart from me, I'm not sure that he knows who's here. Uncle is the one who has been communicating with him, and from the way he's been talking to me, I don't think that he's made a point of discussing Violet. In fact, I'm almost certain he hasn't. He keeps referring to it as "The Water Project" and never mentions anyone personally.'

'But for Violet, it's obviously personal. That's the main reason why she's here.'

'Exactly!'

'Then it's fairly important that she doesn't leave without having tried harder to find him. She needs to lay her ghosts to rest.'

'Yes, but we have no idea at all where he might be. His family village completely distrusts strangers, and it wouldn't surprise me if by tomorrow, it was deserted.'

Though it was cold enough to make him shiver, Faraday was reluctant to go back inside. There were no stars, presumably because of the mists that constantly rolled in and around the hills, and there was no moon to illuminate the garden, only the pale light from the hotel's dining room. They were standing close, holding each other's forearms, and he could feel the warmth of her, and her shivering as well.

'We can go in,' he said, 'or I can put my arm around you.'

'I don't want to go in,' she replied, 'but I am cold.'

He moved forward and put his arms around her, so that she was nestled against his chest, her hair against his cheek. He could feel her body beneath her dress, and his hands stroked it gently, giving warmth to it, seeming to know it instantly as a place where they were welcome. They stayed like that for a minute or two, in silence, and without the need to kiss.

'It has always seemed odd to me,' he whispered in her ear at last, 'that hot air rises and cold air falls, yet it's always colder at the top of the mountain.'

She pulled back and pushed him on the chest. 'You do say the craziest things at the oddest moments!'

Then she kissed him—for quite a long time—before he spoke again.

'I met a guy in the market today that I'd met before on the way to Hoi An. He's a mountain guide from a local tribe, but there's something about him that is very savvy, and I'm pretty sure he would have no trouble finding out what's going on in these parts. I trust him. Why don't I give him a call and see if he'll help you? It needs to be now, because he's planning on leaving tomorrow.'

She shook her head in disbelief, as if he hadn't noticed that she'd just kissed him.

'Alright,' she said, 'but let's go inside, because it's freezing. Then I want to hear about your discovery of the forged painting, and what you're going to do about it.'

TWENTY-TWO

While he recounted the simple facts as they'd revealed themselves in Hanoi, he realized that he was close to leaving the whole affair behind him.

'If I'm sounding somewhat ambivalent in my attitude towards the forger,' he reflected, 'you have to understand that there have been years when I've considered myself a phony. It had to do with the ease with which I first began to sell paintings, the uncalculated but fortuitous timing of my choice of subject matter and the public's awareness of wildlife, culminating in the commissions from the Paladin Foundation. I didn't respect my work, because I imagined my peers didn't either, so self-doubts followed me through my twenties like uncontrolled erections. I knew other people had them, too, but it was what they did to *me* that mattered. These still linger.'

'The erections, or the self-doubts?'

'Okay!' He laughed. 'Both. So, I held no grudge against the man who'd been paid to copy my panda. I actually thought he'd done a damn good job—though I couldn't tell him that, obviously. No, if I have any resentment, it's against the man who I believe paid for the copy, thinking he could pass it off and make a quick profit, knowing that only a handful of people had ever seen the original. I have a number of reasons for being angry at him, not the least of which is that I once considered him a friend.'

'And you're certain about who it is?'

'Oh, yes, I have no doubt at all.'

They were sitting on a plump sofa beside a roaring fire in the hotel lounge, Caroline with her feet tucked underneath her as she poked at the burning logs with a fire iron, and Faraday with his legs stretched out before him, a glass of Armagnac in his hand, which was rapidly dispelling the cold that had penetrated his bones from the walk in the garden. They had the room to themselves.

'I'm pretty sure that this week, I'll get to confront him, provided I can convince the gallery that I need to meet him face to face if there's going to be a deal. He's due back in Hanoi in a day or two, and the gallery owner impresses me as a woman who wouldn't let anything stand in the way of a sale. We'll see.'

'What will you say to him?'

'I'll say, "Fuck you, Kenneth! When are you going to learn how to spell?"'

'To spell...?'

'It was the spelling on the painting that gave it away.'

'Is that *all*? No purple rage, no spit in the eye, no blackballing by Sotheby's and Christie's...?'

'No. I'll probably have a drink with him.'

'You Brits are amazing! I want to know what else this friend did to you.'

'Well, that has to do with a woman.'

Caroline put down the fire iron and sat up straight. Now she was interested. 'Tell me.'

'I'm not sure it's appropriate ... or relevant.'

'I've just kissed you; it's both appropriate *and* relevant. Now tell me.'

'Well, her name was Helene. We lived together for eight years.'

* * * *

But who and what was *she*? He only saw what could be easily seen: the hips, the hair, the hands and mouth, the bursting suitcase, the clothes that spread across the bedroom floor, stiletto heels and shapely ankles, lipstick on wine

196

glasses, and duty-free cigarettes for all her friends. She was an air hostess. She came and went like an equinoctial wind: three days away, then two at home. She was Helene.

And he only heard what could be easily heard: the cab in the street outside, the front door flung open, the inevitable conversations on the cell phone while struggling with luggage and keys, the suitcase landing on the bed, the fridge door opening, wine glasses on the kitchen bench, the pop of a champagne cork, the rustle of stockinged feet on the stairs up to his studio, and the inevitable, 'Well, aren't you pleased to have me home? You can stop working now.'

And who and what was *he*? He was a painter, always working. He had to work, or else there was no reality. He worked alone. In place of conversation, he had thoughts. The thoughts were only partial, unexplored, not needing to be fully formed, because they never saw the light of day. When they had first met, the party noise was so loud he hadn't needed to speak. Safe from investigation, he'd grinned at her outrageous sexuality and could have been anybody she wanted him to be. They fell into bed— because that was what she wanted, she said. Actually, despite her sexual appetite, she often fell asleep quickly. Alcohol tended to do that.

'Do you love me?' she had asked as time went by.

'Of course I do,' he replied.

'Then why won't you say so?'

'I just did.'

'No you didn't; I did.'

She was always in the air, and even when she landed, she was still flying. He was always on the ground, working. The thoughts that he never released into conversation were packed away out of habit. Even when he emerged from his studio to keep her company—on those two days when she wanted to have fun—his baggage weighed him down, as if in her absence, it had become heavier and heavier.

She was Helene. And one day, after eight years, she didn't return.

* * * *

"So, what happened?'

'She took another lover.'

'You mean this so-called friend—what was his name—Kenneth?'

'Yes.'

'Did you know it was happening?'

'I didn't see, and I didn't hear, because I wasn't looking, and I wasn't listening. I didn't own her, so it wasn't like I'd lost property; and she wasn't dragged away against her will, so it wasn't abduction. One day, she just left, and she didn't return.'

"But after eight years, you must have been hurt! Weren't you angry with your friend?'

Faraday laughed. 'Angry? All he'd done was lay his hand upon her knee and whisper in her ear; that's what men are supposed to do. Whether the woman then chooses to join him in a hotel room in Paris is up to her. Once she decides to go there, she has found her reason, and it's easy for her. You see, to be able to betray a lover of eight years, you need to find a truth that will not be rebutted, a truth that opens the door to all the truths that must follow—the ones that will ultimately justify the betrayal. She found her truth.'

'And what was her truth?'

'That I wasn't fun. She was right; I'm a boring bloody painter. It isn't that I don't like having fun, but over the years, I have unconsciously developed work habits that are difficult to unlearn. Whatever the distractions, the easel has become the one mistress with whom I'm constant. But for her, if I refused to have fun—something she identified as a need for herself—it must have been because I wanted to thwart her. And if I was intent on doing that, it showed something worse than a lack of empathy; it showed an unconscious desire to control her, rather than love her for who and what she was. That was her truth … and I accepted that.'

198

'Is that what she told you, in so many words?'

'That's what I deduced.'

'But did she actually *tell* you that was the reason she left?'

'No, we never discussed the reason.'

'You never discussed the reason? And how long did she stay with this fellow, Kenneth?'

'I have no idea. It was none of my business.'

'Holy shit, Anton! You were together for eight years, for Chrissake! How long ago was this? How many relationships have you had since? … No, I don't want to know that; it's not my business. But there's no one permanent, right?'

'There's no one permanent.'

'Then have you ever thought you may have a commitment phobia? Have you ever thought that maybe you *wanted* this Helene to go, bearing in mind you haven't even spoken to her about it since—and maybe, just maybe, you use painting as your prophylactic, to protect you from catching an emotional infection, in case it harms you?'

'No.'

' "No", what?'

'No, I haven't ever thought that.'

'Oh, Christ, I'm going to bed… Let me know in the morning if this guide of yours is able to help us.'

And with that, she unfolded her feet from beneath her, leaned over and kissed him lightly on the top of his head, and left the room before he could think of a response.

He continued the conversation alone with himself, ordering a second glass of Armagnac for company, and when that was finished, he, too, went to bed. There wasn't anything he could think of that he wanted to say to Johnston about Helene, if ever he should meet him; it was too long ago now. But he wondered if she was the reason they had ceased contact, as he had always presumed, or whether there were other reasons that Johnston had dropped out of sight. Someone must have planted the rumour that he might have disappeared in the Mont Blanc Tunnel fire, and for some reason, he'd accepted it. Was that Ralph who'd suggested it—and was his acceptance of it a sign of his willingness to draw a line under the cause of Helene's leaving? Or was it Johnston himself who'd had reason to plant the rumour? But in telling all this to Caroline, he'd clearly been warning her that he had been to blame—selling himself short when it came to his feelings, in other words. Was this his way of protecting himself against the chances of further hurt? Christ, Anton, grow up; all she'd done was kiss him.

TWENTY-THREE

Duc came up the hill to the hotel at first light and waited for Faraday outside the lobby. He was wearing his same hunting and fishing jacket over what appeared to be traditional Highlands garb: a black woollen smock trimmed with red, and short black trousers under a loose loincloth that exposed a sturdy pair of calf muscles and an incongruous pair of mountain-climbing boots. His head was wrapped in a length of scarlet cloth. By all appearances, he had prepared himself for the return to his village, while not quite surrendering the Western world from which he was returning. The rucksack that accompanied him everywhere was clutched between his knees.

For whatever reason, he could not be persuaded to come inside the hotel, preferring to squat outside the entrance and wait while Faraday went to rouse the two women. Violet was an early riser, Caroline less so, and it was thirty minutes or so before the three of them gathered in the dining room and discussed what they wanted to achieve. Simply put, it was to discover whether or not Uncle's cousin could be located before Violet was due to depart, and whether or not his role in the water project was still viable.

The task, as Faraday then explained it to Duc, did not call for a mountain guide, so much as an interpreter who could win the confidence of the villagers and investigate what was happening. There was no need to explain the nature of the problem to Duc as being anything other than an employment matter. The details of an employment offer, engaging the services of Uncle's cousin (the village chief, Nung Ton Phuc, who had now gone missing), were what Violet had come to confirm. As soon as Faraday began to hint at the history of this particular village of Nung people, however, Duc stopped him immediately, as if a cultural boundary line had been crossed and it was not a subject for discussion.

'We only look for one man,' he answered severely, 'not for whole history.'

Further, he was adamant that no information would be forthcoming for a carload of Westerners turning up, as had happened the day before. Perhaps Faraday could come, he accepted, but definitely not the women, and they would take a motorbike part of the way, then walk into the village without drawing attention to themselves. Faraday should dress for walking, and Duc would return in half an hour with the bike.

This, then, was how it started, with Faraday on the back of a noisy Yamaha, clutching onto the waist of a Dao tribesman who was dressed in a bizarre combination of tribal costume and safari hunter's garb, rattling down mountain tracks and along the berms of flooded paddy fields on a crisp morning that was still waiting for the sun to fully rise, on a simple mission to find some information for a young woman who had kissed him on the lips the night before, in a way that had already changed him by morning. He had no idea that this exhilarating ride into the countryside was leading him on an adventure that would alter his view of the world forever, because at this stage, the mission seemed so simple and finite in its objective—nor did he know that the man whose waist he clutched for support was going to prove critical to his survival. But when he came to look back on it, he would recognize that there was a quality to that morning that made it ripe for adventure—a lightness and crispness to the air, an other-worldly unreality about the landscape, exotic, remote, and intensely foreign, that made the mere act of being there an adventure in itself.

The dark mountains glowered down on them as they revved and stuttered through the foothills, and wispy white clouds danced skittishly

202

about the peaks, as if waiting for instructions. Water flowed with pristine clarity down man-made aqueducts to irrigate land that had been flattened and retained, planted and harvested by persistent hands that relied on the grace of nature not to destroy it. Here on the valley floor, and wherever gravity's pull on soil and water could be defied, it was the beauty of man's stubbornness to survive that augmented nature, decorating it with a human pattern that nature tolerated. The two men rode noisily through the silent landscape, one hugging the other despite being a stranger to him in all respects except for the commonality of their organs, trusting that man to maintain his balance and not tip them down the sharp shale embankments to a painful death; two men, each with their own thoughts that neither could express above the noise of the motorbike and the wind in their ears, even if they wanted to, and neither with the slightest idea of where this ride was to ultimately take them.

After nearly an hour of tortuous travel, they reached the village that the two women had apparently visited the previous day, and which Duc had not needed directions to find, though the route he chose avoided the road that had allowed Violet and Caroline to travel there in the relative comfort of a car, as if he somehow despised such an obvious convenience. It was, Faraday also noticed, a route that avoided the settlements along the way; in fact, it somehow managed to bring them there without any human contact at all.

They stopped two hundred meters short, and Duc laid the bike on its side on the ground behind a bush. He'd carried his rucksack on his chest, like a baby in a papoose, and now he slung it onto his back and stood watching the houses in the distance without speaking. Smoke rose from the trees that surrounded the hillside village, blue and straight, reflecting the coldness of the air. There was no sign of activity among the houses and small huts that constituted the settlement, with the only hint of human occupation, apart from the smoke, being a mud-splattered transit van parked at the foot of a path leading into the trees that camouflaged the houses. In Faraday's eyes, it was a desperate place to build a village, clinging bleakly to a hard slope without any open space for cultivation, and even by late morning, still without the comfort of sunlight.

'Is this it?' he asked.

Duc nodded, cupping his ear.

There was a faint sound like a distant wrecking ball thudding into a thick concrete wall, heavy, mechanical, and relentless in its rhythm.

Faraday watched Duc, and Duc watched the village.

'The death drum,' he said. Then he started walking.

* * * *

The houses, if they could be called that, were mostly built on stilts, which seemed like the only option on the bare scrabble slopes where they were perched. A dog or two, thin and mangy, skulked around but showed little curiosity, and there was an informal corral containing two small, rough-coated horses and a rather tired water buffalo. The drumbeat was coming from a building farther up the slope among the trees, and Duc headed towards it, passing a scattering of thatched-roof huts without attempting to look inside, despite the plumes of wood smoke rising in the cold air and Faraday's acute sense that they were being silently watched. Here and there, signs of vegetable cultivation and fruit trees gave evidence of permanent settlement, but the infertility of the ground suggested that produce was wrought with difficulty. In a clearing of earth pounded flat, they came to a round clay-and-schist building considerably larger than the houses they'd passed, and at its open doorway, an old man sat cross-legged beside a vertical temple drum. With metronomic regularity, he beat it slowly with a soft-headed mallet, counting the intervals with a measured nodding of his head, eyes closed and softly humming.

Duc motioned for Faraday to stay while he bent his head and entered the hut. The old man's eyes remained closed. Incense burned on an altar at the doorway. A cock crowed. In the intervals between drumbeats, the silence screamed. Then Duc re-emerged, led by a woman dressed in the indigo garb he had seen at the market the day before, but with strips of coloured cloth sewn into the sleeves of her shirt, and wearing a headdress that resembled a soft, flat cushion. Her face was dark and heavily lined, and her hands were stained with indigo dye. She acknowledged Faraday with her eyes, momentarily surprised, but without apparent hostility, then led them back down the slope to one of the huts they had passed earlier.

The hut had two rooms and a bare earth floor. There were no windows, and the door opening was small and low, forcing Faraday to double over in order to enter, and it took some minutes before he could adjust to the lack of light. They squatted on the floor by a charcoal fire in an open hearth while the woman prepared hot water, and she and Duc spoke quietly. As his eyes began to slowly penetrate the gloom, Faraday realized there were two small children in the doorway to the second room, who gave away their presence as soon as he spotted them by giggling and showing the whiteness of their teeth. Faraday smiled back in the dark, then concentrated on Duc's exchanges with the woman, trying to get a sense of what they were saying. Soon he heard the rustle of fabric and light footsteps on the earthen floor, and he realized that the two children had come close to him and were lightly touching his jacket, tempting his attention.

The tea, when it came, was bitter and served in tin cups, graciously but without ceremony. Faraday was too big to squat comfortably, and unaccustomed to it besides—too big altogether for this small hut. He suggested to Duc that he would wait outside, but Duc demurred firmly, telling him he wouldn't be welcome on his own outdoors.

'There has been death. The spirits must not enter the houses. The village stays inside until the spirits depart. We are strangers. We are a bad spirit.'

'Then why have we entered this house?'

'So they know where we are.'

'Do they feel threatened by us?'

'No, they will see us depart. It is the spirit of their ancestors they most fear. The village priest is not here to appease the spirits, so they will stay indoors until he returns to make a sacrifice.'

'Is this because of the deaths? Who has died?'

'It is the sickness. Seven people from this village are died, and many from other village. This woman tell me where the men have gone. The one you are looking for is their Chief, Nung Ton Phuc. The elders will not speak. Only this woman.'

Faraday's legs ached. In contrast to the warmth of the valleys through which they had ridden, it was cold on this mountain out of the sun. He wasn't dressed for it. He could feel the children's hands in his jacket pockets, and he knew there was nothing there. The guidebooks said not to ruin their teeth by giving them sweets. He had no sweets, but there were small local currency notes in the pocket of his trousers that he couldn't reach while sitting down. The thought of standing preoccupied him until his legs began to ache even more. Duc and the woman talked on. The children built up the courage to poke him on the arm. He reached behind himself and poked them back. The three of them giggled, and Duc and the woman frowned. They talked until their tea was finished, drinking it slowly, then Duc pressed his hands together in respect and stood up. With some difficulty, Faraday got to his feet as well.

Outside, the light was blindingly bright. Joss sticks burned on the crude altar at the entrance, and their clothes smelled of the wood smoke filling the room in which they'd sat. Neither the children nor the woman followed them out, and the small change in Faraday's pocket stayed where it was. They clambered back down the hill and onto the road, where their motorbike was hidden behind a bush some distance away, passing the van still parked at the foot of the path leading into the village. It was what the French called a *camion*, an enclosed panel van with rear doors and no windows, the sort of vehicle that might be used in another place to take trays of onions and tomatoes to market—but not in this place. Duc tried the doors and found them locked. He walked on without commenting, and Faraday followed, the ache gradually easing from his legs and the acrid smell of wood smoke evaporating from his clothes. The melancholic thud of the funeral drum followed them, its lament echoing out across the valley.

Before they reached the motorbike, Duc stopped abruptly. Feeling the pockets of his jacket, he took out a Swiss Army knife, then turned and scurried back to the panel van. Faraday watched at a distance as he selected a tool from the knife and inserted it between the rear doors, working it vigorously before throwing them open and climbing inside. In the darkness of the van, only his boots and backside were visible, until he emerged again and closed the doors behind him. He now had something else in his hand beside the knife, and he carefully put whatever it was in one of his zippered jacket pockets. Offering no explanation, he continued walking.

By the time he retrieved the motorbike from the bushes, Duc still hadn't shared what he'd found out in the village. Faraday was not willing to ride all the way back to Sapa without knowing, so he pressed him. The village, it seemed, had been hit by the virus, just like a number of other villages in the area. Seven people had already died, and a number were sick. It was rumoured that as many as eighty people had died in the immediate region already, and the authorities had been through, ruthlessly culling the poultry. The Nung, as Faraday well knew, didn't have a commercial flock, only domestic chickens, and these had been dispersed into the forest so they couldn't be captured, as evidenced by the cock he'd heard crowing. The problem with this particular tribe was that they blamed all sickness and disaster on evil spirits, and they relied on the priest and medicine man to invoke the ancestors to help appease those spirits who were offended, as well as by making animal sacrifices to them. At the time of the outbreak, the shaman who possessed these powers was in the mountains with a number of the men from the village, and the man that Faraday was seeking—Uncle's cousin, the village chief—had gone to find him. Meanwhile, fearing the ghosts of the dead, including those who had just died and required a proper farewell to the realm above, the remaining villagers had to stay indoors and honour the ancestors in ritual worship until the shaman returned. All of this Duc reported as if it were quite normal and understandable. What did concern him, apparently, was the reason for the absence of the men and the village priest. It was their activity, he was convinced, that would have offended the spirits, and he spent some minutes pacing back and forth on the roadside while he tried to find the words to explain it.

'Spirit of ancestor and spirit of mountain same! Mountain protects our people, allow us to pass and shelter. It is not for sale. No one must command it. The mountain is part of heaven. When the mountain is angry, we all suffer. I tell them.'

'You tell who?' Faraday asked. 'Did you tell this to the villagers?'

'I tell this to those people—the people you know. You meet him.'

Faraday was bemused. 'What people that I know?'

'You meet him in Hoi An.'

'... You mean that man, Sam, from the Paladin Foundation?'

'The Nung make this mistake before, and suffer. Green Beret soldier is enemy of our enemy—but enemy of my enemy is not my friend. The only friend is the mountain. They must stop taking from it.'

While at this stage Faraday had little idea what Duc was referring to, he did get the clear impression that he'd discovered that the Nung were working for Paladin, and that's what he wanted to clarify.

'So, you believe the village men have been employed by your man, Sam? Is that what you're saying?'

Duc shook his head angrily. 'It is sacred land where they go. I know how to find them.'

TWENTY-FOUR

On the hour's ride back to the hotel, Faraday's mind tried to absorb this new information about Paladin. Somewhere in these hills, he could discover the explanation to the question that had baffled him ever since Hoi An: what were they doing here, and what had caused Sam to avoid his attempted discussion about Kenneth Johnston? Duc seemed adamant that what they were doing was wrong. Yet these were the people who were responsible for Faraday's career and prosperity. Should he stay quiet about his doubts, or should he follow through and try and put them to rest?

By the time they made it back to the hotel, Duc's revelation that he knew how to find them had convinced Faraday that he'd pay him to help track them down. The decision lifted a load from him. Though he had no idea what would be involved, he made it sound as if he and Duc were planning little more than an extension of their search for Uncle's cousin to another village not far away. He couldn't be absolutely sure when he'd be back, he told Caroline cavalierly, but he'd been told to prepare himself for some hard climbing and to carry protection against the threat of rain and cold. As he pointed out, many people accepted the challenge of climbing Mount Fansipan, the steepest and highest of the highland peaks, and they saw it as the highlight of their holiday.

To Violet, he gave the impression of being rather keen on the prospect of vigorous exercise and fresh air, as if finding Uncle's cousin would just be a bonus.

'Are you fit enough?' she asked sceptically, eyeing him up and down.

'That does it, Violet,' he retorted. 'I've tramped the world in search of wildlife; a little mountain in Vietnam will be like a stroll in the park.'

'Well, you don't have to do it on my behalf,' she snapped. 'But I appreciate your offer.'

After checking with Duc, he assured them that he'd be in safe hands, saying he expected they might spend the night somewhere in a village, if necessary, and be back by the following day, hopefully in time for dinner. Whether or not this was true, he didn't know, but he didn't want to be dissuaded, and he reminded Caroline that he had her cell phone number if there was any change in plans. Besides, she was now keen to put together a story about the effects of the epidemic on the villages in the Highlands, so she could file it with her news agency (the anticipated story about the Vanderbilt Foundation's water project being off the table for the time being). Her gratitude for his offer to help Violet in this way was tempered with puzzlement at the suddenness of his decision.

'Are you sure?' she asked, more than once.

'Absolutely!' he insisted. 'It'll be fun.'

But he was forced to suppress the thought that he might be doing this in order to dispel the impression he'd given the night before that he was a boring bloody artist with no sense of adventure or fun. Hopefully she wasn't thinking the same.

Then, after quietly confirming with the hotel's reception that he'd have no trouble checking back in, he vacated his room, put his baggage in storage, and purchased a rucksack from a shop in town, which he stuffed with a change of clothing, two packets of chocolate biscuits, and his camera before meeting Duc and his motorbike in front of the market and setting off again in the direction from which they'd returned that morning.

Oh, yes—and he left an envelope at reception to be given to Caroline that night. In it was a note:

The things a man will do for a woman's kiss! Perhaps when I get back with your tribal chief, I'll deserve another?

Once he'd sealed the envelope and handed it over, together with the shawl he'd purchased the day before, he wondered if he should take it back … but by then, it was too late.

They continued beyond the Nung village for half an hour or so, until eventually, the track petered out, and the terrain became too dangerous to negotiate by motorbike. Duc was not forthcoming about the direction he was taking, and as he set off on foot, Faraday had no choice but to follow, sure that with his long legs, he would have no trouble matching the pace of his much shorter companion.

The drumbeats they'd heard at the Nung village continued to haunt him, drumbeats that signified a death, announcing the departure of a soul to the realms above. It was a haunting sound, so full of melancholy that no composer could possibly match it, and as they climbed deeper into the mountains, throughout the day he heard it many times, telling him that death was spreading to the remote villages.

By late afternoon, when his leg muscles were searing with pain, his lungs were burning with the effort of extracting oxygen from the rarefied air, and his clothing was saturated from the gut-busting effort of negotiating the slopes of Mount Fansipan, his only thought was physical survival. They slid on their bottoms down muddy slopes and crawled on hands and knees up shale banks, following a path only Duc was able to see, on the assurance that this was 'the quick way'. Whenever they crossed a man-made track, or even a narrow suggestion of one previously trod, Duc treated it with disdain. If the mountains were the roof of heaven, it seemed that the only way to get there was to follow the route to hell. They crossed creeks that would become torrents at the first rainfall, and they hauled themselves up embankments with only honey thorns for handholds. Blood coloured the sweat on Faraday's soft artist's hands, and he felt certain that it filled his virgin hiking shoes, too. Leeches landed on his neck and forearms, extracting violent curses from him along with his blood. And all the while,

211

ahead of him, Duc's sturdy calf muscles, inexplicably unscathed by thorns or razor-sharp rocks, pressed on relentlessly, as if he were out for a brisk stroll.

On and on strode those sturdy calf muscles of the little man in front until, after nearly four hours, they landed in a clearing that housed what was to Faraday's eyes a vision of Arcadia: a peaceful encampment of thatched mud-brick houses, wood smoke rising, chickens scratching, and figures moving peacefully in the twilight, winding down for the day.

Duc patted Faraday on his stomach and smiled. 'Walking makes us hungry. We stay here and eat with family.'

If he had said anything else, Faraday might have sat down and cried, such was his exhaustion. The motivation for his coming on this journey was now long forgotten, and the only motivation that remained at that moment was his need for rest.

What Duc meant by 'family' was not quite clear. He'd said that his tribe was from Sinho, many miles away, and the people who greeted them were certainly not his wife, children, or parents—not even distant relations, or the same tribe, judging by their appearance—so perhaps it was the fact that they were fellow Montagnards that made them 'family'. Some sort of tale was told, incomprehensible to Faraday, but punctuated by knowing looks and body language that spoke of disapproval on one hand and support on the other. Whatever Duc told them, they were aware of what was going on and honour-bound to offer hospitality, which included everything Faraday could have wished for: food, alcohol, and sleep.

The alcohol was a fiery rice wine, which they drank copiously until all the aches in Faraday's long legs and ill-conditioned back melted away. The food was based around a cockerel specially killed for the occasion, its head sliced off with one sharp machete blow on a wooden block as their host held it firmly by the legs in one hand. The blood pumping from its still beating heart was then collected from the severed neck in a bowl to be whisked and added to the mix of ingredients that would fill the spring rolls that the women prepared after plucking, skinning, and de-boning the bird, so that every morsel was available for their consumption.

The village elder, his wife, and two generations of children, plus the two guests, sat cross-legged in a circle in the smoke-filled two-room hut, where later that night, Faraday would sleep on the earth floor by the fire, using his rucksack for a pillow, dreams swirling like clouds through his alcohol-infused brain, too numerous to be remembered in the morning.

He woke with a thick head, aching muscles, and the communication skills of a deaf mute, wondering what the hell he was doing there. Was Duc deliberately uncommunicative, or was that just his style? Where were they, and where were they going? How long was it going to take to get there, and what was he expecting when they arrived? How could he thank his hosts—and who were *they*, anyway?

They offered him a bitter tea, which he was unable to drink, so he asked for water: copious well water to slake his thirst as he sat cross-legged on the floor, nodding and smiling. He wanted a crap, but he didn't know where to go, let alone how to ask, so he left the hut and wandered into the trees, emptying his bladder and bowels, feeling awkward and disoriented. He couldn't go back to Sapa, because he had no idea how they'd come. Roads and tracks had already been left far behind, and around him were thousands upon thousands of acres of uninhabited forest, uncharted rivers and mountains, and eventually China, stretched along 1350 kilometres of inhospitable border.

Returning to the hut, he found Duc preparing to leave.

'I tell them you thank,' he said. 'You take photo and show them. Now you are family.'

Everyone lined up under Duc's instructions. The whole process was unfamiliar to them and their faces showed their bafflement. 'Smile', Faraday instructed. Failing to get a response, he pressed the shutter, then showed them the picture on the back of his camera, and they passed it among themselves in silent awe.

Then they left, Duc angrily forbidding Faraday from trying to give them money. Faraday still had no idea where they were heading, yet he suspected the day would be no easier than the one before. His muscles already ached so painfully that he was soon unable to keep up, and Duc had to drop back to check that he was okay.

'Not far,' he said. 'You take *hạt thiêng*. Make muscle good.'

He opened the zip pocket on his jacket where he'd placed whatever he had found in the back of the van at the Nung village. Taking Faraday's hand, he placed six black seeds in his palm, the colour and size of star anise.

'Sacred seed,' he announced enigmatically. 'Good medicine.'

At Duc's urging, he chewed two of the black seeds he'd been given. They were hard and bitter, but within minutes, he miraculously felt his hip and knee joints begin to ease. Perhaps they were like the coca leaves he'd chewed in South America. After an hour, he took one more, and the stiffness in his back from lying on the hard earth floor all night disappeared as well. For three hours, they continued to climb, boulder-hopping across river beds, heading north, as far as Faraday could tell from the position of the sun through the open-canopied forest, all while navigating a trail visible only to Duc and never pausing to reassess or check their position.

Finally, Duc decided to stop so they could both drink water from a stream. Faraday took one of the packets of chocolate biscuits from his rucksack that he'd bought in Sapa, and finding that the biscuits had melted and congealed together, he broke the packet in half and shared it. The further they'd gone into the mountains, the greater was Faraday's fear that he'd made a dreadful mistake. Having placed all his trust in his guide, he now came to the grim realization that he was entirely dependent upon him for his survival. If Duc dropped dead, then Faraday was effectively dead as well; he had no way of sustaining himself in the wild, let alone returning to civilization. This realization played on his mind so forcefully that he wondered if there was something in the 'medicine' seeds that was making him paranoid. His pains had gone—but so had his nerve. It was not a fear that he wished to voice, for of course, it would be an admission that the other man now had complete power over him, and that admission would be grounds for paranoia in itself.

As if aware of his thoughts, Duc cheerfully assured him that they would soon reach their destination.

'Not far now,' he said. 'One hour only. You walk good?'

'I think so ... but how do you know where you're going with no trails and no compass?'

'I know mountains, and I have compass in my head. This way quicker than trails.' He laughed happily, clearly at home in such an environment.

'Alright, but how do other people find their way? How would the Nung tribesmen or the man from Paladin come here? They can't all have compasses in their heads.'

Duc laughed again. 'Oh, they follow mountain paths, but too slow for us.'

'Is this why they wanted you as a guide?'

'They can go anywhere they want with GPS. No need for guide then. No, they want I tell where they find what I give you: *hạt thiêng*. Places where no guides, no people, no tracks. I know all the mountains. In village and city, I am Duc, but in mountain, I am king! ... Good joke?'

'Good joke. Very good.'

So, there *were* tracks ... somewhere. There had to be tracks, for wherever they were going must be a location known to the Nung tribe, at least, including the village elder, the priest, and a number of the tribesmen, who he was certain would not possess GPS. And since they were now getting close, that meant that were Faraday to find himself alone and lost, he'd eventually stumble across one of those tracks and have a reasonable chance of finding his way out, provided the weather conditions allowed it. If that was some help for his insecurity, the best help of all was Duc's good humour.

'And what they're looking for is not elephants, but this ... seed?' Faraday asked.

'No elephants. *Hạt thiêng.* I tell you that.'

'I don't get it. Why do they want this seed?'

But he couldn't get Duc to explain further.

The stream they'd drunk from ran, as all streams do, downhill, and they did the same, following along its bank, sometimes forced by narrow-sided gullies to wade in the bed of the stream itself. After an hour or so, as Duc had predicted, they stumbled across a barely visible path and smelled wood smoke, signalling the proximity of a settlement. At this point, Duc stopped, unslung his rucksack, and started to unzip it. Before he could reach into it, however, a loud shout rang out, and three tribesmen emerged from the surrounding trees to confront them, wielding machetes. The one who had shouted the challenge advanced on Duc and snatched his rucksack, questioning him excitably and gesticulating at the surrounding trees and the stream they'd been following, not just upset by their presence, but by their sudden appearance out of the forest, which had clearly surprised them.

For Faraday, watching these events unfurl with the curious sense of slow motion that accompanies a cloudburst of adrenalin (heightened, he came to believe later, by the hallucinogenic properties of the 'medicine' seeds he had been chewing), there was only one possible outcome. That involved the inevitable discovery of Duc's black pistol, which Faraday felt certain would be found in the rucksack—a discovery that would surely be followed by an ensuing melee involving machetes, which would in turn lead to the decoration of the verdant green adjacent undergrowth with the bright crimson of fresh blood. The blood, quickly blackening as it dried, would be his blood—and that was such a sufficiently frightening thought that he shouted at the top of his lungs the only words that spontaneously sprang to mind.

TWENTY-FIVE

'We're from Paladin!'

The words echoed through the trees and into the encampment before them with a clarity that seemed to stun both captors and captured alike. The machetes were lowered as a suspicious examination of Faraday took place, and Duc contemptuously demanded his rucksack back, inching forward, forcing the tribesmen to retreat. Was it the word *Paladin* that had stopped them in their tracks, or was it the sudden burst of a foreign language?

'Are they Nung?' Faraday whispered.

'They Nung.'

'Tell them about Nung Ton Phuc.'

'I tell them.'

After an animated discussion among themselves, one of the tribesmen signalled with his machete that they were to follow. The other two circled behind them and prodded them forward with the sharp points of their weapons, the Montagnard fellowship of the previous night now a distant memory. They threaded their way through the trees, passing hastily built grass-covered huts that appeared to be empty. Grey mist clung to the treetops, and the air was cold and damp.

From out of the dense trees, they suddenly emerged into a wide clearing that was open to the sky. The light brightened, and for a brief instant, there was a glimpse of a mountain ridge rising above them, black against the mercury-coloured storm clouds, and through those clouds, a brief ray of sunlight illuminated the scene like a theatre spotlight. At the edge of the clearing was a thatch-roofed hut, larger than the others, which Faraday and Duc were pushed towards until they stood in the doorway, peering in. It was a storehouse filled with what appeared to be sacks of grain.

As rain started to fall, one of the tribesmen pointed inside and commanded them both to wait. Duc, seemingly unmoved by the order, lunged forward and snatched his rucksack back.

'We come find Nung Ton Phuc!' he shouted aggressively in English, perhaps for Faraday's benefit. Then he repeated it in his own language, leading to a heated exchange with one of their tribal escorts, followed by an indication that Duc was to follow them back out of the hut, presumably to find the elusive chief whose whereabouts had prompted their journey.

As his guide left the room with their captors, an eerie silence entered—one that Faraday, as an only child raised by a Ndebele nanny and cook on a remote farm in Matabeleland, recognized as the arrival of the ancestral spirits, come to mediate between the past and the present. On a more mundane level, it was the silence of the mountains, the forest, and the mists, a silence that absorbed all sound, even that of his own breathing.

He sat down on one of the sacks, suddenly too exhausted to stand. The muscles and joints that had screamed their complaints at the need to keep moving throughout the day now surrendered all feeling and ceased to respond to any signals from his brain. His head drooped, and he longed to stretch out, trying to hold onto the anxiety that would keep him alert, but like a drowning man, fearful of losing his grip on the buoyancy of consciousness.

The unreality of the world into which he had plunged twenty-four hours ago was so blindingly intense that, in his mind, he couldn't find a clear path back to the point where he had entered it. Somewhere on the previous day's climb into the mountains, he'd seen quite clearly that Caroline's kiss and his fulsome admission that he was, as Helene had believed, just "a boring bloody painter" had spurred him to prove (to Caroline, or to himself?) that the easel wasn't the only mistress to whom he was willing to give himself. As the thrilling relief from pain induced by the anti-inflammatory effects of Duc's magic seeds had flushed through his body, he'd convinced himself that he was doing this to prove that he didn't have a commitment phobia, and that painting was not a prophylactic that he used to protect himself from 'catching an emotional infection', as Caroline claimed.

But they weren't yet even lovers. Why this sudden drunkenness on the part of his emotions? Surely he was confusing his desire to impress a beautiful woman with the real motive for his impetuous decision to take off into the mountains. That motive had its origins in his reason for coming to Vietnam in the first place, and meeting Caroline and Violet Dunleavy had finally given it definition: because the Nung tribe were working for Paladin, he had to believe that finding them would bring him closer to Johnston. He was chasing his past, not his future.

Soon the rain began to fall with such conviction that the water cascading off the roof of his shelter looked like a waterfall. He shook his head. Had he slept, or had he merely been lost in a reverie? Staggering to his feet, he stepped outside, closing his eyes and tilting his face up to catch the cascade of water, willing it to clear his head. His breathing was shallow, and his heart pounded. Duc had warned him that the air was more rarefied the more they climbed, but the rain made it thinner still. Returning inside, he collapsed back onto the sacks. The sense of dependency that he'd felt towards Duc while climbing the mountain was now rendered absolute by his condition. There was no way back down the mountain without him, and quite likely, no way of surviving the tribesmen's open hostility without his language and leadership. Whether he'd placed himself in this position on Caroline's account, or on account of a misplaced belief in his sixth sense—that he was destined to encounter Kenneth Johnston—was no longer relevant. Survival was now all that mattered.

At the moment when the rain abruptly stopped and he lifted his head to look out the doorway, it was almost immediately filled with the figure of Duc, water dripping from his saturated clothes and blood dripping from his severed cheek and ear, which he held together with one tightly clenched hand. In the other hand, he held his knapsack and his gun.

Faraday stumbled to his feet. 'Duc…?'

As Duc started to respond, his words were suddenly drowned out by a howling scream, as if the mountain itself were being blown asunder. Faraday staggered to the door. The scream was mechanical. He recognized it. It was the scream of air being violently compressed and then combusted before exploding into life in a turbojet helicopter, parked just meters away in the clearing in front of where they stood.

Faraday gasped in dismay. How could it have landed there without his knowing? How deeply had he fallen into unconsciousness? Had the torrential rain drowned out the sound of its landing, or had it sat there unnoticed when they'd arrived, under camouflage netting? The flimsy shelter shook as the exhaust hit, and the scream rose in intensity as the rotor blades began to spin, turning the rain-soaked vegetation into a giant water blaster that flooded the doorway and blew them backwards.

Shouting obscenities, Faraday grabbed Duc by the arm. 'What the fuck…?!'

'American!' Duc shouted back. 'I find him!' The blood pouring from his severed ear and cheek saturated his hunting vest as the gun in his hand wandered uncontrollably.

In the doorway, a large black figure suddenly blocked the light. He was clad in a blood-red puffer jacket, and his deep voice carried over the roar of the engine. 'Come quick, mon! No time to fuck about!'

* * * *

So, a helicopter took off from a jungle clearing in the monsoon rain. Violence and the absurd logic of madness that plagued Vietnam swirled about them, as if they were trapped in a scene from *Apocalypse Now* that had been dropped on the cutting room floor. What was that about? How long had this sense of apocalypse been building?

The pilot was Vietnamese. Duc sat beside him in the passenger seat with one hand cupped to the cloth that stemmed the blood from his bleeding ear and cheek, and the other hand still clutching the pistol that he hadn't lowered since bursting into the hut. The noise from the engine was deafening as the chopper slowly rose from the clearing, wobbling unsteadily, its rotor blades uncomfortably close to the surrounding forest canopy. Faraday struggled with his seat belt and peered down at the figures in the clearing beneath them, catching sight of the upturned faces of the tribesmen dressed in indigo that blended so perfectly into the deep shadows of the mountain forest, until they abruptly disappeared as the helicopter turned on its side and veered away across the treetops with alarming speed.

Above him was a set of earphones with a mouthpiece, similar to one that the pilot wore. He put it on, fiddling with the switch on the side.

'Sapa,' he said. 'Take us to Sapa.'

There was no sound in his earphones. He reversed the switch and spoke again; still no sound. The system was turned off. He shouted the instruction again at the top of his voice, but the pilot's eyes didn't flicker as he concentrated on the way ahead, climbing out of the steep-sided valley surrounding the encampment and into the swirling mists that shrouded the mountaintops.

Jamaican Sam had shouted the same instruction to the pilot as he'd shepherded them into the helicopter, and he had to hope that he could trust him. Had he helped their departure solely because of the threat of Duc's gun, or was he spiriting them away for other reasons? What might have happened if the helicopter had not been there when Duc had made his dramatic entrance, followed by a group of tribesmen carrying machetes? Sam had seen the tribesmen off, but how would events have unfolded if they hadn't been able to escape?

Duc was not forthcoming, preoccupied by the severity of his wound. 'Not safe,' was all he'd muttered. 'Not safe here.' The skin of his cheek had hung down, exposing the bone, as he removed his hand to rip open his rucksack and pull out a tee shirt to stem the blood. His eyes never wavered from the open doorway, and his pistol had remained trained on it while Sam shouted at the tribesmen, finally getting them to retreat.

'Fuck,' Sam had cursed, 'I don't know what's gone on here, but something sure has upset these people. They're very protective, very tense. The sickness has got them frightened. Then the damned shaman stirs them up about strangers being bad spirits, and the chief has his work cut out for him keeping a lid on it all. How's your guide? Is he going to be alright?'

'Not unless he gets some medical treatment quickly.'

'Yeah, well, hopefully the chopper will have you at the hospital in a few minutes, and you'll be safely out of here.'

That was it—no other explanation—and Faraday was in no state to wait for one.

* * * *

The chopper traced the contours of the mountain ridges and the valley floors, staying alarmingly close to the treetops, so that all Faraday's energy was consumed by his concentration on impending danger. There was nothing in the terrain below that he recognized, but he was aware from the position of the fading light that they were heading south. Anything north would have had them crossing into China in minutes. Duc, too, paid close attention to the ground beneath their feet, and he no doubt could recognize it, for he seemed satisfied with the direction they were taking.

The scream of the engine and the relentless drumming of the rotor blades were hypnotic, and Faraday's mind flipped uncontrollably between images remembered from his viewing of this movie in his bedroom at the Rex Hotel in Saigon, and Jamaican Sam's last words before he'd escorted them through the hostile phalanx of tribesmen to the safety of the helicopter.

'When you're dealing with indigenous people, mon, you need to take the high-level view and respect their culture. They believe in spirits, and we believe in science. Ecology needs the two. Take care, now.'

Why had he said that? What possible connection could that have had to what they had just witnessed? He'd treated them like two trampers who'd inadvertently gotten lost and stumbled into a village clearing. No mention of their previous meeting in Hoi An, no excuses, no pretence of elephants. No questions asked.

Within minutes, they suddenly emerged from the mist and started gliding down a mountain slope towards a sizable town in the distance, its tiled rooftops touched by the pale light of a sinking sun. Duc tugged at the pilot's sleeve and mouthed an instruction to him, pointing as they got closer. The chopper flew in over a lake, banked right over a cluster of buildings on a ridge that Faraday recognized as the Victoria Hotel, then began a fast descent into a field behind what looked like a newish public building. As their skids touched the ground, the pilot shouted at them and waved his free arm, telling them to get out. He barely let them clear the rotor blades before immediately taking off at speed, heading back up the mountain towards the mists in the rapidly fading light.

'Hospital!' Duc shouted.

They stumbled across the stiff grass and through a door that led down a corridor to a public waiting room. Fluorescent lighting flickered blue, and the smell of antiseptic was reassuringly familiar. The mad world of the mountain evaporated as if it had never existed.

The hospital was in chaos, staff running distractedly from room to room in face masks and latex gloves, corridors lined with anxious relatives and patients lying on gurneys. The reality of the exploding epidemic was blindingly clear; their own predicament was puny by comparison.

Duc had to fight for attention before eventually disappearing to be treated, and Faraday sat down to wait, exhausted and sore. There was one last seed left in his pocket, and he took it. He'd lost track of time and realized he'd been too busy to think about Caroline, who must by now be alarmed by his disappearance. They'd been gone for two days, and now night was falling. His cell phone was in his backpack, turned off, and when he retrieved it and turned it on, he found four missed calls: one from Ralph and three from Caroline.

As keen as he was to speak to Caroline, he would put off calling her until he'd had a chance to find out from Duc exactly what had happened, and whether he'd managed to find Uncle's cousin, for that would be her first question. There were so many questions. The one he had come to Vietnam with had finally been answered by Madame Roulet, and now, in comparison with the new questions that had arisen, it seemed almost trivial. Copying a painting would probably be, in Johnston's words, a harmless little scam of no consequence. Faraday was sure he'd track down his involvement eventually, but the exposure of Paladin as a chimera had far more serious consequences, and not just for himself as its sometime beneficiary. As he sat in the waiting room, physically numbed but now mentally active and alert, watching the emergency unfolding around him, he experienced a mixture of excitement and trepidation, waiting for Duc to tell him what he had found out.

He still didn't know what Jamaican Sam and Paladin were up to, for nothing he had seen or heard made sense. Whatever it was, it obviously wasn't what Sam had previously pretended. It had nothing to do with tracking elephants, and it wasn't welcoming of discovery. Duc claimed they were collecting seeds, but why were they so intent on hiding and protecting that fact with such violence? Was it possible that they were not only operating outside of the Paladin remit, but highly illegally? It seemed inconceivable that people with the stature and credentials of the Paladin Foundation would condone such behaviour. Yet no amount of poring over the entrails had helped him divine their meaning, so now his only hope was that some clue lay in the events that led to Duc's attack.

… Unless there was something he'd missed—something that Johnston had told him in the past that he wasn't understanding.

TWENTY-SIX

The mood within the hotel was subdued. Almost without exception, reservations were being cancelled as the news went out that the coronavirus flu toll in the area was climbing to epidemic proportions.

'They don't handle these things well,' the duty manager complained to Faraday as he checked back in. 'It is not a person-to-person virus; we know that. But tourists and people in the city are not being told, so naturally they don't want to take the risk, and we lose business.'

'I feel for you,' Faraday sympathized. 'But why is it spreading?'

The manager shrugged. 'If I could answer that...'

Caroline and Violet, he confirmed, were in the hotel at that moment, but Faraday wanted to shower and change before calling them, so he claimed his luggage and went to his room. The conversation he'd had with Duc at the hospital, after he'd been patched up and before they'd parted, had not adequately explained what had gone on back at the Paladin encampment, but it had left him with something approximating an explanation for why Violet's philanthropy had been rejected. The spread of the virus had spooked the tribe into taking to the hills, expecting to be blamed by other tribes, or the authorities. Experience had taught them to expect retribution; that was their fate. The best he could say was that his impulsive decision to head off into the mountains in search of Nung Ton Phuc had produced a result of sorts, but the full details of their trip would be better kept to himself until he could make sense of them.

While the shower cleaned him up, sluicing a mixture of mud and blood down the drain, it didn't revive him. The anti-inflammatory needs of his muscles and joints weren't being met by Duc's seeds anymore, and the adrenalin that had pumped through his body over the last few hours had left him with a hangover. The comfort of bed was calling to him, but so was the need to explain his whereabouts and what had happened to him.

Once dressed, he decided to knock on Caroline's door rather than phone her room. When she called out asking who it was, he replied 'Room service!' in an obviously false voice, then waited nervously, trying to remember how things had been between them when they parted.

After a few moments, she threw the door open and stood glaring at him with a slightly short-sighted frown of disapproval.

'You took long enough,' she protested.

As well as the scowl, she also wore a tentative smile. She wasn't wearing much else, though; he'd obviously caught her in the middle of dressing, and she'd grabbed a towel to cover herself. He stepped forward and kissed her, long enough for it to be more than just a friendly greeting, but not long enough to stop her from taking issue with him.

'Where have you been, Anton? I've been calling you every hour, and you wouldn't respond. We've been worried sick. What happened?'

'I can't begin to tell you,' he mumbled. 'But I'm pleased to hear you were concerned —and with good reason. I'm battered, bruised, and exhausted, but by some miracle, still alive. Sympathy and a stiff drink are the least I deserve.'

He rolled up his sleeves and showed her his arms, which had borne the brunt of the damage as they'd fought their way through the undergrowth in Duc's determination to take 'the fast way', avoiding tracks. Even more alarming than the scratches were the size of the insect bites. He'd developed a dull headache, which he attributed to stress, and he now felt embarrassed about his foolhardy actions in charging off up the mountain when his body was clearly in no condition to attempt such a venture.

Caroline took his hand, closed the door, and sat him down on the bed. 'You look dreadful. Lie down and rest.'

He stretched out and let her remove his shoes, then she lay down beside him and undid his shirt so she could stroke his chest. When he woke later during the night, she was breathing softly beside him. He lay awake, thinking about the events in the mountains, until exhaustion claimed him again, and he slept until Caroline shook him awake and announced that breakfast service would finish in an hour, and Violet was waiting for them downstairs.

It seemed that Violet had been waiting impatiently since Caroline had called earlier to tell her that Faraday and Duc had returned the previous night. Now she quizzed him closely on Duc's account of his meeting with Uncle's cousin.

'You say he spoke to him and told him why you were there? That you'd come to talk about the water project? Did they discuss that at all?'

'No, Duc was not aware of any of the details. As far as he was concerned, we were looking for Nung Ton Phuc because we wanted to know if he was willing to take the job.'

'And what was the answer?'

'That he didn't want to be involved. His exact words were "Water not safe from sickness." '

'Meaning...?'

'Duc presumed he was talking about the village wells. It seems that some villagers avoided vaccinating their poultry as required by the government because they believed it would damage the fertility of the birds—or maybe they were just bloody minded—and when the authorities arrived, they could be in serious trouble, so they panicked and quickly killed the birds and threw them into the old wells.'

'Well, that's the problem with wells everywhere in the Third World,' Violet insisted. 'Bores aren't so easily contaminated, but you need power to drive them.'

'Anyway, those were the words he used. Nung Ton Phuc said "water", and Duc presumed he meant "wells". I don't know what language they spoke. If the response makes no sense to you, the sentiment, at least, was clear. He'd changed his mind.'

'But why did they attack him?' Caroline asked.

Faraday hesitated. He hadn't pressed Duc firmly enough on this. The tension and latent violence had been high from the minute they'd first stumbled into the clearing and been surrounded by tribesmen. If he could have explained the reason why, then he'd have the answer to all his questions about Paladin and Jamaican Sam's presence there as well.

'Mostly they're wary of being blamed when things go wrong, so they take to the hills. It's the curse of being on the losing side. The shamanic explanation for all threats is that the ancestral spirits are angry. Strangers in the high mountains are seen as agents of enemy spirits. Duc was nosing around. He saw things and disturbed people unwittingly, so they attacked him.'

'What sort of things?'

'He said there were storage huts where people were bagging something up. And there were, by his account, quite a number of tribesmen ill and being tended to in a makeshift field hospital. He said it was not tribal medicine treatment, but Western medical treatment. There was something about that which puzzled him. He was warned off, but he didn't take the warning quickly enough, it seems. They were extremely hostile to our presence.'

'My God, it sounds like you were both lucky to get out!' Caroline exclaimed.

'In a way, I'm relieved,' Violet decided. 'Meeting Nung Ton Phuc never felt like a good idea to me, and I was only looking for a way to make up for my teenage stupidity. The past is the past and best forgotten. I think that we can safely say now that this project isn't going to happen.'

It was not in her character to dwell on setbacks or disappointments. There were too many other things that needed to be done.

'I'm really sorry, Violet,' Caroline apologized. 'I feel responsible for dragging you out here for nothing.'

'Don't be silly girl. We're dealing with people and cultures that are so far removed from our view of life that we can't hope to understand their fears and superstitions. All we can do is try and help them on their terms. If you think what's happening here is hard to accept, you'd better come with me to Africa. Chickens are more valuable there than people. It's not your fault; it's nobody's fault. When this epidemic is over, maybe we'll try again.'

As worthy as this sentiment was, Faraday felt certain that Uncle's cousin and his tribe were never going to be an instrument for Western philanthropy. Whatever was going on with Paladin up in those mountains, it was anything but philanthropic.

It was agreed that there was nothing further to be gained by staying in Sapa, and they would return together to Hanoi on the following morning's train. Their reserved tickets needed to be rescheduled, but that was not a problem, as visitor bookings had dropped off completely, and there were plenty of empty compartments. It was a day train and took eight and a half hours to reach Hanoi. Caroline had work to do, as did Violet, while Faraday suspected that he would mainly sleep the journey away. Though he'd spent the previous night in Caroline's room, he had slept for nine hours undisturbed, and despite the feeling that they were on a path towards something more, their relationship was not at the point where he could assume they'd share a railway sleeper together.

During the two days he was away, Caroline had been gathering material for a story she was filing with her news bureau on the spread of the epidemic to surrounding villages, and she headed off after breakfast to interview local government officials, excited because her bureau chief, Sinclair Baines, had told her he liked her work and wanted more.

Duc had said that he intended to go out to the Nung village near where he'd left the motorbike hidden, and Faraday had asked him to call the hotel on his return, partly to check how he was faring with his wounds, and also because he wanted to pay him for his services. What that payment should be was a matter of conjecture, for Duc had not sought any reward or even hinted at what he charged as a guide under normal circumstances. The fact that he had almost been killed made these circumstances decidedly abnormal, and Violet was determined that the payment should reflect that fact.

'When you put your life in someone's hands,' she pointed out, 'and they take care of you, then how you pay them is partly a reflection of how much you value your own life.'

In the end, they settled on four hundred US dollars a day, for which Duc was very grateful. He arrived, looking impervious to his facial damage, just as they were finishing breakfast, and Faraday went outside to meet him.

'I find what your friends do in the mountain,' he said, tapping the side of his nose disapprovingly. 'I find them in the *camion* when we go to Nung village first time.'

He put his hand in his jacket pocket and pulled something out in his fist, then took Faraday's hand and dropped what he was holding into it. They were the black seeds he'd given him to help fight his pain and fatigue.

'They same bags that I see when I go look for Nung Ton Phuc. They take from the mountain.'

'But why are they collecting these seeds?'

'Special medicine. Only find in mountain in special time. I tell you: they not protect elephant; they protect area from people. Kill people who come there. Kill me. Kill you. Lucky you friend.'

'I'm not a friend.'

Duc shrugged. 'You not enemy. Spirits accept you.'

'Is this seed valuable?'

'Only to people who live in mountain. Seed is sacred; must not be taken from mountain.'

'Why?'

'It grow only there. No seed, it grow no more. Spirits protect.'

'You mean without seeds, there will be no trees? Do the old trees die once they've seeded? Is that why they mustn't be taken?'

'Four years before seeds. Only in these mountain. Very rare.'

230

Duc hesitated. He was a man who did not offer information unless asked, and there was something about his manner now that suggested Faraday needed to find the right question.

'When you met the American, Sam, at the market and told him you didn't want the job, did he tell you exactly what that job was going to be?'

'He want I make a map.'

'Of…?'

'He want to know everywhere *hạt thiêng* trees grow across border.'

'In China?'

Could the explanation for Paladin's presence be as simple as a desire to recover and propagate a rare species of plant that only existed in a remote area of the world? Faraday wanted to believe that, but if so, why the secrecy, and the willingness to use violence to keep intruders away? And how did it square with Johnston's claim that Paladin had an influence and agenda that went well beyond saving wildlife?

Faraday gave Duc an extra two hundred dollars, forcing it on him, and bid him farewell with some sadness. The man had saved his life—he was sure of that—and his values shone so brightly that language and culture could not dim them.

Returning to the hotel reception desk to claim a bag he'd put in storage, he was presented with an envelope. The message read: *Fansipan cable car station coffee shop at 2:30 p.m. Kenneth.*

TWENTY-SEVEN

Finally! Ever since the man from Christie's had knocked on his studio door in London, Faraday had sensed that his journey would end with him confronting Kenneth Johnston. Now that moment had come at last, and he was ready for it.

There were brochures at the hotel promoting Sunworld Fansipan Legend, but he'd paid little attention to them, and he wasn't prepared for what he found there. The hotel concierge had doubted that it would even be open, on account of the burgeoning epidemic forcing the closure of public venues and health officials telling everyone to stay away from crowded places. But he'd phoned ahead for him and was told that the cable cars were running and the queues were short.

Faraday's taxi dropped him off in front of a faux palace with an enormous car park that might have sat comfortably in a Chinese theme park licensed by Disneyland, but which in Vietnam seemed like yet another foreign invasion in a country that had suffered too many. Inside was a ticket hall modelled on Grand Central Station, with roped-off lanes leading to sales booths in expectation of visiting hordes. But the hordes had been decimated by the threat of the virus, and barely fifty people were passing through, incognito behind their white gauze face masks.

Johnston's message had said *coffee shop at 2:30 p.m.,* and Faraday was fifteen minutes early. The coffee shop was empty. The staff, who must have

232

been used to having five hundred customers to serve, decided to ignore him. So, he found a seat by himself that gave a view of the entrance while he thought about everything except what he was going to say to this man who, it seemed, had been lurking in the shadows of his life for twenty-five years, a benefactor, a nemesis, an enigma. The note left at the front desk had not caught him by surprise so much as raised an unexpected question in his mind: who was really following whom on this journey?

When Johnston entered in a light-fawn linen suit (only a little crumpled) with white shirt and tie, checked himself at the doorway until he spotted Faraday, then walked towards him with his rather short-legged military gait, a thin-lipped smile on his ruddy face, it was as though they were still in London and had just seen each other yesterday.

'You've lost your hair,' Faraday said, not getting up.

'And you've put on weight,' Johnston replied.

He stepped forward and pulled out a chair, as if this were where they always met. A waitress arrived simultaneously, and he started to wave her away, then changed his mind.

'Never drink coffee in Vietnam,' he advised. 'They stew it to death. *Rượu rắn.*'

The girl looked surprised, then bowed and trotted off.

If there were spirits in the room whispering in Faraday's ear, they were momentarily confused. 'What the fuck are you doing here in Vietnam, Kenneth? Pretending to track bloody *elephants*, for God's sake?'

'Don't you think they're worth saving?'

'Don't be facetious,' Faraday snapped. 'We both know that's a cover. As if collecting census information on the *Elephas maximus* was the best use of Paladin's time and money anyway… I thought your brief was to save the bloody world. And what's that field operative with the cultured Caribbean accent doing wearing a solid-gold Rolex and a Hugo Boss puffer jacket? Doesn't he know he's not supposed to make money off of wildlife? Which reminds me: what did you think you were doing, commissioning a copy of *my* panda painting? Were you short on petty cash?'

Johnston's face didn't alter. Though his sandy hair had thinned considerably with age and his jowls had begun to droop, he still had a calculating poker player's ability to remain impassive. His eyes, however, gave him away, flicking impulsively like a lizard's, identifying and locating the position and temperature of everything within view.

'Now, don't let's be getting off on the wrong footing, laddie.' He smiled, laying on his Scottish brogue. 'Are you accusing me of something nefarious? I'm still in a state of disbelief that you should have stumbled your way into this godforsaken place ... let alone that we haven't seen each other for two decades or more ... let alone that for you, it doesn't seem nearly as surprising as it seems to me—and why that should be the case is puzzling enough without you accusing me of something that I don't even know if I should feel guilty about. So, why don't we start again?'

The waitress returned with two wine glasses and a bottle. She fussed about getting them off her tray and onto the table, not having a clue what she should do, until Johnston took over and dismissed her.

'You asked me what the fuck I was doing here, and then gave me the answer,' he continued calmly. 'So, what the fuck are *you* doing here? Better still, why don't we have a glass or two of snake wine to settle our nerves and celebrate old times?'

He unscrewed the bottle cap and filled the two glasses. The bottle had something dead inside it—presumably a snake.

'It tastes like shit,' Johnston observed cheerfully, 'but it helps protect against evil spirits, and the plague. When you finish the bottle in one sitting, you're supposed to eat the snake, and that'll give you an erection that'll last a month—not that you'll be able to feel it. But it's harmless compared to the water. Whatever you do, don't drink the local well water. Are you aware that people are dying? Of course you are. The poor, ignorant Montagnards think it's a sign that their ancestors are angry and need to be appeased. No point in telling them different. Here, bottoms up!'

234

He downed his glass without waiting.

Faraday tried to remember when he'd last drunk with Johnston, and whether the man had knocked it back so greedily then. Yes—the night they'd had dinner at the *Alouette*, after sealing the deal on the copyright fee for the Harbinger Collection, Johnston had sunk seven Courvoisiers in a row—and Helene had matched him glass for glass. They'd been looking for the snake in the bottom of that bottle, as it turned out … and they'd found it.

'You went missing,' Faraday accused him now, raising his glass. 'Dropped out of sight as though you'd never existed. What were you doing—faking your own death? Now it seems you're known as the "bagman" in wildlife circles; a feeding frenzy sets in when you come to town. Jamaican Sam melts into the shadows at the hint of your name, and Jason Turnbull buys another property. What's going on that's caused Paladin to suddenly show its face in Vietnam, Kenneth? I thought you said secrecy was your strongest weapon. "Paladin works because it is totally private", you said. "Don't ask me to name Names," you said, "because that would be more than my life is worth." Now here you are, as large as life, with a regiment of Nung tribesmen in tow, gathering seeds while pretending that you're tagging elephants in an area that any local tribesman can tell you hasn't seen an elephant since the dawn of time, and never will.'

He shuddered as he swallowed the liquor. The snake must have died as a result of drowning in it—but that wasn't going to stop Johnston from pouring another.

'They told me you'd mentioned my name when you were in Hoi An,' he replied with an attempt at an impish grin. 'Then when I heard someone was showing an interest in that bloody panda painting in Hanoi, I could have guessed it would be you. It should never have ended up at Christie's; that was just someone being greedy.'

'Why did you get it copied?'

'I was persuaded by a colleague.'

'You knew it had never been reproduced, so you felt it was safe.'

'That was the idea.'

'Was the colleague Madame Roulet, or someone at Paladin?'

Johnston hesitated. 'No, she was the... Actually, I've never met her, but she's a contact of someone I work with at the British Embassy in Hanoi. She knew the artist who could do it. It was meant to be just a harmless little scam that would be a way of paying back a favour. It backfired. No harm done. Did he do a good job, the artist?'

'Not bad.'

'Your reputation's intact, then. Are you sure you wouldn't like to buy it? Artists in Vietnam don't earn much money, you know...'

'Get fucked. Destroy it, or I'll accuse Van Heeren of fraud. He wouldn't like that—and you'd like it even less. And what about the set of lithographs—set number one hundred and twenty, that you skimmed off the top?'

'A present for the same Embassy colleague. You're not going to forgive me, are you?' Johnston lamented, not with particular sadness. He topped up Faraday's glass.

'For copying my fucking painting...?'

'For Helene.'

It was a lightning strike. Faraday pushed back his chair and stood up. 'Did you come here to brag about your sexual conquest, Kenneth? Have you ever thought you might have penis envy?'

He thought about walking off, but immediately felt the stupidity of that and sat down again.

'You didn't love her, and she didn't love you.' Johnston smirked. 'So what the fuck are you getting upset about?'

* * * *

Where there's lightning, it's always followed by thunder. The flash of anger

236

behind his outburst had obviously been building inside him for years, and once he had another storm cloud to bump into, it exploded.

'You're right,' Faraday said. 'Helene and I weren't in love … and that's not the issue between us.' He was embarrassed by the crudity of his outburst, but also, paradoxically, by its lack of ultimate conviction. Every man knew that if he felt violently disposed towards another man, he hit him first and hit him hard—preferably on the chin. It was obvious that he hadn't felt strongly enough to get violent; he'd merely acted like a playground child. But it wasn't the thing with Helene that had triggered his anger; it was something far more difficult to explain.

'The issue between us is more serious than a bit of sexual jealousy,' he conceded. 'It's the suspicion I have that you corrupted me—and I needed very little persuasion. All that money you funnelled my way for a few bloody paintings of animals… Tell me it wasn't another of your "harmless little scams". Tell me the truth about Paladin. Make it simple. Tell me what the fuck you're doing here.'

With blinding clarity, he realized that this was the real point of his journey. This was the fear that he had pushed aside for all those years, and this was the only man who could answer for it. Was he the accidental beneficiary of a deliberate scam, or was the scam just an opportunity that Johnston couldn't resist tacking onto the brilliant fundraising concept of the Harbinger Collection?

'Don't tell me, Anton, that you resent Paladin for kick-starting your career? Isn't that a bit ungrateful?' His smile was almost a smirk.

'Whether I should be grateful or not depends on who or what Paladin really is, and whether I was producing symbolic images to help inspire a commitment to conservation, or merely providing you with an opportunity to engage in some sort of rip-off.'

About to sneeze, Faraday felt in his pocket for a handkerchief—and found another of the black seeds that Duc had given him. His body still ached with fatigue, and it was starting to overwhelm him again, which was

237

not surprising, considering the physical challenge he'd endured. If his survival had been partially down to the seeds, then it wouldn't hurt to take another; he couldn't afford to collapse now that he had Johnston in front of him. It had been a long journey to reach this moment. Besides, there was the issue of Uncle's cousin, Nung Ton Phuc, the village chief. He'd nearly forgotten about him.

He put the seed down on the table to test Johnston's reaction.

'You know what Paladin is,' Johnston stated, bluntly ignoring it. 'You seem to be thrown by the sight of it operating publicly. Am I right?'

Faraday put the seed in his mouth and pointedly cracked it between his teeth. 'It was you who described Paladin to me,' he answered. 'It's a network of influence, you said. You and Van Heeren despised the efforts of the World Wildlife Fund as no more than shakers of collection boxes and self-righteous do-gooders who were incapable of stemming the tide of nature's extinction. Paladin, you boasted, could achieve more in one high-level phone call to save the Amazon rainforests than a hundred thousand wild-eyed volunteers chaining themselves to trees could achieve in a decade of protests. Was that the message of the script? Did I hear it right, or did I misunderstand? Because it doesn't square with what I see here.'

Johnston shrugged. 'What *do* you see here?'

'I see a conservation group claiming that it is tracking a rapidly declining population of indigenous elephants, and recruiting local hill tribes to help them.'

'Good. That's what you're meant to see.'

'... Only that isn't the sort of thing that Paladin is supposed to do, and even the local hill tribes know full well that there are no elephants in this area for you to track. So, that means you have another reason for being here—and don't tell me you're just collecting seeds. Why the secrecy?'

Johnston waved him away scathingly. 'Paladin's goals are not going to be achieved under the scrutiny of the world's media, Anton. Get real. Membership secrecy is the key to the whole fucking thing. Surely you get that?'

238

'Well, if it's dependent on secrecy, then eventually it will fail.'

'Why?'

'Because somebody who knows those Names will let it out.'

'Like who?'

'Well...'

A name immediately sprang to Faraday's lips. It had been lurking there since his phone conversation from the Metropole Hotel, the day he'd called to announce that he'd tracked down his painting.

'... someone like Ralph Lutyen. He must have the delivery names and addresses for the sets of prints you ordered.'

'Let's talk about that painting of yours,' Johnston suggested, as if he hadn't heard what Faraday had been saying. 'The bloody panda that you're so upset about.'

He didn't wait for agreement, but reached for the bottle and topped up his glass again.

'Everyone sees this cute and sexy, lovable bear that they want to cuddle. You saw a bewildered animal, ill-equipped for survival, imprisoned in a cage for brain-dead humans to gawk at while kidding themselves that they cared about nature. That's how Van Heeren saw it, too. That's why he bought it, remember?' He snapped his fingers, trying to get Faraday to keep up with him.

What was he driving at? Where did he think this was heading? Van Heeren had loved this explanation for some reason.

'Van Heeren tells everyone that sentimental do-gooders will never save the world,' Johnston continued. 'He reminds them that the Hutus swept through Rwanda, hacking nearly a million Tutsis to death, and when they came across gorillas, they hacked them to death, too. Why? He claims you can see why when you look at your painting.'

He gave one of his toothless smiles, but it was all too enigmatic for Faraday. He hadn't a clue what the other man was trying to say.

'Is there a point to any of this?' he asked.

'The point, Anton, is that if we're to talk about wild animals, we need to include mankind in that definition. If we leave him out of the equation, there will be nothing else left to save, for mankind is the most dangerous predator on earth.'

'Well, good luck with that one,' Anton replied. 'Unless nature's got a scheme we haven't learned about yet, nothing's going to control our determination to destroy the planet—and ourselves with it. That's one thing I do understand.'

'Don't be so pessimistic, laddie,' Johnston proclaimed in mocking tones. 'We're not alone in this, you know; there are people in much higher places who think the same. How do you think Paladin gets to be here, doing whatever it is you think we're doing? '

'What are you saying? Your presence in the mountains has government approval or something? What was that about you working with someone at the British Embassy? And tell me about the seeds you're collecting.'

* * * *

The rain started in earnest; the rain was always starting in earnest in Vietnam. For six months of the year, it was the northern monsoon, and for the other six months, it was the southern monsoon. As affirmed by Trih, the font of all local knowledge in Chau Doc, you didn't buy the conical *Nón-Lá* hat according to the size of your head, but according to the width of your shoulders, for it wasn't designed to protect you from the sun so much as to shelter you from the rain. Trih and Kenneth Johnston would have made a famous pairing. Between the two of them, the whole of life could have been treated as a harmless little scam.

The windows of their cable car gondola ran with water, and the clouds surrounded them, so they had no view to wonder at. Johnston had led the way out of the coffee shop and into the cable car station, marching straight to the head of the waiting queue and flashing a pass that somehow allowed him to commandeer the first car for the two of them alone. They sat opposite each other, Faraday facing forward, Johnston facing back.

For Faraday, the enveloping clouds were a relief. His head for heights had been tested and found wanting by the chairlifts when skiing with Helene years ago, and a twenty-minute ride up to the highest peak in Southeast Asia was not something he would have chosen for himself. His relief, however, was to be short-lived.

Johnston insisted on reading from Sunworld's tourist brochure, adopting the role of guide. ' "Admire the breathtaking view of the Muong Hoa Valley and the mountains of the Hoang Lien Son range",' he insisted with a sweep of his arm, ' "as you are transported to the temple where the sky and earth meet harmoniously, converging yin and yang, and all sorrows seem to disappear, leaving only peace and satisfaction remaining in the soul." '

He put the brochure down and sat back with that reptilian smile that said nothing, but could have meant anything. Prompted by a new and sudden twinge of unease, Faraday looked closely at the gondola doors, wondering if they were capable of being opened from the inside.

' "Peace and satisfaction remaining in the soul", Anton. Isn't that what we're all seeking?'

At that moment, the clouds broke, and a shaft of sunlight lit up the mountainside and the valleys below. Faraday had no choice but to look out, then down. Christ, it was beautiful... Beautiful, but scary. The uncontrollable power of shifting tectonic plates that had thrown up the mass of these mighty mountains eons ago was not quite as impressive as the persistence of humans in the centuries since then to scratch away at every valley, mound, and shelf capable of revealing soil fit for planting food. Green and gold paddy fields thousands of feet below them shone iridescent in the sudden, startling sunlight.

Faraday sat back and closed his eyes, vertigo rendering him dizzy. There was something he wanted to say about it—something that would speak in humanity's favour, rather than continue the easy, endless derogation of the species that seemed to now discolour every conversation. Wasn't man a part of nature, too? Wasn't man's drive to survive as awesome as the upheaval of the earth's crust, the germination of seeds in spring, the precision of the sun's arrival each morning? Who was left to put in a good word for their own species?

TWENTY-EIGHT

It was over, and they knew it. The Victoria Hotel dining room was empty; all other guests had gone, and they had it to themselves. Not surprisingly, chicken and duck were off the menu, and Violet and Caroline chose the basa fish. Faraday, remembering how he'd cast the handful of dry food into the hole in the deck of the floating fish farm at Chau Doc, could not forget Trih's words: 'It is broken rice and duck shit. Very good. Makes them grow fast.' Nor could he forget the flash of silver light as the fish flew from the water, like the snakehead fish of his imagination.

He had the green papaya salad instead.

Violet was in a surprisingly good mood, and was determined that her companions should join her in it. Perhaps it was a profound relief she was experiencing. She'd come to Vietnam out of a sense of guilt, carrying what she believed was a dirty secret from her past. The secret, once revealed, had proved to be not so dirty after all, and the guilt had likewise been misplaced. What remained was her genuine desire to help people who were prepared to help themselves. That desire had only momentarily been thwarted, and by events beyond her control.

'Imagine how we'd be feeling,' she said, shaking her piece of bread at Caroline, 'if we'd come two months earlier and got the poultry farm up and running, only to have this rotten flu epidemic strike. At least we haven't got that hanging around our necks. People think doing good for others is all upside. They don't know the half of it. It's damned hard work!'

'The only one guilty of "damned hard work",' Caroline complained, 'is Anton—and none of it was his problem in the first place.'

She'd chosen to sit opposite Faraday, and the candle on the table between them was doing the same thing to her eyes as the candle on the first night they'd met in Can Tho, which suddenly seemed a long time ago, and so remote from the events of the last three days that he was struggling to put it all in context. When he looked down at his hand on the tablecloth, it took him some time to realize that Caroline had reached out to touch it in a gesture of apology, or sympathy perhaps, and both she and Violet had been waiting for him to answer while his concentration had drifted, just like his vision. Parts of his body felt numb, as if he'd left them out in the cold.

'... Was it?' Caroline prompted.

'Was it what?' he asked blearily.

'Your problem...?' She squeezed his hand and frowned. 'Are you alright?'

'He's exhausted,' Violet interjected. 'Look at him. He needs food, and the best glass of French wine this hotel can find.'

She waved her hand around to summon waiters, all of whom had developed a malaise uncharacteristic of the Vietnamese, an inattention born of depression. The epidemic had everyone on the verge of despair.

'Your problem turned out to be my problem,' he said, removing his hand and feeling his brow, 'the human manifestation of the snakehead fish. Do you know about the snakehead fish? It's not like the cute little aphrodisiac they put in a bottle to help sell crap wine; it's a vicious predator, unchanged since the dawn of time, and it's seriously evil. It dresses itself up in the guise of the good guy, the white knight, the emissary of hope, and it's given a free pass to go wherever it pleases, and where it pleases to go, I know— I just know—it's up to no good. But it has a free pass, so what do I really know? Nothing.'

He hadn't told Caroline where he'd been that afternoon, or of his meeting with Kenneth Johnston. He was rambling. Was it a fever, or something else that was affecting him? Could it be those damned seeds he'd been chewing? They'd worked because they'd numbed the pain in his muscles, but now he was feeling numb all over, as if he'd overdosed. Perhaps he just needed to rest until it passed.

'Who is this person?' Caroline asked, confused. 'Are you talking about Uncle's cousin? Is he the "snakehead fish"?'

'He's talking in riddles,' Violet declaimed, hurrying the conversation along because she didn't want it to hold up ordering the wine. 'When men talk in riddles, it means they don't know what it is they want to say. Be patient; it will come.'

'Did I tell you what Nung Tong Phuc and the other tribesmen were doing up in the mountains,' Faraday asked, 'and why they attack anyone who comes near?'

'You said they were working for that wildlife organization you mentioned—the one you do the paintings for,' Violet said impatiently. 'Tracking animals, or something.'

'They're protecting an area that contains a unique plant that seeds once every four years. It grows nowhere else, and they're collecting the seeds and flying them out.'

'Well, that's good, isn't it?' Caroline asked. 'That's the sort of thing environmentalists do. You made it sound as though they were up to no good.'

'When people are prepared to kill you when you wander into their territory, it does tend to make you think they're up to no good,' Faraday murmured. 'Or is that quite common among you NGOs, Violet? Are you territorial by nature?'

The wine arrived.

'Thank God!' Violet exclaimed. For a little woman, she had big appetites. After taking a healthy sip, she waved his question away. 'We know that about the Nungs,' she insisted. 'We learned it in the Vietnam War, right, Caroline?

They were the Green Berets' secret weapon, remember? And they're outsiders who've always been under attack. There are a billion Chinese just across the border to the north, and how many million Vietnamese to the south, trying to squeeze them out, and all they've got to protect themselves is the spirit of their ancestors and some impenetrable mountains.'

We rely upon that, Faraday said to himself, echoing Johnston's words that afternoon. *How else could you keep a billion evil spirits at bay?*

'Well, it clearly suits Paladin's purpose,' he concluded out loud. 'But that purpose escapes me, I'm afraid. I simply can't see why a secret group of big-hitters like the Paladin Foundation would be interested in supervising the collection of seeds. Yet I'm reluctant to be cynical about them, because what they represent is also to some degree what I represent.' They were, after all, the springboard for his career and his subsequent identity, he might have added.

Violet delivered a dry cackle. 'Honey, you've got every reason to be cynical! Anyone who isn't cynical hasn't been paying attention to life. And being a cynic, there's nothing to stop you from believing that people are equally motivated by self-interest as by altruism. It makes good financial sense to save habitat, and the wildlife that goes with it, because the economic benefits derived from the virtuous circle of nature's activity is measurable. There's no future in being a lord of the universe if the universe is being destroyed before your eyes. But all the little things we do may not be enough, because the world is reaching the point where it can't sustain us; there are just too many of us. The longer I live, the clearer that becomes. Fact is, the world is polluted with people, and none of them matter—except to each other.'

Johnston had said pretty much the same thing. It was such an easy thing to say. But for Faraday that night, conversation was difficult for him to muster. He could feel the tide running out, leaving him like a beached fish. His adrenals were drained, his brain flaccid, but worst of all, he couldn't see, not beyond this moment, for the present carried with it the sad feeling of inevitability that it only existed to instantly become the past. His quest to find the instigator of a counterfeit painting had turned out to be a journey of desperation, to find the one thing that had always been missing: his own validity as an artist. And in his heart, he knew he had failed to find it. He'd been no more than a convenient tool for people who gave little thought to it—people who gave little thought to anything, it seemed, particularly failure.

'I'm going to bed,' Violet announced after devouring her meal. 'You two don't need a chaperone; you need to be alone.'

But once alone, they had little to say, perhaps because each was waiting for the other to ask the question that was on both their minds: did their friendship have a future? They agreed that getting some sleep was a necessary objective, particularly for Faraday after the exertions of the last few days.

'You look terrible,' Caroline said kindly. 'Why did you go out this afternoon when you were feeling so tired? Wouldn't it have been better to get some rest?'

He wasn't ready to tell her. Everything done, everything said, was like compost; it needed to rot down if it was to become fit to feed the ground from which meaning could grow. He didn't know where to begin … so he didn't.

'When we're back in Hanoi,' he said, trying to show her something of what he was thinking, 'I want to see whether Madame Roulet can follow through on her offer to obtain the copy of the panda painting, if for no other reason than to complete the circle. Then, I guess, my mission in Vietnam will be complete. And you…?'

'First up, I want to file my story with the news bureau. Then I need to visit Uncle and tell him what's happened. Violet wants to come with me. Although she was putting on a brave face a few minutes ago, I think she's having trouble swallowing the suggestion that the hill tribes are spreading this virus by polluting their own water. Like me, she can't see the sense in that. I don't know … I get the feeling she wants me to work for her in some way.'

'Do you think you will?'

This time, he took her hand. It was cool and soothing to his touch. His own hand was hot, like his forehead and his neck, and his head was throbbing with a deep internal thud that followed the rhythm of his heartbeat.

'Perhaps,' she replied, not entirely sure. 'My goal is to write news journalism, as I told you. That's where I see myself, and I don't want to be distracted from achieving that. Maybe I can work for her on the side. What do you think?'

He turned her hand over and peered at her palm, as if reading it. 'Let's talk about it tomorrow. Right now, I feel like death, and I won't do justice to the question. Tomorrow night, though, I'll be all yours.'

* * * *

His vertigo was real. No amount of mind control could overcome it when swinging thousands of feet above the valley floor.

'If you wanted to get to the top of the mountain the other day, this is the way you should have come,' Johnston had chided him, 'seated comfortably in a gondola. That whole intrepid adventurer thing is much too hard.'

'Yes, I can't imagine you ever doing it. I was being chivalrous and trying to find the head of the tribe that your man Sam has working for him.'

'Chivalrous, indeed. Why were you looking for him?'

They'd cleared the air about Helene, and trivialized the forging of the panda painting, but Johnston had revealed nothing to explain why he'd set up this meeting. Now, it seemed, he was evincing some interest in what Faraday was doing there.

'A woman called Violet Dunleavy—a charity donor from the Vanderbilt

Foundation—had arranged for him to work on a project here in the mountains, but when she arrived, he'd gone missing.'

'So, you set off to find him for her?' Johnston clapped his hands in admiration. 'How bloody chivalrous of you! The urge to do good is irrepressible.'

'And what are you doing here, Kenneth?' Faraday demanded. 'You're not an environmentalist; you're Van Heeren's emissary. Are you up to anything good?'

'Ha!' Johnston barked appreciatively. ' "Emissary"! I like it.'

It was his chance to make up a lie—or even to tell the truth. He chose neither. Instead, he pointed back down the mountain over which they were riding, as if having listened to Faraday's thoughts speculating on the survival skills of tribal people driven into the inhospitable mountain mists to scratch the rocks in search of enough soil to sustain themselves.

'Belief is a powerful thing,' Johnston proclaimed, peering down at the quilted patterns created by the tireless endeavours of the rice farmers on the slopes far below them. 'And once it is firmly embedded, it's impossible to shift.'

'What are you saying?' Faraday asked, still looking for an explanation as to why this meeting was taking place.

'There are one billion people across the border beyond these hills,' Johnston mused, 'just itching to invade. But the Montagnards believe the spirits of their ancestors patrol the mountains, protecting them. Without that belief, they wouldn't have toiled away for generations, creating such elaborate survival systems. Blind belief, Anton—we rely upon that. How else could you keep a billion evil spirits at bay?'

'Are you saying that it's only ancestor worship that protects them from invasion?'

'Belief, Anton. Belief. We all have it, including non-believers. It's what gets us up in the morning. In the Middle Ages, the Catholic monsignor would ride through the Italian countryside each season and instruct people where to plant their crops. God's command. Because grapes could grow in crap soil on steep hillsides where arable farming wasn't possible, that's where he told them to put them. Now everyone thinks that grapes grow best in steep, infertile soil. Try and tell them otherwise, even though the infallibility of the Catholic God is pretty much a thing of the past.'

'I don't quite get the connection,' Faraday protested. 'Tell me something that I can believe about Paladin. You're not here saving animals, so what the fuck *are* you doing? You haven't explained the seeds.'

At the top of the mountain, the cable car slid to a halt.

'What's more important, Anton: saving animals, or saving people? What would you say?'

The doors were thrown open by an invisible hand. Faraday didn't know what to say; it was a question that answered itself.

They stepped out of the gondola and looked up towards the peak.

'There's a temple here,' Johnston announced, 'or we could walk to the summit and pretend to look at the non-existent view. I'm not much for walking. Let's do the temple thing.'

Inside the temple, the only feeling of belief Faraday could detect was the developer's belief that tourists might be impressed by a pagoda that housed pseudo-religious statues built on top of the highest mountain in the country. An information board for visitors proudly proclaimed in five languages that Fansipan Legend could welcome two thousand guests per hour on its aerial ride to the heavenly peak.

'Two thousand people per hour,' Faraday noted incredulously, 'for ten hours a day, three hundred and sixty-five days a year, at thirty-five dollars a pop: that's a shitload of people and money, by anyone's standard. How is believing in the ancestors going to protect your tribesmen…?' He turned around. '… from that sort of invasion?'

But Johnston had gone. And after Faraday had checked the toilets without success, he quickly returned to the cable car station, just in time to see a red gondola pulling away from the dock with the sole figure of his one-time benefactor inside, not even glancing back to see what effect his unannounced departure might have had. So, Faraday was forced to buy a ticket, and of course, when he reached the bottom, there was no sign of the bastard anywhere, nor any means of contacting him.

TWENTY-NINE

While Caroline poured her thoughts into her laptop, and Violet alternately read and drowsed, the paddy fields and bleak railway sidings of Yen Bai and Phu Tho rolled past their carriage window. Faraday slept fitfully, elbows propped on the table between them, head sliding out of his hands and waking him with a start, until he was forced to move to a vacant row of seats and curl up like a foetus. How could two days of tramping have reduced him to this?

It wasn't over. *Of course* it wasn't over. Instead of learning the answers to questions that he'd harboured for years, he'd just been saddled with new ones—and the only person who could answer them had stood him up like a fool. No wonder he'd avoided telling Caroline. It was enough that he needed to redeem himself in his own eyes, without facing the challenge of redeeming himself in her eyes. He might not be a man of action, but he was stubborn, and he reacted badly to deceit. So, despite his crippling fatigue, he would hunt the truth down as soon as they reached Hanoi.

* * * *

The woman at the desk of the British Embassy in Hai Bà Trưng was used to fielding enquiries for passport renewals and visas. Her responses were programmed to deal with those issues, and few others.

'Are you a British subject?' she asked from behind her cotton mask.

'Yes.'

'And you have a valid passport?'

'Yes.'

'Do you want a passport renewal or visa application?'

'Neither. I wish to contact someone through a member of the Embassy staff: a Mr Johnston.'

'How do you spell, please?'

He told her. She consulted a telephone directory beside the phone on her desk while he held onto the edge of the desk for support, feeling himself begin to waver. The heat that had been burning up his body all night, and on the train back from Sapa, had suddenly turned to cold.

'No Mr Johnston at this Embassy. You have wrong name perhaps, or wrong embassy?'

'Let me speak to someone on your diplomatic staff—someone senior. It's important.'

She asked him to wait while she left her desk and went in search of help from a higher echelon. Faraday was forced to sit down, his head now spinning alarmingly. He wondered if he had food poisoning; he felt his gut convulsing, as if it wanted to reject something. The woman returned and asked him to follow her down a corridor to a small waiting room where someone would join him shortly. There was a water cooler with paper cups on a stand, and he helped himself, inadvertently spilling the entire cupful on the floor, his coordination suddenly collapsing. In the corridor outside, he heard men's voices, and through the glass partition, he thought he recognized one of them behind his gauze mask. But as soon as the door opened and Faraday stood up, he collapsed into the startled arms of a complete stranger.

The next thing he remembered was waking, from a long and vivid dream, in what turned out to be a hospital room to which he had no memory of being admitted. The depth of dreaming was so intense that it seemed akin to departing into another life. He dreamed of Africa: his childhood. He dreamed of colours, smells, and sounds that had embedded themselves in his past. And he dreamed of floating through time and space in a capsule that was his body, peacefully free of gravity, untethered. There was no sense of time, no physicality, no hunger, no pain, no fear.

As he discovered later, he had been in a coma for ten days, hooked up to saline drips and fever-reducing drugs. He was alive, they said, because his immune system was better than ordinary. Despite the coma, he had been aware of being attended to, but only in the sense of feeling a nearby presence. Of physical sensation, there was none; that came when he began to emerge from his deep sedation, and the involuntary urge to cough took over his body. He coughed and coughed until his ribs ached and his throat was raw. It was the coughing that pulled him from the depths of unconsciousness up to the surface of awareness.

Doctors and nurses passed his bed in occasional blurs, like spirits in shrouds, their touch as light as butterflies, their voices like whispering ghosts.

Then he became aware of a man in the room, waiting—material, not ethereal.

He heard snippets of what the man was saying, words, not sentences—words that floated past him in the murky water of his brain like bait dropped into a deep ocean, sinking slowly, tempting a fish to strike. The fish was his consciousness.

The man had a name: Proctor.

The man had a mission: to talk to him.

But he couldn't talk, because he had no strength, and though he recognized his own name when Proctor used it seeking a response from him, he struggled to understand his identity, the time, the place, and his reason for being there. So, he focused on listening, until the meaning of words triggered whole sentences in his own mind, and the desire to respond grew gradually stronger.

'He's a painter; he paints animals,' he heard Proctor say.

Yes, he was.

'Is that what he was doing here?' someone else asked.

No, that wasn't what he was doing here, he thought. What was it?

He drifted in and out of consciousness. Sometimes when he woke, he was alone. Sometimes there was a silent person stripping his bed, wiping his body of excrement, filling his veins with fluid.

Then there was Proctor again. He heard his voice close to his ear: 'Can you hear me, Mr Faraday?

Yes, he could.

'You have contracted a dangerous virus and are now in hospital. Do you understand? I want you to try and acknowledge me if you can. Can you hear me? Are you able to speak?'

He forced himself to respond. Once he made it to the surface, he'd be able to swim.

'Ah, your eyes are opening! Good. Take your time. My name is Donald Proctor. You were taken ill when you came to see us at the British Embassy. You were trying to locate someone: a Mr Johnston. Is that right? Take your time, now.'

Little by little, it started to come back. Whole sentences formed that he didn't have the energy to speak. He'd been in Sapa because… He'd gone to the Embassy because… He was traveling with Caroline because…

Where was Caroline? Was she alright? He needed to call her.

'Do you understand why you're here?' Proctor asked. 'The tests show that you have a virulent strain of the coronavirus, and we need to know how and where you picked it up.'

Proctor was patient. Gradually, he teased it out of him: where he'd been and who he was with. Faraday could only manage a few sentences at a time. He got to Sapa with Caroline and Violet, then stopped. Was he too tired, or was some instinct telling him not to go into the mountains?

Proctor then left him alone, suggesting he'd return after Faraday had rested. But not before telling him, 'The man you were asking about, Kenneth Johnston—I'm afraid there is no one of that name working at the British Embassy. If it's important to you, and when you're better, the Embassy staff might be able to help you track him down.'

'Wait,' Faraday protested, struggling to sit up. 'Are you saying Johnston has no connection to the Embassy at all?'

'No, he isn't known to us.'

But even in his weakened state, Faraday was sure he'd never referred to him as *Kenneth* Johnston. And why was someone from the Embassy staff interested enough to sit beside his hospital bed just to assure him that his enquiry was misplaced?

* * * *

Sleep, alternating with coughing consciousness, gradually cleared his mind. And when Caroline entered the hospital room without warning, he suddenly realised that his life had changed almost without reference to him. Contrary to his long-held assumption, he was not alone. Neither of them said or did anything consciously that made this obvious, but clearly they each held an assumption about the other that seemed to confirm it.

Someone at the British Embassy, finding his cell phone when he collapsed, had called the last number he'd dialled and found it was Caroline, so she'd known what had happened to him and where he was taken, but she hadn't been allowed to see him until he'd been confirmed as not being contagious.

Perhaps, he thought, after she'd left and they had tentatively agreed on the arrangements for when he was to be released from hospital, these things were far better left unsaid. Perhaps trying to explain them only exposed them to doubt and misunderstanding. The kiss they couldn't exchange was more telling than the one they might otherwise have shared. For whatever reason, it was clear that she was waiting for him to be discharged, and he was counting on joining her as soon as he could. They were lovers who'd never made love, the best of friends who'd known each other for only a few weeks. If he was delirious, perhaps that was what was needed in order for him to surrender to another.

When the coughing died and he was cleared for release, she came to collect him, and they returned to the hotel above the flower shop. She'd booked him back in his own room, where he spent the next two days sleeping and mulling over events, only venturing out with her to eat. Her story had been well received by the news bureau, but because she was only a freelancer, any follow-up would rely on her own initiative. Meanwhile, she was busy with hotel staff work, as she needed to get some money coming in while also considering Violet's job offer and trying to locate her brother, who had apparently made up with Uncle after their row and was working nearby in Hanoi.

He didn't tell her the full story about his reasons for having gone to the Embassy on the day they returned to Hanoi, or about his disquiet around what he'd seen while tracking down Uncle's cousin, and for reasons he couldn't explain to himself, he chose not to tell her the full details of his meeting with Johnston in the cable car. It seemed that he was still trying to decipher that event. But he did tell her about Johnston's admission that he'd collaborated in the production of the counterfeit painting.

'And tomorrow, if I'm up to it, I'm going to have the pleasure of confronting Madame Roulet again and seeing whether she's managed to follow through on her offer to sell me the copy that was presented for auction at Christie's. That should then be the end of the matter—the end of my journey. And you?'

Caroline looked a little doubtful. Violet had left Hanoi well before Faraday had been discharged from hospital, leaving him a note wishing him a speedy recovery and expressing her appreciation for his help in trying to unravel 'the unholy mess in Sapa'. As a postscript, she had added, 'The upside of all this is that I have found a remarkable young woman to help me in my work'.

But what exactly was that work?

'Am I going to add you to the crowd of NGOs that are clambering all over the Third World, trying to salve the First World's conscience?' Faraday asked. 'Because as worthy as it sounds, I can't help feeling that gratuitous intervention in problem societies only helps to shore up the cause of those problems, making them even worse. I'm reluctant to admit it, but it seems to me that human nature is a virus that's resistant to good intentions; it simply mutates into a new and more virulent strain of evil.'

Caroline scoffed good-naturedly. She knew he was freewheeling in order to tease out her thoughts, but she also knew there was an element of truth in what he was saying, and that was why she had doubts.

'A part of me says that I want to do something worthwhile; that's what draws me to investigative journalism. But there's another part of me that says I don't want to just coat-tail on someone else's bandwagon,' she admitted. 'I've been reading about the places where her Foundation works, like Bangladesh and Ethiopia and the Congo. Do you know anything about them? Do you ever give them a moment's thought? Come on, you're a man who cares about the planet.'

'No, I don't,' he had to admit. 'I know they're fucking cot cases, but that's about all I know, truth be told.'

'You're right. The more I read, the more the problems seem too big. Did you know that Ethiopia, despite all the wars and famines, has ninety-four million people—and the median age is eighteen? What rate must they be breeding at for the *median* age to be just eighteen? And Bangladesh, where nobody has anything, is the most densely populated country in the world, with a hundred and sixty-three million people. Kinshasa, the capital of the Congo, where we're always being asked to send money, is forecast to have thirty million inhabitants within the next twelve years, and that's just one city. None of them have clean water or decent food, so how do we explain it?'

'It's nature: the lower the chances of survival, the higher the birth rate. Nature's laws.'

'I like Violet, and I admire her a lot, but would I have concluded that

258

the provision of fresh water should become my life's work in the face of figures like this? I don't think so. I have *always* wanted to be a journalist, asking the questions rather than providing the answers, believing that asking the right questions was more important than believing you had the answers. I have an awful feeling that what she's offering may be no more than a worthy job that gives me the warm fuzzies, but makes no goddamned difference in the end. Isn't that awful?'

'Well, it may be awful, but it's honest, at least.'

That night, he and Caroline slept together for the first time, cautious and tentative at first, before allowing themselves to be swept along in a rip tide of excitement and surrender that eventually cast them in the small hours of the morning onto a beach of contentment that Faraday, for his part, had never visited before. *So that's what they mean*, he thought as he finally drifted off to sleep, *don't fight against the current; just relax and let it take you.*

The next day, his physical energy levels were higher than at any stage since he'd contracted the virus, and after Caroline left for work, he felt up to walking the thirty minutes or so to Madame Roulet's gallery on Pho Trang Tien at the southern end of Hoan Kiem Lake near the opera house, taking his camera in case he got a chance to record the quality of the work being turned out by the gallery, so he could show it to Ralph when he returned to London.

It was a fine but smoggy day, with the usual film of diesel-laced humidity waiting to mingle with the sweat that inevitably rose to the surface of his skin at the slightest exertion in Vietnam. The mood in the street was subdued. The face mask business was booming, and the newspapers in the hotel lobby were fixated on only one subject, which was the burgeoning scale of the epidemic and media speculation around the two great fears: was it mutating, and could it become transmittable human-to-human? At the Foreign Language Bookshop on Trang Tien, he stopped and bought copies of the international editions of *The New York Times* and *The Guardian*, which he would read over lunch.

When he reached the gallery, he found that Madame Roulet had gone out.

'She has gone to the food market,' a young male assistant informed him, 'and will be back after lunch. Two p.m.'

'Oh, whereabouts is the market?' Faraday asked. "I might see if I can run into her.'

It was behind them, apparently, somewhere down the alleys off Pho Trang Tien, in the vicinity of a department store, the name of which he failed to catch. Searching for it would at least help kill time until he could return in the afternoon, so he set off to wander, wondering whether he was quite as fully recovered as he'd assumed earlier that morning, for his breathing was still suspect.

After ten minutes or so, he found himself standing in front of a fruit stall, squeezing jackfruit with a toothless stall holder who kept saying, 'Tasty, tasty!' and nodding his head in encouragement. Instinctively he backed away with a silly grin and raised his defensive camera. *Click* ... and *click, click, click*. In that moment, he thought of himself painting again—for the first time in weeks—but not animals. He toyed briefly with the idea of buying a selection of fruit and taking it back to the hotel for dissection to reveal the luscious flesh beneath the forbidding shells, the creamy, faintly rotting interiors carrying hints of baser pleasures. The odious smell of the durian, they say, has to be overcome before the soft pulp yields itself to the lips and tongue. Perhaps he could paint it thus.

The East was on the rise, and the West was beginning to crave its images. (Not for the High Street print shop or the suburban wall, but for Belgravia, Manhattan, and the Boulevard Haussmann, according to Ralph, who could spot a trend faster than anyone.) *But hold on*, he thought, *resist the idea!* This task wasn't for him; it was for younger painters who needed the money and could work themselves into a convincing patter about the great *Breath of Life* that filled the lungs of Asia, the laser light that illuminated the world from the eyes of the tiger. That wasn't him at all.

Lowering his camera, he glanced up to see Madame Roulet selecting vegetables from a stall in the distance, her crisp decisiveness and conservative but elegant attire standing out in the indigenous Vietnamese shopping crowd. Having completed her purchase, she crossed to an adjacent spice stall and slipped her shopping bag into the hand of a man who was negotiating a purchase there, an act that was at once both domestic and affectionate. The man looked familiar... It took him a moment, but it was the shaved head that did it.

Faraday raised his camera again and took three shots in rapid succession. It was the man who had sat beside his bed in hospital, the man in the face mask who identified himself as Proctor from the British Embassy, the man who told him he didn't know any Kenneth Johnston, and who had been so keen to know his movements prior to his catching the virus.

THIRTY

Retracing his steps away from the street market back to Pho Trang Tien and then on to the Metropole Hotel, where he knew he could find a comfortable place to sit down and reassess the situation before deciding whether to confront Madame Roulet after 2:00 p.m., Faraday's initial thought was that, surprisingly, Johnston had told him the truth behind the commissioning of the counterfeit painting. He really did have a colleague who worked at the British Embassy, and he could see, with the connection to the gallery owner being so close, that copying an unknown painting could have seemed like a 'harmless little scam' with a reasonable chance of succeeding. Still, it was a greedy thing to have done. Who really needed the money? Was it Johnston, because he just couldn't help himself, as Ralph was at pains to point out? Was it this man Proctor who had appeared at his bedside, clearly intent on denying any knowledge of Johnston or his activities? Was his public servant salary insufficient enough that he would be tempted to pass off a painting that might yield a thirty-thousand-pound windfall if offered for sale in London? Or was it Madame Roulet herself—as wife or mistress—who was the intended recipient of the windfall?

She'd said that the original purchaser was keen to on-sell, but she hadn't expected him to be back in Hanoi until after the weekend. That was nearly three weeks ago. If she'd been referring to Johnston, then she would by now have been warned of who she was dealing with. And wouldn't Proctor have been told this also?

All this filtered through Faraday's mind as he drank an iced Campari and soda on the pavement outside the Metropole. Johnston's frank admissions had removed the need to unmask him. Faraday no longer cared whether he'd skimmed money off the commissioning of the print portfolios, which was why he hadn't bothered to return the two phone calls from Ralph that were waiting on his cell phone. It didn't matter anymore. But he'd come a long way, and he owed it to himself to see how it all played out. So, he scanned the papers for a brief update on the spread of the coronavirus, finished his drink, and sauntered back to the gallery, getting there at a quarter past the hour—where he was surprised to be welcomed by Madame Roulet like a long-lost friend.

'Mr Anthony, I feared I had lost you!'

'Lost...?' he asked cautiously.

'Yes, I expected you three weeks ago, but I feared you must have left Hanoi.' She was vivacious, almost flirtatious, and clearly pleased to see him. There was no hint that she knew his true identity.

'I *did* leave Hanoi,' he explained ruefully, 'but unfortunately I became unwell and ended up in hospital. But I survived. A long story, madame, but you never left my mind—and no, I am not contagious.'

She laughed, hand to mouth, and involuntarily stepped backwards. 'Oh, *mon Dieu!* Then I am so glad you are better, and of course, my commiserations. You will be pleased to know I have your painting!'

'You do?'

'*Bien sur*. That is why you are here, no?'

'I thought perhaps... No, excellent! I look forward to seeing it.'

'*Au moment...*'

She left the room and was gone for several minutes, causing him to fret that perhaps she was phoning someone. But no; when she emerged, she was struggling with a large cardboard package that she could only drag across the floor. Her assistant, it seemed, was not available to help.

'I must ask your assistance,' she pleaded. 'The frame is a little heavy for me to remove from the packaging. Could you…?'

They laid it on the floor, and while he gripped the sides of the carton, she pulled until the painting emerged. It was 850 by 850, just like the original, but now in a heavily gilded ornamental frame totally unlike the original, which it had clearly picked up somewhere along the way since it was offered at Christie's, presumably to add 'value' to it. Madame removed a Hockney lookalike from a display easel and replaced it with the panda, so they could both step back and admire it.

'*Voila!*' she exclaimed, her hand on his arm. 'Exactly as the photograph, do you not agree?'

Of course, he'd seen it before, in his kitchen the day that Appleby had called unexpectedly—the day that had triggered this whole journey for what at the time seemed like a simple quest, but which had inexplicably turned into an odyssey of Homeric proportions. Like a man who had plunged into a pool to retrieve a key, only to find the pool deeper than he imagined, he came to the surface and took a deep breath. Surely now he was on the brink of discovering the full truth.

'Who is the vendor again…?'

'He prefers to remain unnamed.'

'I am just curious that he chose to commission this subject. You said something about him working at 'the Embassy'. Was that the British Embassy?'

'No, no, it is another Embassy. But you have not told me what you think! I particularly like the composition: the tunnel of heads all looking in one direction, and at the end of the tunnel, the bear, captured in brilliant light. Such simplicity!'

'Simplicity is a complicated effect to achieve,' Faraday mumbled instinctively. It was a stock response. 'But generally, I would have to agree that your copyist has done a good job—apart from two errors in the inscriptions.'

'Two errors…?'

'Yes, the word "morning" is spelled incorrectly, because it was intended to have a different meaning, and of course, the signature is not that of the artist. If I understood you correctly, the artist for this particular work is the man you introduced to me when last we met, and his name is Hien, not Faraday.'

Madame Roulet was an intelligent woman, and she did the intelligent thing in not immediately replying. Instead, she advanced on the painting and bent down to squint closely at the two inscriptions in question. *Yes*, he thought, *you have a very nice derrière, and the next few minutes are going to be quite interesting.*

'Morning is the time of day, no? The beginning time?' she asked pertly.

'Unless spelled with a "U" in it, when it becomes a time of sorrow or regret. The original artist was referring to the sad fact that pandas are prone to infertility and therefore don't have any surety of achieving the destiny that drives all creatures on earth, which is the ability to reproduce.'

Madame Roulet straightened, crossed her arms, and tilted her head to one side, her lips pursed thoughtfully. 'That is rather poignant, if true, and not something one would be aware of, Mr Anthony. So, I must ask how you know this—or are you playing with the meaning in order to amuse me?'

They held each other's eyes while Faraday reached into his pocket, took out his wallet, and removed his plain and simple business card, which he read aloud before handing to her. ' "A. J. (Anton) Faraday". I must apologize for deceiving you, madame. But I know the original painting rather better than I know this one, though I have seen this one before as well, when it was offered for sale in London, and it is partly a tribute to the skill of Mr Hien that I have pursued it here, as well as curiosity about how he was able to copy the original. You partially explained that when you showed me the photograph last time I was here, and the source of that photograph has since been confirmed as our erstwhile friend, Kenneth Johnston. So, now I guess we have to decide what to do next.'

The cloud that passed over Madame Roulet's face was not entirely unexpected, but what she said was a complete surprise. 'Who is Kenneth Johnston?'

'The man who commissioned this painting…?'

'No, that is not his name; I have never heard this name. There seems to be confusion. My client is not that person—but I will not tell you my client, because of confidentiality.'

Well, it seemed reasonable enough that she would protect the man he had seen her with in the market, if he'd judged their relationship correctly. And if it was Proctor who was indulging in the 'harmless little scam', there was probably no reason why Madame Roulet needed to know the name of the person who had put him onto it in the first place. 'Paying back a favour' is how Johnston had described it.

There are skills some women possess that men have no hope of understanding, let alone replicating, and Madame Roulet displayed a skill in the next few minutes that would leave Faraday in awe. Admittedly, he was struggling to keep up with the subtleties of her twists and turns, being decidedly light-headed from his exertions, but he was resigned to the fact that she would outwit him even under normal circumstances. What should have been a tense confrontation, involving accusations of criminality, instead turned into a calm and elegant dance, like a tango tinged with the pathos of impending loss.

'Well,' she surmised wistfully, 'as you have already completed a version of this painting yourself, Mr Faraday, I presume you will not be in a mood to offer me the price necessary to buy this one.'

'No,' he smiled, 'but thank you for acknowledging that.'

'Then I will have to hang it on my wall and wait for someone else to come along and recognize its merits.'

'Is that wise, when it has knowingly been signed as if it were genuine?'

'This is Vietnam, Mr Faraday, not London or New York,' she said flatly.

'Quite so! And what would it take to persuade you not to hang it on your wall?'

She hesitated demurely, as if being asked if she would accept a kiss upon the hand.

'Five thousand dollars,' she replied, 'but that would include a guarantee.'

'A guarantee...?'

'Yes: that I would never allow a copy of a genuine Faraday to be offered for sale in my gallery at any time, no matter the price or the vendor's power of persuasion.'

Faraday took out his credit card. 'And would I get a discount if I offered to leave the frame with you and took only the canvas and the protective packaging?'

* * * *

By the time he got back to the hotel—by cyclo rather than taxi, because he'd learned that taxis refused to negotiate the one-way street—he was exhausted. It was to be expected. The hospital had discharged him into convalescence, not running all over town, and if the sheer exertion of walking wasn't going to get him, the heat and humidity would do it on their own. He leaned the package containing the painting against the wall, turned on the air conditioning fan, and collapsed onto his bed, unable to distinguish the difference between success and defeat. Yes, he'd finally tracked down the painting ... but he'd been relieved of five thousand dollars in the process, and he still didn't know the name of the person who'd commissioned it.

The New York Times and *The Guardian* were giving front-page attention to news of the spreading virus, treating it like a deepening cyclone that was forming out at sea. Would it move away and dissipate, or would it turn towards land and devastate the country? Speculation as to why it appeared to be spreading rapidly was focused on whether the feared mutation had occurred and human-to-human transmission was taking place. *Give a journalist a typewriter, and he'll create an apocalypse,* Faraday thought, albeit from the safety of his own recovery. It was transmitted by infected poultry—that was well proven—and the cockerel they'd killed and eaten in the mountain village on the first night of their trek to the Paladin encampment was coalescing in Faraday's mind as the most likely source.

Duc's cell phone number was still in his dialling list, and he decided to call it, firstly to warn him of his suspicions and to check that Duc hadn't contracted the disease as well, and secondly out of concern for the state of his injuries. Not surprisingly, the number was reported as unavailable, as was the messaging service. Hopefully he'd made it safely back to his own village, which would be too remote for such communication. He sent a short text instead in the hope that it would be transmitted when he came within range.

Then his own phone rang, and it was Caroline.

'I've tracked Tuan down, and we've arranged to meet tonight at seven,' she said excitedly. 'If you're up to it, I'd really like you to come.'

'Who's Tuan?'

'My brother.'

'Your Vietnamese brother?'

'Yes. I told him about you and how you'd kicked the virus, and he's keen to meet you. I didn't realize, but he's right in the middle of this thing.'

'What does he do?'

'Molecular biology. He's a science nerd.'

'I thought you didn't like him?'

'It's alright now. He apologized for his behaviour, and he's made up with Uncle. He said he was under a lot of stress at the time. Look, you don't have to come…'

'I want to. Pick me up before seven. I need to rest. The day has caught up with me.'

He slept fitfully, thinking about Duc and the way he'd held his face together so nonchalantly after having it severed by a tribesman's machete. Had he contracted the virus from that meal also, or was infection a matter of luck—bad luck? And he thought about Kenneth Johnston, the ultimate sponsor of the tribesman's machete attack in an encampment that, according to Duc, harboured a number of sick people in a makeshift field hospital. Could that be due to human-to-human infection, or was Nung Tong Phuc correct in fingering contaminated well water as the source? And he thought about those seeds that had sustained him when his body was crying out in protest at the unaccustomed pain and exertions to which he'd subjected it—the same seeds that Paladin had been harvesting. What was so ecologically significant about them that a man like Johnston—a 'London and Geneva' man, as Ralph so often described him—would personally travel to Vietnam to oversee their harvest?

When Caroline knocked on his door, he was already showered and dressed, and the sight of her blew the last dust of fatigue off of him, so he drew her down on the bed in an embrace that threatened to make them late for dinner.

'You're better,' she said with a laugh, coming up for air. 'A *lot* better! You must have had a successful day.'

'I've had a very successful day. At least, I think I have. I've found the counterfeit painting, the object of my search in Vietnam. What's more, I am now its proud owner.' He got up and brought the packaged painting back to the bed, then drew it out of the carton and held it up for viewing.

'It's beautiful!' she exclaimed. 'So sad and haunting. I never thought...' She paused as if caught by surprise, biting her lip.

'Remember, I didn't paint it,' he pointed out. 'This is just a copy.'

She shook her head. Whatever it was that had crossed her mind, she decided not to share it. 'So, who was it that tried to sell it at Christie's? Was it your friend Kenneth Johnston, or someone else?'

'Someone that Johnston was paying off with a favour. I don't know for certain who that was, but I have a fair suspicion. Madame Roulet swears it was someone else altogether.'

'She's protecting someone.'

'Obviously. She tried to put me off the track by talking about someone from another embassy, not the British one. Perhaps it's true, but it just doesn't feel right.'

'So, who delivered the painting back to her gallery?' Caroline asked.

'I have no idea.'

'What does the consignment note say?'

'What consignment note?'

'There's a plastic pocket with a pink invoice or consignment note in it on the side of the carton—behind the open flap.' Caroline pulled the envelope off the side of the cardboard packaging and took out its contents.

' "Sam McAvoy, c/o United States Embassy, Hanoi". Does that name mean anything to you?'

Sam! Of course: Rolex watches and Hugo Boss jackets.

'I can guess at it. The United States Embassy address might explain a few things, too. In the absence of Kenneth Johnston, I had someone at the British Embassy down as the culprit, but it seems I may have been wrong. It doesn't mean that he didn't know about it, but this suggests someone else was the intended beneficiary of the scam: a colleague of Johnston's who was owed a favour—just like Kenneth said.'

'So, mystery finally solved? You're now the proud owner of a copy of one of your own paintings, which you have very generously paid for. That must feel weird. I'd have been angry as hell, but you seem to have no trouble with it.'

She pushed him back down on the bed and peered at him curiously, not convinced that she knew what he was thinking or feeling. 'Is that the end of the matter?' she asked.

He pushed her gently to one side and sat up. 'It's the end of my search for the painting,' he replied thoughtfully. 'When I phone my agent and tell him that I had to buy it back, I'm sure he will be very amused. But is it the end of the matter? Of that I'm not so sure. You said the other day—about wanting to be a journalist—that asking the right questions was more important than believing you had the answers. I realize now that I never did ask the right questions about Paladin, even though they were begging to be asked. I think that's because I didn't want to hear the answers. It was easier for me to believe that I'd gotten a lucky break, and that was the end of it.'

'You're talented; that's why you're successful. It has nothing to do with luck.'

He smiled. 'Thank you. But I'm not talking about painting now; I'm talking about something far more important. It's about what you do when you know something is wrong, but you can't put your finger on it. Do you ignore it and hope it goes away, or do you look for the evidence, no matter how difficult, embarrassing, or dangerous that might be?'

'You trust your instincts; you look for the evidence.'

He kissed her. 'You're quite a girl, Miss Brinkley. Why did I know you'd say that? Now, where are we meeting your brother?'

THIRTY-ONE

It was the restaurant where they'd eaten on their first night in Hanoi, four weeks ago, when they shared the fish hotpot. Once again, she demanded the table by the fountain. They were early—or rather, her brother was late— which was good, because it allowed Faraday to order a large, cold beer and down it quickly, without having to defer to the drinking habits of others.

Tuan was thin and intense, a bloodless type whose most appealing facial feature was a permanent expression of surprise. What it was that surprised him soon became apparent: the thought that other people were not as smart as he was. For Faraday, this quickly became an excuse to play dumb.

'You must know,' Tuan challenged him, 'where you were infected by the virus. I mean, it is not difficult to identify the possible sources. We know it is by ingestion, in one form or another, of avian faecal matter or blood. How did you catch it?'

'Oh,' Faraday mumbled, rubber-lipped, 'I don't know. I think I must have been the victim of foul play.'

'Anton!' Caroline snorted. 'Be serious. Tuan genuinely wants to know. It's his job.'

'To infect people?'

'To find a cure. That's right, isn't it, Tuan? Tell him.'

'My specialty is antigen-presenting cells. They trigger the adaptive immune response and are the reason you are still alive,' Tuan announced authoritatively. 'Specifically, receptor molecules.'

'You're over my head,' Faraday conceded, fearing that a pleasant evening sharing a bowl of fish hotpot could easily degenerate into a lecture in microbiology. 'Is it possible to explain your specialty in simple terms fit for a layman?'

Well, there was no holding him back now. It took a while for Faraday to train his ear to listen, because Tuan may have lost his American manners and failed to adopt Vietnamese manners in their place, but his voice was full-on. Whether he liked it or not, he was an American college graduate through and through, with all the self-certainty that acquired knowledge mandated by an authoritative institution can bestow.

If Tuan had possessed any self-awareness, he might have replied that no, he couldn't explain his specialty in simple terms. Instead, he launched into a dense explanation of the role of dendritic cells in activating cytotoxic T cells, and the vital role of killer cells and memory cells, and the whole battleground of the auto- and adaptive immune systems in which pathogens were identified and destroyed. Faraday doubted that he really cared whether his companions understood. For him, it was just stream of consciousness.

'This so-called "influenza virus" has chosen to be incubated in poultry, the perfect breeding ground, and there will always be outbreaks, as long as people are stupid enough to concentrate their flocks. But human beings concentrate in dense flocks also, and we can expect that at any time, we will become its preferred carrier. Then it will spread person to person. That is what I research.'

'Well,' Faraday said at last, 'I'm surprised you can do this research here in Vietnam. It sounds extremely complex.'

'Do you think we Vietnamese are not up to such a complex task?' Tuan demanded.

'No, no, not at all. I was inferring that the technical resources required for such research must be enormously costly.'

'My company has the resources,' Tuan responded confidently. 'And it will be obvious to you why we are based in Vietnam when you see what is happening right now—and what happened to you.'

'Of course. It makes sense. Well, I have a simple question for you: why did I survive, when others, who may well have contracted the virus from the same source, died?'

'Because your immune system released antiviral elements that induced apoptosis in the infected cells. Most likely, you had a high number of CD8 T cells.'

'… And they didn't.'

'They didn't.'

'Well, that's simple then. Here's to CD8 T cells! Now, let's order. But I have one other question: how serious would this virus be if it learned to become transferable human-to-human?'

'Geometrical progression would spread the disease—person-to-person—worldwide in thirty-eight days. During the 1918 Spanish flu epidemic, more than fifty million people died worldwide—and that was caused by the H1 influenza strain picking up genetic material from the avian flu strain in domestic ducks. This variant will be far more dangerous if it develops the same ability.'

'Shit!'

'And besides, in 1918, no one travelled like they do today. So, multiply by ten.'

* * * *

Their dinner was finished early, which suited Faraday, because he could feel himself waning. He was still a long way from fully recovered, and he couldn't stop yawning. Tuan was neither an eater nor a drinker. He subsisted on the nutrients fed by blood cells to his brain, and he seemed baffled as to why anyone would want to lead a conversation away from the topic of microbiology, as quite clearly in his view, this was where the origin and meaning of life were to be found. Even the fish hotpot was source material for his topic of choice.

'Star anise,' he exclaimed, holding up a whole seed that he'd fished from the broth. '*Illicium verum*. Produces shikimic acid, a valuable synthesizer. To you, it is just an herb. Nature has all the answers; that is the lesson of microbiology.'

* * * *

'Did that go as you hoped?' Faraday asked Caroline as he settled up the bill once Tuan had left.

'It was pretty much what I expected,' she admitted. 'I can see now why Tuan argued so strongly with Uncle over the duck farm proposal. To him, it must have seemed like the stupidest idea in the world. And he was right, as it turned out.'

'Well, he gave me his business card, so he must be anticipating meeting again. I'm surprised, given the way I kept yawning.'

They walked back to the hotel the long way, choosing to window shop while they thought and talked, each mulling over the conversation for different reasons. For Caroline, it must have been a salutary reminder that the person she had grown up referring to as her 'brother' was so different from her as to be almost an alien species. Would she continue to try and maintain family ties, or was it already evident that they had become strangers? Hers was probably a feeling of loss.

For Faraday, the conversation had been a reminder of how close he had come to losing his life, but for the existence of a receptor molecule on the outer membrane of a cell that might not otherwise have received the signal to defend itself. They'd commented frequently in the hospital on the fortitude of his immune system, taking blood samples with indecent frequency, but there was nothing in his lifestyle that could have accounted for it. Was he just 'lucky', therefore?

'I need to do some research,' he said, stopping in front of a computer store window. 'I don't have a laptop with me, and my cell phone screen drives me mad. I think I'll buy an iPad.'

'There's no need to do that; borrow my laptop.'

'You'll need it for work.'

'Not for the next few days. What is it you want to research, anyway?'

'Things.'

' "Things"…?'

'Unexplained things: whispers, fleeting faces, footsteps, hints that I've failed to understand. I know something is wrong, but I can't ask the right questions because I know nothing about it.'

'Know nothing about *what?*'

'Precisely! This whole Paladin thing, and the man from the British Embassy taking such an interest in me and my movements that he was monitoring my time in hospital. Then he turns out to be connected to Madame Roulet, and you spot the consignment note that shows Paladin's Jamaican Sam works for the US Embassy.'

She examined his face closely, frowning, unable to help. 'Borrow my computer in the meantime. If you still don't know what you're looking for, you can come back and buy your own.'

The following morning before heading off to work, she gave him her laptop and password.

THIRTY-TWO

Faraday had decided he'd browse the internet until mid-afternoon, when it would be early morning in London and he could call Ralph. It was not at all obvious where he needed to start. The Northern Highlands were where the mystery was seated, and he needed to read all he could on the history of the area and the treatment of the Montagnards. But most of it proved to be superficial and written for tourists. There were sidebars on wildlife and conservation activities, but much of it was repetitive and culled from press releases, as was to be expected from the internet, where misinformation was likely to be repeated just as frequently as fact. But what was he looking for?

Violet's story of the tribesmen who elected to fight for the US Army in guerrilla actions against the Viet Cong was repeated on the web. The simple explanation was that the traditional enemies of the hill tribes were the Vietnamese themselves, who had historically taken every opportunity to wipe them out. When the US Special Forces ran for cover at the end of the war, they left their Montagnard allies behind to be executed, persecuted, and almost obliterated by the North Vietnamese government. The mountains running north from Sapa to the Chinese border were the steepest and densest in the region, and that's where they had retreated to hide. But what was Paladin's interest in the region? If it was as innocent as the collection of seeds to ensure the survival of a rare plant species, why the secrecy, and why the need to police their activity so violently?

Whenever he found himself ready to start a painting, it began with an unformed concept, a feeling and a mood rather than an articulated idea. That was where he sat now. He had a feeling, and the feeling was that he already knew the answers he was seeking. It was simply that he hadn't found the questions to elicit them.

It never had been about 'a harmless little scam' involving a painting of a panda. That was just the wood smoke that had lured him into the forest. Within the forest, tracks led in all directions, and what had made them were the people who had trod there and the destinations they were pursuing. Which one did he need to follow?

Johnston had said to him in the gondola that the behaviour of the Nung tribesmen had been driven by their desire to protect their sacred land from 'a billion evil spirits'. That could only have been the billion Chinese who lived across the border, and who, as recently as 1979, had invaded from the north, according to the man on the train at Lao Cai. 'We count on that', Johnston had added, suggesting that the severity of the tribesmen's defence against intrusion suited Paladin's purpose well. But what was that purpose—the mere collection of seeds?

'When elephants hide, it is not from the tiger, it is from man.' It was Duc who told him that. He decided to write it down, like an annotation on the side of one of his paintings. Was it Duc's way of stating where mankind was positioned in the hierarchy of nature's predators, or was it a more obscure allusion? Was he suggesting that where something could not be found, it was not necessarily because it did not exist, but because it was safer for it not to be discovered? The camp was not meant to be discovered. Nung Thon Phuc was not meant to be discovered. Paladin was not meant to be discovered—and non-existent elephants were their camouflage.

At noon, Caroline called.

'How are you feeling?'

'I'm fine. A bit tired, but otherwise fine. I'm surfing the web. Why?'

"I just got a call from Tuan. He wanted to know which hospital you'd been in, and whether you're going back for blood tests. He wanted to confirm your name, because apparently I hadn't told him. I gave him your number.'

'Why does he want to know?'

'He's a microbiologist; he works with blood. Ask him. You saw what he's like. It'll be to do with his job. He did say that he's working on this current virus, and he made it sound like he was in the know and we wouldn't understand. He's always like that, so I didn't bother to ask questions. The one thing I do know is that he's paranoid about the Chinese, for some reason. That might just be his American schooling though. He said, "We have to get there first, before the Chinese do"—whatever that means. See if you can find out what he actually does.'

'How's the table-laying lesson going?'

"I can think of something else I'd rather be laying..."

'Well then, it's quite possible that you and I may be compatible.'

It was brave talk, but he wasn't as well as he pretended. This virus killed people, and it had nearly killed him, wreaking havoc on his lungs, ears, nose, throat, and eyes. He still had no energy, and a wavering mind that wanted to lead him to bed—and not to make love, but to sleep. His passionate night with Caroline had drained the small residue of reserves that he had obviously been saving up ever since Helene had left him—reserves that he had preserved in order to assure himself that he had not been rendered impotent by her rejection. But now that he had expended them, he felt empty.

Leaving the laptop and stretching out on the bed led him down a steep slope, forcing his body and mind to abandon all efforts to remain in the conscious world. And as he sank, he gave himself up to it, with no thought about how he would return. Try as he might, he couldn't get Caroline's image to follow him as he sank, or Helene's, or anyone else's; he sank alone.

But what he dreamed then was to stay with him for days, interrupted only by coming events—until eventually, the events merged with the dream.

'Did I wake you?' Caroline asked needlessly as he sat up with a start when she entered the room some hours later. 'You looked dead to the world.'

'I was totally knackered,' he mumbled, 'and I was dreaming. Something vivid that I'm sure I've seen and heard before, but I don't know where.' He shook his head to clear it.

'Nice dreams, or nasty?'

'All I can remember is a voice saying, "The genius; the genius to do that", but I can't remember who or why.'

'Were they talking about your painting?'

He laughed as she joined him on the bed and kissed him. 'No, they definitely weren't talking about my painting. But that reminds me that I need to call Ralph and tell him I've got the panda back.'

* * * *

The phone rang for a long time, until it was eventually answered by a woman he didn't know. He asked for Ralph and told her his name, then was left hanging while she disappeared. There were voices in the background, but he couldn't make out what they were saying. The waiting went on so long that he was starting to think she must have forgotten, until Ralph's assistant, Robbie, came on the line.

'Anton?'

'Robbie, for fuck's sake, I'm growing old here! Where's Ralph?'

'Anton? You haven't heard?'

'Heard what? I'm in Vietnam.'

'Ralph's in hospital.' His voice broke. 'Anton, it's dreadful! Just horrible!' He was choking.

'What happened? What was it, his heart?'

'There was a break-in. They tore the gallery apart. Ralph had been working late…'

'You mean he was *attacked*…?'

'It's just so senseless. There never has been any money kept here. I told the police that. He must have struggled, and they just beat him viciously. He's in a coma.'

Faraday closed his eyes and took a deep breath, thinking. 'Robbie, I don't believe what I'm hearing.'

'They may have broken his neck, Anton. Snapped it! What if he should be paralyzed? There was no need for that—no need at all. There was nothing for them to steal.'

THIRTY-THREE

This attack, so random and pointless, and so far away from Faraday's current fields of danger, only served to highlight for him the impersonal nature of fate. If Robbie was to be believed, Ralph was an ill-chosen victim, undeserving of the violence into which he had been swept. The animist religious beliefs of the Montagnards allowed that spirits could be good or bad, and both were ever present and active in the natural world. Was this just a broader explanation for the concept of fate? Why couldn't he, an irreligious Westerner, be similarly accepting of events? Why did he feel so compelled to scrutinize them for meaning, and why did those meanings have to be so empirically founded on fact?

When Tuan called him the next morning, Faraday had trouble even remembering who he was. His mind had been totally preoccupied with the disturbing news of Ralph, and he'd forgotten his conversation with Caroline.

'Tuan? Yes, of course: Caroline's brother. I'm sorry, I was in the middle of something.'

'She told you I'd phone…?'

'Yes, she did mention something like that. You wanted to know which hospital I was in?'

'She told me; I have that. Could I meet you? There are some questions.'

'What sort of questions?'

'I'll explain when we meet. Are you busy now?'

'Not unavoidably so, no.'

'There is a noodle bar on your street called Lucky Pho. I will meet you in one hour.'

Oh, God, Faraday thought, *do I really need to subject myself to another lecture on the impenetrable subject of pathogens and antigens?* He realized he didn't much like Caroline's brother, and he put that down to a prejudice he'd formed as a result of Caroline's story of how he'd treated her when she'd first arrived in Hanoi. It would have helped if Tuan had a likable personality, but he simply wasn't Faraday's type, so the best he could do was put his prejudice to one side and try and be pleasant.

'Now *you'll* be able to answer this question,' he said with false bonhomie as he sat down in the noodle bar an hour later. 'How is it that every bit of unwashed food scrap in a flyblown market gets thrown into a bucket to make soup, and nobody dies from it?'

'Sterilization,' Tuan responded without hesitation. 'Prolonged high temperatures kill all bacteria. If you cook maggots long enough, they are safe to eat. Full of protein, in fact.'

'I wish you hadn't told me that, Tuan. I'll be looking closely at every grain of rice on my plate from now on.' He laughed lightly, but Tuan's thoughts were already on something else.

'Your blood,' he said.

'My blood? What about my blood?'

'Would you let me take a sample?'

'Well, I feel like I've given enough blood samples at the hospital to supply a disaster-area triage unit for a year... Why would you want me to give *you* a sample?'

'You know what I do?'

'You're a microbiologist.'

'My company, Nui BioLab, has received blood samples from all Hanoi hospitals since the coronavirus outbreak began. I checked your name: you are T3308.'

'What is T3308?'

'You are. That's your blood sample number.'

'Oh.'

He was going to say something about patient confidentiality, but he realized that would sound uncharacteristically precious. Still, it was a bit of a surprise to think that his blood was not only readily identifiable by Tuan's company, but was already in their possession.

'Are you contracted to conduct tests? Is that why you receive samples from the hospitals?'

'Yes; we have the expertise. The Vietnamese government has no capacity to deal with this epidemic, and sending samples overseas is not efficient.'

'And now you want another sample from me. Why? Haven't I provided enough already?'

'It's because T3308 is the sample that interests me.'

'I'm sorry, but you'd better explain to me why. Frankly, I prefer to keep my blood to myself; it's a little quirk of mine. Every drop will be needed, should we ever have to defend England again. I think it was Churchill who planted that idea in me, and I've never been able to forget it.'

Levity was wasted on Tuan, and the historical reference was unfair; who the fuck was Churchill?

'T3308 had more CD8 T cells in the blood than normal. During and after infection, the body makes antibodies against the virus. Blood tests can detect these antibodies, but this requires one sample from the onset of disease and another sample several weeks later. Thus, results are not available until the patient has recovered, or died. You are fully recovered, and your sample differed from others. It is important to know whether your blood has changed.'

'What is CD8 T?'

'A virus-killing immune cell.'

'And how come my blood's got it?'

'That's what we want to know.'

284

'Alright. But first, *pho*; I need to get my strength up.'

When it came, in the blink of an eye and piping hot, he realized that the stuff was addictive. He'd consumed it over the length and breadth of the country, and it never disappointed.

'So, you believe this CD8 T chap got me through by helping kill the virus; is that where we're at?'

'That's an oversimplification. The virus has genetic material wrapped in a layer of protein, which has a lipid membrane coating. When the protein breaks down the infected cell wall, it allows the virus to be released to attack uninfected cells. As they continue to destroy their host cells, more and more copies are released to attack other cells, until the body is overwhelmed. The body's first line of defence lies in the innate immune system, which generates antigens. The second line of defence is the adaptive immune system, which uses the antigens as its starting point and creates a living memory of the microbial invaders, in order to defeat them. T cells and B cells are at the heart of this adaptive response. My research is in T cells.'

'Well, as a microbiologist, you must be feeling extraordinarily lucky,' Faraday suggested brightly.

' "Lucky"…?'

'To be right here in the thick of it while an epidemic is raging. How many samples do you get to study?'

'We are not lucky. We have been working very hard for a long time.'

'I'm sure you have. I didn't mean "lucky" so much as "fortunate" … to be in the middle of an epidemic. And what sort of progress are you making, do you think?'

The last time Faraday had shared a bowl of *pho*, he'd been with Duc in the marketplace in Sapa. He'd made the mistake of eating a whole chili from the bottom of the bowl, but he wouldn't be making that mistake again.

Frowning, he paused. There was something there, but he couldn't identify what it was.

'I can't tell you any more,' Tuan continued. 'We are not alone in seeking an antiviral treatment, and that is all I will say. Vaccines are valuable, but viruses mutate. In my line of work, it is how we survive the viruses that matters.'

Tuan had an intellectual conceit—or self-assuredness—that translated as cold arrogance. Opportunities for social niceties slipped past him unrecognized.

'Well, I was only wondering—as I imagine everyone must be—whether you think protection is any closer. You're not alone, as you say, so presumably, you swap information with others. Or is it a case of who will be first to win the prize? I presume there's a lot of money in it.'

'It isn't just the money. It is far more important than that.'

'Sure, I get it: it's human lives. But there must be a rush to get a treatment onto the market. How close is it?'

Tuan closed his eyes, as if wrestling with his impatience at having to find simple words to explain a complex subject to an ignorant layman.

'Human trials take years,' he sighed. 'They can't be rushed. If anyone thinks they can, an even bigger disaster will result.'

'But once you get one, right, then this thing can be knocked on the head?'

For the first time since he'd met him, Tuan smiled. 'The world is blind to what is happening, Anton. In China, they have been deliberately producing hybrid viruses with the potential to acquire mammalian transmissibility by reassortment with the human influenza viruses. So have we; we call it "research". If such a mutation escaped, and the pathogenicity in man was anything up to twenty percent, then a pandemic affecting five hundred million people could result in one hundred million deaths. What use is money then?'

He smiled again, coldly. No, not likable, Faraday thought, but probably the right man for the job.

He agreed to give him another blood sample and went with him to the hospital by taxi, returning to the hotel mid-afternoon. If he had lacked a direction for his internet searches the day before, he now found himself drawn to Tuan's research and his apocalyptic warnings about pandemics. By the time Caroline returned from her hospitality training sessions, his mind was swimming in it … but it wasn't until the urgent knocking on their door later that night that the whole thing started dropping into place.

* * * *

He and Caroline had both been naked. The air conditioner creaked. It was too hot to make love, and their minds were too active for sleep.

The sudden banging on the door was loud and insistent. Faraday drew a sheet over Caroline and grabbed a dressing gown for himself.

'Who is it?'

'Tuan.'

He almost fell into the room when the door was opened, oblivious to the scene in front of him. Without offering an explanation, he opened an envelope he was carrying and tipped its contents onto the bed before turning to Faraday. 'You know these?'

They were the seeds Duc had given him—the seeds that had sustained him through the pain and exhaustion of his journey into the mountains.

He picked one up and cracked it between his teeth. 'Yes, I know these.'

'Did you take them before or after you developed the viral symptoms?'

'Before.'

'*Only* before?'

'Only before. Where did you get them?'

'They changed your T cells. You had no antiviral treatment at the hospital, but your T cells had changed.'

'Is that what you came here to tell me with such urgency?'

Tuan's frame was light at the best of times, but under the burden of whatever it was he was carrying, it now seemed about to break.

'This is the source of an extract we are using to manufacture an antiviral medication recombinantly. We insert its DNA into E. Coli bacteria for large-scale laboratory production of the enzyme. The scale of production was suddenly expanded some months ago, without explanation, and a new control group was established for clinical trials. The control group is in the area where the epidemic has spread, and it has been returning hundreds, now thousands of patient statistics that are being collected as part of Phase 3 clinical trials, when Phase 1 and 2 trials have not yet been completed. I have to ask why, because I am a scientist. This is not how good science works.'

Neither Faraday nor Caroline knew how to advance the conversation, because its subject matter was beyond them. As they glanced at each other, both confused, the question that troubled them both was why Tuan had ended up at their door late at night to unburden himself.

'Has no explanation been offered?' Caroline asked.

'I have raised serious concerns about the methodology used in Phase 1 and 2 trials, and questioned the priority being given to this drug as a palliative treatment, but our parent company insists that all our resources be put into it.'

'Where do you think the resources *should* be going?' Faraday asked.

'The problem is vaccination, not palliative treatment. If we don't achieve a vaccine that's effective, then we are wasting our time. Once a transmissible mutation is on the loose, we'll have a pandemic.'

'Are you talking about the Chinese experiments?'

'It's not just the Chinese. I told you, we have a program, too.' He stood up abruptly. 'But I shouldn't be telling you this; we are forbidden to speak about it.'

'So, why did you come?' No, Faraday really did not like him, though he could see that he was genuinely disturbed.

'Because Caroline is my family.'

Then he fled for the door.

'Tuan, stop!' Caroline shouted. 'What are you telling us? Are you in some sort of trouble over this…?'

'The CD8 T cells have to be developed before the virus invades. This product will not save anybody who hasn't taken it before infection, and even then, the after-effects can be fatal...' His voice trailed off.

'How so?' Faraday asked.

'You can trigger the immune system, but in some people, that can't be stopped. I have spoken out about it, and now I'm in danger... It isn't science; it's greed.'

As they listened to his footsteps running down the stairs, the bleakness of his words echoed in the room.

THIRTY-FOUR

August in Hanoi is a month to avoid. Outdoors, there is no escape from the heat and humidity; it claims everything. When it rains, the storm drains erupt with fountains of brown water, and street market awnings collapse their contents onto the stall holders who shelter beneath them. Then, at the first break in the downpour, the street traders unwrap themselves and their merchandise from the clear plastic shrouds that protect them to begin again the endless pursuit of petty commerce that characterizes daily life in Vietnam.

Inside the British Embassy building in Hanoi, the heat and humidity were kept at bay by solid masonry walls, double-glazed windows, and Japanese heat pumps. Even so, Faraday, sweating heavily, would have liked it to be a good ten degrees colder.

The receptionist asked if he had an appointment. Yes, he had; he'd phoned Mr Proctor earlier, he replied. He was asked to wait in the same room where he'd collapsed on his previous visit, but not for long.

Proctor was reserved but welcoming as they went up to his office overlooking Hai Ba Trung. It was cool, quiet, and spacious, but remarkably uncluttered. Mr Proctor was not a paper-pusher.

'I monitored your progress,' he confided as they entered, 'and I was delighted that you recovered so quickly. Your case is of particular interest to us, as you may be able to help with identifying the source of your infection.'

He motioned Faraday into a chair on the other side of his desk. The desk was more of a meeting table: three chairs on one side, and a large, swivelling executive chair for the man who ran the meetings on the other. The desktop was bare except for a large white pad and a computer screen off to one side.

'It occurred to me to get in touch with you, but we've been run off our feet with this epidemic thing. However, you've taken the initiative and beaten me to the gun. So, thank you for that.' As he spoke, he took out a business card from a drawer and slid it across the desk.

Shifting forward in his chair, Faraday reached out and took it, only to find that it told him nothing at all. 'I'm sorry, remind me again,' he asked innocently, 'are you with Home Office or Foreign Office?'

'Foreign and Commonwealth,' Proctor replied with a hint of institutional pride. 'In the dark ages, when I first joined as a lowly administrative assistant, it was Foreign and *Colonial*—very non-PC. That tells you my age. "Colonial" is a word we've had to purge from our lexicon, yet it doesn't seem so long ago. You'd probably have some views on that.'

DONALD PROCTOR, CMG. No department, and no job title. A plain, uncluttered office, bare of any personal effects. No regulation portrait of Mrs. Proctor and child on the desk, just a large drawing pad with a collection of doodles on it—doodles that Faraday (because he was drawn to that sort of thing) would have liked to turn around so he could interpret them.

' "CMG"! That sounds lofty,' Faraday observed. 'Someone obviously appreciates your work.'

'It's given to those who hang around long enough.'

'And which department of the Foreign and Commonwealth have you been hanging around in?' Faraday asked.

That was better, he thought, *let's stop the niceties*. It was time to show that this wasn't a social call.

But no, Proctor was not inclined to stop the game. 'The Human Resources Group.' He smiled apologetically. 'It's extraordinary how language has become the agent of inflated pomposity. Staff are now "resources"—vital commodities, like precious metals. I suppose we can blame America for that. I prefer plain language myself. "Personnel" will do, though within the Consular Directorate, which gives it a rather broad brush. Hence my involvement with this influenza thing. We can't leave it to the Vietnamese alone. We take responsibility for our own subjects when they're here, like with you. But I'm digressing. Things have gotten so much more serious since you first came down with the virus. It's quite alarming, and I'm conscious that we didn't fully cover enough ground with you in hospital to enable a conclusion to be reached about how you contracted it. I hope that's what you've come to tell me. Tea? Can I get you some tea? Coffee, perhaps?'

Proctor didn't wait for him to reply, but pressed a button on his desk phone that was apparently installed for just that purpose; no need to speak. Or perhaps the person on the other end had been listening the whole time.

'It seems counter-intuitive, but hot drinks really do cool you down. I don't quite know how that works, but…'

Christ, the man was good, Faraday thought: cool as a cucumber.

'… Let's talk about where you've been, and where you might have picked up this filthy thing.'

'I could speculate,' Faraday said, 'but it would only be speculation.'

'Then let's speculate together.' Eyebrows raised, expectant. 'You started your journey, as I recall you telling me in hospital, in the Mekong Delta. Did you go there to paint—I seem to remember you saying you're a painter of wildlife—or did you have some other purpose in mind?'

'I was trying to locate a gallery that might have sold a counterfeit copy of a painting of mine—a painting of a panda that I'd sold to the Paladin Foundation in Geneva. The copy was done by someone here in Vietnam,' Faraday replied carefully. He watched Proctor's face for a reaction, but there was none.

'Ah, they're incorrigible copyists. Any luck?'

292

'No. I spent three days travelling up and down the river, wondering how on earth people can live in that environment and just how that filthy water can sustain so much life.'

'If we are to believe what they tell us,' Proctor said, his tone rather implying that he did not in fact believe it himself, 'life as we know it started with a single-cell bacterium lying in such water—just a primitive bug, going nowhere, doing nothing. Then the bug farted. That's how it all began: under water.'

* * * *

It didn't go at all how he'd imagined it would. The moral indignation that had incited Faraday to action wasn't sufficient to goad Proctor into admitting having a connection with the painting, and lacking proof, Faraday had to resort instead to exchanging a half hour of elegant but unproductive banter—something at which Proctor was an expert practitioner.

Then, just when he was beginning to question why he had come there, so convinced that he would find answers to questions he hadn't yet even asked of himself, the tea arrived, carried on a lacquered tray by a young Eurasian woman who had mastered the art of soundlessness. In acknowledgement of her silent footsteps and ethereal calm, Proctor and Faraday lapsed into silence also. Without looking at either of them, gaze fixed solely on the two blue porcelain cups and the bamboo-handled porcelain teapot, she gently set them down on the desktop, as if to spill one precious drop would be a sin unforgivable in heaven. With just the faintest rustle of her silk *ao dai*, she turned and left as she had come, without a word.

'It takes time to adjust to Vietnam,' Proctor advised, completely ignoring what Faraday had been saying before the interruption. 'It can't be done in a few days, or even a few years. Have you noticed they don't bow when greeting or leaving you? They stand erect. The Japanese bow to the waist and beyond, guided by the most complex set of rules, and they bow all the time. The Japanese, on the other hand, are the most ruthless murderers of any peoples over whom they have sway, yet they are mortified by any breach in their ritual politeness. The Vietnamese do not bow, nor do they have any interest in killing other people—unless those people are intent on killing them. Interesting, don't you think?'

'I haven't been here long enough to comment,' Faraday admitted. 'The only thing I'm sure of at this stage is that it is most unwise to take anything here at face value. But that could be said of anyone, not just the Vietnamese.'

Proctor raised his eyebrows, but was otherwise unmoved. '*Bien sur*, Mr Faraday*, bien sur*! An attitude which would hold all of us in good stead, if only we could remember it'.

He reflected on this a moment, as if disappointed that there weren't others present to share his erudition.

'The place I always start,' he continued, preferring his own direction to the one Faraday might want to follow, 'is the map. It explains almost everything. From the Gulf of Tonkin in the north, to the Gulf of Thailand in the south, the Indochinese Peninsula stretches for sixteen hundred kilometres and encompasses Thailand, Cambodia, Laos, Vietnam, and Southern China, with all their diversities of race and culture. Imagine the history; imagine the tensions! But look at the map, and you'll see that Vietnam itself stretches the entire length of that peninsula along its coastline, so long and thin that it is almost an outline, as if someone had taken a thick pencil to the outer edge of that map. The Vietnamese live in that thick pencil line, and after everyone has had a go at pushing them into the sea, they are still there, and what is most remarkable is that they are still a distinct ethnic group. The Chinese have failed to absorb them; the Chams and the Khmers are marginalized minorities. I find this quite remarkable.'

He was in full swing now, the tone of an academic lecturer colouring his voice, chair starting to tilt back, hands circling as though he were massaging his own erudition.

'You and I, being of Anglo-Saxon stock, would have interbred by now and thus be unrecognizable. Good God, one only has to walk down any British High Street to see the proof of that! But the Vietnamese have no time for miscegenation. They don't even have time for those of their own who emigrate overseas. They're regarded as soft-bellied cowards and traitors, and while the American troops did their best to plant their own seeds, you'll find very few Amerasians have chosen to remain; it's simply too hard for them.'

Did he look towards the door that the young woman had silently closed behind her? Faraday thought so, but he couldn't be sure.

'They've fought hard to remain who they are, and that's a lesson the French and Americans had to learn the hard way. Would you have gained a sense of that as you travelled around, or were you preoccupied with your forensic pursuits among the country's galleries?'

'Funny you should mention that, because I've got the impression that Vietnam is being invaded again.'

That got his attention. 'Good God! By whom?'

'NGOs.'

'NGOs...? You'll have to explain.'

'Well, they're everywhere. I may not have told you, but I received my first major commission for painting threatened wildlife species from The Paladin Foundation—an NGO whose executive director is a chap named Kenneth Johnston. That's who I was asking about when I first came to the Embassy. I'd run into him in Sapa.'

'Yes... As I said, I don't know him or his organization. He has no connection whatsoever with the Embassy. What do they do here, exactly?'

'They claim to be tracking elephants by satellite for a census. At least, that's what they say publicly.'

'So, they're conservationists. Good! That's what I thought. I'd like to get to that part of your story eventually, if you have time, because we need to eliminate all possible sources of your infection before you got to the

Highlands. Perhaps we could make a list of the places you've been since arriving in Vietnam…?"

He pulled open his desk drawer and took out a lined notepad, then removed a pen from the same drawer and adjusted it, ready for writing. It was a heavy silver pen, not unlike the Mont Blanc knock-offs that Trih had purchased in the market, except that as he began to write, Faraday could see that it had an ink cartridge and a nib rather than a ballpoint.

Proctor's writing style was fluid and rather flamboyant, as if he was conscious that he was providing a transcript that would be read by others. He started with a heading, which he then underlined. ' "Contact with Potential Sources of Infection",' he read out loud as he wrote. 'Surely we have established two locations that deserve investigation immediately: the Mekong Delta, and the Northern Highlands. Where else might there be? This might be of interest to the WHO. Who else have you told about your travels?'

Faraday was surprised, both by the sudden call to action and by the direction of it.

'No one,' he replied. 'No one has asked. The hospital seemed solely intent on my recovery, rather than how I'd obtained the virus. Nobody even raised that question. I was perfectly well until I came back from Sapa, and from what I've been reading, this outbreak is confined to the Highlands. It had already spread there before I arrived. You're not suggesting that I might have caught it elsewhere, are you? Because if I did, why wouldn't others have caught it, too?'

Proctor pinned him with a slightly accusatory gaze, his pen hovering above the page as if deciding what needed to be written next. Then he laid down his pen and sat back in his chair, joining his fingertips together and closing his eyes, as if searching for visual clues.

'Hmm…' Pursing his lips, he sat forward again slowly. '… I can think of one obvious explanation, Anton—may I call you that?—but I have to say that I am not a virologist, and it would be dangerous for me to speculate. Let's leave that to the WHO people. But tracing your movements and identifying the people with whom you've had close contact might be better done here in the Embassy than letting it fall to the Vietnamese authorities who—dare I say it?—do not treat unwelcome events with any great sensitivity or understanding, particularly where foreigners are involved, if you get my meaning.'

Faraday spun around and looked towards the door. Had he heard the latch click? Open, or closed? Or had he just imagined it? Perhaps he was being paranoid. When the air pressure changes inside a room, the door can sometimes spontaneously adjust itself. The air pressure had just changed; that's what he'd felt. Something unidentifiable had stirred in the room, and seeking release, it had imperceptibly altered the atmosphere in a way that disturbed him. There was a hint of a smell—no, more a *memory* of a smell— and a feeling of translocation, familiar, but struggling to be remembered, something from the past rather than the present.

He frowned, trying to gather his thoughts. He was definitely still far from fully recovered.

'Wait a minute… You just said you could think of one explanation as to why I might have contracted the virus when no one else had. What did you mean?'

That wasn't it; that wasn't what had triggered the feeling. But it would do for the moment while he tried to identify what it was. It had something to do with the hospital. That's why he'd imagined a smell. Of all the senses, smell has the strongest link to memory. The imagined smell was a marker dye.

Proctor looked surprised. 'Why, simply that you, fresh from London, had no immunity, whereas the locals have had generations of exposure and have developed resistance—that's what I meant. But look, this is not my subject, and I don't even know whether such a hypothesis is credible in biosecurity circles, so it's not something I'd want to advance. I'm more concerned that we can hand the WHO people a log of places, activities, and contacts, free of amateur speculation on our part, but as full of detail as your memory will allow. That should be our aim, so the more you can recall about your journey, the better … and of course, about the people you've met, like this Mr Johnston.'

That was it! Yes, it was the hospital. He was beginning to recall something: a mood, a sensation, a far-off sound stirring beyond the mist of his fevered palsy. He'd heard these words before, he was sure. 'We need to know where he went and who he met.' It had been Proctor speaking, and Faraday had been only semi-conscious. But what if he had responded to Proctor's questioning in that state and had since forgotten? What if he'd already told him things that he was now planning to spring on him? He felt certain that something was returning to him, and he needed to leave the door open to it.

Meanwhile, he realized that Proctor had subtly and effectively wrested the focus of the meeting away from him. It wasn't any longer the illegal activities he'd unearthed in the Highlands that were going to be examined under a spotlight; it was his own activities.

And while tracing his footsteps, he apparently had a duty of care to tell Proctor (and whoever was listening at the door, or down the Cat 5 line from that communication device masquerading as a telephone on his desk) everything he knew about Kenneth Johnston, as well. Oh, really? No; Faraday shook his head secretly to himself. He wouldn't be doing that, thank you. He'd be damned if his intent was going to be hijacked in that way.

If one thing was clear, it was that Proctor wanted to play the role of a health official, when he was quite clearly a very different animal altogether.

THIRTY-FIVE

Faraday pushed back his chair and stood up again, feeling his fever returning. He wasn't comfortable sitting and preferred not to be facing his adversary.

Proctor got to his feet as well.

Now that they were both standing, the office seemed suddenly smaller—closer to the size of a boxing ring, and this must have been felt simultaneously by both of them, for they moved, as if by consent, to opposite ends of the long window that looked out over the Embassy compound to the swarm of motorbikes and scooters that choked the streets of Central Hanoi at every hour of every day, endlessly rushing like blood cells around the body of the city, keeping it alive. It was not a rush hour phenomenon; it was perpetual, eighty million people rushing about in pursuit of their own little plan for survival, all with smiles on their faces. There was no prospect of his ever coming to understand them in anything but the most superficial way. Even if he chose to live among them, how could he inherit their history? What had Caroline said? 'You'll never know what's not being said' ... which was also true of what was going on in this room.

'So, just to get this straight,' he confirmed, 'Kenneth Johnston has no connection with the British Embassy, and you know nothing about Paladin's activities in Vietnam; is that right?'

He knew he needed to get it right, because he wasn't used to this type of game. Moral indignation wasn't going to get him through on its own, though moral indignation was the fuel that he needed to keep him going.

'Affirmative to the first,' Proctor replied briskly. 'I would need to obtain confirmation of the second. Someone here might know them.'

'Well,' Faraday observed, 'I'd be grateful if you could let me know for sure, because Johnston and I were friends for many years, and I would like to try and contact him again to discuss something I've learned about what's going on in the Highlands.'

He might be an artist, and he might look a tad foppish and unkempt at times, but that didn't stop him from seeing what was happening. He was convinced that these bloody Whitehall bureaucrats had gone rogue, when they should have been working for the people who paid their taxes. They thought the world was run from their diplomatic offices. Well, it wasn't; it was run by people out of their sight. That had become apparent with every step along his journey thus far, and he wasn't going to stop until he finally showed it for what it was: people playing at God.

But he had to be careful, because he had started to reach the point where everything he saw and heard began to have meaning. Intuition had inestimable value, but it never trumped facts.

Returning to his chair at the desk, he pulled towards him the lined notepad on which Proctor had been writing. The other man made no attempt to stop him.

Beneath the heading, *Contact with Potential Sources of Infection,* he had written, *Mekong Delta and Northern Highlands.*

'Shall we just record your progress through the country,' Proctor asked pleasantly, 'and not dwell on speculation? What we do know is that you have survived a particularly virulent strain, and what we don't know, *mutatis mutandis*, is whether the necessary changes have occurred in that strain yet to allow it to be passed from human to human. Or would that be more correctly *mutatis mutandum*? My Latin is rather rusty.'

'As you say,' Faraday reflected quietly. 'There are people far better qualified to identify lines of investigation than you or me, so why don't we let them do it? I'm more than happy to talk to the WHO people, if you wish to call them.'

If Proctor took this as a dare, he didn't show it. He was too well practiced for that.

'That is a perfectly sensible suggestion,' he answered, almost enthusiastically. 'There I was, rushing us towards some magical determination of cause, down the old eureka path to glory, when I don't know the first thing about what we should be looking for. I don't know what I was thinking. We'll get you in front of the experts just as soon as you're ready for them.'

With this, he sat up energetically and made a gesture towards the phone, as if he were about to pick it up and call for the cavalry. But the gesture was a little too obvious and not sufficiently sincere.

'There is just one thing,' he cautioned, pulling his hand back. 'There are bound to be questions about what you were doing in Sapa, and why you're trying to contact this Johnston fellow. I wonder how we should handle that, bearing in mind that they'll probably want to speak to him, too. You know that foreigners are being asked to register with them.'

Faraday's laugh in response caught him by surprise. It was not a laugh that could be mistaken for humour.

'Then I'm afraid I won't be able to help them, Mr Proctor. You'd have a better idea of Kenneth Johnston's whereabouts now than I do, seeing as he claims to be connected to the Embassy.'

'Ah!' Proctor laid down his pen and eased himself out of his chair. It was time to go for a wander again. 'We keep coming back to that, don't we? Remind me why again.'

'He's the reason I'm here—the reason I came to Hanoi, as it turns out.'

'Because…?'

'Because of the bloody painting! This is where it originated, here is where I met the forger, and Johnston was the person who provided the original image for him.'

'Good heavens. You mean you actually met the person who painted your counterfeit? Were you angry?'

The door opened silently, and the young Eurasian woman in the silk *ao dai*, who had earlier brought them tea, now bore a tray with a stack of dumpling baskets and dipping sauces, which she set down on Proctor's desk, and without bidding, proceeded to lay two places with white napkins and blue-and-white bowls and chopsticks. Her movements, graceful and measured, seemed almost deliberately at odds with the tension in the room.

Faraday waited until she'd finished, then made a point of thanking her politely. Clearly Proctor had planned this in advance. Once she'd left and closed the door, he thought about Proctor's question. This was one of the cards he had to play, so he needed to be careful. Had he been angry at all, or had he felt no resentment towards the forger whatsoever?

'No, I wasn't angry. In fact, I was quite excited.'

'Excited? How interesting.' Proctor's handling of the dumplings, serving his guest first with an assured display of dexterity with his chopsticks, showed an assimilation of Asian etiquette that could only have come from some years of service in the region. It also revealed an eagerness to get to his first mouthful, and only when that had been achieved did he turn his mind back to Faraday's reply.

' "Excited", you say. On account of…?'

'Being at last able to confirm my suspicions, or failing that, to learn something completely unexpected. I'd travelled a long way to come to that moment, and I was certain of its source. The panda was the only subject that had never been reproduced, and the only person I could finger as having access to it was Kenneth Johnston—which he subsequently confirmed.'

Proctor appeared more interested in the matching of chili and soy sauces to his next dumpling than he was in what Faraday might next reveal.

'So, we've arrived at the point where this story of yours began.' His chopsticks hung in the air between his mouth and his bowl, but the mildness of his interest was feigned. He was interested, alright—but buggered if he was going to show it. The painting had only ever been a harbinger of other things, and now that the journey in search of its source was nearing an end, the 'other things' would inevitably become the focus.

The chili sauce was hot, and Faraday coughed. When it came to chilies in Vietnam, he was learning, he was inclined to be overconfident. They weren't the mild-mannered things he bought from his Waitrose supermarket back home. Almost immediately he felt himself sweating, and he momentarily recognized a familiar feeling from his days in hospital—a sense of falling. Was it the chili, or was it his fever? He put down his dumpling bowl and chopsticks and wiped his forehead with the linen napkin, looking for water.

… Water! It must have been the water he drank in the market in Sapa with Duc that day that had infected him. The water must have been drawn from a contaminated well!

'I have to ask,' Proctor sighed, as if the effort of maintaining his attention was beginning to tire him, 'how had you tracked it down?'

'Oh, quite simple, really. I stumbled into a gallery, run by a certain Madame Roulet, that obviously dealt in copies, and I told her that I was looking for something by A J Faraday. In response to my enquiry, she offered to sell me a copy that had already been made—though she didn't call it a "copy". You understand that the word "original" has a certain flexibility in Vietnam. *Ob-la-di, ob-la-da, life goes on.* Seems that the original purchaser was keen to on-sell, and if I was interested, she would get in touch with him—which might take a day or two, because she wasn't exactly sure of his whereabouts at that moment, but she did expect him to be back in Hanoi after the weekend.'

'And she told you his name was Johnston?'

'No, I asked her if her client was also involved in wildlife conservation, like me. It seemed like a nice, oblique way of extracting the confirmation I was seeking. But her answer was not what I was expecting at all.'

'Oh…?'

'According to Madame Roulet, he works at the Embassy.'

Proctor put down his chopsticks and wiped his mouth with his napkin. His sigh and his facial expression, not to mention his body language, made every possible attempt to convey his exasperation. 'Here we go again,' he complained, 'the "Embassy connection" lark that I hear time and time again. Whatever this woman thinks, or whatever she has been told, I have to repeat that we have checked our records, and your Mr Kenneth Johnston is *not* an employee of the British Embassy, and has never been an employee of the British Embassy, and that is absolutely official. This woman—what was her name…?'

'Madame Roulet. You may know her?'

'Why would I know her?'

'Well, you have clearly been in Hanoi a reasonably long time, and you seem to have an ear for French, which presumably puts you at ease with the French community, so I thought… She's an attractive woman; I'm sure you'd remember her.'

'I'm sorry, I can't recall meeting her. But unless you are about to tell me that the person she was referring to as the customer for her forged painting was not Kenneth Johnston after all–Yes? No?–then I'm afraid that she has got it wrong. As I have already said, it is far from uncommon to discover people implying a connection with the Embassy for a multiplicity of reasons, so, if you don't mind, could we please put that assertion to one side and concentrate on what really matters here, which is how you came to contract the virus.'

That's funny, Faraday thought. After serving tea and dumplings and waffling on about the origins of man, as if filling in time on a slow day, Proctor was now all business and wanting to move on. Clearly, it was Madame Roulet whom he wanted to quickly leave in his wake.

Well, Faraday thought, *I'll come back to that when the moment is right.* Meanwhile, he was starting to get a feel for how to read this man. Perhaps

Proctor was now aware of that, and that was the cause of his suddenly abrupt manner. But Proctor was a professional, so he would know better than anyone if his composure had slipped.

'So now, here I was in Sapa. As they say, the perfect spot for a weekend away, though it was to prove somewhat longer than the weekend I'd planned, because I was helping out a friend in trying to trace a local, which led me unexpectedly to spend two days with a guide trekking through the mountains. I had no idea when I left how quickly the crisis was developing there. I don't think anyone outside the Highlands knew, because the authorities had obviously kept a tight lid on it, and even now they can't be trusted. It caught us all by surprise.'

'Why did you choose to go into the mountains? Surely that was … how shall we put it … an unhealthy decision during an epidemic? You must have had strong reasons.'

'My reason for going into the mountains? It was prompted by what my guide learned in the Nung village where we'd gone in search of a tribal chief, who was supposed to be the beneficiary of my friend's poultry farm project,' Faraday explained.

'What was this thing your guide learned?' Proctor was forced to ask.

'Among other things, the reason the men of the tribe had disappeared into the mountains.'

'Which was…?'

'I'll come to that shortly. In the meantime, my personal reason for going on up into the mountains in pursuit of these missing men was due to a sudden conviction that it would somehow lead me to the elusive Kenneth Johnston, the man at the heart of this enquiry, about whom we seem to have some disagreement as to his affiliations and role in the grand scheme of things.'

'Oh, so there is a grand scheme afoot, is there?' Proctor snorted. 'I can't wait for it to be revealed. But in the meantime, what on earth made you think you'd find Johnston by going up into those mountains? I thought you said he was an executive director, not an intrepid adventurer who would trek off into the wilds of Vietnam's highest mountains.'

Proctor's eyebrow was arched in precisely the manner that gave expression to mock irony, but his body had stiffened in anticipation. He knew they were getting close.

'Yes, it was completely out of character, one would have thought,' Faraday agreed nonchalantly. 'But that only shows how wrong one can be when it comes to character, I suppose. I'm sure there are people trained to never make assumptions about character, but sadly, up until now, I've not been one of them. Naive and trusting; that's been me. Taking things at face value. I've never had reason to do otherwise, until now.'

'And now?'

'Still naive … not so trusting!'

He smiled grimly. Wasn't that the truth?

'You still haven't told me: what made you think you'd find Johnston there?'

'Ah! Because I'd seen someone else I knew from Paladin in Sapa—an American by the name of Sam McAvoy who claimed that their mission was to do a census of elephants in the wild—and then the tribesmen talked about some sort of project up there.'

At this point, Faraday stopped. He'd given him enough for the moment. Now it was time to judge his reaction.

Proctor hesitated. He was still working the story over in his mind, trying to be sure there was nothing of relevance that he'd missed. 'Which convinced you it must involve Johnston? Tracking elephants?'

This was a man who liked to thoroughly inspect the ground he had just covered before he moved forward. He not only swept in front, he swept behind himself as well. That was a good habit to adopt; he must remember it. But significantly, he hadn't reacted to Sam McAvoy's name.

'Let's put it down to instinct,' he replied simply.

'Yes, let's do that,' Proctor agreed. 'It can be a good thing, or it can be a dangerous thing. But at least now we can say that your impetuous decision to go off into the Highlands put you right in the front line when it comes to exposure to the virus. I don't think there's any doubt about that,' he added, making a new annotation on his notepad. 'And that's what you found them doing: tracking elephants?'

'No. They were collecting rare seeds—bags full of them.'

Proctor was ready for him. 'They were collecting seeds?' he scoffed in disbelief. 'How prosaic can that be? They're conservationists, for heaven's sake! That's the sort of thing that conservationists *do*. Couldn't you have told me this at the outset, rather than persisting with that line about elephants? I'll concede that they might need some sort of local permission if they're taking away fauna on any scale, but it's hardly the sort of activity that requires the protection of an Embassy.'

He was clearly tempted to pursue this line further. The opportunity to ridicule the Embassy claim was hard for him to resist, but the fact was that Johnston had made the claim, and Faraday wasn't going to give it up. Right now, though, he didn't need to persist with it.

'Let me come back to that later,' he said. 'It was Paladin itself that was running the elephant census story. That was the line I was given in Hoi An by the American, McAvoy, whom I subsequently saw at Paladin's encampment, so they obviously want people to believe that's what they're doing. But whether they were running a plant propagation exercise or a census of elephants is not as important as the manner in which it was being conducted. Effectively, they had control of a vast area of remote mountains bordering China, and they had a standing army of hostile tribesmen, willing to attack anyone who entered it. Now, for a seemingly benign non-governmental organization, that does raise some questions, don't you think?'

'Does it? From what I've heard and read, the Highlands have always been the domain of the Montagnards. No one has ever succeeded in rooting them out. They guard it with their lives. It sounds to me as though

Paladin found a convenient ally who allowed it to get on with its conservation work uninterrupted. That would be my take on it. Not to put too fine a point on it, Anton, but do you think it might be possible that these suspicions of yours are the product of a fevered imagination? Let's not forget the state you were in when you first arrived back in Hanoi and called on us here at the Embassy. You were not a well man, you should remember. When you collapsed and were taken to hospital, I was called upon to monitor you because we feared we were about to have a dead British subject on our hands. You won't remember any of that, I suspect, because you were unconscious for days.'

'Yes, I accept that my imagination was fevered. But my memory wasn't, and now that the fever has passed, I can delve into my memory again and begin to connect the dots.'

'Well, you are an artist, after all. And what sort of picture have you come up with?'

'Let me take you back to the day I collapsed. It was the duty officer who came to answer my enquiry about Kenneth Johnston's status here at the Embassy, I presume. Is that how it works?'

'That's right. And he would have told you what I've told you: that at that time, we had no knowledge of a Kenneth Johnston, and he most certainly was not attached to this Embassy in any role, nor, as far as I have been able to ascertain since, has he ever been an employee in any capacity in Her Majesty's service, secret or otherwise.'

'But the duty officer, whoever he might be...'

'Gerald Bromley.'

'... Gerald Bromley had the good sense to check me into hospital and to tell you about my enquiry, which you thought sufficiently important that it warranted visiting me in hospital, more than once, presumably in order to satisfy me that my information about Johnston was wrong. Well, that really was service above and beyond the normal call of duty.'

Proctor let his exasperation show. 'As I've already explained to you, we are taking this epidemic extremely seriously, and responsibility has fallen to my watch. If British citizens are going to become victims of it, then it will be *our* job to help them. Don't think the Vietnamese will give a damn that you're British. *That's* why I was at the hospital. *That's* why I needed to know where you had been and who your contacts were. *That's* my damned job, *plain and simple.*'

Faraday smiled. He wasn't amused, but he was pleased; every step that Proctor took now was going to sink him deeper into the quagmire of his own evasions. The only way out was for him to reach for the relative safety of a retraction and admit to at least some of what he was covering up.

'Shall we return to the subject of the counterfeit painting, then?' Faraday asked.

'I thought we'd dispensed with that?'

'No, we merely put it to one side. When I challenged Johnston about it, he said he was doing a favour for a colleague here at the Embassy. 'A harmless little scam' was how he described it. Well, I think we both know who that someone was, don't we? The only thing I couldn't decide when I saw you with Madame Roulet in the market yesterday was whether she is your wife or your mistress. When a man and woman display affection for each other in public, I am more inclined to say she is the latter, but shopping for vegetables together is sufficiently domestic that I'm willing to be proved wrong. So, which is it: wife? Mistress…?'

To his credit, Proctor remained unmoved. It was possible that he gave a small involuntary shrug, but what he didn't attempt to do was speak; he merely inspected his nails, as if trying to decide whether it was time for a manicure.

'So, that's another thing that convinces me of Johnston's connection to this Embassy. Combine that with the fact that Sam from Paladin, the Jamaican-American I met in Hoi An and then again at the encampment in the Highlands, is the person who has been dealing with your Madame Roulet.'

To give him his due, Proctor showed no hostility at having been deliberately led into a trap. Instead, he chose the best course available to him.

'Anton, I have no choice but to offer you my sincerest apology.' He spread his hands in surrender. 'It was a foolish thing for them to have done, and unfortunately, I felt obliged to protect my wife. Yes, you are quite correct: Marie Roulet and I are married. As you have pointed out so clearly, the art world in Vietnam has not yet caught up with the rules that govern authenticity in London or New York, and I'm afraid she was too easily persuaded to organize a reproduction of your painting, not realizing the consequences. So, when you came to us asking about Kenneth Johnston, and I became aware of your identity, I was immediately concerned for my wife—even though, as you now know, she has no personal knowledge of him.'

'Her client was Sam McAvoy,' Faraday confirmed, 'Jamaican Sam. It was his name on the consignment note returning the painting from England.'

'Well, that sounds like an obvious giveaway. He'd hatched the idea with Johnston after meeting my wife at some sort of function here in Hanoi, and unfortunately, I became aware of it because my wife and McAvoy were friendly, and I'd been party to their conversations about Christie's turning down the painting for sale and possibly exposing it as a fraud. I thought they had done a very stupid thing. When you turned up, I was concerned to know whether you'd come because you knew all about it. My denial was driven by a very understandable need to protect my wife, and also, I must say, by the poor reflection on myself and the Embassy.'

'You denied knowing Kenneth Johnston.'

'I don't know him; I know *of* him ... from Sam.'

'You denied having dealings with Paladin.'

'I ... we ... do not have dealings with Paladin, other than socially, through Sam. I was aware of them, of course, but they are *non*-governmental, and our relationship with them is exactly as I've described. I have never met Johnston, and the circumstances under which the panda painting was produced were not known until you revealed them to me today. I doubt that my wife is aware of them. All she knew was what Sam told her: that the photograph was of an original that no one else would have seen. As I have said, my view was that it was a very ill-advised venture, but…'

He spread his hands in supplication. Proctor was not the wily old trout waiting in a dark pool to rise to the tempting bait of Faraday's challenge; no, Proctor was the dark pool.

'I believe that Jamaican Sam was here in the Embassy the day I came back from Sapa,' Faraday said quietly. Was he sure of this, or was he making it up? 'He was on your side of the counter,' he added, 'not the visitor's.'

'Who was?'

'Sam McAvoy, the American from Paladin. He wasn't on the visitors' side; he was on the *in*side. What's more, he was on his way to find out who was asking about Kenneth Johnston. I don't suppose there's any point in asking whether *he's* one of yours, by any chance?'

'Oh, for heaven's sake! Now you're being absurd.'

Proctor was suddenly showing a different side of his personality. He'd been exposed as a liar, and the only response he could adopt with any credibility was that of a man bound by higher duties than a duty to the truth. He was angry because he'd probably thought he could outwit Faraday in the delicate dance around the facts in which he'd been engaged so far, but he'd been undone by Faraday's slow reveal. He didn't like it.

'I'm going to tell you something.' He leaned forward, elbows on his desk, fists clenched so that the muscles in his arms flexed and the veins on his neck stood out, in much the same way as they probably did when he lifted the dumb-bell each morning in his daily exercises. 'If you continue to run conspiracy theories, you are not only going to try my patience, but you are going to undo the goodwill I have extended to you on account of the ill-judged behaviour of my wife and her friend Sam, for which I have already apologized. I'm not going to say it again: Kenneth Johnston has no connection with this Embassy. Sam McAvoy has no position in this

Embassy. What the Paladin Foundation does in Vietnam is their business, and theirs alone. Tracking elephants, collecting seeds—they can do whatever they bloody well want to. Sam was here the morning you called after returning from Sapa because my wife's gallery was closed that day, and he had a package that he wanted me to give her, as you now know. It was a *coincidence*. Do you understand? A *coincidence*, nothing more. There is no bloody conspiracy.'

THIRTY-SIX

'That's it?' Caroline complained in disbelief.

That night, they were both equally deflated. They stirred their favourite fish hotpot round and round with an uncharacteristic lack of enthusiasm. The journey had taken so long, and now it had come down to this.

'He admitted to being involved with copying your painting, but denied even knowing your friend Johnston? That's bull crap. What are you going to do?' she asked.

He hadn't yet told her the full story, so he couldn't give her an answer. It was too soon.

'Well,' she said, 'I can't get the look on Tuan's face last night out of my head. He told us that these seeds that the Paladin people are collecting are the key to a new antiviral drug, and that the experiments he's been working on relate to mutations for which there'd be no vaccination. What he was saying should scare the bejesus out of us! You can't tell me that the British or American governments don't know about this. There's no way Paladin would be doing this on their own; they're just the ones with the free pass to get in there. People need to be told the truth. There's no information getting out.'

'For good reason.'

'Yes, but *we* know. We have a duty to tell others,' she insisted.

'What duty? What we've learned is scary, but we haven't learned anything that will change the health situation. It's an outbreak, not a pandemic. Cross your fingers that it goes away.'

'Cross your fingers and hope to die, you mean. Tuan told us that the Chinese are carrying out equally dangerous experiments. Did you challenge your Mr Proctor with that information?'

'Yes, I did, actually.'

'And what did he say to that?'

'He didn't deny it.'

* * * *

Of all the body's organs, the brain is the greediest consumer of energy. The session had drained Faraday, and he needed a break from it. He pushed back his chair, circled the desk, and crossed the room to look again at the view outside. Proctor followed him.

The window was double-glazed, and Faraday leant his forehead against it. The glass was relatively cool, the colder air from the heat pump above falling invisibly down it like a waterfall. Because of the double glazing, there was no sound at all from the traffic streaming past, only the sound of the air conditioning. Take away one or more of the senses, and the body tends to float, as if in water. That was what Faraday felt happening to him. He could see the frenetic pace of movement on the road outside, but could not link it to sound. He could sense the heat outside the window, but his forehead was cold. It was, in a much milder form, how he had felt drifting in and out of consciousness in the hospital for … was it really three weeks?

'I think you'll find,' he answered absently, 'that your people are well aware of what Paladin and Kenneth Johnston are up to. He says he's one of yours.'

The windowpane wasn't cold enough; the warmth from his forehead had quickly dulled its ability to refresh him. The clear focus that had directed the energy he'd brought to this confrontation began to blur.

314

Johnston was one of *them*. Yes, Johnston was definitely one of them; that was something he needed them to admit. But that was only part of it. There were other, more important things than that—things that he had deposited around the cluttered room of his mind that he knew were there somewhere, but which he couldn't find in the gloom.

'When you say that,' Proctor replied calmly, after just the slightest pause, 'I presume you mean that Mr Johnston is a British citizen. I'm quite sure we are satisfied of that.'

'No, I'm saying that the British and American governments have to be involved.'

Standing up had not been such a good idea. Christ, three weeks of fever and delirium, during which he'd lost ten kilos or more in weight, and he'd only been out of bed for a week; how could he expect to be at his best? Perhaps he should sit down again and take things slowly.

He pushed himself away from the window and walked carefully back to his chair, reaching for the edge of the desk to steady himself.

'The world of our imagination is filled with infinite wonder,' Proctor continued confidently. 'I'm sure that's a quotation, but I can't safely provide an attribution. Suffice to say that there is no end to the possibilities we can imagine. One of my recurring delights is to lose myself in the labyrinthine twists and turns of a John le Carré novel, imagining myself at the centre. Well, not exactly at the centre, but shall we say, close enough to the action to be able to put my ear to the door. But as much as I admire his writing and his undoubted success in drawing me in, I invariably put the book down feeling that I have travelled through the imagination of the writer, rather than the reality of the world as I know it, here in the rather dull, dumb interface where we conduct our relationships with other countries. So, I am bound to ask what it is that makes you think we should have the faintest interest in what one of the countless NGOs in this country gets up to? Do you see where I'm coming from?'

'So, you're denying that Johnston is one of yours,' Faraday questioned, making sure that he got it right. 'Is that how I should understand it?'

He already knew. He already knew that this slippery bastard was busy wrapping himself and the whole fucking Western world, whatever *that* was, in cling foil. To preserve it, or to hide the stench? Should he have expected anything different?

So why was he here, he wondered? Was it merely to close the gap between what he knew and what he suspected? And how would that change anything anyway? If he was looking to salvage his pride after having been so naively deceived for so long, it wasn't going to happen as a result of this man admitting to an official complicity in Johnston's activities. It was going to take a massive rehabilitation of his own sense of worth and entitlement, for that was the real damage that had occurred. That was what was driving this inquisition: the need for restoration of Anton Faraday's belief in himself.

Leaning against the wall, hands in his pockets, and looking down into the street, Proctor appeared disinterested in the view outside and indifferent to his visitor's challenge. His nose was slightly wrinkled, his lips pursed, as if he'd had a thought that annoyed him, and had then let it slip his mind without his face yet realizing it.

'Let's get to the bottom of this,' he said, returning to the desk and pretending to a duty of care. 'I did take the liberty of checking Kenneth Johnston's credentials following your initial enquiry. You had pointedly asked whether he was an employee of Her Majesty's government, and I, coming from the human resources side of things, looked into it, and could find nothing to suggest he was engaged in government business. What I did find was that he holds a reasonably high-profile position in the Paladin Foundation for the Environment. But you know all this, because your name features quite prominently in some of their news clippings as well. I'm going by what can be found on Google. These days, it is our most important tool for intelligence-gathering.'

Smiling, he wiped his hands across the drawing pad on his desk, as though he was smoothing a metaphorical blanket that covered the fanciful imaginings of his guest. 'Does that concur with what you know of him, or is there more of which I'm unaware?'

Of course, Faraday thought, that was bound to be the way he'd play it.

'Paladin is just one of many NGOs operating in this part of the world,' Proctor continued, 'because, as I'm sure you know, the wildlife and ecology in Southeast Asia have taken quite a hammering. Mr Johnston was here in Vietnam, I presume, on account of the work that his organization was involved in. But we at the Embassy do not have much contact with these organizations, because, as their name implies, they are *non*-governmental, and it is precisely that status that they are keen to preserve if they are to have the trust of the local authorities. But you would know better than I what projects interest Paladin.'

Faraday reluctantly concluded that he wasn't going to wear his opponent down. He needed to play a tiebreaker.

'Okay!' he said abruptly. 'Let me tell you what I think this is all about. The Chinese have been working to develop a broad-spectrum antiviral agent, at the same time as they have been creating hybrid strains capable of passing easily between humans. Let's stop pretending that Paladin is an independent conservation body, shall we? When I started researching treatments for bird flu, I learned that the product most touted as a protective agent is synthesized from shikimic acid, found in plants like Chinese star anise. Guess where that comes from? It grows in the mountain provinces bordering Vietnam. 'Coincidence', Mr Proctor! A good reason, you might think, for encouraging a fearsome hill tribe to keep the bloody bastards out of the mountain forests where *we* Westerners are allowed to operate. "We" being us, and us being the good guys. What do you say?'

Proctor said nothing. He was looking at his fingers again.

'Apparently, it requires thirty kilos of star anise to produce one kilo of shikimic acid,' Faraday went on, 'so my first thought was that those were the seeds that Sam McAvoy and Paladin were flying out in their helicopter. The problem with that is that oseltamivir, the product synthesized from shikimic acid, doesn't bloody well work. Besides, those seeds weren't star anise. I know star anise when I see it, because I keep encountering it in fish hotpots and particularly good versions of the national soup. No, those seeds are a totally different kettle of fish, as I discovered just yesterday, when I received a visit from an acquaintance of mine. He wanted to know how an anti-inflammatory agent had got into my blood that he, a microbiologist, could not explain away, until I told him that I had been consuming this particular seed, given to me by a Montagnard to relieve my physical aches and pains during my trek through the Highlands. What kind of bloody *coincidence* was that?'

Proctor turned his eyes back to Faraday, and they weren't friendly. 'Cut to it, please. We're out of time.'

'Paladin has been used as a Trojan horse to operate in a sensitive area where you—that is, the British and American governments—don't otherwise wish to be identified. You've probably now spirited Johnston out of the country, so he can't be linked to it.'

'That's it?'

'That's it.'

Without further comment, Proctor leant in and addressed the telephone on his desk. He didn't bother to pick it up. 'You'd better come in,' he said.

The two men then sat back and waited, holding each other's eyes: Proctor's impassive, Faraday's unable to disguise his keen anticipation.

It wasn't altogether a surprise when the door opened and Jamaican Sam sauntered in, no longer in his Hugo Boss puffer jacket, but in a regulation white shirt and striped tie: an Embassy man. The question was, which embassy?

'I believe you know Sam McAvoy.' Proctor's introduction was devoid of irony.

McAvoy didn't bother to acknowledge Faraday, but drew up a chair at the end of Proctor's desk. 'We gonna own this thing?' he asked.

'Might as well,' Proctor replied. 'Mr Faraday has a vivid imagination, as

318

you would expect from an artist, and I have a saying that 'When the truth is hard to believe, lies make better traction'. Rather than let him make up a story, let us tell him the truth, and trust him to respect it. I have no reason to think that he won't.'

'Okay.'

Sam turned to Faraday and nodded curtly, dropping the Jamaican accent. 'Sorry about the painting. It was Johnston's idea. Nothing personal on my part, you understand. It won't happen again.'

As casual as that, Faraday thought, but not with any anger; the painting was long since forgotten.

'Paladin provided us with access to an area of acute sensitivity, just as you surmised. Kenneth Johnston facilitated that for us. Yes, we have a major concern about China and the direction that some of their research at the Harbin Research Institute might be taking. There have been universal calls from the scientific community for a moratorium to be imposed on such research, for safety reasons, but the Chinese consistently ignore those calls. Once, it was nuclear proliferation that concerned us. This is far more serious. Imagine if this current epidemic were a strain that transmitted human-to-human.'

'Are you saying that the Chinese might be prepared to unleash such a strain deliberately?'

Sam turned to Proctor, who was busy inspecting his nails.

Proctor's smile was reassuring. 'Sam isn't saying that, are you, Sam?'

'No one would be crazy enough to do something like that,' Sam replied. 'Not unless they knew how to protect themselves, and even then…'

It was a thought that hardly required articulating.

'But it isn't just the Chinese who research mutations of the virus, is it?' Faraday interjected. 'Vaccination isn't effective unless you can stay ahead of it, and the only way to stay ahead of it is to be able to predict it.'

Now it was Faraday and Sam McAvoy. Proctor chose to sit back.

'I don't know whether you're telling me or asking me," Sam said. "I'm a field officer, not a scientist, but it would seem reasonable that every possible resource should be thrown into staying ahead of this thing. You're right: vaccination is the only protection. But development of treatments doesn't just stop on that account.'

'The seeds you were collecting…?' Faraday asked.

'A member of the *Illiciaceae* family that one of the microbiology research groups has identified as being of interest. We wanted to secure its supply rather than letting someone else do so.'

'… Like the Chinese?'

Sam shrugged.

'Is it Nui BioLab that's investigating this plant?'

Sam looked at Proctor with an expression that suggested he thought this entire conversation was a mistake of Proctor's making, and he looked at his Rolex watch to make the point that the whole thing had already gone on too long. 'Look, Anton, we're drowning in facts here. The simple story is the one we need to stick with; that's the one I can vouch for. Is there a reason why you can't accept the seriousness of what you've been told?'

'So, this is all about China.'

'Vietnam has always been all about China. It has never been about Vietnam.'

'And Paladin is just a cover, a fraud.'

Proctor decided it was time to intervene. 'Let's be thankful that they chose to take up the cudgel on our behalf, shall we? Correct me if I'm wrong, but you don't truly have a problem with their involvement in the well-being of our wildlife, do you? So, why so squeamish about their involvement in the well-being of humanity? If I'm right, your main concern is that their publicly expressed *casus belli* may be insincere, so let's examine that. I take it from what you've said today that it's offensive to your moral code that any group should be allowed to pursue an agenda that is not public. You're not alone in this. We Western democracies are quite unique in insisting that every act that affects our lives should have our consent. But that isn't how the world works.'

His tone had shifted so completely that Faraday could now see that the man he had been sparring with all morning had been a characterization of a civilized public servant. The real man was nobody's servant.

'So, I'll explain something for your benefit. The central dilemma in the world of intelligence is that external threats in peacetime may be just as real as in wartime. So, what should we do, then? Do we work secretly to defend ourselves in peacetime as we would in wartime, or do you insist we provide our enemies as well as ourselves with full transparency?'

Faraday took the view that Proctor's questions were rhetorical, but he needed to participate if he was going to draw him out further. Both he and Sam were trying to close the door on the threat of a man-made pandemic. That was too easy.

'You're making a case for secrecy,' he suggested, 'but that just paves the way for any self-appointed group to operate without our knowing it.'

'Alright, then. I wanted to bring you face to face with the democratic paradox. You apparently have some idea about the individual having a right to know everything. So, how is the individual going to respond if the Chinese decide to release a pandemic as a weapon of war? There are some who believe that the world is polluted with people—that we're some sort of pathogenic organism. What we've been talking about might be seen as a solution to that. What's your view?'

It was difficult to decide about the man. Was he truly so cynical, or was he teasing Faraday in order to provoke him?

Before he could think of a response, the door opened, and the young Eurasian girl entered, bearing another tray of drinks.

'Good timing!' Proctor enthused. 'My daughter knows me too well. All this talking calls for a cold drink. And while we enjoy that, I'd like you, Anton, to consider where your loyalties lie, and how you will bear the burden of the knowledge you believe you possess. For I think we're almost done talking, don't you?'

Caroline looked at him in disgust. 'I don't believe what you're telling me! You might as well have been having a tea party. How could you let them get away with that, Anton?'

She took out her cell phone and looked for a number.

'What are you doing?'

'I've been telling myself I want to be a proper journalist, but all I've done is file a few crappy travel stories about new hotels and beach resorts with luxury spas for corporate wives that are too greedy to give up their calories. This is a real story, and if I want to be a real journalist, I need to tell it.'

'But there's nothing here we can tell.'

She wasn't listening. She found a number and dialled it, then stood up from the table and walked away to a corner of the restaurant where she couldn't be heard.

Faraday ordered a bottle of snake wine. God knows why—he hated the stuff—but he was in a mood to get drunk. And why not? His mind and body were already fucked, so what difference would inebriation make? Whatever had driven him forward on his journey over the last few weeks had suddenly vanished. He felt like a stolen vehicle that had run out of gas and been abandoned at the side of the road, the thieves vanishing into the dark night, their hyena laughter dying on the wind.

When Caroline returned to the table, she had the flushed cheeks of a woman who had just been propositioned. There was no need for tea candles to light up her eyes.

'… Well?'

'He said yes.'

'Who said yes, and to what?'

'Sinclair Baines, the bureau chief, said I could file a story on the epidemic if it presented a new angle not already being covered, and provided that my facts and attributions check out. To begin with, he said no. He said their senior correspondent for the region has all the contacts with the World Health Organization and government departments, and he wouldn't want me treading on his toes. But when I started to tell him my angle, he changed his tune—even though he's sceptical.'

'What angle?'

'You know, what Tuan was telling us last night, and what you found out was going on up in the Highlands. The fact that we're doing the same thing as the Chinese, working on mutations and antiviral medicines that will have no chance of stopping it if it gets out.'

She leaned forward and gripped his hand. 'I'm so excited, Anton. You know that this is what I want to do with my life, and here at last is a story worth telling! Oh, and another thing: he wants me to write down everything I know and take it to him personally in three days' time. The bureau gets lots of free travel and accommodation deals, and you and I are going to spend those days in Halong Bay while I put this thing together. What do you think about that? If anyone deserves a rest, it's you.'

THIRTY-SEVEN

The free tickets for the boat and vouchers for a hotel on Cat Ba Island were delivered to their hotel the following morning. The hotel manager rang to say she had a packet for them, marked 'urgent', and it seemed to contain tickets. Her curiosity was apparently too great for her to curb, because the packet had already been opened when he went downstairs to pick it up. *Old communist habits die hard*, he thought. In Russia, too, they were still going through your luggage whenever you left your hotel room. He gave her twenty US dollars.

'A brief holiday,' he told her with a smile, 'but we'll be back in three days' time, if you wouldn't mind keeping one or two things for us in storage. Oh, and I have a painting as well. Nothing valuable.'

Two nights in a four-star hotel, and another on a luxury junk, sounded like the perfect antidote to what he'd been through, and it would give him an opportunity to look life in the eye. What Faraday needed more than anything was a chance to let go of his preoccupation with conspiracy theories and return to the everyday rhythm of normal living, whatever that was. What Caroline needed was the time and space to consider what was worth writing about in all the speculation that swirled around them. After three days, she'd know whether she had a story worth filing, and to some extent, that would determine what to do with the offer that was on the table from Violet Dunleavy, and how she would respond to Faraday's eventual return to England (something that neither of them had discussed).

So, they got up early the next morning and caught a minibus out to Hai Phong and on to the Halong Bay boat harbour, where an army of anxious touts was massed, ready to fight over the corpses of the diminishing number of foreign travellers. A damp grey fog hung over the port, and the air was heavy with desperation.

'Too many seagulls and not enough scraps!' Faraday shouted as they sought the boat on which they were booked.

'Don't engage with them!' Caroline shouted back. 'Just follow.'

He was happy to obey.

Caroline stopped to ask for directions, and a man in a tour guide's uniform looked at her tickets and pointed them towards a wooden junk.

'Most of the cruises have been cancelled because of the epidemic,' Caroline explained, 'so we're getting a boat to ourselves.'

There were six cabins on the junk, but theirs was the only one booked. As the crew waited anxiously for more custom, it looked as though that was the way it would remain, until the tour guide arrived on the dock to say that they had one more last-minute booking, and the crew would be changed to reduce their numbers, leaving one man on the wheel, one man in the galley, and another on drinks and dishes. It was a lesson in free-market economics in a country that was apparently communist in name only.

The last-minute arrivals were an English-speaking German couple who seemed determined to turn the journey into a social occasion, treating Caroline, with her local knowledge and language skills, as a de facto guide, thereby rather spoiling the privacy that they'd hoped for.

Faraday made it quite clear that he was not in the mood for conversation, then retreated to the aft deck, where he was able to indulge his thoughts about the day spent at the British Embassy and ponder the cause of his niggling dissatisfactions. Despite the hours of discourse (and the main dish that had finally been served to him: 'Vietnam has always been all about China. It has never been about Vietnam'), he was left with that same feeling that an Asian banquet could leave, where despite being filled up, he was inexplicably hungry still. And why not? There were clearly key ingredients that had been left out of the recipe, not the least of which was a convincing explanation as to Kenneth Johnston's role in it all.

When eventually their boat got underway, it slid through the slate-grey opaque water with a buoyancy that defied the crude thickness of its heavy timbered hull, the slowly revolving crankshaft of its diesel engine pounding out a rhythm like the funeral drumbeat that had echoed through the hills from the nearly deserted Nung village north of Sapa. Water defined Vietnam; it filled the air like a bronchial inhalation and saturated the ground until it dissolved into the sea. Halong Bay was where the land had drowned, leaving hundreds of steep bare rocks exposed above the surface like the facial spikes of a giant submerged dragon, and the boats that navigated their way through the mists of this vast water world did so with a quiet caution, as if trying not to disturb the dragon from its sleep.

'They say they were dropped there by the gods,' he heard Caroline explain to the German couple. She was in travel writer mode.

'Why?'

'To protect Vietnam from invasion. Out there is the Gulf of Tonkin: China's backyard. The islands act as an obstacle course, and the water is reputedly home to a giant sea snake that will devour ships that fail the enmity test. That's why all the prows of these vessels are carved with spirit figures: to propitiate the dragon.'

'What is "propitiate"?'

'Appease; make it happy.'

'Ha ha! We like happy dragons!'

The man was chatty—and snap-happy, too. Everything had to be photographed, including his companion, Caroline and Faraday, the boat, and every little islet they passed. He was going to be busy; there were nearly two thousand islands to be covered off if he wanted to do the job thoroughly. From the way he was dressed, he looked like he planned to scale each one as well: sturdy boots, sturdy legs, and action man clothing. It was evident that he liked Caroline, but Faraday, less so. His female companion was the reverse; she smiled politely, but didn't speak. If they were looking to hook up with new friends, Faraday thought, they were out of luck.

'And sharks?' the German woman asked, breaking her silence. 'Are there many? The water is so…'

'Polluted, yes,' Caroline agreed, taking responsibility for the country as if it were her own. 'That's Vietnam, I'm afraid.'

'Perhaps we will have some soup with fins for lunch.' The man laughed. 'That will be one shark less, ha ha!'

Peering over the side, distancing himself from being captured by inanities, Faraday pondered the impenetrable depths as they slid through its turpentine layered surface with an apologetic stealth, as if unsure of the wisdom of being here in this strangely prehistoric world. In the Mekong Delta, it had been the snakehead fish that had haunted the soupy waters; here, it was the dragon. There was always something in Asia, it seemed, waiting to get you if you wandered into its depths.

At lunchtime, they stopped at a small island fishing village, anchoring off while a table was set on the aft deck for the four passengers to eat together. The island had caves one could visit, according to the captain, and Caroline translated his suggestion that they take the inflatable dinghy with outboard motor and go exploring—a suggestion which the Germans received with enthusiasm, but which Faraday declined, for the good reason that he lacked the stamina for anything other than an afternoon nap.

'Anton has recently been in hospital,' Caroline explained. 'He's still recovering, and I have work to do.'

'Oh, but we will be quick! It would be so nice…'

Renate and Karl (for those were their names) prevailed upon Caroline to join them, and finally the three went off together, returning an hour later with the flush of shared exertions on their faces and an elevated level of bonhomie from which Faraday felt excluded.

'I think they're looking to have some excitement,' Caroline whispered as she joined Faraday in their cabin. 'They're very Club Med. We'd better be on our guard, because I can't afford to be socializing once we check into the hotel.'

Cat Ba Island was their destination, barely five hours' sail if they went there directly, but the captain chose a circuitous route to help fill up the day and emphasize the complexity of navigation involved in threading their way around the myriad islands with no static horizon or dominant landmass for reference. The plan was to check into the hotel mid-afternoon, and Caroline was eager to get started on her story. They had two full days and nights scheduled ashore before returning to the boat, and then, after a one-night sleepover on board somewhere further out among the islands, they would return to Hanoi and face the verdict of the sceptical bureau chief.

'What if I can't do this?' Caroline asked. 'What if it turns out that the sum total of everything we've learned is no more than what is already known by others—and nobody cares?'

* * * *

Within a day, it was apparent that Caroline's fears were well founded. Silent and morose, she glared angrily at her keyboard, filling their hotel room with such a dark energy that Faraday, happy for the opportunity to just doze and read, was finally forced to sit up and give her his attention.

The enthusiasm that had inspired her to bring her story to the world was obviously proving difficult to sustain when she tried to define exactly what it was that she wanted to say.

'The thing is,' she admitted, 'the internet's an echo chamber for any claim you want to make. Whether it's fantasy or fact, there'll be a bunch of willing believers, and an equal bunch of emphatic deniers. Social media is supposed to be the new participatory democracy. "Information gotta be free", is the modern mantra, "or else we'll all be held hostage to the tyranny of Them."

It's a sexy viewpoint, but it's bullshit; nothing is free, and now all information is tainted. So, what's the point of searching for the truth if nothing can be trusted?'

What Caroline had discovered after a day spent wandering down the Google path into the forests of misinformation was how easy it was to fall down a rabbit hole and not be able to find a way out.

'The bureau isn't going to buy a story from me if all it does is warn of the dangers posed by a potential pandemic. They have people with much better creds than me to do that. Nor are they going to buy a conspiracy theory from me, not if I can't connect the dots—and not even if I can, probably.'

No, that was something Faraday had learned for himself from Proctor and McAvoy. Once an accusation could be tainted with the odour of 'conspiracy theory', it was damned near impossible to eliminate the stench.

'Drop the theories,' he advised. 'Just report standalone facts. Let other people create their own theories from it. Don't be in the business of false news.'

But what *were* the facts?

' "Under the cover of conducting a census of endangered elephants in the wild, the Paladin Foundation has been harvesting a rare plant in Vietnam's remote Highlands, which is believed to have medicinal properties that might lead to the development of an antiviral treatment." Is that a provable fact?' she asked.

'Yes,' he replied. 'It can be verified by me and by Tuan.'

' "In order to guard against other people—particularly the Chinese— intruding into the area, Paladin has recruited an outcast tribe as mercenaries to protect their activities." '

'Can we say outright, "the Chinese"? That's speculation,' he cautioned.

'But Proctor told you that.'

'Yes, but he wouldn't tell *you* that. He'd likely claim that he didn't know what you were talking about. His business is diplomacy.'

'Alright, Sam McAvoy, then; he's clearly a US agent, and we have proof of where he works. His involvement throughout can't be denied, and he was adamant about the Chinese threat. He openly admitted it.'

'Says who?'

'You.'

'Am I the only source for your story? It's starting to sound dangerously like a conspiracy theory to me. You'd need to get these people to admit it directly in print. And even then, so what?'

'You're not helping!' She was frustrated but adamant. 'The information about the work China has been undertaking at the Harbin Research Institute to develop virus mutations is all over the internet,' she declared. 'Nobody is going to deny that fact. The international scientific community is outraged by it.'

'Alright,' he allowed, 'that might be worth mentioning at this time. But it's not a new story, presumably. Is the news bureau going to credit you with a major scoop when there's no evidence of the virus mutating? Isn't that just scaremongering?'

'Why are you being so obstructive? We know that Nui BioLab is involved in the same work, because Tuan hinted as much the other night. And we know that the British and American governments are party to it, because Kenneth Johnston as good as told you.'

'Ah!' He wished he didn't have to be so discouraging, but he couldn't avoid stating the obvious. 'I think you'll find, my love, that Kenneth Johnston is a dead end.'

* * * *

Cat Ba Island lacked charm, but they needed to get out of their room and stretch their legs and lungs, so they decided to walk down to the dock and look for a bar. It was a warm night, and the streets were pleasantly quiet after the frenzy of Hanoi. Faraday's slow rate of recovery was beginning to frustrate him. In one sense, that was a good sign: he was impatient to be well again. In another sense, it was a signal that his mind was ready to move on. With the saga of the panda painting now behind him, his original purpose for being in Vietnam had ended. He'd learned the truth behind the lucky break that had kick-started his artistic career, and it was neither a surprise nor a disappointment; it was what it was.

But he wasn't in a mood to extend his stay on account of Caroline's journalistic ambitions. The heady pleasure of falling in love seemed to have possessed them both, and he knew that no matter how tempting it was to lie in the soft bed of delusion, the hard ground of reality would never be far away, for in the real world, love's cycle of intensity tended to be short. She'd sensed it in him on the night when they'd first kissed in Sapa, challenging him to admit that he may have a commitment phobia, using painting as a prophylactic to protect himself from 'catching an emotional infection'. He hadn't admitted it then, but what if she was right? Besides, there was nothing in her history to suggest she was any different. She was far too modern and independent to be seduced into subordinating her long-term ambitions to romance.

So, as they held hands and enjoyed the ease of each other's touch and company, he realised that the avoidance of the discussion about their next move, beyond their return to Hanoi with her story, came down to their inability to measure the strength of their feelings for each other. It was a subject that neither felt confident to broach.

'I think I need meat!' he exclaimed. 'Let's look for somewhere that does a good red steak.'

They found it at a seedy Korean barbecue house on the waterfront, the sort of place that was dark enough to hide the dirt and whose tiny kitchen was hidden behind hanging strips of plastic. But once the brazier was on the table and the coarse blade steak was giving off smoke, he didn't care too much about the hygiene. Bamboo shoots and shiitake mushrooms were tossed on, and the whole thing was doused in fermented soy. Finding a red wine to accompany it was out of the question, but there was Korean beer to wash it down.

Caroline was not hungry.

'If the virus *were* transmissible human-to-human, how would it take place?' Her mind was still buried in her story.

'Through saliva, faeces, and … coughing, presumably. Same as Ebola.'

'So, it wouldn't be inevitable that everyone in contact with someone who had it would also contract it?'

' "Mammalian transmissibility"—isn't that what Tuan called it? And the figure he mentioned was twenty percent. So, no, not everyone would necessarily get it.'

He wanted to drop the subject and enjoy his food, and as if on cue, voices from the doorway of the restaurant threatened to prevent him from doing just that.

'It's your German friends,' he whispered, 'Renate and Karl.'

* * * *

With hindsight, could he—should he—have seen anything in this encounter other than what he saw at the time? Probably not.

Cat Ba was small enough that tourists were bound to run into each other, and there was nothing in the German couple's manner—other than their overt friendliness—that justified snubbing them. The fact that Karl was brandishing a bottle of rather good red wine that he hoped Anton might help him to consume (Renate was not into red, it seemed) tipped the balance in favour of asking if they could join them at their table.

Caroline, though passively accepting, was not in the mood. She was suspicious that the Germans had in mind a degree of intimacy somewhat beyond just sharing a meal together. Perhaps she had picked up that feeling when she went ashore with them in the rubber duck. Whatever had been said or hinted at, it wasn't something to which Faraday had been party, so he wasn't looking for it.

Karl was keen to talk about wildlife. Somehow, he had picked up on

Faraday's connection to the subject (Caroline must have told him), and as a fellow photographer, he felt that they were kindred spirits. He'd come to Halong Bay, he said, to compose a geographical photo essay. Already, in the multitude of images he'd captured, he could sense that there was a spirit to the place that he had never encountered anywhere else. His frustration was that the wireless internet connection in the hotel was insufficient to transmit the files that he wanted to send back to his editor in Germany.

'How have you found the internet?' he asked.

Faraday admitted that he'd had no cause to use it, not having a laptop with him. Caroline had found it sufficient for her purposes; she was just doing searches that didn't require much data usage.

'And the cell phone signal also,' Karl complained, 'it is very poor, don't you think?'

Again, Faraday hadn't used it. But Caroline had no problems. It was a small island, after all.

The one thing Karl couldn't complain about was the quality of the red wine he'd bought. By chance, he'd stumbled onto some shelves at the back of a spice bazaar that were stacked with thirty-year-old French vintages. 'Burgundy, Bordeaux, Rhone, *mein Gott*: a trove of treasure!'

Faraday made a point of getting directions from him.

'And what do you do with your time on the island?' Renate asked.

'I sleep,' he replied wearily.

'He's recovering from the flu virus,' Caroline explained.

'And you?' Renate asked.

'I'm a journalist. I have a story to complete.'

'Oh? What is it about?'

'The epidemic.'

'Ah, so you write about Anton,' Karl joked. *'Prost!'*

'Prost!'

No, nothing much there. It was all pretty inane. If anything disturbed him, it was the thought that Renate reminded him too much of Helene—

that surface composure that so easily masked what lay beneath.

'What is there new to write?' Renate asked enigmatically.

Caroline looked at her sharply, as if she were being belittled.

Safely back in their hotel room, uncompromised by any rash promise to meet up again, Anton fell asleep in minutes, while Caroline continued to commune with the internet.

THIRTY-EIGHT

Day two.

Caroline shook him awake.

'It's started,' she hissed. 'It's all over. My story's dead. Dammit, fuck it—I was too late.'

He struggled to sit up. 'What the hell are you talking about?'

'Didn't you hear me? Exactly what we were talking about has happened, and now I have no story. It's all over *The Washington Post* and *The Guardian*. I was too damned timid, wanting to get everything right, when what I should have done is just go in with all guns blazing. Now I'll never get the chance.'

Her Irish eyes were so black that they would have made obsidian look pale—and with more than just a hint that this was all Faraday's fault. He levered himself upright. There was no room for sympathy or excuses on his part. It was the end of sickness; that was clear.

'Well, for fuck's sake, what are they reporting?'

'It's jumped—like a flea. It's done just what Tuan said it would do.'

'Where?'

'In China.'

'Who says?'

'*The Washington Post* says! The World Health Organization says! Tuan says!'

'Tuan...?'

'He's sent me an email. Won't answer his phone. "Now do you believe me?" he says. "I tried to tell you. Now do you believe me?" And there it is in *The Washington Post* overnight: "China fights influenza outbreak—closes border with Vietnam and Laos. Rapid spread raises fears virus may be transferable human-to-human".'

'Okay, okay. Let me read it.'

There wasn't much more to the story, other than the fact that all movement in and out of the Guangxi Region had been halted, and the WHO had been advised. It was the Chinese who were voicing fears that the virus might now be transmissible by humans, not the Vietnamese.

'Well, that's one good thing we can be grateful for,' he concluded. 'It isn't the Chinese releasing a virus mutation—not unless they're deliberately infecting their own people. Where's Tuan's email? What exactly does he say?'

She found it for him.

Caroline, Sorry. I tried to tell Uncle and you. Now do you believe me? The situation is very dangerous. As a scientist, I cannot be silent about what is happening. Too many will die. Tuan.

'What did he try and tell you? I was there. We didn't say anything about not believing him.'

'He must be referring to the argument he had with Uncle. He tried to warn him not to help set up the poultry farm. He must have had some sort of premonition.'

'He's a scientist; scientists don't have premonitions. Get him on the phone.'

'I've tried, but there's no connection. See if your phone will work.'

Faraday hadn't used his phone for days. The last call he'd made was to Ralph. (Christ, he needed to call Robbie and find out how Ralph was recovering...) He gave Caroline his phone and went to have a shower, making it quick in case he missed out on what Tuan had to say.

He needn't have bothered. Tuan's phone wasn't answering.

'The network says there's no connection to that number. I can't even leave a message.' Caroline passed the phone back to him. 'And you've got two new messages. I need to go for a run, clear my head.'

She was already dressed for it. He couldn't tell how long she'd been up, waiting for him to wake. It was another reason why he was impatient to recover his strength: he was spending too much time sleeping.

She pecked him on the cheek and left quickly. He got dressed, wondering if she would return more determined than ever to write her story, or whether he should be prepared for a day wandering the limited tourist attractions that Cat Ba Island had to offer.

The first of his cell phone messages was chillingly stark:

RALPH DIED YESTERDAY. FUNERAL IN 8 DAYS. CALL ROBBIE URGENTLY

Faraday walked back into the bathroom and looked at himself in the steamed-up mirror. The face that looked back at him was vaguely familiar, like someone he felt he ought to know, but it certainly wasn't him. It was older and gaunter than the person he would have recognized as himself, but that wasn't what made it the face of a stranger. In this face, the eyes to the soul were different. Somewhere on his journey through Vietnam, the last vestiges of naivety and optimism had departed from him. He'd left the cloistered confines of his painter's studio and ventured out into a world that bore no resemblance to that of his imagination. And in this moment, he wasn't sure that he was fit to survive in it.

Someone had killed the man that had anchored his life for the last twenty years. They'd broken his neck. And now, as he watched the reaction on his own face in the mirror, the only tears forming on his cheeks were the drops of condensation from his shower congealing and running down the glass.

He looked at his watch. London was six hours behind Hanoi; he'd call Robbie later that afternoon. He brushed his teeth and went back to the bedroom, glad for Caroline's absence. He needed time before he could respond to her inevitable questions.

The second message was a voicemail notification. He called his message bank to listen to it, struggling to understand. After replaying it twice, he was confident that it was Duc trying to contact him, and he was saying something about Nung Tong Phuc. But he couldn't decipher it, so he sent back a text message saying he'd call back in a few hours' time.

In light of Ralph's death, he could no longer sit it out on Cat Ba Island, pretending to recuperate while Caroline struggled with an angle for her story. His heart and mind were already on their way back to London. He needed to be at the funeral, and he needed to think that through before Caroline returned. It was the defining moment that he'd known would have to be faced eventually. Once he left Vietnam, was it likely that he'd ever return? How quickly would the strength of their relationship be exposed once they were apart?

When she returned to the room, flushed and out of breath, he told her immediately about the contents of Robbie's text message. He didn't mention his decision to return to London in time for the funeral.

'I don't think we're going to make any progress sitting here,' he explained. 'Neither of us is in the mood for a holiday, and if we were, this isn't the place we'd want to be. Let's see if we can cut it short and get back to Hanoi.'

Caroline was in immediate agreement. She, too, was anxious to get back, it seemed. Her story was going nowhere in the absence of Tuan, and she was relieved to see Faraday's new-found impatience. Perhaps she could see that his strength was returning, and with it, she was hoping for a revival of the indignation and determination that he had taken into his confrontation with Proctor. Her mind was obviously on the warnings that Tuan had given them, and she guessed that she needed to find him if she was to achieve her ambition and get to the heart of a worthwhile story.

Running down to the port, she'd established that their junk was moored in the harbour, and if they checked out of the hotel after lunch, they could re-board, overnight somewhere in Halong Bay, and be back at Hai Phong in the morning.

'Great!' he agreed. 'We're of one mind.'

Before then, Faraday wanted to be sure to visit the spice shop with the French wine collection, because he'd be damned if he was going to spend the night floating through Halong Bay without something decent to drink. And once he'd had that drink, he'd be better prepared to tell her of his decision to return to London.

* * * *

Once they were packed and ready to check out, Lutyen's Gallery in London would have opened for the day, and he could make the call that was preying on his mind. While Caroline dealt with the people at the front desk, he wandered outside, saying he'd be back in a few minutes once he'd picked up his wine from the spice shop.

Robbie's voice had that flat tone that eventually comes when the irreversibility of a tragedy has been accepted. 'Of course he had enemies, Anton. Nobody can deny that. He sat at the top of the gallery trade for over thirty years. Even when the auction houses took over the art world, they couldn't compete with his standing among collectors. He could make or break an artist's reputation and wipe millions off the value of a Sotheby's sale just by raising an eyebrow. You know that.'

Robbie had been with Ralph for most of those thirty years, and may even have been his lover at one time. Lutyen's—the man as well as the business—had been his life.

'What are the police saying?' Faraday asked.

'The police are very, very polite, and very, very unwilling to say anything. Anton, it would not surprise me if they thought it was an inside job and I was under suspicion. That's how I feel about everything. I'm afraid to ask questions or to show my true feelings. You know, of course, that Ralph's parents are still alive. They are completely distraught and bewildered. I just pray the police don't tell them the details, because it could very well kill

339

them. Ralph was badly beaten—tortured, even—before they broke his neck. It must have been some sort of choke hold, they're saying, forcing him to open the gallery safe. But there was nothing in that safe, I'm absolutely certain. Ralph kept no secrets from me; I'd know.'

'So, what were they after—money?'

'Anton, we don't handle money; you know that. What kind of person would pay cash for a fifty-thousand-pound painting? And the amount of drugs Ralph has taken in his life wouldn't fill a matchbox. But so many of these crims now are meths monsters; they go mad and tear the place to pieces. Their minds are perforated like Swiss cheese, and they can snap without warning. They didn't just destroy the gallery, they trashed his house as well—slashed his beautiful paintings, smashed his Lalique glass collection, and threw the contents of every cupboard and drawer onto the floor. I shudder to think what they would have done to me if I'd happened to be there when they broke in. It doesn't bear thinking about, Anton.'

'Are you saying they did the Holland Park house on the same night?'

'Within an hour of attacking him at the gallery, the police think. Either he told them something, or they went there leaving him for dead. Nobody knows.'

'Then they must have known what they were after, Robbie. What could it have been? If anyone would know, it has to be you. Did they find what they came for at the house? What was it? Had he made an enemy? I hate to say it, but was he blackmailing someone?'

'Anton, please…'

'Robbie, Robbie, we both know that people came to Ralph asking him to make paintings legitimate that sometimes weren't right. His word could be worth a lot of money…'

'Ralph would never! Not ever. Never!'

'Alright, Robbie, I'm on your side. My God, I'm on Ralph's side; how could I be otherwise? But either way, it's not hard to imagine that someone could be fucked off if he hadn't done what they wanted—fucked off enough to send in a squad of goons to exact revenge, who then lost it and went too far. It has to be a possibility.'

Robbie went silent. Was it the line? Had he lost the connection? Caroline was walking down the street, coming to find him.

'Robbie, it has to be a possibility.'

A sniff, a cough, a sigh. The connection was fine.

'Ralph was very fond of you, Anton.' His voice was tired. 'There were times when it made me jealous, but I came to terms with it, and I have always liked and trusted you, and hoped you felt the same.'

'Of course I do.'

'Ralph never kept anything valuable here or at his home. He was too sensible for that. Anything he really valued, he kept in a safe at Kitty and Simon's apartment.'

'You mean at his parents'?'

'Nobody would think to break in there. I can tell you because you're a trusted friend. Now I wish he had kept something in the safe at the gallery. It might have saved him if those monsters had found something worth stealing.'

Another sniff, another cough, another sigh. He was entitled to be taking it badly.

'I know how this must be affecting you, Robbie, and I'm sorry I'm not there to help. But I'll get there as soon as I can, and whatever happens, I'll be there for the funeral.'

He rang off, thinking about his last conversation with Ralph and wondering about the contents of that safe at Kitty and Simon's apartment.

THIRTY-NINE

'You are a naughty man,' Karl said, wagging his finger.

The tone and gesture had the camp over-familiarity of a cabaret host from the days of the Weimar Republic. It needled Faraday's stolid Anglo-Saxon reserve, making him prickle.

'Now I will not get to photograph the Cat Ba langur. How will I explain this after traveling so far, and when there are so few left in the world? Naughty Mister Anton and naughty Fräulein Caroline must leave the island urgently, and there is not another boat to come and collect poor Karl and Renate, because all travel is stopped for the health emergency. But I forgive you, because I like a man who paints wildlife, and so we will enjoy each other's company, no—the four of us?'

Like fuck we will, Faraday thought.

'We weren't aware that returning early would mean that you had to return early as well. The cruise agent didn't tell us that,' he replied coldly. 'I'm sorry if it's spoiled your visit.'

'Ach, I am teasing! Tell him, Renate, how I tease.'

'We are not minding,' Renate explained. 'It is okay.' She shrugged. Maybe she found Karl's shorts too short and his legs too bare, also. Big boots, big calf muscles, and nearly invisible ankle socks: it was a strange look. Caroline had decided to stay in their cabin. The mere sight of these two running down the wharf as they boarded had raised her hackles, which were already high enough to make Faraday tread lightly around her.

The crew were the same three that had brought them out from Hai Phong: a skipper on the wheel, a kitchen hand already preparing their evening meal, and a deckhand who doubled as a drinks steward and had brought them three beers as they sat on the aft deck, watching Cat Ba receding into the afternoon mist. Faraday was sitting there because he did feel some sort of obligation to be civil to them, but he had no intention of allowing them to draw him into making a night of it. He was hoping he could get a cell phone signal, as he was anxious to call Duc, and there was a conversation with Caroline waiting to be had.

'Ah, I am hungry!' Karl announced, smacking his lips noisily. There was an enticing aroma wafting from the galley, and his beer was empty. 'Perhaps we will see a sea eagle fishing, then I will photograph it and send a copy to you so you can paint it, *ja*? You must give me your email.'

Renate went and leaned on the gunwale, gazing out across the water at the myriad steep islands, clearly bored with her companions. She was slim and athletic, and each movement held a hint of contained energy, as if she was suppressing an urge to stretch her limbs and subject her muscles to a mentally imposed resistance. She needed a gym or a squash court; inaction and the sound of Karl's voice were suffocating her. Faraday was certain that they weren't a couple, but he couldn't guess as to why they were together.

'*"Leben und leben lassen"* is my rule: "Live and let live", Anton. This way, we are all friends, and we reach our destination just the same. You must return to Hanoi quickly, and so we have no choice but to do the same. *Leben und leben lassen*. Will you not have another beer?'

The deckhand had arrived at Karl's bidding with three more bottles. Faraday waved him away. He was concerned that the farther Cat Ba receded into the distance, the more likely it was that a cell phone signal would do the same.

'Ha ha, "You Germans love your beer", you are thinking. Am I right?'

'I wasn't thinking that at all. Excuse me… I was thinking that we should be heading west towards Hai Phong, and yet we seem to be pointed due east. Maybe I should go up to the wheelhouse and talk to the skipper. The cruise agent may not have explained to him that we are not wanting a scenic tour.'

Besides which, he was feeling restless, and sitting across the table from this man was not helping. He stood up. The skipper, as he recalled, had shown little if any willingness to converse in English when they'd boarded. He might need to get Caroline to come with him.

Renate turned her attention back to them, tossing her head in the air as if someone had just dropped an easy catch. 'Karl...?' she enquired impatiently.

'Es ist ein Gefallen,' he explained to Faraday. 'I asked the captain to make a small detour.'

'Es ist kein Gefallen!' Renate snapped. 'It is not a favour. We are passengers, too.'

'Sure, sure, we all understand this thing. Anton ask to return a day early—*Das ist ein Anfrage*—and they ask us to agree. "Okay," I say, "but I need the red-haired monkey to see for my work, and how will I do that now?" So, they tell me we can stop near another island before it is night, and on this island is a deep grotto with an underground lake surrounded by trees, where the monkeys come to feed. While we do that, they will cook our evening meal, and then ... on our way again. Okay? *Das ist* okay, Anton, my friend? A nice thing to do for a painter of wildlife, I think, so we hope you will come with us, too, to see these things. And Caroline, also. We make a nice appetite for our *Abendessen* and sleep like babies in our wooden *Bett*. Is this a good thing to do?'

Anton sat down again. Renate sat down, too. Fair enough; he was thinking solely of himself. The Germans had as much right to the trip as they did, if not more; they'd actually paid for it, which was more than Faraday and Caroline could say.

'I'm sorry,' he apologized. 'I had a sudden vision of them wanting us to take in every sight along the way. What you've arranged is absolutely fine, and I'd be interested in joining you. But first, I need to make a phone call, and see if there's anything Caroline needs.'

* * * *

The layout of the boat was designed to provide sleeping and eating space for twelve passengers, with the saloon containing the galley and bar open to the aft deck on one side, and open to a central passageway housing six double cabins on the other. At the end of the passage were the crew's quarters, as well as access to the engine room behind a spiral staircase that led up to the top deck, where the wheelhouse was located.

Being not quite ready to frame a conversation with Caroline, Faraday made his way towards the spiral staircase, hoping to find somewhere private where he could phone Duc. Knowing there were no other passengers on the boat, he tried the cabin doors on either side of his own in case an empty one had been left unlocked. At the end of the passage, one of the doors opened to reveal an open suitcase and women's clothing spread out on the bed. Embarrassed, he quickly closed the door again and started up the staircase. Then he stopped and stepped back down again. Making sure that he couldn't be observed from the aft deck, he tried the handle of the cabin opposite the one he'd already opened. This was also unlocked, and on the bed was a rucksack and a camera bag with its contents laid out neatly on a green felt cloth.

Two people. Two cabins. His instincts had been right: they weren't a couple.

He climbed the stairs and found a place behind the wheelhouse, looking down onto the boarding platform at the stern of the aft deck. There was a strong smell of diesel exhaust coming from the engine room, and the dull thump of slowly revolving pistons echoed through the thick wooden frame of the boat. His co-passengers were out of sight beneath him, and the wheelhouse door was shut. He took out his phone and called Duc.

'I find the elephants!' Duc announced. His voice sounded faint and far away.

'What elephants?'

'I tell you before.'

Faraday struggled to remember. Sapa was such a distant memory now. 'Tell me again.'

'There are no elephants.'

'Yes, that's what you told me.' He shook his head. 'So, now you're saying that you've found them?'

'Not elephants; they are wells. The wells are the elephants.'

Duc speaking in riddles, Faraday's mind still fighting off meth-fuelled intruders in Ralph's gallery, and Caroline waiting for him: nothing was making sense.

'Nung Tong Phuc say, and I not understand. "Water not safe from sickness", he tell me. You ask him to find villages with old wells, and he think you know something. Understand?'

'No.' This was too difficult.

'You know what American do—the one in the market at Sapa, black man? We see him at the place in the mountain. He help us leave in helicopter.'

'You mean Sam?'

'He asked me to map all mountain villages with wells across the border, while finding the *hạt thiêng* seed. I said no. Remember?'

'I didn't know that's what he asked you. I thought he asked you to map where the seeds grow. And then Nung Tong Phuc told you the well water was unsafe?'

'All the tribes who have the sickness from birds have wells. My people guard our wells and have no sickness, then we catch someone try to poison it.'

'But—'

'The American want me to go in Zhuang, not Viet side.'

'What is Zhuang?'

'Guangxi, China. Now the sickness is in China. You understand?'

'Jesus!' He couldn't comprehend this. What was Duc saying—that someone was deliberately poisoning wells, and Paladin had wanted him to go into the Chinese Highlands and identify village wells there?

'Duc, can you stay there a minute? If we get cut off, stay by your phone. I'll be as quick as I can. I just need to work something out.'

Now, how did he do this? He knew it must be possible, but he'd never done it before. Was it a special app...?

'Hey, Siri, how do I record this call?'

'... Hello, yes, hello?' It was Duc answering, not Siri.

'Stay there!' he shouted.

Clattering down the stairs, he threw open his cabin door. 'Caroline! Stop everything and listen to this! Go ahead, Duc, repeat exactly what you told me.'

He pressed the speaker button and held the phone up for her to hear. When Duc had finished, she failed to respond, looking up at him slightly myopically, seemingly unable to speak. Faraday had a vision of his bus companion from Marble Mountain looking quizzically at his cell phone and wondering why it had gone quiet, and further wondering whether he had been wise in calling this *Tây trắng* Westerner with such dangerous news, when all he knew of him was that Faraday had persuaded him into a trap that had left him with his cheek hanging off, and without ever properly explaining why.

He cleared his throat. 'I'm sorry, Duc. I don't know what to say.'

'These your people?' Duc asked. He didn't wait for a reply. 'Bad people. Very dangerous. Did you know this?'

'No, no, I had no idea, I promise you. But...'

He watched as Caroline, as if in slow motion, pushed aside her laptop and stood up, bending forward and shaking her black hair as though it had birds nesting in it. She breathed deeply, exhaling the air with loud and forceful contractions of her abdomen. He watched and waited until she was ready to say something, trying to assemble his own thoughts. When she stopped and turned towards him, he stepped forward and put his arms around her.

'Duc,' he mumbled into the phone, 'whatever you do, please be careful.' His voice was hoarse. 'Protect yourself.' It seemed so inadequate. 'I'll text you when I … when I … know something.'

Caroline stepped back and took off her glasses. She was clear-eyed and focused now, her voice hard-edged with anger. 'We need to find Tuan,' she declared. 'I know that he's in danger.'

'Why? What else have you found out?'

She went back to her laptop and passed it to him. 'This is what it's all about. This is why we're in danger, and why Tuan is an even bigger danger to them than we are.'

He sat down and began to read out loud. ' "FDA Fast Tracks Coronavirus Treatment: Govt and Defence Prioritized".' He looked up. 'What's this from?'

'Reuters. An hour ago.'

' "The Food and Drug Administration has approved a new antiviral medication in response to the alarming spread of new strains of the coronavirus now infecting people in Southern China and the Vietnam Highlands. CD8MAGNA has been developed by Nui BioLab, a wholly owned subsidiary of Swiss pharmaceutical giant Anglo Swiss BioLab, for early-stage treatment of infection"… Jesus! This is impossible! Tuan told us the testing takes years. He said it may not be safe. What did he say? "This product will not save anybody who hasn't taken it first"…'

' "And even then, in some people, the after-effects can be fatal"…'

' "Using a unique fast track modelling system that overcomes the extended delay of conventional human testing, Nui BioLab, based in Hanoi, has convinced the FDA that the seriousness of the current epidemic warrants speedy release of the new product, which works by blocking the

348

neuraminidase (NA) enzyme from escaping a host cell and replicating, thereby inhibiting the virus's ability to spread through the body." '

'But in some people,' Caroline interrupted, 'Tuan claims the immune response can't be stopped. He warned them about it—and that's why he claims to be in danger.'

' "The US Government has placed an initial $2.8b order for stockpiling by defence and security agencies. The United Kingdom and Germany have announced similar orders." ' Faraday stopped reading. 'Money. It's all about fucking money.'

'Tuan knew about this, Anton. That's what he wanted to tell us, but he was too scared. He knew that they were deliberately spreading the virus. We need to find him.'

'I never saw this coming,' Faraday admitted.

His disgust was equally with himself as with Charles Van Heeren, president of Anglo Swiss BioLab and founding chairman of the Paladin Foundation for the Environment, ably served by Kenneth Johnston and Sam McAvoy (and who else but Donald Proctor?). For them, it was just business—but on a scale that trivial little people like Anton Faraday, a painter of animals, couldn't even imagine. He'd come nowhere near unravelling the truth of what was going on. His outrage had been focused on the forging of one of his paintings, and the deception of Paladin's pretence to be concerned about the dwindling number of wild elephants. Proctor must have been struggling not to yawn in his face. And for Johnston? It was all in a day's work.

What would have happened if he hadn't collapsed in the Embassy that morning? Would he have accepted some bullshit answer and just returned to England? Probably. But he hadn't; he'd ploughed on, getting deeper and deeper in the mire of human perfidy, and dragging Caroline into it with him.

'We need to find a way of getting safely out of here and back to London. I'm going to call Duc back and see if we can record something you can use. And we need to track down Tuan and make sure that he's safe.'

FORTY

In Halong Bay, the tide rises and falls by three meters or more. At high tide, a razor-sharp pinnacle of limestone rock can be a comfortable ten feet below an inflatable rubber dinghy of the type that Karl, Caroline, and Faraday occupied as they approached the mouth of the cave to which the captain of their luxury junk had pointed them. At low tide, that same rock can rip a hole in the bottom of the boat that would see it sink in seconds.

The captain of the junk hadn't told them about the tide, so they had to work that one out for themselves. One thing that was immediately apparent to Faraday was the high tide mark around the entrance to the cave that housed the grotto with the underground lake, which by Karl's account was the feeding and resting place of the langur that he'd come to observe. That mark was a good twenty centimeters above the entrance of the cave, suggesting that at high tide, salt water flowed into the grotto and, presumably, the lake that it housed.

The white-headed langur that they'd come to see (whether of the Cat Ba subspecies or the broader Francois langur species was something that Karl had failed to explain) was destined to remain unobserved. The water level was a good meter and a half below the cave entrance, and not even Karl with his sturdy boots and bulging calf muscles was inclined to stand on the side of the skittish boat and clamber up, a tidal miscalculation that was causing him great frustration.

'The captain told me now is the right time,' he swore. 'I told him this is important. We go around the rock and look for another entrance, or else we wait for the tide to rise.'

It seemed that the object of Karl's search lay tantalisingly out of reach, and he was determined that they stay until he managed to get ashore.

'The male and the female look the same,' Karl informed them intently, 'except that the female has a white pubic patch, and the male does not. This I wanted to photograph. It is why I came on this journey.'

'Well,' Faraday replied laconically, 'they live in dark caves, so I guess that helps the male know where to aim. But couldn't you just Photoshop it in?'

It was a joke that was lost on Caroline and Karl both. Not that anyone was in a mood for joking. She was furious that Faraday had agreed to them coming on this jaunt, because she could see no reason for going out of the way to be nice merely because they'd caused the Germans to have to change their travel plans, let alone what they were now dealing with.

'Why are you Brits so damned polite?' she'd hissed at him in their cabin when the insistent knock on the door had come, accompanied by the German's booming voice.

'Because we're sick of going to war. Besides, I promised them, and we're going to have to eat together, so being unpleasant will merely ruin the meal. It'll only be an hour at most, and being out on the water will give us time to think.'

'So, all of us will be off the boat, leaving the crew free to go through our luggage. There's no safe in this cabin. Did you think of that?' she demanded.

The boat's engines had stopped, and Karl's boots pacing the wooden deck outside their cabin door were becoming increasingly impatient.

'Well,' he said, looking around, 'give me your passport and credit cards, and I'll put them in my money belt. And why don't you put your laptop and phone out of sight in your cabin bag and close the zip; then you'll know if they've been nosing around when we get back. The cabin door will be locked, and if anything's missing, there are only three people who could have done it. And I …' He looked around at what he could do to show that he was following his own advice. '… I'll put my cell phone under the mattress—and more importantly, I'll put my bottle of Nuits-Saint-Georges under there as well. Satisfied?'

What she really wanted was for him to stop creating diversions and find the words to explain to her why they'd been so easily deceived by Paladin and Proctor that they'd not even thought to connect them to Tuan's warnings. It was now obvious that the stakes had been so high that Tuan had every reason to fear for his safety. And where did that put them?

'We need time for all this to sink in' was all he'd offered as he adjusted his money belt under his trousers waistband. But he knew he was palming her off, and going to look at monkeys was the last thing she wanted to do. To make things worse, Renate had started down the steps to get into the boat, then suddenly stopped and announced that she would stay on board.

'I am too tired for monkeys,' she said offhandedly, and Karl had accelerated away without giving Caroline a similar opportunity to opt out.

'Let's get back,' Faraday suggested now that they weren't going to be able to enter the cave.

But Karl ignored him. He gunned the motor and steered the inflatable off around the jagged rocks of the island, forcing them to hold on or be tossed overboard, until eventually he found an overhang to what appeared to be another cave, where he clambered out awkwardly, taking the boat's bowline with him.

'I will check for an entrance.' He tied off the bowline on a spindly bush and disappeared into the shadows.

'Are we supposed to just wait for him?' Caroline asked.

'He'll be back. He's left his camera bag.'

They had no option but to wait. The sea rose and fell gently, like a monster quietly breathing, and a black kite swooped down to inspect them. When Karl returned, muttering in frustration that the cave came to a dead end, Faraday decided he'd had enough.

352

'Look,' he said, 'we're going back. You can return and wait for the tide to rise, but we don't have the time.'

It wasn't really a suggestion so much as an instruction. He'd done his dash. He didn't owe these Krauts anything, and pissing about looking for monkeys made a mockery of what had happened to Ralph, and what was happening to people in the Northern Highlands. Their mothership was anchored five hundred meters away. Sunset was drawing close, and twilight in the tropics was usually only an hour behind.

'But you must see them!' Karl insisted. 'You are a painter of wildlife!'

Foolishly, Faraday allowed him to take the tiller, so once more they headed back to the first cave, where Karl killed the engine after convincing himself that the tide had risen enough and he could now pull himself up out of the boat. He was strong, heaving himself up with grunts of determination until he was sitting triumphantly on the entrance ledge. In the process, the rubber dinghy slid away from the rock face, leaving Caroline and Faraday floating out of reach.

'I will lift you up,' Karl commanded. 'Throw me the rope.'

Faraday moved to the outboard motor and pulled it into life, then he steered them in a slow circle, staying away from the rock face.

'I said we're going back, Karl. If you wish to stay, I'll send the deckhand to pick you up. Alternatively, you can drop us back and return on your own. What will it be?'

Karl looked at his watch and glared at Faraday, but his flash of anger was short-lived, and he reluctantly offered a smile of surrender.

'*Der Kapitän spricht.* You are in command. Please allow me to climb in the boat, and we will return.'

Though his words were gracious, there was no doubting that he was furious at being made to feel impotent. Faraday moved forward to allow him to slide off the ledge into the bow of the boat and then, keeping hold of the helm, he turned them out towards the mothership.

His thoughts were already on other things, and he took Caroline's hand as they puttered slowly back towards the privacy of their cabin. He was starting to compose in his mind an explanation for what had happened to Ralph that would make sufficient sense to himself that he would be able to repeat it to Caroline. Now that he knew the venal reality of what his onetime benefactor, Kenneth Johnston, had been up to, he could only feel sadness and disgust. But he worried that he might not be the person Caroline needed if she was to take on such adversaries, for he could feel in the strength of her grip on his hand that nothing was going to deter her from exposing them.

FORTY-ONE

The inflatable tender bumped into the stern of the wooden junk, and Karl tied the painter to the bottom rung of the ladder, then climbed onto the boarding platform and up the ladder, calling out, 'Ahoy, ahoy, the sailors return!' like some comedy character from *The Pirates of Penzance*.

Faraday killed the outboard motor and held them tight and steady so that Caroline could climb aboard as well. A deck-mounted swing davit hung above them with two ropes for lowering and raising the boat aboard, but that was a job for the deckhand.

'Are you going out again?' he shouted, but Karl didn't answer, having disappeared inside.

As Caroline cleared the ladder, Faraday followed. There was no sign of the deckhand or Renate, and they passed through the galley, where the kitchen hand was already plating up an evening meal, presumably for the crew. The appetizing smell of prawns, fried onions, and chilies filled the air as the cook worked the galley's griddle plate, calmly ladling spoonfuls of cooking oil from a huge pot beside the stove into a mound of fried rice and bamboo shoots with lemongrass and kaffir lime leaves that Faraday recognized so well from his leisurely wander through this schizophrenic country of peace, friendship, and violence that always slept with one eye open.

The sound of raised voices stopped him before he reached his cabin door. It was Renate's voice, and the meaning of the rapid-fire German eluded him, though the tone made it perfectly clear that she was angry and alarmed. Karl, his hand on the door jamb of the cabin where Faraday had earlier seen the woman's clothes, looked sharply back down the passageway at Faraday, then quickly turned and entered the room opposite, firmly shutting the door.

There was no time to dwell on this scene, for Caroline's face when he entered bore a message of its own: something was very wrong.

'My laptop's gone!' she exclaimed.

'What?'

'The whole bag—it's been stolen! I told you we shouldn't leave the boat. I should have followed my instincts.'

Faraday shook his head. 'No, it makes no sense. If it's one of the crew, they'd know they couldn't get it off the boat, because we won't leave without it.'

'What if it's hidden where we'll never find it? How long would they have to wait until we gave up and went away?'

'Was the cabin door locked just now?'

'Yes.'

Faraday went to the door and looked down the passage to the crew's quarters. He turned to Caroline.

'Was your phone in the bag?'

'Yes.'

'Was it still turned on?'

'Yes. I'd been trying to call Tuan. It's never turned off.'

Faraday lifted their mattress with one hand and slipped his other hand underneath, sweeping it from side to side. He felt the neck of the bottle of Nuits-Saint-Georges, pulled it out, and placed it on the floor, then he swept again until, with relief, he locked onto his cell phone. He held it up.

'How good is your hearing?' he asked. 'My guess is that it was the deckhand or the captain. The crew's quarters are at the end of the passage, and the wheelhouse is directly above. I'm going to call your number, and if we're in luck, the phone will ring. We'll have one chance at it.'

'Then what?'

356

'How do you mean?'

'So, it rings—then what?'

The thought that she was better equipped than him for all of this returned. He leaned forward and kissed her lightly on the cheek, then bent down, picked up the bottle of Burgundy from the floor, and smiled ruefully. 'A weapon.'

At the end of the passage, they stopped beneath the spiral staircase and listened carefully. The only sound was the muted creaking of the ship's timbers and the gentle slapping of seawater against the sides. Faraday put the wine bottle under one arm, opened his phone, and searched for Caroline's number.

The phone at his ear rang twice before an answering ring came from somewhere nearby. The sound seemed to travel within the timbers of the boat, circling the walls of the stairwell and the passage. Caroline pressed her ear to the door of the crew's quarters and shook her head.

Faraday looked up the stairs to the wheelhouse, then spun on his heels and peered back down the passage. Four times it rang out before abruptly stopping.

They looked at each other, not speaking, their eyes searching each other's for the thought that each felt forming in their own mind. The sound hadn't come from the quarters in front of them, or those above; it had come from beside them.

Faraday looked to his right, then to his left, and finally took his best guess, knocking firmly with the butt of his cell phone. 'Renate!'

Behind him the door opened, and Caroline gasped.

A sharp pain in Faraday's back forced him to wince and look down at the gun in Karl's hand.

In front of him, the door opened, and Renate looked at him impassively. She, too, was holding a gun. She stepped back into the room as a large boot was planted in his back and he was sent sprawling forward onto the cabin floor, dropping the wine and his cell phone. Both boots pursued him, one landing squarely on his hip bone, paralyzing his leg, and the other exploding into his rib cage, emptying him of air. He rolled away sideways, vision focused solely on the boots and the thick legs that propelled them as they moved quickly towards Caroline, whose screams of outrage identified her as a greater source of potential trouble than the agonized body lying flat out on the deck, unable to move without sharp needles of pain running through his groin and into his spine.

He watched helplessly as Karl wrenched Caroline's arm up behind her back, pulled her head back sharply by her hair, then threw her across the room onto the bed. The wine bottle that had been in Faraday's hand rolled gently across the carpet towards where Renate stood looking down at him. Her face and voice were expressionless. 'You came back too early,' she said. 'Now we have a problem.'

Caroline stood up. Beside her on the bed, her computer bag, laptop, and cell phone were in plain view. 'Who the hell are you?' she demanded. 'What the fuck is going on?'

As if to remind himself that he had an important role as well, Karl hit Caroline with the butt of his gun, and she fell to her knees, choking on the words of defiance that had sprung up in her throat.

Faraday's impotence shamed him. He struggled to sit up, but couldn't.

'Is violence part of your plan,' he challenged, 'or are you making this up as you go along?' But even his voice lacked strength.

Despite the pain, if there was a clear thought that occurred to him in this moment, it was that the more violence these people were willing to exhibit, the lesser the chance that they'd let them walk away in the end. They weren't after computers; they were after information, and once they had it, the threat that information presented would still be alive in the people from whom they'd obtained it.

'*Sarkasmus*, Mr Faraday. Very British,' Renate sneered. She nodded curtly at Karl. '*Geh raus.*' Her tone was emphatic. As he'd earlier suspected, she was the one in charge.

358

'We'll go outside, and you'll give us what we need,' she announced calmly. 'It was not planned this way, but this is how it will now happen.'

As Karl marched towards him, Faraday mentally checked the zones of his body that might be capable of movement. One leg and two arms were heavily compromised by rib damage, and his head, reeling with the hyper-clarity of a massive adrenalin rush, seemed to be the sum of his undamaged inventory. One more heavy kick could eliminate any of those parts instantly, leaving him crippled. But as he prepared to throw all his strength into catching the swinging boot in mid-air and attempting to topple its owner, Karl stopped, bent down, and dragged him by his shirt into an upright position.

'Get up,' he commanded.

Now that he was sitting, he could feel the paralysis in his leg being sluiced with blood from his racing heart. In a minute or so, he expected he would be capable of standing. The pain in his ribs was something he would have to bear. His immediate objective was to avoid another damaging blow from those boots.

'Okay, okay,' he gasped. 'There's no need to hurt Caroline. I just need to catch my breath.'

He reached out for the bed and made a show of agonizingly rising onto his knees and then, with half-stifled cries of genuine pain, he pulled himself unsteadily to his feet and stood, swaying and clinging to the bedspread, watched by his adversaries, who were clearly unconvinced that he would make it, and by Caroline, who had rolled over onto her back and was nursing a bleeding cut to her temple from Karl's gun.

'It would help,' he whispered through clenched teeth, 'if you said who you are and why you so badly need our phones and laptop.'

Renate started to cut him off, then seemed to change her mind.

'Once we have your passwords,' she said with a chilling smile, 'we will be able to tell you that.'

Karl rammed his gun into Faraday's ribs and propelled him forward, with Renate and Caroline following. He moved slowly, holding onto the walls of the passageway, each step lancing pain through his body. The galley chef had gone, taking the crew's meals with him and leaving the empty gas rings burning. The crew, Faraday realised, had been changed at the last minute before they left Hai Phong, so he had to assume they had been hired by these people.

Out on deck, he gratefully sank into a chair at one of the tables. Caroline was pushed into a chair facing him, and their two captors sat at each end, Karl holding his gun and Renate holding Caroline's computer bag and a laptop of her own. She emptied the bag and pushed its contents towards Caroline.

'To save time, you will open these with your password, please.'

Caroline glared at her, not moving. 'Why did you even take them if you couldn't access them?' she demanded.

Renate removed a USB stick from her own laptop and held it up for them to see. She looked at Karl and smiled without humour. 'I can easily access your laptop in five minutes with this software, but you returned from your monkey cave too soon. What is done is done, *ja,* Karl? Now you can save time by doing it for me, and we can end this thing.'

Caroline remained unmoved. 'End what thing?'

'What is on your laptop and what is on your phone: that's what I want, with or without you.'

Karl leaned over and casually slapped Caroline across the face, hitting her so hard that her chair tipped and nearly deposited her on the deck.

Faraday tried to get up, but ended up doubled over from the pain in his ribs. 'Who hired you?' He grimaced. 'Was it Anglo Swiss? Was it Paladin?'

Renate ignored him. She picked up Caroline's phone, looked at the screen, then placed it back on the table. 'This needs a fingerprint to open.' She glanced up. 'Karl, *bitte.*'

Karl leaped up and took Caroline's arm from behind, squeezing her hand in his giant paw until it was spread flat on the tabletop. With his spare hand, he picked up the cell phone and pressed her index finger onto the home button. Renate watched dispassionately, then reached across and took the phone from him. Calm and unhurried, she frowned slightly as she scrolled through the phone's history.

'Tuan Brinkley, Tuan Brinkley, Tuan Brinkley... No answer, no answer, no answer.' She didn't look up. 'Give me the four-digit code for this phone, and the password for your laptop, or Karl will break your fingers.'

Caroline winced under Karl's grip. Cheek red and swollen, the cut on her temple dripping blood, she looked at Faraday for guidance. He broke her gaze, looking away in shame, unable to help.

'Do it,' he muttered. 'They'll access it anyway.'

As she reluctantly gave them the information they wanted, Faraday scrambled through his mind, trying to piece together the consequences. Clearly they wanted to find Tuan, but they must have had his phone number and email already, so this was not going to get them any closer. The story she'd been drafting for Sinclair Baines had gotten nowhere beyond the speculation about Paladin collecting seeds in the Highlands. Everything else had happened since they'd decided to leave the island and return early to Hanoi. There was nothing for them on the computer or her phone other than Tuan's vague warning. Once they were convinced of that, then the threat Caroline and Faraday posed to the people who'd hired them could be shown to be baseless.

Clearing his throat, he tried to sit up. 'Look, I don't know who you work for or what you're hoping to find out, but you'll soon see that Caroline has no information that's a threat to anyone. Her brother believes he's in danger, but we don't know why. He's gone to ground. Instead of adding to your employer's problems by harming us, just put us ashore somewhere and don't tell us anything more. Take the computer and the phone as evidence of what I'm telling you. I repeat: we know nothing that's a threat to anyone.'

Renate looked up from the computer screen. 'Karl, get Anton's phone.'

'His phone is missing?' Karl asked. '*Mist!* We know he has one, because he was using it earlier.'

'*Das ist offensichtlich.* Take him and search the cabin,' Renate commanded.

'We need your phone, Anton,' she added. 'It has to be there somewhere. Karl can beat you, or he can beat Caroline, so just find it and give it to me. *Verstanden?*

The chef had returned to his station in the galley and was busy cooking again, ignoring them as they passed, apparently unaware of Karl's gun and Anton's crippled gait.

There was little point in Faraday mounting a false search. He knew where the phone was: it had slid under the bed on the floor of Renate's cabin when he'd fallen. But finding it would lead them to Duc, and the voice message he'd left before Faraday had spoken to him about the poisoning of the wells. Thankfully he had not managed to record that last conversation, but the initial message from Duc would be enough to put him in danger.

Faraday was vaguely aware that he could not talk himself out of this situation. The pain and the fear were overwhelming him, and the instinct for survival was pressing in on him, so that the horizon of his consciousness was shrinking closer and closer to his immediate physical space—a space filled with pain. He leaned against the wall of Renate's cabin for support and clutched his chest, sure that he could feel the jagged edge of a broken rib.

'I can't bend down,' he said quietly, 'but it's probably under the bed.'

Karl gripped his face in his giant hand and squeezed it like a lemon before slamming his head back into the wooden wall with a grunt of annoyance. The wine bottle still lay on the carpet, and he picked it up and placed it on the bed, then got down on his knees and lifted the bedspread, his enormous boots and fat calves laid out in front of Faraday and his arms sweeping the floor beneath the bed in search of the phone.

Faraday stared. The wine bottle! With a gasp, he fell forward fumbling for its neck, tripping over Karl's legs, desperately trying to keep his feet as they became entangled and the man beneath him started to rise. His palms were wet and slippery, his knees trembling, his mind fogged. As he felt himself begin to fall, he raised the wine bottle above his head and smashed it down with all his might on the back of Karl's skull. The force of the adrenalin driving him was so great that the bottle exploded, dousing him and his victim with the deep blood red of the Burgundy. Karl's huge body collapsed heavily, first forward onto the bed, then off the bed and onto the floor, his head already swelling with a contusion that suggested he would struggle to regain consciousness.

Heart thumping, ribs screaming with every movement and breath, Faraday gingerly bent down and recovered the gun from the man's open hand. The cell phone, his only connection to safety, remained out of sight, and he frantically fished for it with his foot, every movement of his leg sending needles of pain into his groin, the pain blanketing his vision and numbing his brain. Holding onto the bed for support, he reached down and swept the floor with his spare hand until his fingers found the phone and he was able to straighten up.

He looked at the gun, sliding the safety catch on and off with his thumb, grimly aware that he did not know what he was doing. The crankshaft of the ship's engine was beating in time with his heart. He thought he could hear the rush of water against the ship's hull outside the cabin; they were underway again. Slowly, holding onto the bed and wardrobe for support, he shuffled to the door and cautiously peered into the passageway that led back to the galley. The cook remained preoccupied at his wok, stirring his fried rice and chili prawns. Was he party to all this, too? That would make three of them, including the deckhand and the captain in the wheelhouse.

He had to get to Caroline. There was no hiding and no escape.

With the pistol held behind his back, Faraday hobbled towards the flaming grill, tentatively attempting to adopt a smile of appreciation, bending in to sniff the aromas arising from it as if all was well.

His act was unconvincing. The cook jumped back and grabbed a long knife, brandishing it at him and calling out a warning. Advancing on Faraday, he sliced the air with his blade, ignoring the pistol that now hung limply at Faraday's side, forcing him to retreat backwards until he was pressed up hard against the hot stove. Faraday reached behind him, searching for the wok to use as a shield. Feeling a handle, he gripped it hard, pulling it towards him. It wouldn't budge. He pulled with all his strength, and the large pot filled with cooking oil fell over and tipped its contents into the flames of the grill, where it overflowed onto the wooden deck and over the feet of the cook before igniting with a roar, instantly filling the galley with smoke. Screaming, the cook lunged at Faraday with his knife, undeterred by the pistol that Faraday now held out in front of him, but then he slipped on the oil covering the floor and fell backwards with a terrified shout, his trouser legs on fire.

The flames instantly took hold of the wooden galley's tinder-dry cabinetry and deck, and the smoke was thick and acrid. Through it, Faraday could see the deckhand searching for the source of the commotion, but hesitant to advance into the flames. Then the deckhand was joined by another figure, presumably Renate, calling out for Karl. Everyone was coughing, Faraday included.

'Karl, bist du est?' Renate shouted. 'Bist du est?'

No answer. She disappeared from view. The deckhand shouted out to the cook, who was struggling to get free of the flames, as was Faraday, who turned back towards the cabins just as a shot was fired. The shot ricocheted off the metal gas bottle next to Faraday and entered his groin. He doubled over as if he'd been kicked, swatting the air ineffectually with his gun, unable to make the connection between the surge of anger and fear that gripped him and the muscles in his hand required to trigger the weapon he was holding. He hesitated, caught in the inertia of shock, then fired off two wild shots, which sent the deckhand stumbling backwards and out of sight.

The flames were now ferocious, and his way out was blocked. Two large gas bottles sat next to the stove, and the threat of an explosion loomed large. Even if he risked it and got through the flames without being burned, he would be greeted by at least one person with a gun and a clear view of him, so he hobbled back towards the guest cabins.

At the other end of the passageway by the crew's quarters, he could see a fire extinguisher. The ship's fire and smoke alarms were now ringing deafeningly. Blood was soaking from his wound into the pocket that held his cell phone, which he transferred into his shirt front. A second was becoming a minute; a minute was becoming an hour. His mind was racing, but not fast enough to save him. At the bottom of the stairwell, he took the fire extinguisher from its bracket, and holding that in one hand and the pistol in the other, he slowly climbed, gritting his teeth in pain. The pain from the bullet wound was leaching into his thigh muscles, and they struggled to bear his weight.

Darkness had fallen suddenly. Smoke from the galley billowed out onto the aft deck, and flames had begun to light up the water beside them. The wheelhouse was empty, the engines stopped. The captain, agitated and screaming, was leaning over the top deck rail, crying out to whoever would respond from below. As Faraday came up behind him, he spun around and started to raise the shotgun he was carrying. Faraday's instinct was to try and release the foam extinguisher, but one hand was still holding Karl's gun, and as he fumbled to grip the canister, the gun went off, and the captain fell face forward into him.

The shock of what he'd done momentarily paralyzed him. His heart was racing as waves of nausea pulsed through him. Renate had Caroline held at gunpoint, and his only way down onto the aft deck was via a ladder that would make him a sitting duck for anyone below. There was no way to get to Caroline, short of surrender, and even that was unlikely to be effected safely.

He'd killed people. The horror of it numbed him. Unless they escaped the boat, anyone left behind would die as well.

Then, like a fog suddenly lifting, his mind cleared. He dropped the fire extinguisher onto the deck. Taped to its side was a clear plastic envelope containing the inspection certificate. He ripped the envelope off and threw the certificate away, then placed his cell phone in the resealable packet before putting it back into his shirt and buttoning it up tightly. Finding the safety on Karl's pistol, he slid it the opposite way, then buried the gun deep in his trousers pocket before moving back to the wheelhouse and climbing over the railings. With the engines stopped, the boat sat dead in the water. It was a short jump.

Everything hurt. His head was spinning. Taking a deep breath, he jumped feet first overboard.

FORTY-TWO

At night, fish are attracted to light on the water, as anyone who has witnessed cormorant fishing on the Nagara River in Japan—as Faraday had—will be well aware. It was one of his more interesting painting subjects: the string around the cormorant's throat making it impossible for it to swallow the fish, the tail of the fish protruding from the bird's mouth, and the reflected flame on the water with which the fisherman attracted the catch lighting the scene. The cormorant was not a threatened species, but the method of fishing was increasingly so.

The fish in the waters of Halong Bay were no different from fish anywhere; they would be attracted to light as well. But it wasn't the light from the flaming boat that worried Faraday as he lay on his back in the water, quietly inching his way along the boat's waterline towards the stern. It was the blood seeping from the wound where the deckhand's bullet had entered him. Blood notoriously attracted sharks and barracuda.

The inflatable dinghy remained tied to the boarding ladder, and the two ropes from the deck-mounted davit still hung down, waiting to be attached so the dinghy could be hoisted on board. With his broken ribs and damaged hip knifing him with every movement, he slowly hauled himself onto the boarding platform. The galley fire now engulfed the interior as if an incendiary bomb had exploded, and acrid smoke belched through the aft doors. Renate had pulled the table away from the flames and closer to the stern. The deckhand lay motionless at the galley entrance. Caroline was on her knees, one cheek bleeding from a jagged wound that seemed to indicate she had been struck again, this time most likely by Renate.

Renate herself was preoccupied with packing the computer bags. Despite the drama and the encroaching flames, she was calm and methodical. Faraday took the gun from his pocket, trained it on her, and released the safety. Her gun lay on the table beside her. If he fired a series of shots in quick succession, at least one was bound to put her down. Yet he hesitated. He wasn't a killer; his instincts drove him to find another way. Besides, if he were to kill her, he would have no way of knowing who she was or why he and Caroline had been targeted. If he tried to rush her, he was sure her athleticism and training would make her quicker and more accurate than anything he could manage in his crippled state, and once he went down, Caroline's chances of survival went down, too.

As he lowered the gun, a deafening explosion tore the galley and forward quarters apart, rocking the ship and knocking Renate off her feet. But he knew that there were two gas cylinders; the second one would explode at any second. Faraday pulled himself up onto the deck and half fell, stumbling towards her as she started to rise. His damaged leg gave way on him, and he struggled to stay erect, giving her a chance to look up and then launch herself through the air at him.

His gun clattered loose from his grip and his broken ribs tore apart as she landed on top of him. The pain was so intense that his entire body convulsed with it. His muscles went into spasms, and he was helpless, unable to move as she reached back into her waistband and pulled out a knife that glinted in the light of the fire behind her.

He didn't hear the shot, but he felt Renate's head fall onto his as if she were giving him the kiss of death. Then her body fell sideways, and he saw Caroline standing over them, holding the gun that he'd dropped.

Another explosion rocked the boat.

'Gas cylinders!' he shouted. 'We've got to get off before the fire reaches the fuel tanks!'

Rolling over onto his knees, he felt for Renate's pulse. It was faint, but it was still there.

'Take your satchel and climb down into the dinghy. Hurry!'

'What about you? Are you alright? You're hurt!'

'I'll be fine. I need to find out who these fucking people are. Hurry!'

She ran for the bags on the table and then for the ladder while Faraday searched Renate's pockets. Empty.

He slapped her hard across the face. 'Wake up, wake up! If you want to be saved, tell me who you are.'

Her eyes flickered open, then closed. How had this thing gone so badly wrong? They'd simply planned to steal information and had both ended up dying. Had it been their intention from the beginning that Faraday and Caroline would die once they'd learned what they came for? How could what they knew be so important as to warrant that?

'Alright,' he muttered to himself, 'I know the answer.'

He searched for her pulse again. Nothing.

He stood up painfully, face lit by the encroaching flames. Looking down at Renate's inert body, he was overwhelmed by a feeling of exhaustion tinged with despair. Sweat poured from his brow and ran down his back. In horror and disgust, he screamed at the top of his lungs. Pain was prodding him like a persistent and sadistic picador, but it was the darkness in his heart that pained him so indelibly.

As he staggered towards the stern ladder, the flames reached another of the junk's gas cylinders. The explosion threw him into the steel stanchion of the deck-mounted davit, and he reached out instinctively to try and hold on. What his hands found was the swinging rope that hung down above the dinghy in the water. He tumbled over the guard rail, hanging onto the rope for dear life, and slid down it as the junk's upper deck started to collapse and flames began spreading down into the engine room towards the fuel tanks. Falling forward into the dinghy, he crawled towards the rope painter that tied them to the ship's ladder, fingers feverishly feeling for the knot. Thankfully, it was a slip knot. The rope fell loose into the water, and with Caroline's help, he pushed the dinghy away from the stern.

As they began to drift with agonizing slowness away from the burning hull, he felt for the fuel tap on the outboard motor and pumped the diaphragm to fill the carburettor, then knelt in the bottom of the boat with his hand on the pull starter. But his ribs wouldn't let him do it; he was close to passing out from the pain.

Caroline reached over him and took the pull handle, pulling on it three times. The motor burst into life. Then she took the tiller and steered them away out towards darkness.

As if by design, the petrol in the outboard motor ran out in less than five minutes. Had that been part of Karl's plan to keep them away from the boat while Renate went through their files undisturbed?

They sat in silence as the wooden junk burned to the waterline, cremating the five dead people on board and taking them towards a watery grave. The night was warm, but what they had been through left them chilled and shivering. Lying down in the bottom of the boat, they wrapped their arms around each other, too tired to talk, too confused to think, until the comfort they took from each other's bodies and the relief they felt in being alive became their blanket.

If love is the fitting of two people into one, there must be curves and hollows waiting and wanting to be filled; physical, emotional, and spiritual. Somehow, they had found them, without either ever having identified them in advance or even having known the strength of their wanting during the time of waiting.

So, was this how the story was destined to end?

As Faraday lay back with his head resting on the inflated pontoon of the ship's tender, his pulse was weak, breathing shallow, mind drifting. The sky and the sea were lamp black, and the flames from the burning junk were painted in cadmium red and yellow ochre, the edges flickering in titanium white. Though the night air was in the thirties centigrade, his skin was cold and clammy. The volume of blood draining into his pants from his open wound suggested that an artery may have been ruptured. If so, the internal haemorrhaging might be worse than the external bleeding. He was vaguely aware of this, but the dissociative amnesia brought on by shock protected him from the heightened anxiety of dwelling upon the danger of something he could not resolve.

As his mind ebbed and swirled and his eyelids drooped, the red and yellow flames from the burning junk morphed into a flaming sun. Feverishly he peered into its shimmering haze, finding familiar shapes he'd long forgotten. Aware that he was hallucinating, he followed the imaginary sun into a dreamscape from his distant childhood. In the dream, the sun beat down relentlessly on parched red earth, and in the purple shadows, people squatted patiently, waiting for rain. On the horizon, where a ragged line of mountainous rocks had been pushed up by the ancient crush of slow-moving tectonic plates, wispy clouds formed. A soft breeze arrived across the plain, bringing with it the rustle of locusts, like scouts on the wing, and soon the wind would be up and roaring, the topsoil ripped from its resting place and flung into the wild, open, unresisting atmosphere. The sunset was magnificent: shafts of orange light refracted through the dust, mirrored like fire in the black pupils of those who watched and waited.

Caroline stirred gently, aware of his broken ribs and weeping wound even though she'd momentarily fallen asleep, exhausted. Her pulse was steady and slow, her breathing soft and even. Though she, too, had killed to survive, it hadn't shocked her in the same way. She slept now in order to refresh, to wake and confront those who had dared contrive this affront. She was the stronger of the two. She would have no doubts, only determination.

Faraday fought to return from the African plain. The air shook with memories, and his heartbeat slowed to match the tempo of a generator whose sound filtered through the wild sage and olive trees behind the house of his youth. *Thump, thump...* Down, down his blood pressure dropped, and he fought against the weight of his descending eyelids.

Would Johnston have ordered this? He could have asked him what he knew on the mountain. No one knew better than him who Faraday was. The bully smells out the weak, knowing he'll never fight back, and Faraday was weak in Johnston's eyes—a man who could be bought, who hid from life in his attic, afraid to expose his moral credentials to the harsh reality that he was just a tool in 'a little harmless scam'. Why would he want him killed?

Across the water, the burning hull creaked, reluctant to sink, and from its bowels it emitted a growl like a dying animal. The flames sprang into life anew, this time orange instead of red, and black had been added to the mix. The fire was in the engine room, heating up the fuel tanks.

And McAvoy? He'd had his chance on the mountain, too. Instead, he'd summoned a helicopter. He'd seen Faraday for what he was: a man willing to buy a story. 'Look, Anton, we're drowning in facts here,' he'd said. 'The simple story is the one we need to stick with; that's the one I can vouch for.'

'There's no need to kill you,' he might have said.

Proctor, then? But why Proctor? Who was he?

Unable to hold these thoughts, he slid into a reverie, less distant than the last, when he'd been dangerously ill. Back then, he'd sensed there were other people in the room, but his eyelids had been too heavy, as they were now, and his hearing too submerged in the thick oil of sickness. He'd lacked both the energy and the will to wake.

Far below him, he could now vaguely see himself lying in a room that had the air of having outlived those who came before him. Where was he? Later he would come to know, but if he couldn't see it clearly, perhaps he was just imagining it.

By the window of the hospital stood a middle-aged European man in a white short-sleeved shirt and grey trousers. The creases in his shirt sleeves emphasized the muscles in his arms. He was stocky, with a thickening waist, and his thinning hair had been shaved close. Leaning against the wall, hands in his pockets, looking down into the street, he appeared disinterested in the view outside and indifferent to his surrounds.

'I want to be called the minute he comes around. And if he mentions the name Johnston, I need to know.'

Then, darkness. The darkness was a black canvas in a room devoid of light. He watched it as if he were waiting for an eclipse to appear, his body floating in a void without stars, adrift, unremembered, weightless, removed. There was no sound, no touch, no tethering gravity—only time and darkness.

Faraday's heart kicked as if he'd been prodded by an electrode. Stirring, he moved his broken ribs away from the weight of Caroline's head.

He had no fear. The dream of death was quickly forgotten. He waited calmly, listening to the flow of blood moving through him, driven by that fluctuating pulse. He sensed that he was waiting for the light of his past life to overtake him and illuminate the darkness, willing, out of nothing, an explosion of memories to erupt, creating brilliant showers of crimson and yellow, waiting for impasto volcanoes of titanium white to splatter the surface of the blank canvas of his consciousness.

Here on the gently floating boat, his blood was draining away, but he was not dying.

'Ah, your eyes are opening. Good! Take your time. My name is Proctor. You were taken ill when you came to see us at the British Embassy. You were trying to locate someone: a Mr Johnston. Is that right? Take your time, now.'

The patient's eyes had opened, but the man at his bedside sounded as if he were speaking into the end of a long, hollow pipe, and his face swam in and out of view as if the room were under water.

The blades of the ceiling fan had turned slowly, but too fast for Faraday's retinas to register. Like the wheels of a car in a celluloid movie, they'd kept breaking loose and spinning backwards, pulling his attention away from the man beside the bed whose insistent tone demanded his focus. Faraday cleared his throat of mucus and forced his head to the side so he could see the man more clearly.

'Proctor,' he murmured in Caroline's ear.

The dying animal in the stricken hull across the water growled again as the fuel tanks expanded in the heat and finally split. The flashpoint of cheap diesel from India is fifteen degrees lower than that of well-refined fuel; it only needs a flammable ignition source and vapor to ignite it. The wooden hull of the junk was all the lighted wick that it needed. The diesel gushed out of the tanks.

Oil spreads far and wide on water.

Caroline's eyes opened, and she lifted her head. Her hand came up and gently stroked his cheek. 'We escaped,' she whispered. 'It's Tuan they're scared of. It's what he might have told us.'

She kissed his eyelids until they opened, pushing back her sleeve and stroking his damp hair, the smooth skin of her forearm brushing against his cheek.

Her arm, her arm…

Now he remembered: it was from *Apocalypse Now*, which he'd watched in his room at the Rex Hotel on the night after he'd arrived in Vietnam. The Americans had been at a village, inoculating children against polio, and before they left the district, an old man came running after them, screaming that the Viet Cong had returned. When they went back to the village later, they found that the children's arms had been hacked off and thrown in a pile—the very arms that had been inoculated—and Marlon Brando, as Colonel Walter E Kurtz, mumbled, 'The genius to do that'.

And if not Proctor, who?

The lamp-black water became stained with monastral blue as the diesel spread across its surface towards them, and the snakehead fish lurked beneath, out of sight.

Faraday turned his attention from Caroline's arm to her face, in his mind tracing the line of her mouth, the curve of her jaw, and the smooth concavity of her temple where it disappeared beneath the sweep of her hair. She didn't need make-up. Her eyes and mouth, cheeks and neck didn't need any help from anyone. But if he was to paint her, he now realized, it wouldn't be the physical form he'd need to reproduce; it would be what lay within. And who knew of another person what that really was?

Turning away, he looked out into the darkness—and saw that the sound of the generator he thought he'd recalled from his African youth, its tempo keeping pace with his heart, came from the engine of a fishing boat whose red and green navigation lights showed that it was headed straight towards them.

THE END

About the Author

A.I. Fabler is the pen name of the New Zealand-born author, who spent a large part of his working life in London, New York and Sydney, initially in journalism and advertising, before moving into senior corporate roles in property development and financing before writing fulltime. He is the recipient of a number of screenwriting awards, and his political satire, "Agenda 2060: The Future as It Happens" was published in 2021, described by Kirkus Reviews as 'A laser-focused, irresistible lampoon of woke culture'. He has two further novels due for publication in 2022 and 2023 including Book Two in the "Agenda 2060" series, and a noir murder mystery set in seventies New York titled "A Song for Leonard".

www.aifabler.com

www.ingramcontent.com/pod-product-compliance
Lightning Source LLC
Chambersburg PA
CBHW070203120726
47909CB00001B/235